Praise for D. Reneé Bagby's *Adrienne*

Joyfully Recommended "Adrienne is a fantastic exploration of a magical universe full of intrigue, supremacy and creative characters... I was held spellbound through the complete narrative. This is a wonderful love story that I enjoyed immensely."

~ *Rosemary, Joyfully Reviewed*

"Wow! ADRIENNE is an exquisite example of world building, and D. Renee Bagby kept this reader on the edge of her seat... I was biting my nails in reaction to all the perils, betrayals, danger, treachery, hope and joy that are such integral parts of this splendid romance. Get it, read it, keep it."

~ *Vi, Romance Reviews Today*

"D. Renee Bagby has written a highly intensified novel. You can truly relate to the characters, and more importantly to their emotions... The novel also flowed absolutely wonderful, and you just have to continue reading to see just where these two will go, as well as what is on the next page..."

~ *Denise, ParaNormal Reviews*

4.5 Stars and Reviewer's Choice Award "D. Renee Bagby delivers a wonderfully written fantasy that takes you to new realms. Wonderful characters take you to new heights of fantasy, not to mention passion. Time well spent on this wonderful book."

~ *Renee Kautz, Historical Romance Reviews*

NORTH PORT LIBRARY
13800 S. TAMIAMI TRAIL
NORTH PORT, FL 34287

Adrienne

D. Reneé Bagby

NORTH PORT LIBRARY
13800 S. TAMIAMI TRAIL
NORTH PORT, FL 34287

A Samhain Publishing, Ltd. publication.

3 1969 02110 5191

Samhain Publishing, Ltd.
577 Mulberry Street, Suite 1520
Macon, GA 31201
www.samhainpublishing.com

Adrienne
Copyright © 2008 by D. Reneé Bagby
Print ISBN: 978-1-59998-757-6
Digital ISBN: 1-59998-523-3

Editing by Carrie Jackson
Cover by Anne Cain

This book is a work of fiction. The names, characters, places, and incidents are products of the writer's imagination or have been used fictitiously and are not to be construed as real. Any resemblance to persons, living or dead, actual events, locale or organizations is entirely coincidental.

All Rights Are Reserved. No part of this book may be used or reproduced in any manner whatsoever without written permission, except in the case of brief quotations embodied in critical articles and reviews.

First Samhain Publishing, Ltd. electronic publication: July 2007
First Samhain Publishing, Ltd. print publication: May 2008

Dedication

To my dad, who gave me my first romance novel and my love of reading.

To my mom, who knew I could and would do it before I was totally sure what *it* was.

To Ms. Morse, my high school English teacher and my very first beta reader (and editor).

To Mr. Boyle, my college Creative Writing professor, who taught me to write for my audiences' tastes as well as my own.

To Panya, who—as my beta reader—was forced to put up with the dynamics of a romance novel when she normally reads straight fantasy.

To Terez, who has to put up with my whining before, during and after the writing process.

To my husband, who has to put up with everything.

To Liz, my first fan—even if we never did finish that comic.

And, to Samhain Publishing, Ltd. for giving me this chance to unleash my madness, uh, creativity on the world.

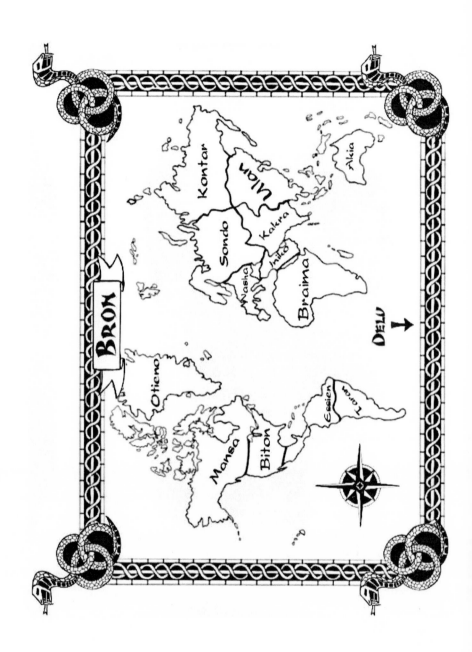

Chapter One

March 17, 2006

Adrienne shuffled papers around the desk. She cupped the phone between her head and shoulder so she could lift a stack of folders with both hands. She had put the pen on the desk earlier. By all rights, it should still be there. It couldn't have gotten up and walked away. Adrienne would like to think she would notice a walking pen...and have a camera handy, because no one would believe her otherwise.

"Adrienne? Adrienne, are you listening to me?" the woman on the phone asked in an annoyed voice.

"Yes, Mother, I'm listening to you. I'm also in the middle of grading tests. The Scantron machine picked today of all days to break. I promised Ms. Evers I'd get the tests graded and the mid-semester marks on the website before I left for the night."

"Why couldn't this Mrs. Evers person do that herself? You're a teacher's aide, not a teacher, Adrienne."

"I know what I am, Mother." Adrienne sighed. She checked the spot directly in front of her. The pen hadn't been there the first three times, but she might have overlooked it.

It wasn't there.

"And *Ms.* Evers isn't married—yet," Adrienne continued. "Her fiancé dropped by with plane tickets earlier today. She wanted to put him off because of this whole mess with the midterms, but I wouldn't let her. I'm not doing anything important and I don't have to catch a plane. I'm driving. Besides, I prefer night driving. Less people on the road."

Against her better judgment, Adrienne moved from behind the desk to search on the floor in her immediate vicinity. She hadn't put the pen on the ground, but it never hurt to check in case she'd knocked it off the desk while looking for it.

"I just called to let you know I'll be home tonight after I finish. I've already finished with the tests and now I'm calculating grades. It won't be but another hour, at most." What started as a simple conversation had turned into a two-hour-long lecture.

"That's just my point, honey. Your father and I don't want you attempting a three-hour drive so late at night," her mother complained.

"I'll be fine. Aha!" The pen was on her chair. How it had gotten there, she would never know and didn't care. Ten minutes had passed while she searched for the stupid thing.

Her mother asked in concern, "What?"

Adrienne shook her head even though her mother couldn't see her. "I found my pen. Look, Mom, I gotta go. I'll get to the house in another four hours. Don't wait up. I'll be fine. And make sure Castor and Pollux stay out of my room."

The muffled voice of her father filtered through the phone. Adrienne couldn't make out what he said.

Her mother translated, "Can't you let your father come get you?"

"And be home without a car for a week during spring break? No way. Bye, Mom."

"Wait, Adrienne—"

She hung up the phone. Her mother liked to argue a point until the other person gave in just to shut her up. The only other option was to cut her off. Sure, Adrienne would catch an earful once she got home, but she had won herself a few hours' reprieve.

It was almost eight o'clock. The darkness outside turned the glass of the window near the desk into a mirror. Instead of looking out and seeing the campus below, Adrienne's light brown eyes stared back at her. She smiled at her reflection. Her hair looked horrible. She smoothed a few errant black strands back over the rows of braids that graced her head. It didn't help. She would have to redo the braids when she got home.

This late at night, on an empty campus, no one would see her to care what her hair looked like. *If they could see me in the dark*, she thought with a quiet laugh. Adrienne's cinnamon-brown complexion had the uncanny ability to turn her invisible on dark nights.

Speaking of night, if she didn't get to work soon it would end and she would be stuck on the highway in morning rush hour—exactly what she wanted to avoid.

Pen in one hand and a calculator in the other, she tallied the midterm grades of the students from the Introduction to Literary History class. Adrienne was glad she'd already taken Ms. Evers's course. The teacher used harsh and rigid rules in her classes because she loved the subject. That love had transferred to Adrienne, and in another two months, she would graduate with an honors degree in literary history.

The only thing she looked forward to more than graduation was spring break. That time had come, albeit an hour later than what she had quoted to her mother. Adrienne punched in the last grade, gathered up her stuff and bade farewell to the English department building.

She made sure she had her car keys in her hand and Ms. Evers's office keys in her purse before the building door closed behind her. After hours, the door had an automatic lock that needed a key code Adrienne didn't know, since she was a student.

Adrienne followed the lighted path to the parking lot a few yards away. Her car seemed to smile at her, like it knew they were headed home. The restless movements of her hand made her keys jingle at her side. Just a few more feet and she would be on her way home for rest and relaxation.

"Spring break has officially started," she declared.

"Yes, it has," agreed a man from the shadows.

Adrienne gasped in surprise. She clutched her purse to her chest as the man who had spoken stepped onto the path in front of her.

There was another man with him. He kept to the shadows the large oak trees cast in the lights of the street lamps.

It took a while for Adrienne to register the face of the man who had spoken. He'd traded his designer shirts and tailored slacks for a non-descript black tee shirt and jeans. He'd even covered his blond hair with a black skullcap.

"Josh?" she asked to make sure.

"In the flesh, teacher's pet."

Adrienne gave a nervous laugh. She took a step back from the men. "What are you doing on campus this late? I thought you would be halfway to Europe...or someplace equally as expensive."

"I thought I would be too," he said with an offhand shrug. "I mean, I had the tickets and was all set to leave. Just one problem. Go on, ask me the problem."

Something didn't feel right. Adrienne looked around for an emergency phone. There wasn't one in sight.

Figures, she thought.

She looked back at Josh and her car, which was a few steps past him.

"What's the problem?" she asked, hoping to stall until one of the night security guards came along. Maybe he wanted to scare her. It was late at night and people had to get their jollies somehow. She wished they had chosen another target, but as one of the last remaining students on campus, she was the lucky winner of the booby prize.

"You," he said flatly. He started up the path towards her. "I pride myself on having pretty good scores. I mean, I pay enough money for them," he said with a chuckle. "This semester has been crap for me, though. It took me a while to figure it out, but it's all started and ended with you."

"Me?" she asked as she backed up more. She needed to get back to the building. Adrienne may not know the code, but there were still a few teachers there doing last-minute grades.

"I knew I would have to be careful with the bribes these last two semesters. Seniors are under more scrutiny. All my planning went to pot when I found out our teacher was a lazy bastard and he left it up to our peers whether we should pass or fail the senior sem."

Now she understood. "You plagiarized that paper. I might have overlooked a quote here or there, but I found the exact same paper on the internet. I had to point it out to the professor," she explained in what she hoped was a stern yet somewhat sympathetic voice. She didn't feel any sympathy for the lazy prick. He only needed to think she did.

Josh's sneer let Adrienne know he didn't buy it. "Who, in turn, took it to the dean of the English department and then the president of the school. I've been expelled. Seniors don't get second chances. One mistake and you're out of there, bucko."

"Oh, shit." Adrienne turned tail and ran. The building wasn't that far away. She could make it.

Why had she worn a long skirt today? She grabbed handfuls of the skirt and hiked it up to her thighs so she could run faster.

"This was your one mistake, Adrienne," Josh yelled after her.

She screamed when someone tackled her. She barely had time to raise her hands to keep her face from bouncing off the ground. Her assailant flipped her onto her back in one move. It was Josh's friend.

Adrienne hit him with her purse and kicked him. The man grunted. Her attack didn't seem to faze him in the least. He smiled at her and beckoned her to hit him more. She obliged him because she might land a lucky hit and get away.

"How do you like Greg? He's an old buddy of mine from back in high school. We used to con idiot girls into sex, then tally up our points with a few other friends. I won, even though some of those twits needed convincing, like you." From his back pocket, Josh produced a credit card-sized digital camera. He clicked a picture.

The flash dazzled Adrienne. She squeezed her eyes shut before he flashed another picture. Stars danced around the backs of her eyelids.

"Don't do this."

"That's what the other girls would say. 'No, please,' or 'Stop, don't do this, I beg you'. In the end, they all loved it. It's not like I'm going to kill you or anything. I'm going to take some nice little pictures of Greg and you. Not showing Greg's face, of course. After spring break, you'll go tell the dean you switched out my paper with one you found on the

11

web. Call it academic jealousy or some shit like that. Make up something that sounds plausible and pathetic. You look like you can do pathetic."

"Like hell I will," she screamed. "Let go of—"

Greg pressed his hand over her mouth, cutting off her high-pitched command and her ability to yell for help. She continued swinging her purse while scratching his wrist with her free hand.

"Or else these pictures end up all over the campus grounds and website... Oh, and I might send a few copies to your parents."

"Dude, quit talking and cuff her already," grunted Greg as he caught another smack in the face from her purse.

In her struggles, Adrienne saw an emergency phone near the door of the English building. *Typical*, she thought angrily.

Maybe she would get lucky and a campus security guard would happen by.

Josh pocketed his camera and pulled out a pair of handcuffs. When he got close enough to Adrienne to cuff her, she changed targets and whacked him with her purse.

He clutched his mouth and hissed through his fingers. "Damn it, Greg, hold her."

Greg reared up and planted his fist in her stomach.

All the air left Adrienne's body. Her assault on the two men was forgotten as she tried to get breath back into her lungs. One of the men took her purse away while the other stretched her arms over her head and snapped the handcuffs around her wrists.

"Take her in the trees while she's still out of it," Josh commanded.

Adrienne could only glare at the smirk Josh threw her way.

Greg grabbed the chain of the handcuffs and used it to drag Adrienne towards the trees.

Josh patted one of the oak trees as he walked past it. "Never thought these stupid oaks would be useful for anything—other than firewood." He bent over and pulled off one shoe and sock and tossed the sock towards Greg.

"Gag her, too. Don't want campus security getting nosy."

Gemmabulan 17, 6954

The forty-eighth King of Ulan, Malik, showed all the signs of a man well past the limits of boredom.

He held a crystal goblet that he twisted back and forth, which made the liquid inside swirl and slosh over the edge. The droplets splashed on the polished marble floor of his twenty-step throne dais and on the edge of his black leather boot. He'd slung his other hand over the arm of his throne so his fingers could make lazy circles in the fur of his pet, Feyr—a giant black panther-like cat whose temperament usually matched that of his master.

Feyr let out an angry growl every few breaths. The cat's vocalizations indicated Malik's mood wasn't all that it seemed. His outward calm, a façade he perfected years ago, served to hide his true feelings from the people around him—like the only other person in the room, a honey-colored leman who had her head buried in his lap.

Malik couldn't recall her name and didn't care enough to try. She wasn't the woman he wanted.

He wanted his bride. Her absence had caused his fouler-than-normal mood. Malik had three months to find a suitable bride and marry her before he had to forfeit his throne.

Locating his bride was supposed to be an easy task. Forty-six generations ago, Malik's ancestor had cast a spell on the royal bloodline that would locate a perfect mate for each heir to the throne. Malik's woman had yet to be found.

With time running out and Malik's patience at an end, the leman before him had better start to please him soon or he would take his frustrations out on her.

Feyr let out a loud roar.

Malik looked away from the leman to the throne room doors. They had opened without his permission. He watched High Chancellor Travers enter the room. The palm-sized glass orb he held completely engrossed the man.

"If you value your present health, Travers, you will give me a good reason for your intrusion."

Travers jerked to attention. He looked around himself, then at Malik. He cleared his throat, coughed a few times, and then said, "Sorry for the interruption of your time with Lady Juven, Majesty."

Malik shifted so his weight rested more on one hip. The movement made Travers jump.

The man rushed out, "I have located your bride, sire." He held out the orb as proof of his statement.

"Bitch," yelled Malik. He dropped his crystal goblet, balled his fist into Juven's thick brown hair and jerked her away from his lap. The crystal goblet shattered on the marble floor and sent droplets of crimson liquid running down the throne dais stairs like rivulets of blood. Juven had bitten him...hard. Malik's other hand cracked across her face. The force of his blow sent her flying down the stairs. Feyr followed her progress. He snapped at her feet and growled every time he missed.

"Feyr."

A single word from Malik halted the cat, who was primed to attack the woman once she stopped rolling. Feyr stopped one step above Juven and sat on his haunches. He glanced up at Malik, then back at his prey with a tiny chirp of impatience.

Juven clutched her face. Malik saw fear in her light brown eyes. "Forgive me, Majesty," she cried.

"You remain unscathed only because I refuse to sully my good news with your blood," Malik snapped. He ignored Feyr's whine at the news of Juven's pardon. "You have lost my favor, Juven. Return to the others."

Juven tripped over herself in her hurry to get out of the throne room.

Feyr climbed the dais steps and resumed his place at Malik's side. He growled when Malik patted his head.

"There will be other times, Feyr," Malik whispered. His words were meant for Travers. The man would know true pain if he brought false hope. Malik's bride wasn't a subject to be mentioned lightly or joked about.

Malik straightened his clothing and sat. The rage he'd displayed only moments before disappeared like the small piece of lint he flicked from his shoulder. The pain and damage of Juven's bite healed without Malik having to concentrate on it. Such magick was as involuntary as his heartbeat, and happened when needed.

"Well, High Chancellor, why is she not here? I wanted *her* brought to me, not *news* of her," Malik said.

"She is located on an alternate Bron, Majesty. The parallel dimension caused the delay of the blood spell—or that is my guess. Only you are strong enough to handle an interdimensional portal."

Malik took the compliment even though he wasn't sure he could handle a portal that bridged dimensions. He'd never tried before.

For his bride, he would make it work.

"Show her to me."

Travers nodded. He spread his hands away from the orb, which floated and expanded.

"What is this?" Malik roared.

The orb showed two black-clad men with a bound-and-gagged woman—his intended bride he assumed—held between them. The larger of the two men was using a knife to cut the woman's clothes away.

Malik snapped his clawed hand towards Travers. The other man grabbed his neck and gasped for air. Malik said in a harsh tone, "If this is your idea of a joke, High Chancellor—" Rage choked his words when one of the men manhandled the woman's bare breast. The woman's muffled cry and Travers's yelp of pain mingled with each other.

"*You're hurting him.*"

"I want to hurt him," Malik growled.

"*No, you want to hurt* them. *I suggest you hurry up before they get much further.*"

Malik made an angered noise before flinging his hand outward. The motion sent Travers careening into the throne room doors. The sound of the man's pain as he hit didn't alleviate Malik's mood. He looked at the two men in the orb.

"She is your bride," Travers croaked. He tried to stand with the help of the wall but ended up in a heap on the floor.

"Get out."

Travers nodded and crawled out of the room. The doors closed after him.

Feyr leapt from the throne dais, landing in front of the orb. He glanced back at Malik with a questioning look.

Malik said, "You are not coming, Feyr. This is between me—" a sword appeared in his hand and he pointed it at the assailants, "—and them."

He pushed his power through the sword. It hit the image with a loud crack. Instant, cold fear hit Malik mere moments after the interdimensional portal formed. His breath fogged.

This was his bride's fear. He could feel her emotions, which proved her identity. And the feeling of it added to his overwhelming need to see the blood of both men smeared on his sword.

The larger of the two assailants had his back to the portal. The man's companion, who faced the portal, would be able to see Malik— and his own imminent death—if his attention wasn't so focused on the woman.

Their mistake.

Malik hurtled his sword like a spear towards the bigger man's back. He leapt from his throne and followed the sword's path. The time had come to claim what was his.

Chapter Two

Greg knelt between Adrienne's legs. His pants were unzipped and he had a leer on his face. Behind her head, Josh snapped picture after picture.

Adrienne wanted to twist away from Greg but he held her knees in a painful grip. Her hands were stretched over her head so the handcuffs could pass around the leg of a cast-iron bench.

Josh had decided to handcuff her to the bench so his hands would be free to work the camera. Adrienne didn't understand why no one saw the flashes and came to investigate. Where was the night security guard?

Why hadn't she kept her mouth shut about the paper?

She should have let her father come and get her.

She squeezed her eyes shut in hopes of blocking out everything. Tears seeped from the corners of her eyes.

"Get ready, bitch," warned Greg.

He grunted.

It took a moment for Adrienne to realize nothing was happening. In fact, Greg had let her go.

She knew it!

It was a prank. A stupid, elaborate joke, but a joke nonetheless. She would open her eyes and Greg and Josh would be gone, leaving her to try to figure out how to get out of the handcuffs.

Something hit the ground near her head. She opened her eyes.

Josh stood with his hands grasping air since he had dropped his camera. His attention wasn't on her any longer, but on Greg.

Adrienne looked at Greg. The sock in her mouth muffled her screams, but that didn't stop her from doing it.

Moonlight filtered through the treetops and glinted off a sword that protruded from Greg's stomach. He had released her legs so he could grip the blade.

She kicked at him to get him away from her. When that didn't work, she twisted her hands, grabbed the handcuffs and pulled herself closer to the bench. Her gaze never left Greg.

Movement in her peripheral vision made Adrienne look at Josh. He took two steps back, then turned and ran. She tried to call after him. He was leaving her. A sword-toting maniac had appeared and Josh left her chained to a bench.

He didn't get far. The sword was ripped from Greg's body and was sent spinning after Josh. The blade whistled as it cut the air. The spin of the blade caused Josh's head to come sailing back towards Adrienne when the sword separated it from his neck. It landed a mere inch from her leg.

There were two faint thuds. Adrienne looked up to see the sword had gotten stuck in a tree and Josh's body had collapsed. She looked at Greg.

Blood gushed from his wound. He would be dead soon, as well. Adrienne didn't want to be next.

She struggled against the handcuffs. Ignoring the pain in favor of saving her life, she leaned back and shoved with her foot at the same time. There was no way Josh had gotten real handcuffs. She hoped they were novelty cuffs and would break.

The handcuffs didn't give. She would wonder how Josh got real handcuffs later. For now, she had to get free.

It was time for a different tactic.

The benches weren't bolted down, so she should be able to tilt it enough to free herself. She braced her shoulder under the bench and pushed. The bench scraped as it slid backwards but didn't lift. She tried again.

More scraping.

Frustrated tears flowed down her face.

The sound of a twig snapping wrenched a startled cry from Adrienne. She forced herself to turn and look at the killer. He looked strong enough to cause her severe damage without the use of his sword.

She shied away from him when he stopped in front of her. He reached out to her and she squeezed her eyes shut.

Malik lowered to his haunches in front of his bride. With a thought, he ended the shielding spell he'd erected around her before his attack had started. Little droplets of the assailants' blood fell to the ground—blood he hadn't wanted to taint his bride's skin.

The suffocating chill of her fear continued, enveloping his body. He had caused that fear. Killing the two men while she watched showed poor judgment on his part. He would make it up to her at a later date. His priority was her freedom.

Once she saw that he meant her no harm, she would stop being scared of him. And he could regain a measure of his original warmth. Malik remembered his father telling him that he would feel his mate's emotions and she would feel his. He hadn't known this was what his father meant.

He reached out with the intention of removing her gag. Instead he brushed his fingers across her cheek. She flinched away from him.

Her reaction made him focus. There would be time to get to know her feel later.

He removed her gag then cupped her bound hands in both of his. She tried to pull away but he held her.

"Don't hurt me," she rasped.

"I do not plan to, my lady," Malik soothed in a low, soft voice. Her language, while remarkably similar to Otieno's, felt cumbersome in his mouth. He wanted to use his own but decided the magicks needed to bridge the communication gap could be better used elsewhere.

With a single thought, he melted her chains. His bride's earlier struggles had torn the skin around her wrists. Blood seeped from her wounds and coated her hands.

It was simple enough to heal her the way he had melted her chains, but Malik couldn't help but make the act more intimate. He brought her wrists to his lips and breathed the healing magicks over her skin.

His bride opened her eyes and watched him. He smiled at her. She looked confused.

Correction, she was confused. The emotion felt like itself instead of a temperature. Malik knew he wasn't confused, so the emotion belonged to her.

The chill of her fear ebbed away. He took that as a good sign. With slow movements, he rose to his feet and pulled his bride to stand next to him.

She snatched her hands from him and rubbed her wrists. The feeling of her confusion intensified. She looked down at her hands, then back up at him.

"What?"

"I am Malik of Ulan, my lady. Your servant," he said with a bow.

"My... Huh?"

"And your name?"

"Ad...Adrienne. Adrienne Backett."

Malik told himself to stop staring at her so intently. The feel of her fear had returned and she looked ready to run. He reached for her hand to hold her at his side.

"I should go home now," she said with a tug of her hand.

"Would you leave in such a state of disarray?"

Adrienne looked down at herself and gave a cry of shock. She snatched her hand away from his and pulled her shredded shirt together over her naked breasts.

Malik swept out his hand. A cloak appeared out of nowhere and he placed it over Adrienne's shoulders. He brought the ends of it together in front of her. She grabbed the edges of the cloak with a murmured thank you.

He smiled at her bowed head. "Such as this is my pleasure, my lady, as I would do anything to make you happy." He stepped closer to her, which forced her to look up at him. He asked softly, "Shall we return?"

"Return? Yes, I need to go home. My parents will be worried. If you tell me your address, I'll mail this cloak back to you."

"You misunderstand." His voice remained low and soothing. "I meant *my* home." He slid his hand around her waist and pulled her close. The action indulged his baser needs. He recognized the lust he felt. What he didn't understand was his urgency.

Even when he was new to sex he had never felt this anxious to be with a woman. Something about Adrienne made him want to forget all the rules and have her now.

"Let go of me. I'm not going anywhere with you."

Malik bent to place his other hand under her legs and lifted her effortlessly against his chest.

"I'll scream."

"You could, as it is your right. I do not see the merit in it and think you would be better served with rest rather than theatrics."

"I'm not...I..." Her words stumbled to a halt as sleep claimed her.

He smiled at his sweet burden. She would understand once he explained the entire situation to her. He laid a feather-light kiss on her temple before walking back the way he had come.

He brushed his fingers over the hilt of his discarded sword when he passed it. The sword faded and disappeared. It would return when Malik needed it.

"Freeze!"

Malik looked back at the man who pointed a light, and what seemed to be a weapon, in his direction. It wasn't every day someone dared command him to do anything—or threatened him. The sheer novelty of it made him obey.

"Okay, buddy, put the girl down nice and slow and back away."

"Are you the guardian of this place?"

"Yeah. I'm the *guardian*, buddy," agreed the security guard in a humoring tone. He pointed the flashlight at Adrienne. "I want you to put the girl down."

"No. I would not leave her to such an incompetent guardian. Your aid has come too late, as I have done your job for you," Malik said. He moved his gaze to the two bodies the guard had overlooked.

The guard glanced quickly in the direction Malik looked. "Holy Jesus," he yelled.

"I leave the rest to you, then, guardian. You shall leave the girl to me." Malik walked back to the portal. The guard yelled for him to come back, but the novelty had worn off so Malik ignored the man.

The guard ran to catch up. He would be too late.

Malik closed the portal after himself.

A soft sigh from Adrienne made Malik pause and look down at her. For the first time in a long time, Malik felt the burden of his rage alleviating. He had his bride. Everything else would fall into place from this moment forth.

Chapter Three

"Ah, you are awake. I shall inform His Majesty immediately," said a woman from Adrienne's right.

Adrienne, who had started her usual pre-wake ritual of stretching just to turn over and go back to sleep, opened her eyes to see who had spoken.

Her gaze never made it to the owner of the voice. The unfamiliar ceiling caught her attention. It was painted to resemble the sky on a sunny day. There were wisps of clouds and a flock of birds flying by.

Flying by?

She immediately closed her eyes. This had to be a dream. She would open her eyes and be at home in her own room. The sound of a door as it opened and closed made Adrienne open her eyes again.

The scene hadn't changed. The sky was still the sky and it remained on the ceiling. The clouds moved and so did the birds, who were almost out of sight. Maybe the ceiling was see-through? That made a little more sense.

This wasn't her room.

Afraid to move, Adrienne let her gaze track from the ceiling down to the far wall.

The room was big—more like huge. The far wall sported a tapestry with an image she could barely make out. It looked like an intricate knot design.

Her attention strayed from the tapestry to the rest of her surroundings. The bed she occupied seemed to be the only thing there.

Like the room, the bed was huge. Her toes made a tent in the covers that marked the halfway point before the edge. She turned her head and saw the foot of the bed wasn't the only thing far away. This bed was a king times three—maybe four.

Who needed a bed this big? Paul Bunyan?

Adrienne finally worked up the nerve and sat up. She was wrong; other furniture did adorn the room. Several tall vases stood like sentries on either side of each of the large windows. The largest window—it reached from the floor to the ceiling above—had a table situated in front of it. The table looked big enough to seat four but only had two backless chairs.

Where was she?

Looking around hadn't answered that question. The woman who had spoken earlier had left to retrieve whoever this "majesty" person was, so Adrienne couldn't ask her. Had royalty picked her up after her attack?

Her attack!

She looked down at her wrists. The evidence of her struggle against the handcuffs was gone—no scratches, no bruises, not even a little soreness. She ran her hands over her wrists anyway, just to be sure. Nothing hurt.

Then she remembered the man. He said his name was Merrick. No, Malik. He had done something to her wrists. But what? She also remembered trying to get away from Malik but falling asleep instead. Had he taken her somewhere while she slept? The obvious answer was yes, he had. But where and for what purpose?

She looked back at the bed, which made her notice her attire.

Someone had taken off her ruined blouse and skirt and replaced them with a sheer nightgown. She could take it off and wouldn't be able to tell the difference. Whoever had put it on her had a sick sense of humor.

A knock at the bedroom door made Adrienne gasp and grab the blanket to her chin. The person on the other side of the door took that to mean come in, since he pushed the door open and entered.

"Good morning, my lady," Malik said with a smile. "I trust you slept comfortably?"

She nodded dumbly, not sure what to say to the man's obvious good cheer. A million things were appropriate at this moment. Where am I? How did I get here? How long do you plan to keep me? Can I get some real clothes?

None of her questions would leave her mouth.

Her inability to speak could be traced to the man in front of her. Had Malik looked this good last night? He was Asian—his slanted eyes and black hair made that obvious. But his aquamarine eyes and towering height said more than Asian made up his ancestry. She had only come up to his collarbone when she stood next to him the night before.

Malik wore close-fitting dark pants that showed off his muscled legs, and a loose, white button-up shirt covered by a floor-length black vest.

"Shall I fetch breakfast, Majesty?" the woman behind Malik asked.

The voice belonged to the woman who had spoken earlier. She had slanted, dark eyes and delicate features that reminded Adrienne of the older Asian lady who ran the sushi restaurant near the campus. Her black hair was braided and wrapped around her head like a crown, which gave her a regal air that suited her.

Belatedly, Adrienne wondered if this woman had dressed her. Adrienne may not know Malik very well—or at all—but she would bet he suggested the sheer nightgown. Either way, someone would get a piece of her mind.

"Take your time. My lady and I have many topics to discuss," Malik said.

The woman curtsied and left the room. She pulled the door firmly closed behind her.

The sound of the door closing made Adrienne jump. She watched Malik, ready to run in case he tried something funny. Even if he had saved her virtue—and she was thankful for that—he might be dangerous. If need be, she could use the blanket's edge to strangle him in case he had changed his mind about killing her.

Her grip on the blanket tightened as he approached.

"There is no need to be scared of me. I will not hurt you."

"Then stay over there." She scooted across the bed, away from him.

"There is no need to be so cautious, my lady. I merely wish to talk."

"About?"

"Us," he answered.

"What *us*? I only met you last night. Did I live out a lifetime in that moment and not notice?"

He chuckled. "No, you are correct. We did only meet last night." His look turned serious. "Though I have waited for you for a lifetime."

"Waited for me to do what exactly?" She shifted so her knees were under her. Whether to jump at him or away from him, she wasn't sure, but she planned to be ready either way.

"To marry me and rule by my side as the Queen of Ulan," he answered proudly.

Adrienne's mouth dropped open. Of all the things she'd expected him to say, that hadn't made it to the list.

Then the meaning of what he said registered.

She frowned. "The queen of who?"

"Ulan. Of Bron's fourteen kingdoms, it is the second most powerful."

Ulan? Bron? What the hell was he talking about? The countries didn't sound familiar. Geography had never interested her since countries came and went so quickly nowadays.

Malik elaborated, "All that I tell you and plan to tell you will make more sense if I first clarify that you are no longer on Earth."

"I'm no longer what?" she squeaked in horror. She jumped off the bed, happy it was between her and Malik. The man was nuts and she wanted him to keep his distance. "What do you mean I'm no longer on Earth? Where the hell am I? I've been abducted by aliens! Why did you bring me here?"

All of her questions were sound and justified given the situation, but Malik couldn't bring himself to focus on any of them at the moment. The sight of her breasts beneath the sheer nightgown had completely caught his attention. Her breasts had been bare the night before, but it was dark then. The joy of finding her at last had made her state of undress secondary in Malik's mind.

Not so now. Adrienne was safe. Malik could allow himself to think of other things, such as lust.

Imagining cupping her ample breasts made his hands twitch at his sides. He wanted to touch all of her. Her slim waist, her round hips, her long legs—he wasn't picky so long as he could touch her.

The urgency of the night before returned full force.

Malik didn't realize he had started walking around the bed to indulge his longing until Adrienne screamed. The frantic sound and the cold fear that nipped along his senses snapped him back to himself.

Adrienne looked around the room for a way to escape. Malik stood between her and the one door she knew to be an exit. There were a few other doors in the room, but those could be bathrooms and closets and the like. She wanted to get away, not trap herself further.

Her agitation made her feel hot. She fanned herself with one hand, but it didn't help. The room wasn't hot, she was. A sensation like warm oil oozing over her skin had her body tingling. She looked back at Malik to accuse him of drugging her, but the words became strangled in her throat. He simply stared at her. The lust in his eyes was almost a tangible thing.

She took a step back when he moved towards her. The cloth of her nightgown brushed her ankles. She remembered the sheerness of her clothing and screamed as she tried to cover herself with her hands and reach for the blanket on the bed at the same time.

Trying to do both at once accomplished neither. She finally settled on ducking below the edge of the bed and tugging on the heavy bedcover with both hands.

This was a nightmare. She would wake up any second and have a good laugh at her own expense.

Malik's voice jarred her out of that fantasy.

"Forgive me, my lady. I did not mean to stare." His voice sounded strained.

"Then why did you put me in this...this...this thing?" she asked in an accusing tone. Finally, the end of the cover slipped over the edge. Adrienne wrapped herself in it and made sure no part of her body could be seen before she straightened and glared at Malik.

"I did not. Once I brought you back from Earth, I gave you over to the care of your lady's maids. They are the ones who dressed you."

"What do you mean I'm not on Earth?"

"We are currently on a parallel Earth known as Bron."

Adrienne gave him a look to let him know she thought he was nuts. The look turned back to a glare when he laughed at her.

"I assure you, this is a different dimension from the one you are familiar with," he continued. "Bron's months and days have different names, the count for our years began much earlier than yours and many other subtle differences but it is the same planet—third from this solar system's star—merely another version."

"You brought me here...to...to marry you."

He nodded.

"You have got to be kidding me. Even if I bought this pile of horseshit with *your* money, why me?" She pointed out the window. "There are probably millions of women on Bron, just like Earth. Why the hell would you go all the way to an alternate dimension to get me?"

Malik raised his hand and Adrienne stumbled back to get farther away. She sucked in a surprised breath when a glass orb appeared out of thin air, floating over Malik's hand.

"This is not a joke," he assured her.

"Okay, so you can do magic. Big deal. I've seen—"

He reached out with his other hand and pulled a sword out of the air. The same sword he'd used to kill Josh and Greg.

Adrienne tried backing away but ended up on the ground when she tripped on the bed cover.

Malik released the sword, which continued floating, and pointed at Adrienne. He gestured towards the ceiling.

She looked up, thinking there was something to see, then yelped as her entire body lifted into the air. Her yelp turned into a cry of panic when the blanket unraveled. She grabbed at it to hold it in place and it fought against her.

"You can believe me or I can continue," he said with a grin on his lips.

"I believe you. I believe you. Stop it. Put me down," she yelled.

"As you wish, though I preferred to continue."

The blanket stopped fighting with her and her feet were placed on the ground. She sat on the bed in relief. Her gaze stayed on Malik to see what he would do next.

"To answer your earlier question, I first have to explain the history of Ulan and Kakra."

"Of who and who?"

Malik smiled. "I am confusing you and I am sorry."

She was way past confused. Confused was the last rest stop before the eighty-mile stretch she found herself on now.

After a moment of silence, she asked quietly, "I'm not dreaming, am I?"

"No, my lady."

"But—"

A knock at the door cut off what she would have said next.

Malik glared at the door. "Come," he snapped.

The woman from earlier entered the room followed by two younger women carrying trays. The older woman said, "I am sorry to interrupt. I took as long as I could, Majesty."

"Fine." Malik sighed in frustration. He pointed to the table near the windows. "Put the food there and leave. I do not want to be disturbed once the door closes behind you. Is that clear?"

The woman nodded quickly. She signaled the younger women forward and followed after them but stopped when she chanced a glance at Adrienne. Surprise showed on her face. "Are you cold, Highness? I can use a warming spell—"

"Mushira," Malik warned in a cold tone.

Adrienne grabbed on to the opportunity to keep the women in the room. "Mushira? Is that your name?"

"Yes, Highness. The two girls are Hani and Nimat. We are your lady's maids," Mushira answered with an encouraging smile.

Adrienne looked at the girls. They looked close to her age. They weren't Asian—or, she should say, Asian-looking—like Mushira. This wasn't Earth, after all, and Bron might not have an Asia.

Mushira had introduced the girls too quickly so Adrienne didn't know which was which and couldn't match their names with their looks.

The blonde girl to the left of the table was tall and willowy. The smile on her face looked like it was never far from the surface and her green eyes glittered with it.

The other girl was a head shorter than her companion and looked Indian—India Indian: brown skin, dark eyes and black hair. Like Mushira, the girls had their hair braided and wrapped around their heads in a crown.

Both girls stopped unloading food onto the table and curtsied to Adrienne.

She nodded at them with a wan smile and then looked back at Mushira. "So, you're the one who put me in this nightgown?"

Mushira must have heard the accusation in Adrienne's tone. The woman bowed her head and answered quickly, "I'm sorry if the gown is not to your liking, Highness. My only excuse is that I have yet to learn your tastes and therefore couldn't guess what you would like to wear."

"Okay," Adrienne said in complete dismissal of the woman's apology. She didn't care if the woman was sorry. She wanted to be decent. "Is there a robe or something around here that isn't see-through?"

"Of course, Highness. I should have set it out for you as soon as you awoke. I was careless in that regard," Mushira said in a shaky voice. She glanced towards Malik, then rushed over to the closet and rifled through it to find the robe. Once she pulled it out, she all but ran back across the room to present it to Adrienne. "Here you are, Highness," she said with a quick curtsy.

Adrienne didn't take the robe, even though she wanted to. It was perfect—orange, floor-length and terrycloth-esque. Her problem was with Malik. She glared over at him.

He turned his back before she could tell him to. Her attention stayed on him for another few seconds before she trusted he wouldn't turn back.

Mushira helped her out of her blanket cocoon, and then she put on the robe. Adrienne wasn't happy until the front halves of the robe completely overlapped, almost cutting off her oxygen, and the sash was tied in one huge knot. She thanked Mushira.

Mushira stammered out another apology.

Malik yelled, "Out. All of you. Now."

His tone made Adrienne flinch. She watched, helpless, as all three women curtsied on their way out the door. Nothing she could say would keep them there.

He smiled at her and she looked away from him to stare across the room. The food-laden table was in her direct line of sight. The smell hit her as soon as she looked at it, reminding her that she hadn't eaten since lunch the day before.

"Would you like to hear how I came to choose you, now, my lady?"

Adrienne ignored his question to move towards the food. Nothing looked familiar but it all smelled delicious.

She asked over her shoulder, "Can I eat while you talk?"

He joined her at the table before answering, "Of course. I would not dream of making you wait until the end of such a long story."

Malik held the seat for Adrienne and she thanked him automatically. Her good manners ended there. She grabbed a piece of bread and bit into it before Malik rounded the table to sit.

The orb Malik had summoned earlier floated over to the middle of the table and grew. It stopped at the size of a small television. An impressive trick, but Adrienne was more interested in her food.

"Bron is a world in which magicks exist, Adrienne. Unlike on Earth, science never had a chance to stamp it out."

Around a mouthful of meat, she asked, "Is there any way to skip to the important parts that explain why you kidnapped me?"

"A spell was cast to lead me to my perfect mate, and you are it, Adrienne."

"By?"

"By what?"

"Who cast the spell?" Adrienne asked in annoyance. Malik's grin made her think he was being purposefully vague to make her ask questions.

He tapped the orb. A tall Asian man appeared. Malik said, "This man."

"Who is that?"

"Kenji."

"Who the hell is..." she trailed off on a growl. It took a great deal of will to keep from throwing her knife at him. "You're being obtuse on purpose. Stop it."

"You told me to skip to the important parts, my lady. I do but obey."

She sighed and decided to play along. "Just tell me."

"Tell you what?"

"Whatever you were going to tell me. Just tell it your way."

"Are you sure?"

She pointed her fork at him in a threatening manner and he laughed. The sound preceded a soft fuzzy feeling, like touching cotton. It made Adrienne want to laugh even though she felt annoyed, not amused.

Malik began, "Because of stipulations set forth by my ancestor, I must marry before my twenty-fifth birthday or I will forfeit my throne."

"What does that have to do with me and the spell that found me?"

"You said you wished me to impart this information in my own way, my lady."

Adrienne rolled her eyes then signaled him to continue. She planned to ignore him and eat anyway so it didn't matter what he said or how.

The soft, fuzzy feeling intensified.

Amusement tinged Malik's voice as he continued, "In order to answer your question about Kenji and why he cast the spell, I must first explain about the feud that exists between Ulan and Kakra."

Chapter Four

Forty-eight generations ago, Malik's kingdom of Ulan and its bitter rival Kakra were joined as one kingdom under the rule of Derex, Malik's ancestor. Foluke, the combined kingdoms, was the strongest of Bron's thirteen kingdoms.

"Earlier you said there were fourteen kingdoms," Adrienne corrected.

"I assume you know simple math, my lady."

She glared at him.

"Take away two and add one, that is thirteen."

"Get on with it."

Malik tapped the orb again. A red-headed man seated on a throne appeared. Beside him, a small Asian woman sat on her own throne. Two men, one with black hair and one with red, stood on either side of the couple. Malik pointed to the standing man with red hair and said, "This is Kakra." He moved his finger to point at the man with black hair. "This is Ulan."

"Let me guess, the kingdoms were named after them."

"Yes."

Ulan and Kakra were twins and bitter rivals in all things. Their constant fighting threatened to tear Foluke apart. Derex decided to split his kingdom along the Tano River and give each son their own kingdom to rule upon his death. He hoped this would placate his sons and the feuding would stop.

He was wrong. Each wanted to rule Foluke as a whole, not simply a part of it. Derex decided to use his sons' greed against them. He set forth two stipulations on the newly formed kingdoms—only legitimate sons could inherit, and the heir to the throne had to be married before his twenty-fifth birthday.

"Only kids born in wedlock can be crowned."

"No, my lady," Malik replied. "Only *sons* that are *conceived* in wedlock may inherit the throne."

"There's no way to be sure the child was *conceived* in wedlock."

Malik unbuttoned his shirt, smirking when Adrienne stopped eating and watched him. He felt her confusion return along with an edge of fear and a tiny hint of curiosity. His bride wanted to see more of him, and he planned to show her.

He peeled back his shirt and revealed his shoulder, tattooed with Ulan's crest—a coiled serpent. "This crest is magickal and only marks legitimate children, sons and daughters alike, though the daughters will never rule," Malik said.

"Why not?"

"Derex felt women were too stupid and emotional. Kakra agreed. Ulan, however, married a competent queen who could help him rule. His son Kenji did the same."

"He's the one who cast the spell?"

"Yes. Kenji cast a blood spell—the most powerful kind—that would flow through the generations from one Ulanian heir to the throne to the next. Each time, the spell would find the heir's perfect queen, who would be equal in magickal power and rule at his side."

"I don't know magic," Adrienne said in a cheerful voice. "That means I'm not the one you want. Feel free to send me home."

Malik reached across the table and caressed Adrienne's cheek. He didn't need to touch her but doing so proved his point faster. He asked, "Do you feel that?"

"Your hand? Yes."

"No. Warmth. Warmth that makes your skin tingle and your body feel hot. Do you feel it?" he purred. Her small shiver was his answer.

He leaned across the table. A smile curved his lips when Adrienne did the same.

Their faces were only a few inches apart. He could bridge the distance easily. Instead, he whispered, "What you feel is lust, Adrienne. *My* lust for you. That you can feel it is proof that you are my intended bride."

Her lips parted and she gave a tiny gasp. She looked at him with wide eyes.

Malik felt the murmur of her lust on his skin. She had responded to him and he wanted to act on it. He couldn't. He needed to be wed to Adrienne before he could have her.

He threw himself back into his seat with an annoyed growl. "You are my bride and we will be married."

"What if I don't marry you?" she asked. She met his eyes but he didn't see defiance, he saw curiosity, and felt it, too. "If Kakra comes to take your throne, just fight them off. You seem like a good fighter and, I'm betting, you make sure your army is full of good fighters, too."

"I would lose," Malik answered. "Only because Kakra would have the help of Kontar, our neighbor to the north. Derex made them our watchdog. He married his daughter Selene to Kontar's then-king and charged her and her descendents with the task of making sure Ulan's and Kakra's rulers adhered to his rules."

"How long have you ruled, Malik? Where are you parents? Did they step down so you could rule?"

"Kakra had my parents assassinated. My mother when I was three and my father when I was ten." Involuntary vehemence entered his voice.

Talking about his parents annoyed him faster than anything else, but Adrienne didn't know that. While her curiosity didn't cause his anger, the topic of his parents' demises needed to be avoided.

"Why? Why would Kakra's ruler kill them?"

"Hollace knows only greed. He probably thought I would be an easy target once my parents were out of the way, and then he could claim Ulan and re-form Foluke," Malik said. "After my coronation, I had the palace moved to Ulan's Eastern island and an entire navy placed between me and harm."

"My God." Her eyes searched his across the table. She whispered, "You've ruled Ulan since you were ten? But why? Wasn't there a...a...what are they called?"

"Regent," he supplied in a lackluster voice.

"Yes."

"No. There are no regents. There are only rulers and heirs to the throne. That is the way Derex wanted it and that is the way it must be." His words sounded bitter and tasted worse. Malik watched Adrienne for a reaction. Seeing and feeling her confusion and uncertainty made his anger ebb away.

He looked up at the orb, which had changed its image to show all the people and places Malik mentioned. His parents stared out at him. The pain of seeing them returned, even after all this time. With a small push of will, the orb went blank. His parents were gone—as they were supposed to be.

"How old are you now?"

"In three months I will be twenty-five."

"Yeah, that's right, you said that earlier. Sorry," she said absently.

Adrienne didn't mean to ramble. Her mind couldn't fathom being thrust into ruling an entire kingdom at such a young age. At age ten she had played with dolls and dreamt of being swept away by Prince Charming, just like Cinderella and Sleeping Beauty.

She looked at Malik—really looked at him. Here was Prince Charming—scratch that, he was a king—*King* Charming, and he had definitely swept her away. Except away meant a whole new dimension where her nearest neighbor might kill her to get more power.

Her hand clenched where it rested near her plate. Malik's parents' assassinations, while tragic, held a more immediate concern for her.

She was in danger.

"What is the matter, my lady?"

"You want me to live here," Adrienne whispered. She pushed away from the table. Whether to run from Malik or from this new horrifying future, she couldn't be sure. She just wanted to be away.

Malik stood as well. "Adrienne—"

She yelled, "You want me to put my life on the line to secure *your* kingdom and squeeze out an heir or two—male, I might add. Are you nuts?"

He replied in a normal, calm tone, "My sanity is quite intact, I assure you. As to the other, I would protect you."

Adrienne laughed humorlessly at his proclamation. "Protect me? Protect me! I've seen your type of protection. His head rolled past my feet." She inched back towards the bed and the door beyond it. "No way! No way in hell am I staying in this crazy place. I'll be killed before my next birthday," she predicted. Her slow escape to freedom ended when the backs of her legs hit the bed. "Send me home. I don't know this place and I couldn't care less about it. Find someone else to play martyr. I'm not it."

"It does not work like that, I am afraid, Adrienne. The spell found you, thus you belong to me."

He followed her. No, it looked more like stalking.

She tried not to be scared of what she saw in his eyes. Malik had told her repeatedly that he wouldn't hurt her, and she gathered from his explanation that he couldn't have sex with her until after their vows. Keeping that in mind proved difficult when the look in his eyes made her feel like she was on his menu.

She pleaded again, "Please, send me home. I don't care about some stupid spell. I do care about dying an untimely death."

Malik closed the gap between them, his body a hair's breadth from hers. He bent his head and held her eyes in an unbreakable gaze. "None shall harm you so long as I rule here," he vowed. "None would dare try."

Adrienne swallowed. She tried to turn her gaze away from his and realized she couldn't. She felt as helpless now as when Josh and Greg grabbed her, but Malik hadn't touched her. He hadn't impeded her escape in any way—except she couldn't break eye contact or run.

"You can't force me," she said with a conviction she didn't feel. "No priest, or whatever, will marry us if I don't say yes."

Malik moved his hand to her cheek and she flinched. "The Mage Guild master needs to hear nothing from you, Adrienne. She does not need your consent and will not ask for it. All she needs to know is that the spell my ancestor cast found you."

All of a sudden, Adrienne could look away. She tore her gaze from his with relief and didn't question why she'd held it as long as she had. Malik had done something to her, nothing else made sense.

"I don't want this. I don't know you," she said in the barest of whispers.

"You will come to know me after the wedding," he said matter-of-factly. He moved his hand from her cheek to cup her chin, though he didn't make her look at him. His thumb rubbed gently over her cheek. "Now that I have found you, I will not hesitate to make you mine."

The feeling of paralysis returned. She wanted to turn out of his grasp but couldn't.

"Just like them," she whispered.

"Who?"

Adrienne looked up at him, proving herself wrong. She could move, just not away from him. "Josh and his friend, the guys you killed. Josh wanted me to do what he wanted—what was in his best interest. To hell with how that would make me look or what would happen to me." Her gaze bore into his. "When I refused... Well, you interrupted what happened when I refused. Funny how this time I doubt someone's going to jump out of nowhere and stab *you* with a sword."

Malik's hand dropped from her chin. Remembering his parents had hurt, but Adrienne's words hurt worse. He didn't want to be compared to the men who had attacked her. They'd wanted to hurt her. He offered her the life and the privilege of a queen, and her only concern was the vague possibility of an assassination attempt in the far-off future. He knew it would only be an attempt, since he planned to protect her.

The first person he needed to protect her from was himself and his lust. In his bid to keep her near him, he had used a light paralysis spell—involuntarily. He hadn't meant to call the magicks, but neither did he stop them. Adrienne's comparison held a ring of truth. She had refused him and he immobilized her with the intention of...

No, he wouldn't have. She had to be pure on their wedding day. He knew her to be pure now—his magicks had discerned this while he healed her. He looked forward to introducing her to the carnal side of life and had hoped such an experience—an awakening—would happen tonight after their wedding ceremony, once he had calmed her fears.

"One week," he said as he stepped back from her.

"What?"

He took another step back. Being so close to her made him want to forget the ceremony and Derex's rules and have her at that moment. Such wants were dangerous when his magicks seemed to be heeding subconscious promptings.

"I will give you one week to grow used to Ulan and life on Bron."

"If I don't, then what?" she asked, hope coloring her words.

"Regardless of whether you have come to accept your situation here or not, in one week you *will* marry me."

"And to hell with what I want, huh?"

Malik moved to the bedroom door. He put his hand on the knob and turned back to look at Adrienne. She glared at him. Heat licked at his skin, painful heat.

The heat, a familiar feeling for him, belonged to Adrienne. She was angry.

"Once we are wed, your opinion and happiness will be important to me above everything else. However, I cannot let your momentary ill humor and disorientation hinder me from keeping the kingdom my parents died for."

He watched a tear slip down Adrienne's cheek and steeled himself against the pain it caused him. His time had run out and he couldn't handle this in any other fashion.

A week would test the limits of his control. The small amount of time it took him to explain his past and Adrienne's future had him wanting to rip the clothing from her body and run his tongue over her skin. He'd almost made good on the urge three times that he remembered. A week was all the time he could give her and hope to remain noble. He knew she would understand one day. Until then, he planned to make her comfortable and happy.

He opened the door, but instead of walking through it, he beckoned to the people waiting in the hall. Mushira, Hani and Nimat entered and two extra people followed. Malik gestured to them and said, "You have already met your lady's maids."

Adrienne nodded. Her gaze traveled to the extra woman and the man who stood next to her. The woman looked like a warrior. She definitely had the height for it. Adrienne guessed the woman had four inches on her.

Unlike Mushira, Hani and Nimat, the woman wore pants instead of a dress. There was a sword strapped to her hip, a small baton hung from her opposite hip and the armbands on each of her wrists sported small throwing knives. Her dark brown hair was pulled into a severe ponytail that reached her shoulders. It made her amber eyes look all the more pointed and catlike. Except for the stern look on the woman's face, Adrienne thought she looked very pretty.

The man by her side, who was similarly dressed and armed and stern, shared his companion's height. His eyes were a steely grey. And while he had the same severe ponytail, his copper hair went to his mid-back. The man was a toothpick—a broad-shouldered toothpick, but a toothpick nonetheless. He didn't look like he could lift the sword strapped to his side, but Adrienne got the feeling he wouldn't carry it if he couldn't handle it.

Malik explained, "This is Qamar." The woman bowed at the waist. "And Khursid." The man bowed. "They are two of the top five Elite, and your personal guards."

"Two of the top five? What happened to the other three?" Adrienne asked.

"The other three are my personal guards."

"Why do I get two and you get three? That doesn't sound that equal to me."

Mushira sucked in a loud breath. When Malik looked at her, she asked, "May I, Majesty?" She smiled when Malik waved her on, then turned her smile on Adrienne. "You do have three personal guards, Highness." She gestured to the side. The blonde girl stepped forward and curtsied again. "Hani is a trained assassin."

Adrienne immediately took a step back. She gave Hani a wary look.

Hani soothed, "I am for your protection, Highness. I have trained all my life as an assassin but my goal was to serve the royal house of Ulan, not to be a mercenary. I made sure I excelled at every lesson so I could anticipate and better protect you, Highness."

"You don't even know me," Adrienne pointed out. She wasn't sure she wanted an assassin hanging around her as one of her lady's maids.

Malik informed Adrienne, "She will know you in time. Hani's loyalty to the royal house was proven long ago or I would not allow her near you, my lady. To the palace, in fact to the entire kingdom, Hani is a simple lady's maid. Such a ruse makes her your most valuable guard."

Hani added, "However, I am not one of the Elite."

Before Adrienne could ask, Malik supplied, "Qamar, Khursid and my personal guards all went through training in Kakra. Once their training finished and I paid their blade price, they endured challenge after challenge to prove they were good enough to be my...*our* elite, personal guards. Hani went through no such process because assassins are not trained in Kakra. Where exactly they are trained is a mystery I have allowed Hani to keep because of the service she is providing me."

Adrienne quoted, "Fight fire with fire."

"Exactly, my lady. I realize you have had a trying morning and have had to digest a large amount of information all at once. In a bid to see you in a happier, less stressful mood, I shall take my leave and you can become better acquainted with your guards and your maids." He bowed to her. "I shall see you again tonight for dinner."

She watched him leave and close the door behind him.

Dinner? She had barely eaten breakfast thanks to him. She had no intention of letting him ruin dinner for her, as well. That information she kept to herself, for the time being. Another confrontation with Malik had to be postponed for as long as possible.

Mushira moved towards Adrienne. She spoke calmly as though she expected Adrienne to bolt at the slightest provocation. "If Your Highness would like, we can prepare a bath for you. King Malik healed your wounds but decided you might wish to have a soothing bath instead of being sponged off."

She didn't wait for Adrienne to say yea or nay to the idea, but signaled Nimat to proceed with the bath preparations. Hani followed Nimat without prompting.

"You two can wait outside," Mushira commanded Qamar and Khursid. Both bowed to Adrienne, then left the room. Mushira assured quickly, "They will be right outside the door, Highness. There is no need to worry they are going far."

Adrienne didn't appreciate being treated like a child on top of being kidnapped. She didn't care if the woman did it to be nice or not.

"Look, Mushira," she started.

"Yes, Highness." Mushira had a smile of encouragement on her face.

"Stop talking to me like I'm three years old. I'm upset, not a child. I realize you're probably old enough to be my mother, but you aren't, so don't act like it."

In the wake of Malik's departure, fear had turned into anger, and Malik's absence made this woman her target. She hadn't meant to choose Mushira but it had to go somewhere. All these people were the enemy because they worked for Malik.

Mushira jerked back with a look of surprise. She bowed her head. "I am sorry if my actions or words have angered you, Highness."

"I'm not angry at you. I'm angry at that...that..." She made an angry noise. "I can't even think of a word strong enough to describe his supreme jerkiness."

Hani came out of the bathroom holding a foot-tall vase with intricately painted flowers. She ventured forward and held it out to Adrienne. "Perhaps you would feel better if you threw something, Highness. My mother always did when my father angered her."

"Thanks," Adrienne said as she grabbed the vase. She thought about throwing it at the door and knew it would never get there. Too many times people had told her she threw like a girl. She settled for the wall closest to her.

She hurtled the vase with all the frustration and anger she felt. Amazingly, when it shattered on the wall, she did feel better. Adrienne hoped the vase was expensive and well-liked. She pretended it was to increase her satisfaction in breaking it. If it turned out to be expensive, it would serve Malik right.

The door to the room opened. Khursid and Qamar spilled into the room with hands on their still-sheathed swords. Adrienne waved them away. "No worries, just venting. I'm still alive, for now," she said.

Khursid took a step forward. "We cannot allow you to take your own life, Highness."

Adrienne snorted. Thoughts of suicide were the furthest thing from her mind. She had meant her imminent assassination. She shot back, "Well, then your job just got easy. I'm too much of a coward to take my own life. I would rather live out this hell than find out what waits for me in the next."

Neither Khursid nor Qamar looked convinced. They didn't leave or stand down from their tensed stances.

"Oh, whatever. Stand there, then. I'm going to take a bath and then I'm going back to sleep."

"Your bath is ready, Highness," said Nimat as she exited the bathroom. She curtsied. "We will wake you in time for dinner."

Adrienne walked towards the bathroom. "No, you won't. If I sleep through dinner, it's all for the better."

Hani reminded, "King Malik said—"

"Screw him. If *he* wants me to leave this room so he can display me at dinner, *he* can come and drag me out by my hair—'cause I'm not going otherwise," she said with her hands on her hips.

Nimat exchanged a look with Mushira. She turned her gaze back to Adrienne and asked, "Would Your Highness like me to relay this message to His Majesty?"

"Whatever floats your boat," Adrienne answered. Her words caused Nimat to look at her in confusion. "If you want to, you can tell him. I don't care either way."

Mushira nodded to Nimat and the girl left to relay Adrienne's message. Adrienne wondered if she should stick around to hear the reply. She got the distinct impression Malik would deliver his response in person. And he probably wouldn't care if she was occupied with her bath or not. He'd already seen her naked...sort of. She didn't want to give him another show.

"Might as well relax in my bath while I can," she said to herself.

Khursid whispered to Qamar, "I will remain outside while you make sure the future queen doesn't harm herself." Qamar gave the barest of nods to this plan.

Adrienne had all but forgotten about him until that moment. She didn't know if Khursid meant for his words to carry, but she'd heard him.

She waited for him to look at her before she said, "I can tell you and I are going to have major issues with each other in the future, Khursid."

"I don't know what you mean, Highness," he said in a calm, condescending voice.

That's it, she thought, *I'm officially sick of men*. She crossed her arms and returned Khursid's look with one of her own. "You just called me a liar."

Khursid blinked in surprise, the first real emotion he had shown since he met Adrienne. "I would never—"

"I told you that I'm not going to kill myself. That you don't believe me means you think I'm lying."

Khursid dropped quickly to one knee with his arm crossed over his chest and his head lowered. He excused in a stiff tone, "I never meant to insinuate Your Highness would lie, but I am sworn to protect you from everyone, including yourself."

She wanted to throw something at him. Instead, Adrienne turned to Hani and asked, "Are there any other small vases around? It seems I'm going to be venting a lot in the days to come."

Hani's worried features smoothed into a wide smile. "Of course, Highness. I will fetch others. If need be, I will have the pottery smith make vases of varying sizes and shapes specifically for you to vent with." She hurried past Khursid, who stayed kneeling. She didn't look to or wait for Mushira to give her approval of this errand before she ran to complete it.

Adrienne turned to Mushira. "Since both Nimat and Hani have run off, does that mean I have to wait, or are you going to trust I know how to bathe myself?"

Mushira gestured to the bathroom. "It is this way, Highness." Her gaze went back to Khursid. "Highness, what of Khursid?"

Adrienne ignored Mushira's question and looked at Qamar instead. The woman stiffened to nervous attention. She asked, "Are you coming or not? You can't stop me from slitting my wrists from across the room."

Qamar took a hesitant step forward and then looked at Khursid. He had not moved. Her gaze returned to Adrienne. "Does Your Highness wish my presence during your bath?"

No!

Adrienne wanted to scream it for them all to hear. She wanted to be alone. Everything had happened so fast and she was lost in a sea of information and unfamiliarity. She needed quiet and solitude to process it all.

She looked at Khursid, then Qamar. It wasn't to be. Finally she shrugged and said, "If I'm going to be protected by you, both of you, I have to get used to you following me around no matter where I go. Now's as good a time as any."

Adrienne wanted to cry as the words left her mouth. They were in direct contradiction of what she really wanted. Malik forced this all on her. That she had no choice frightened her.

Nimat and Malik entered the room then. He assessed the situation and found himself trying hard not to laugh. Nimat curtsied as Malik passed her.

Malik had been in a funk from the moment he left Adrienne until Nimat came to the throne room and delivered her message. He hadn't meant to upset Adrienne as much as he had. He knew his news would do nothing but irritate her. Who wouldn't be angry to find they were taken from their world and thrust into another?

He'd returned with Nimat with all haste because he expected to see Adrienne in tears. Tears he had seen the beginnings of before he quit her room. Instead, Malik found she had cowed one of his strongest warriors.

When he was sure his voice wouldn't betray his humor at this turn of events, Malik said, "Nimat informs me you do not wish to join me for dinner tonight, my lady."

Adrienne didn't answer him. She didn't look at him, either. Looking at Malik only reinforced all the inevitabilities of the last hour. It took all her willpower not to dissolve to the floor in a puddle of tears.

She looked at the door to the bathroom—her goal. She walked away from Malik's question, ignoring it and him. Mushira, Nimat and Qamar followed her. Qamar entered the bathroom last. She gave Khursid a worried look, then closed the door.

Adrienne didn't relax until she heard the telltale click of the door latch. A sigh slipped from her lips and she sank onto the bench nearest her. She let her head fall into her hands in hopes that it would stop the flow of her tears. They seeped through her fingers anyway. She didn't want to cry in front of a room full of strangers, but this was as private as she would get, and she had reached the end of her emotional endurance.

Malik looked from the closed bathroom door to Khursid. His smile of amusement turned sad. He looked once more at the bathroom door. His future queen was in pain—emotional pain. Time was the only cure—and possibly his absence.

To that end, Malik would leave Adrienne in the care of her maids. Before he took his leave of Adrienne's rooms, one small matter needed attending to first.

"Rise, Khursid."

The man straightened to his full height. He stared at the wall in front of him in a state of attention.

"Be at ease, I will not punish you."

Many warriors carried the scars of Malik's displeasure since they had been denied the aid of a healing mage. Those who tried to hide their mistakes only to have Malik find out later were counted among that number.

"But Majesty, you do not know what I have done," Khursid insisted.

Malik waved that away. "It does not matter. She is upset and rightfully so. The fault is not yours but mine. If it were something truly grievous, Mushira would have voiced the complaint where Adrienne had not."

He patted the man's shoulder and felt him stiffen in reaction. Malik did not take offense. He knew he was a hard taskmaster, but his warriors were the stronger for it. "Return to your post and I shall return to mine. It seems the palace will have to wait to meet my intended queen."

Malik returned to his throne room and the people he had left awaiting his judgments.

Chapter Five

"You had better have good news," said the woman from the shadowed recesses of her study.

The cloaked man bowed to the floating orb that held the image of the shadowed woman. He spoke in a hushed voice so he would not be overheard. "I am afraid not, Excellency. Malik has found his bride. That meddlesome Travers broke my spell of interference. I underestimated his power level. I will not make the same mistake again."

The woman in the orb slammed her hand on the desk in front of her. Blue sparks flew out from the impact point and fell harmlessly in a shower around her. She leaned forward, though her face remained shrouded in darkness. Her voice was rough and angered. "You assured me the interference spell would keep Malik from finding his bride. That was the only way to assure Kakra's ability to claim Ulan. You assured me the interference spell couldn't be easily detected or broken. The fact that you cannot handle a simple royal chancellor makes me wonder if I chose the wrong man for this job."

The man scrambled to make the situation better. He would have rather gone into hiding than report badly on himself, but he knew his other news would cheer his mistress. "I have other news, Excellency."

"Speak!"

The man flinched. The woman's voice carried in the small space and he remained silent, tempting the anger of his mistress to ensure none had heard her angered command. He heard nothing and assumed his conversation remained private. "The girl is from the Earth dimension, Excellency," he said.

Though he couldn't see her face, he knew the woman smiled. A smile he hoped to never see in connection with himself.

"Are you positive of this?" she asked in quiet wonder.

The man sagged in relief and nodded. "I would stake my life on it. Malik retrieved her himself."

A brief silence followed this statement. Laughter flowed out of the orb, quiet at first and then gradually louder. "Excellent! Bring her to me. I don't care how or who you kill to do it. I want her alive and unharmed and delivered to me immediately," she commanded.

The man bowed to the orb. "As soon as Malik drops his guard, the girl is as good as mine, Excellency. She will be yours moments after that."

"She had better be. Another failure means your death," she promised him. "See to it I am not kept waiting long."

The orb blanked before he could answer that proclamation. The man replaced the orb in his robes and hurried away from his quiet spot to plan.

If he had known Malik's bride-to-be would be from the Earth dimension, he wouldn't have cast the interference spell. His mistress could have had her prize years ago. Hopefully her patience would last until he could find the opportunity to carry out her order. As much as he feared his mistress's wrath, he didn't want to face down Malik.

Such a confrontation might be inevitable. He'd heard that Malik's intended didn't have magicks. That would make her the first Ulanian queen to be unequal to her husband in power. It would also make Malik overly protective of her.

But, Malik had to sleep sometime. And guards weren't infallible, as Malik's parents had learned. The man's chance would come and then he would happily deliver Ulan's future queen to her doom.

Chapter Six

The outlook didn't get much better for Adrienne the next morning. She lay on her gigantic bed against her soft, fluffy pillows and stared at the ceiling...sky...whatever...and couldn't think of a single reason to get out of bed.

After a good long cry in the bathroom, she decided to face facts. She was on a parallel Earth, magic brought her there and she had to get married in a week. It made more sense for her to try to learn something about Bron rather than pout the days away—even if pouting seemed like a better idea.

It made her angry to think she had wasted her entire childhood studying and learning and preparing to be a useful part of society. A society she wasn't part of anymore. She had an answer for the age-old question of when algebra and world literature and numerous other subjects would be used in the real world—never.

She had to toss everything aside and learn all new facts. One fun fact was Hollace's refusal to use magic, which meant he wouldn't try to kill her that way. He, like every king of Kakra before him, hated magic. Hollace ruled over a nation of soldiers and preferred the simplicity of a sword or other edged weapons.

Qamar had imparted that bit of knowledge as a way to soothe Adrienne's nerves. It hadn't worked. Who cared *how* Hollace—or whoever—did it? The *wanting*-to-kill-her part had her upset.

"Do you plan to sleep this day away as well, Highness?" asked Mushira.

Adrienne let her head fall to the side. She watched Mushira come into her room—without her permission—and proceed to open all the curtains. The transparent ceiling already let in the morning sunshine, which made opening the curtains pointless. There was no difference and Adrienne would seem petty if she told Mushira to close them. She kept her mouth shut and went back to staring at the sky-ceiling.

"Good morning, Highness," greeted Hani brightly.

"What's so good about it?" Adrienne muttered.

Mushira faced Adrienne with a stern look on her face. "I know last night was trying, but that is no reason to be morose today. The ordeal has passed and the shield around your bed will ensure it won't happen again."

"Oh, I'm sorry," said Adrienne in a snide voice. "The next time I have a nightmare about being raped, I'll scream a little softer so I don't wake you up."

"I didn't. I only meant..." She trailed off with a look of fear.

"Mushira didn't mean to belittle your experience, Highness," Hani excused. "She only wants you to be in better spirits."

"Yes," Mushira agreed quickly. "My tone was lecturing and I didn't mean it to be. I'm sorry."

Great, now Adrienne felt guilty. She'd awakened her entire entourage in the middle of the night with her screaming, then a few hours later, repaid their concern with anger. It wasn't their fault her mind decided to replay the events of her attack in full, vivid detail along with alternate endings and deleted scenes.

"Your ordeal wouldn't have happened at all if I'd had the presence of mind to stay at your side once the sun went down," Mushira continued. "I am not normally this forgetful, Highness, but your sudden appearance has me a bit out of sorts."

"Don't worry about it. You didn't know," Adrienne dismissed.

"I should have predicted it. Ulan is a land of errant magicks. They are attracted to people of strong emotions and great potential."

"Potential for what?"

"To control them."

"I don't know any magic. And why do you keep referring to magic like it's a living thing?"

Hani answered, "Magicks *are* a living entity, Highness. The people of Bron are not born with powers and abilities. If they have the aptitude, they learn to gather the magicks within themselves and shape them to their needs. The more magicks a person harnesses, the more powerful they are. Some—like you, Highness, and King Malik— don't need to gather magicks. They simply seek you out."

"Are you telling me these magicks things caused my nightmare?" Adrienne asked in surprise.

Mushira nodded. "The magicks must have felt your distress and worked to amplify it."

"I get it. I brought this on myself by being depressed."

"I didn't mean to imply—"

"No, no, Mushira. It's okay. I can admit when I'm wrong," Adrienne soothed. She didn't want the woman going into another fit of apologies. Mushira always sounded frightened, like she expected Adrienne to hit her.

A knock at the door caught everyone's attention. Mushira looked to Adrienne. Hani stepped forward with a robe held out in front of her. Adrienne crawled to the edge of the bed and got to her feet. She tied the front of her robe securely before she signaled Mushira to answer the door. Despite the non-sheer nightgown Mushira had produced after her bath yesterday, Adrienne still wanted to be in a robe.

All her preparation and nervousness were for naught. The knock had come from Khursid. Unlike the ladies, he couldn't simply enter Adrienne's room. He had to make sure Adrienne was decent first.

"Good morning, Highness," he greeted.

"Where's Qamar?" she asked without returning his greeting. She hadn't known them very long, but she didn't like the implications of seeing one and not the other.

"She was called before King Malik, Highness."

"He didn't want to see you too?"

"No, Highness."

"Do you know why he called her?"

"No, Highness. Sorry."

Adrienne shrugged.

Another knock. Khursid waited for Adrienne's nod before he opened it. Nimat entered, carrying a tray of food. A man, carrying another food tray, followed her. The man was willowy like Hani but shorter than Adrienne.

The stern look in the man's violet eyes reminded Adrienne of her tenth grade English teacher when he caught someone using "ain't". The look didn't end with his eyes. From his close-cropped white hair to his stiff spine, his whole manner was of stern disapproval. The man couldn't be angry at Adrienne, he didn't even know her.

He and Nimat immediately carried the food trays to the table.

Once she settled her tray on the table, Nimat greeted, "Good morning, Highness."

Adrienne settled on a half-hearted wave.

Nimat gestured to the man with her. "This is Saj, Highness. He is King Malik's lord's valet."

Saj bowed low to Adrienne.

"Lord's valet?" Adrienne asked with a raised eyebrow.

Mushira supplied, "The male version of a lady's maid, Highness."

"Oh." If Adrienne had stopped to think about it before she opened her mouth, the meaning of the phrase would have been obvious. It only made sense. What didn't make sense was...

"What is he doing here?"

Malik entered the room without knocking. Qamar followed in his wake. She bowed to Adrienne, then took her position next to Khursid.

Malik answered, "He is here to serve me as I eat breakfast with my intended queen. I assumed she would not be up to eating breakfast before the court." He nodded to everyone in the room as they bowed or curtsied to him. "I trust the morning finds you well, my lady?" he asked with a smile. He signaled Qamar and Khursid out of the room. They closed the door after themselves.

Adrienne wanted to tell him she'd had a crappy night thanks to her magickally amplified nightmare, but she decided against it. According to Mushira, Malik should already know about her nightmare since he was summoned when no one could wake her. He hadn't shown. That alone proved Malik didn't really care about her happiness or anything else.

She settled on saying, "As well as can be expected, I guess."

"I'm sorry to interrupt," said Saj in a voice that didn't sound sorry at all. "Your breakfast is ready."

Malik went to the table and sat. Adrienne stayed put. She was hungry and the food smelled wonderful, but she refused to sit across from Malik again.

"I don't want you here," she said quietly.

Mushira dropped the serving fork in her hand. Her eyes went wide and she stared at Malik. Nimat edged back to hide behind Saj, whose gaze was on Hani. She had placed herself sideways between the royal couple.

Malik only smiled at Adrienne's declaration. "I appreciate and understand your anger at me, my lady. However, avoiding me will not alleviate these emotions. Also, you will not be able to acquaint yourself with me if I am not in your presence."

"Why now? I have seven days. Why can't you bother me later and leave me alone now?"

"Ten," corrected Malik. He took a sip of his coffee.

"Ten what?"

"The weeks on Bron are ten days long, not seven, my lady."

"Even more reason to leave me alone today," Adrienne insisted. She wanted to kick herself when she heard the whimpering quality of her voice. Pouting like a child wouldn't win her this argument. Malik had proven immune to her upsets.

He nodded at her words. "You are right, of course, my lady. I find I cannot leave you, though."

"It's easy. Get up and leave. The door's right there. Don't let it hit you on the ass on your way out." She pointed at the door in question but Malik didn't move. He continued to smile at her and eat his breakfast. His amusement at her frustration made her angry.

"I have allowed you ten days, my lady. You can allow me to spend that time in your presence. It is only fair."

"What about your kingdom? Don't you have to do *something* as the king?" she asked in a last ditch effort to get him to leave.

"I do. As much as I would enjoy your presence at my side as I attend matters of court and kingdom, I know you will refuse. As well you should. You are new to Bron and I wish to keep the knowledge of your origins secret from the world. It is best to wait until you are comfortable in your knowledge of Bron and Ulan before I present you to the court," he said. "I had not planned to spend all day with you, my lady. Only a few hours. Surely such a small amount of time can be tolerated?"

Adrienne stalked over to a set of windows as far away from Malik as she could get. If he wouldn't leave, then she would wait him out. She could concentrate on the garden below her room and the many people trying to keep the palace grounds beautiful—a task made difficult because the plants didn't seem to want to be cut and fought back when the gardeners tried.

The battle of man versus nature should have been hilarious to Adrienne. It only reminded her of Bron's differences. Ten days wouldn't be enough time to learn everything she needed to convince people she was a true inhabitant.

What would she talk about? One family anecdote and she would give herself away. She couldn't discuss how she and Malik met or anything about her life before he brought her to Bron. The less she said about herself, the more people would want to know and that would put undue stress on her.

There had to be a good reason why she had to keep her origin a secret, but it didn't matter. It constituted another demand—something forced on her by a man who didn't care that he'd taken her from her family and all that she loved for his own selfish ends.

There were so many things she wanted to say, wanted to yell, at Malik. None of them would come out and she knew none of it would make any difference.

She "belonged" to him. That's what he'd said to her. He'd brought her there to be his possession, not his equal. There was no way he would share his power with her. He didn't want a queen, he wanted a placeholder. What better placeholder than some dupe who...

Adrienne startled. The window in front of her cracked with a loud snap, the only warning before the whole thing shattered.

Adrienne cried out and shielded her face. Flying glass whizzed past her.

Another loud crash made Adrienne look up to see what had broken. A three-feet-tall vase had exploded. Bits of ceramic rested on top of a translucent white barrier that surrounded Malik. He looked surprised.

Before Adrienne could ask, Khursid and Qamar rushed into the room. Qamar went to Adrienne while Khursid leapt out the window face first.

"Why did he—?"

"Are you hurt, Highness?" Qamar asked.

"No, I'm fine. What was that?"

A tiny flash of light heralded Khursid's return. He stood before the shattered window. "I could find no intruders, Majesty, and no trace of the magicks used," he said to Malik.

"You just jumped out the window," Adrienne yelled. "What the hell?"

"A levitation spell slowed my descent and a teleportation spell aided my return."

Adrienne was so preoccupied with Khursid's antics that she missed Malik moving to her side. She jerked away from him when he would have touched her cheek.

"Don't touch me, damn it."

Another vase shattered.

Everyone looked at it and then at Adrienne. She stared back at them.

Saj walked over to the first broken vase and gathered the pieces. "It is not well done of you to upset your intended queen in such a way, Majesty. Her Highness will end up destroying the palace if you persist."

"What's he talking about?" Adrienne asked.

"You are right, Saj. I am leaving even now," Malik agreed. He turned his attention back to Adrienne. "I had not expected your powers to show this early. In a bid to keep my palace whole and return you to a more sanguine mood, I shall take my leave of you. You will not see me again until tomorrow. I hope this is satisfactory, my lady."

"No, it's not. I want to go home."

"I am sorry I must disappoint you in that regard."

"No, you aren't. You're not sorry in the least. Just leave."

Malik bowed. "As you will, my lady." He straightened and left the room without another word.

Adrienne sagged. She wanted to sit down but too much broken glass blocked her path to the nearest chair, and she didn't have shoes. Instead, she checked for wounds. When her search turned up nothing, she turned to Saj. "No offense, but can you leave, too?"

"I wished only to aid in the clean up, Princess."

"Doesn't Malik need you?" Adrienne asked. She didn't care if Malik needed him, or for *what* Malik needed him. She wanted the man gone.

"Not presently, Princess. If I could be allowed to help clean the shattered glass, I will make quick work of the task and then be gone from your presence."

"Whatever," Adrienne said. She looked around. Had she really caused the vases and window to shatter? The tension she felt had demanded she break something. In answer to that request, things had broken.

"Is this normal?" she asked.

Hani answered, "No, Highness. As you are new to Bron and magicks, your control is not what it should be. Extremes of emotion at this time will manifest in unpredictable ways."

"Like my nightmare. Great. Now I'm a hazard to myself," Adrienne muttered in annoyance. She looked across the room when a table rattled. "Oh, stop it."

The table stopped.

She looked away from the table to Khursid and Qamar. They stared at her. She said with a smile, "Looks like you were right, Khursid. I may end up hurting myself after all."

"That was not something on which I wished to be proven right, Highness," Khursid replied.

Mushira announced, "No one will get hurt. We merely have to teach Princess Adrienne how to recognize the power she is using and how to control it."

"That's another thing," said Adrienne. "When did I become a princess?"

"As you are not yet queen, you must be given a title that denotes your status. That title is princess," Mushira answered.

Adrienne nodded. The sound of glass clanking against itself drew her eye. Saj put the last of the broken glass on the serving tray. He said, "I will endeavor to remind Malik of this incident in the hopes he will curtail his selfish tendencies, at least until you have gained control of your powers, Princess. After that, I can make no promises."

"You've just given me incentive not to learn, Saj. Thank you," Adrienne quipped with the first real humor she had felt since she got there.

"I am always glad to be of service to you, Highness. I shall take my leave now." He bowed again, gathered up the tray and left.

Adrienne waited for the door to close behind him, then asked, "Is he always so...rigid?"

"Yes," everyone said in unison.

"Ah, King Malik must have ordered the repair of the window," Mushira said with satisfaction.

Adrienne looked at the window she'd broken. The upper pane of the window dripped clear, viscous liquid. Each drop of liquid formed a small portion of glass until the entire window pane was filled.

"None of you guys is doing that?"

"No, Highness. Construction magicks are a specialty. It takes years of training to master," Hani said. She went over and tapped on the glass once the repairs finished. "The construction mages who work in the palace are extremely strong. Fixing this window without being in the room is a testament to that."

"Nice," Adrienne said. She looked back at her breakfast. How many meals would be ruined before she got used to life on this alternate Earth?

෨෬

Adrienne stared intently at the vase in front of her. It was simple, blue and about four inches high with no unique characteristics to cause her fascination.

"You've improved since yesterday, Highness," Mushira said.

"This is easy. I'd rather go back to juggling."

"Perhaps another time. It's better to make sure you are able to split your concentration between floating the vase and speaking."

Adrienne waved at the vase. "Done. Here I am, floating a vase and talking. What's next?"

Mushira pushed down on the vase. It dipped, then returned to eye level. "Keep it stationary, if you would, Highness."

"Sure."

Mushira pushed again. This time it stayed in place—and started laughing. Mushira gasped and snatched her hand away.

Adrienne laughed at the woman's surprised look. "I'm sorry, Mushira. I couldn't help myself." She poked the vase. It laughed harder.

The laughter garnered the attention of everyone in the room. Nimat poked the vase and it squeaked with even more laughter. She looked at Adrienne in awe. "Highness, how do you know animus magicks?"

"Animus magicks?" Adrienne asked. She put her hand over the mouth of the vase, muffling the laughter, but it didn't stop. She needed a top.

A small lid with a round knob appeared.

"That's the ticket," Adrienne said. She plunked the lid down on the mouth of the vase. The laughter stopped.

She smiled at her accomplishment and looked at the others for praise and words of encouragement. Her companions looked stunned.

"What?"

"Where did that lid come from?" Mushira asked.

Adrienne shrugged. "Don't know. I wanted a lid and it showed up. It matches perfectly, too."

"Princess Adrienne, that vase has no lid," Hani said.

"It's right here." Adrienne pointed at the lid. She looked around at everyone. "What's the problem?"

"You have exhibited both animus and materialization magicks but are trained in neither, Highness," Qamar said.

"Materialization would mean the lid existed somewhere in the palace, Qamar," Khursid corrected. "Her Highness performed transmutation magick. She changed some other object into a lid."

"And? What does all that mean?" Adrienne asked. Her actions shouldn't get this type of reaction. This was a land of magicks and she had used them.

"Mages are measured against twenty levels of accomplishment, Highness," Mushira said. "The higher the mage's level, the more complicated the magicks the mage can control." She indicated the vase. "You are using magicks reserved for mages of the sixteenth level."

"Oh." Adrienne stared at the vase. It had seemed a simple enough task to make it laugh when she did it. She'd imagined all the talking furniture in the cartoons she watched as a kid.

Malik entered the room. As had become his custom, he hadn't knocked. Everyone except Adrienne immediately bowed or curtsied to him. He nodded to them all. "What has everyone so distracted?"

Adrienne lifted the lid off the vase. Its laughter had died down to small titters until she poked it. That got it laughing uproariously again.

"It seems I'm doing things I shouldn't be able to." She replaced the lid. To the vase, she said, "It's not that funny."

"Impressive." He came forward and placed his hand on Adrienne's cheek. He smiled. "I would expect no less from my future queen."

Proud. Adrienne felt proud. Her annoyance with Malik's presence changed the second he touched her. She could have pulled away but decided not to, a small concession since he'd given in to her the day before—albeit to save his palace.

His touch was light and it didn't seem like he would do more. She looked up at him. His eyes mirrored the pride she felt.

Malik was proud.

The emotion she felt was his. Knowing he was pleased with her tiny accomplishment made her happy—in a little kid kind of way. Any praise was good praise, no matter whom it came from.

Malik cupped her chin and moved closer. Her breathing sped up. Lust replaced pride. It slunk along her skin, leaving a trail of goose bumps on her arms.

A muted crash made Adrienne jump in surprise. She stepped away from Malik, then looked around for the source of the sound. A three-foot vase in the farthest corner of the room sat at a diagonal because the base had cracked when it hit the ground.

"I didn't mean to break that one. It was actually kind of pretty." Adrienne had forgotten about it. Floating the tiny blue vase for hours on end bored her so she had decided to split her attention between the blue one and the three-foot one without letting Mushira know. Hani had noticed but kept quiet.

Though Adrienne's concentration had slipped, the blue vase continued floating. That made her feel a little better.

"That is why I said to limit your activities, Highness," Mushira scolded lightly.

"The damage is minimal. A construction mage can fix it easily," Hani said.

"I don't want to bother them."

"It is no bother for them to do their job, my lady," Malik said. "Nimat, see to it."

Nimat curtsied, then left the room.

"Speaking of bothering people..." Adrienne said, looking at Malik. She plucked the small vase out of the air before it became a victim of her wayward concentration. Its muffled laughter grew louder. The joke started off cute, now how did she shut it off?

"I promise you will only have to suffer my presence for a short time," Malik said. He smiled when she rolled her eyes at him.

Adrienne sat in the window seat then continued with her levitation practice. "I'd rather not be bothered at all. I'd also rather be back on Earth." She spared him a glance before turning her attention back to the vase. "But we both know what I want isn't your first concern."

Malik had prepared for this. He joined Adrienne on the window seat. It was wide enough to accommodate them both without him touching her, and he knew she wanted it that way.

"Your life here will not be as fearsome as you think, my lady. Beyond myself and our personal guards, there are many mages and warriors who are prepared to stand between you and harm."

"Were these the same mages and warriors who stood between your parents and harm?"

Malik didn't take offense. He knew Adrienne would lash out at him. He had prepared for physical, magickal and verbal abuse before he decided to visit her.

"No. Those charged with my parents' protection were executed for failing in their task."

"Makes you take your job more seriously when your life is hanging in the balance, too, huh?"

"Exactly, my lady," Malik agreed in a cold voice.

Adrienne tapped the small vase. An identical vase appeared next to it, but this one darker. She plucked the lid off and it cried. Water dripped over the rim. She replaced the lid quickly, then asked, "How about I make everyone's job simpler and never leave my room? Protecting me would be much easier if I'm always in one place."

"So would attacking you," he snapped. Malik regretted his words the second they left his mouth. Adrienne's control on the vases faltered. He caught them—one in each hand—before they hit the ground. "I did not mean to say that, my lady. Forgive me."

He held out the vases. He wanted to tell Adrienne how proud he was of her ability to not only animate the vases but to conjure another into being. She had no formal training and yet wielded magicks most mages had to spend decades learning to control. Only her imagination limited her abilities, the same as him.

Knowing she wouldn't want his compliments stayed his praise. She wanted his absence. He couldn't give it to her. "There is no danger here," he offered, instead. "I have learned from my parents' mistakes and do not rely solely on magicks. I have endeavored, in my years as ruler, to make this palace as safe as possible for your arrival."

"So what? Even if the palace is safe, what about the rest of the world? I'm a prisoner here. If you really want to keep me safe, send me home, Malik." She took the vases from him then placed them on the floor.

Malik's eyes narrowed. He kept his silence until Adrienne straightened and looked at him. "Need I remind you of your attack, my lady? I had not thought you would forget it so easily," he said in a cool voice.

"Yes," she agreed, "let's talk about that. Because, God knows, when you aren't winning an argument, bringing up the stupidity of the other party is a sure-fire way to win." She held up a hand, stopping his response. "Spare me."

She looked out the window.

"Then allow me to speak of more pleasant things."

Malik smiled when she gave him a dismissive wave. She may not wish to be a queen, but she already conducted herself like one. In time, she would realize what Malik already knew. They were two of a kind and meant to be together.

Chapter Seven

"Highness, four days have passed," Mushira said.

Adrienne raised an eyebrow at Mushira's reflection in the window. The vases that floated behind her head mimicked her movement—one floated slightly higher than the other. "And your point is what, Mushira?" She'd already had this argument the day before and the day before that. It had become a ritual of sorts.

"You have only six days more and you have not stepped one foot out of your rooms. How are you to get to know Ulan and its people if you never leave your rooms?"

As with the last few times Mushira had asked this question, Adrienne deemed it unworthy of an answer.

Mushira tried another tactic. "King Malik has ruled wisely since age ten. He has made Ulan the third richest and second most powerful of the fourteen kingdoms. As Ulan's queen you will be expected to show off that wealth in the way you dress and are adorned. Would you not like to go to the bazaar and pick out jewels to compliment the outfits King Malik had made for you?"

"If he had the outfits made, then he can pick out the jewelry to go with them."

"Would you not like to tour the beauty of Ulan? There are other, far more beautiful gardens in and around the palace to tempt the eye. Perhaps you would like to see them, Highness?"

"I can see them fine from my perch. Besides, I'll live longer if I don't leave my rooms."

She was only half-joking. The thought of leaving her rooms terrified her. Forget the threat of death. What if she made a mistake or had a slip of the tongue and someone realized she wasn't from this neck of the woods?

Qamar smiled at Adrienne's remarks. "You insult Khursid's and my skills as Elite guards, Highness."

"I thought you two were enjoying the break. You get to sit around all day doing nothing and still get paid. Sounds like a cherry job to me," Adrienne countered.

Khursid, who stood as a stoic guard at the entrance of the room with his back to everyone, finally spoke. "I do not know what a *cherry* is, but your use implies it to be synonymous with easy. A true warrior hopes for opportunities to test his skills, not to *sit around* at his ease."

"You want me to be in danger? That's nice to know. Makes me all warm and fuzzy inside when my own personal guard wants me to get attacked so he can test his skills. What happens if your skills aren't up to par? What then?" Adrienne asked in an amused voice. She waited to see if Khursid would rise to her baiting. Qamar had learned to bait right back. Either Khursid was born without a sense of humor, or he'd had it beaten out of him at an early age.

"That wasn't how I meant my words to be interpreted, Highness. I wish only for your well-being at all times," he replied in a gruff, somewhat defensive voice.

Adrienne recognized the tone. Khursid only became defensive when he feared his words might get him in trouble. The tone also meant Adrienne had the advantage.

Khursid and Qamar couldn't leave the room. Adrienne had made it an order. She wanted to get to know them and for them to get to know her. The one upside to the command was Khursid's inability to leave when she started teasing him, which she did when he acted like an ass.

Her next words were well chosen. "Come now, Khursid, you're telling me it doesn't suck even a little being stuck in here all day and most of the night with five women who do nothing but talk? You could be swinging big pointy objects at your fellow Elite. Wouldn't that be preferable to this?"

Hani and Nimat smothered giggles behind their hands. Mushira gave them a stern look but didn't pull it off since she was trying not to smile herself. Adrienne smiled with them and winked at Qamar, who winked back.

Khursid didn't see this exchange since he hadn't faced them when he joined the conversation. He stood at rigid attention, showing his agitation.

Before Khursid could even start to form an answer that wouldn't get him in trouble, Malik entered and signaled Khursid out of the room. The other man practically left a smoke trail in his haste to be gone. Qamar bowed to Malik and followed her partner.

Adrienne couldn't be mad at Malik for not knocking. She wouldn't invite him in if he did. Somehow she got the feeling he knew that particular fact.

Mushira and the others curtsied quickly, then busied themselves with some task or another on the far side of the room, a small attempt to give the royal couple privacy.

Their conversations never got intimate so the others' courtesy served no purpose. Adrienne usually ignored Malik until he decided to leave. She'd hoped Malik would get fed up and stop visiting. It didn't happen.

"First, Khursid would be stupid to answer that question. Second, Mushira is right, my lady. You need to get out of these rooms and explore the palace. It will soon be yours," Malik said as he approached her. He didn't expect her to answer. He had gotten used to her silence.

For the past four days, he had spoken to her of preparations for the wedding or of their plans for after they were wed. When he felt she had suffered his presence long enough, he left.

Malik considered himself a patient man and knew the day would come when Adrienne would have to suffer his presence all the time instead of a few hours each day. He wouldn't let her continue hiding after they were wed, not unless he joined her. Then they would be occupied with other matters.

Adrienne was prepared to sit and stare out at the gardens. It was what she had done all the days before and she planned to keep doing it. Her silence was childish—knowing that didn't stop her from using the only form of retaliation she had left.

A strange shadow reflected in the window caused Adrienne to whip around. The shadow turned out to be a giant black panther. The cat not only had Adrienne's attention, he had everyone else's attention, as well.

Nimat gave a high-pitched scream and ran for the bathroom. The silence of the room made the sound of the lock turning clearly audible. Mushira edged behind Hani, who looked too scared to defend herself, let alone Mushira.

"Feyr, I told you to wait outside," Malik snapped.

The big cat came farther into the room. His eyes roamed over everyone but ultimately fell on Adrienne. He moved towards her.

Adrienne's gaze scanned every inch of the cat. While the others were afraid, she was intrigued. Its size reminded her of a tiger but it had the sleek shape of a cheetah.

"What in the world is that?" she asked in a whisper.

The cat stopped near her knees. He sat on his haunches and stared at her.

Malik's frown changed instantly into a smile. Where Mushira's and his efforts failed, Feyr's mere presence prevailed. Simple curiosity had made Adrienne break her silence. Malik latched on to this opportunity. "This is Feyr. He has been my constant companion since I was five, a present from my father."

"Fear? What a strange name."

"*Feyr*, my lady, not fear."

"Oh," Adrienne said absently. Her hands twitched at her sides. She wanted to touch the cat, but wasn't sure, given the others' reactions. "He doesn't look twenty."

"He is. The animals in Ulan age slower than anywhere else, Feyr especially."

Giving in to temptation, Adrienne held her hand out to the cat for him to sniff. Instead, Feyr pushed his head under her hand and purred. She laughed at Feyr's forwardness.

She obliged him and scratched his head, then ran her hands over his neck and shoulders. It surprised her that Feyr's fur resembled thick strands of silk beneath her fingers. She had expected it to be coarse.

Feyr bumped his body against her legs and purred loudly. Adrienne laughed and scratched him faster.

Malik inhaled deeply at the sound of Adrienne's laughter. The feel of her joy was intoxicating to his senses. He could become drunk on her excitement if he allowed himself. He hadn't thought he would hear her laughter so soon.

Loath to interrupt, Malik watched silently until Adrienne spoke again. At this moment, he envied his cat. He wanted Adrienne's hands in his hair and her laughter to be for him and him alone.

Feyr tried his best to climb onto the window seat. Malik wouldn't move and there wasn't enough room for all of them. Feyr laid his head on Adrienne's lap instead.

Adrienne scratched Feyr wherever her hands could reach. She cooed at him and hugged him.

A movement from Mushira caused Malik to look away from Adrienne to see what the woman wanted. He had every intention of beckoning her forward, but the fear evident in her eyes told Malik she wouldn't come near him with Feyr there.

He hated to, but he left Adrienne's side to see what the other woman wanted. "Yes?"

"Majesty, I thought perhaps Princess Adrienne would appreciate a companion during the days. Isn't Feyr's mate having her cubs soon?" Mushira asked in a shaking voice.

"*You* want Feyr's cub to reside with Adrienne? That seems an odd request, Mushira. You have to know Feyr would more than likely follow his progeny."

"I do, but—" she glanced at Adrienne and smiled at the girl's laughter, "—she is happier. It's a welcome change. I can swallow my

70

fear of the father if the child would keep Princess Adrienne in high spirits."

"Yes. It is a welcome change," he agreed. He nodded to Mushira and returned to the window seat. He gave Feyr a good-natured thump on his haunch then sat. "I have an offer to present to you, Adrienne."

Adrienne looked up from Feyr. "Sending me home?"

"No. I wish to give you one of Feyr's cubs. Your choice, of course."

Her face split into a huge smile. "Really? A little Feyr for me to take care of?"

Malik couldn't believe how much his heart lightened when Adrienne smiled at him. Was this the effect this woman would have on him? Was this the effect all the queens had on the previous kings? He found himself wondering what her passion would feel like to his senses.

Those were thoughts and questions for a later time. He couldn't let her new attitude distract him from his immediate goal. "Yes. Feyr's mate will have her cubs any day now and I am sure she would be willing to give one to you once they are weaned."

Adrienne cupped Feyr's face in her hands. She cooed at him, "Oh, you cute whiddle puddy you. I get one of your cubs—with mommy's permission. Isn't that great?" She kissed his nose then laughed when Feyr snuffed at her.

His tongue darted out, removing her kiss. *"Don't kiss my nose, if you please."*

Her laughter turned to a surprised squeak. She jumped away from Feyr and he jerked back in response. He looked as surprised as she did. They both leaned forward to peer at each other more closely.

Malik asked in confusion, "My lady? Is something the matter?" Had she realized she should be scared of Feyr after all? He didn't feel any such emotion coming from her. She still radiated excitement.

Adrienne pointed at Feyr and asked, "Did you talk just now?"

"Yes," Feyr answered. He looked her up and down. *"You can hear me."*

She nodded. "I can hear you in my head." She asked Malik, "Is that normal?"

"You are a marvel, my lady," Malik said with genuine amazement. "It is a rare mage who can speak to and understand animals."

"I'm chock-full of surprises, it seems," Adrienne bragged half-heartedly. She didn't know what she had done to understand Feyr. It frightened her a little. She continually manifested different abilities without knowing what triggered them.

"*Power is nothing to fear, Adrienne,*" Feyr assured her.

"I didn't say anything," Adrienne replied.

"*If your thoughts are loud enough, I can hear them as though you had spoken aloud.*"

"Oh. Okay, this is weird." Adrienne resumed petting Feyr while trying to figure out what she thought of this new ability. Her distraction didn't matter to Feyr. He was happy with her petting regardless. He said as much.

Speaking to animals wasn't a bad talent. Adrienne wished she'd had the ability when she'd dealt with Sir Sheds-A-Lot, Crabby and Sphinx—her cats back home. Half the time, she hadn't known what they wanted or how to make them happy.

Thinking of her cats made her homesick. She forced herself to focus on the here and now. She'd already devoted one day to crying and it hadn't solved anything.

She focused on Malik's proposal—Feyr's cub. She smiled when she realized she would never have communication problems with a pet that could talk.

"I think I can handle a cub if I can speak to it." She nodded to Feyr.

He nodded back.

"On one condition," Malik said.

A sigh escaped Adrienne's lips. "I should have known there was a catch. Nothing is free, right?"

"That is correct." The change in her emotions was immediate. Malik knew this feeling from Adrienne all too well since it normally greeted him when he came to visit her. He'd made up his mind. She would be happier for it and he would have the joy of her happiness back.

"You must leave your rooms, starting with attending dinner tonight in the great hall." He crossed his arms and waited for her answer.

He knew she wouldn't refuse. She wanted the cub and he knew she would cherish it. Malik's near-fifteen years as the ruler of a very prosperous merchant kingdom had taught him to recognize demand and to fill it at a price advantageous to him.

"It's a cheap shot using your cat to lure me out of my room," Adrienne finally said, giving in to a last-minute whine before she agreed.

"Feyr actually disobeyed my order. He has accompanied me each time I have visited you. I thought his presence might cause you alarm as it did your maids." He motioned to the locked bathroom door. "With that in mind, I always left him in the hall until I finished. He must have gotten bored waiting for me."

Malik would have to remember to reward Feyr later, though the attention Feyr got from Adrienne seemed reward enough.

Adrienne thought on this. The lack of security outside her rooms still worried her. Was one of Feyr's cubs worth the risk?

Another thought occurred to her—would Malik allow her to stay cooped up once they married? She couldn't deny the wedding on the horizon. There was no way around it that she had found.

Conceding to bribery seemed a better option than showing Malik he had some power over her. He did, but until now he hadn't used it, and she spent her nights worrying about when he would start.

"Me out of my rooms for my choice of Feyr's cubs," she said for her own clarification.

"Yes."

She looked down at Feyr and he stared back at her. "The things I do," she muttered to herself. She held out her hand to Malik then raised her gaze to meet his. A shiver traveled up her spine as his hand surrounded hers. "Done," she said.

Malik squeezed her hand before bringing it to his lips. This was the first time Adrienne had voluntarily touched him and he savored it. He whispered, "Whatever the reason, I am happy for the change in your attitude."

With her hand still clasped in his, he stood. "As I will see you at dinner, I shall take my leave of you earlier than usual. Do you require Feyr's continued presence?"

A muffled squeal passed through the bathroom door. Adrienne rolled her eyes. "If I want Nimat to ever come out, I guess Feyr has to go." She disengaged her hand from Malik's to give Feyr a farewell scratch and hug. The contented cat padded off in the direction of the door without prompting. He tossed a farewell over his shoulder and exited the room.

Malik bowed to Adrienne then followed his cat.

Khursid and Qamar returned and closed the door. Nimat peeked out of the bathroom. Mushira sagged into a nearby chair. Hani dropped to her knees and hugged her arms.

Adrienne looked at all of them in turn. "Why are you all so scared of Feyr? He's such a big sweetie."

Hani was about to speak but Mushira silenced her with a look. Khursid busied himself straightening his clothes. Qamar and Nimat would not meet Adrienne's gaze. This worried her. "What's going on?"

Mushira answered hurriedly, "It is nothing, Highness." She jumped out of her seat and rushed over to Adrienne. "We should find an outfit for you to wear to dinner and figure out what we will do with your hair." She pulled Adrienne from the window seat and ushered her towards the closet.

"Mushira, dinner is four hours away. I think I have time," Adrienne said laughingly. She stared at the gauzy and formfitting contents of the closet. The memory of her first nightgown floated through her head. "Let's keep the sheer material to a minimum, shall we?"

"My mother told me Queen Dione would take nearly four hours to style her hair alone. Though to look at her, you would think her beauty was a natural state and she didn't have to work at it. We lady's maids know better."

Mushira pulled a dress out of the closet and held it so Adrienne could see. Adrienne hoped her face looked skeptical. That was the emotion she wanted to convey.

"You are to be a queen, Highness, and you must look it." Mushira's voice dared Adrienne to argue with her. "This night most of all."

Chapter Eight

The next four hours were spent showcasing outfit after outfit until both women were satisfied. Adrienne adamantly vetoed three of the outfits out of modesty. She didn't have as much confidence about her body as Mushira.

Hani tried different things with Adrienne's hair only to take it down again when Mushira didn't think it quite right. Nimat had to leave over fifty times to retrieve some piece of jewelry or random item that, for some reason, wasn't kept near everything else.

Adrienne excused Khursid and Qamar when it came time for her to change. Khursid happily complied and left without further prompting. Qamar, used to seeing Adrienne in various states of undress, didn't think both guards should be absent. But Mushira changed her mind—if Qamar planned to stay, she would have to help with Adrienne's preparations. As threats go, it provided enough incentive to get Qamar out of the room. She exited in as much of a hurry as Khursid.

At the end of it all, Adrienne was exhausted, both physically and mentally. Dinner time came but she wanted sleep. The multitude of hairstyles had made her scalp ache. After the third hairdo, she asked why Hani couldn't use magicks to style her hair. Mushira explained that a true mage didn't abuse her powers by using them to perform simple tasks because such actions made the mage vulnerable if they were ever caught without their powers. Questions of how a mage could lose their powers were ignored.

Adrienne didn't take offense at Mushira's lack of cooperation in answering her questions. She had grown used to the woman clamming up when it suited her. It only annoyed Adrienne because it meant she had to ask Malik. She didn't want to ask him anything, since he might mistake her curiosity for interest in staying.

She didn't want to stay. Or, that's what she thought before she looked in the mirror. If staying meant she could keep Mushira, Hani and Nimat, she might reconsider. Adrienne had dressed up in the past and she'd looked damned good, if she did say so herself. Damned good looked frumpy and plain compared to the beauty that stared back at her.

The floor-length, spaghetti-strapped blue dress with a neckline directly below her bust showed every curve while shaping a few problem areas. Two translucent blue lengths of fabric were draped over her shoulders to cover her breasts and were held in place with two palm-sized silver medallions in the shape of Malik's family crest.

Adrienne shifted the fabric on her shoulders so it overlapped. The second she let go it moved apart again and revealed more of her breasts than she cared to show.

"I feel naked."

"If you continue to fiddle with your outfit, Highness, you will be." Mushira pushed Adrienne's hands out of the way and resituated the fabric to its original position.

"Do I have to show off this much skin?" Adrienne asked. She looked down at the hip-high slits on either side of her dress. The ribbons from her slippers that crisscrossed up her legs to mid-thigh peeked out at her.

"You have a beautiful body and shouldn't be ashamed to display it."

"I'm not ashamed. I'm modest." She moved the fabric on her shoulders again.

Mushira pushed her hands away and moved the fabric back. Tiny pins appeared in her hand. She placed them at strategic points on the fabric to keep it in place. "There. Now stop touching it."

"Is her hair to your liking, Mushira?" Hani asked.

"Say yes," Adrienne demanded. "She's not taking it down again. My scalp hurts."

Mushira fingered one of the interwoven braids atop Adrienne's head. She nodded. "Yes, this is best. It shows off your long neck."

"Thank God."

"Which one?"

"What? You have more than one god on Bron?"

Malik entered the room before Mushira could answer, with Qamar and Khursid two steps behind him. All three came to an abrupt halt and stared at Adrienne.

"What?" she asked. Their reactions embarrassed her. She looked down to make sure one of her breasts hadn't popped out or something equally mortifying.

Malik smiled slowly. "You are beautiful, my lady," he whispered in awe.

"Agreed," voiced Khursid before he could stop himself. A blush rose up his neck and landed right on his face.

Qamar added, "Mushira, you have outdone yourself this night and will be hard-pressed to top this accomplishment. Princess Adrienne will surely outshine all present."

Adrienne smiled at all of them in turn. "Thanks," she said in a breathy voice.

Malik offered her his arm but Adrienne hesitated.

Mushira prompted, "It's all right, Highness. You needn't worry about your gloves. They are stronger than they look. If, however, they do rip, I will be with you tonight to fix them."

That wasn't why Adrienne hesitated, but she took the out Mushira gave her. She placed her hand on Malik's arm and he nodded to her. She waited for the familiar feeling of warm oil drizzling over her skin but it didn't come. Either her outfit didn't impress Malik as much as he said, or he was controlling himself.

Either way, she appreciated the reprieve, and relaxed. "Let's do this before I change my mind."

Malik chuckled. He gave her hand a pat and proceeded out the door with Qamar taking the lead.

Hani asked, "We are walking the entire way to the dining hall, Majesty?"

"I thought it best," Malik answered in a tone that sounded final.

"I did not mean to question you, My King." Hani bowed her head.

"Huh? How else would we get there if we didn't walk?" Adrienne asked. Malik didn't answer. She looked over her shoulder at Hani to see if the girl would volunteer the explanation.

She didn't get the chance to ask her question again. A few paces behind Khursid, who brought up the rear, three men shadowed the group. Instant fear froze Adrienne's feet to the floor and stopped the forward progress of the group.

"Who are you?" She didn't like unknown people following her, especially unknown people no one acknowledged.

The three men came forward and went to one knee before Malik and Adrienne. No one spoke, which confused her. Adrienne looked down at them in complete confusion. Was this some kind of answer? She looked at Malik for an explanation.

He obliged. "These three men are my personal guards. As I consider myself a fairly good warrior, my guards are mostly for show. However, each of these three men are the most deadly you will ever meet. They are not only first blades, they are also eleventh-level mages." He pointed to each man in turn and introduced, "Bayard, Indivar and Flavian."

The introduction happened too quickly for Adrienne. She was horrible with names. Add in her growing anxiety at the upcoming dinner, and her memory turned to mush. "How do I remember which is which?"

Malik tried to continue down the hall without answering but Adrienne wouldn't budge. He gave a little sigh before answering, "You need not remember their names, my lady. They are unimportant, as I said. Merely for show."

"Humor me," she clipped out through her teeth. Couldn't this dope see she was stalling? Most men would figure that out and let her do it. But no, Malik was too thick for that.

"They wear the primary colors as they are my primary guards. Bayard is always seen in blue; likewise, Indivar in yellow and Flavian in red. Does that help, my lady?" His tone betrayed his slight annoyance over the delay.

Malik felt Adrienne's curiosity shouldn't be for something as trivial as his personal guards. He could protect himself with either sword or magicks quite well. His guards represented one of the only times Malik had ever conceded an argument to his chancellors. Only then did the men leave off the subject, as he hoped Adrienne would do now that he had answered her question.

"Guess it makes it easy to get dressed in the morning if all your clothes are the same color," she said.

Malik jerked his head slightly. The movement sent the Primaries back to the rear of the group where Adrienne couldn't question them. He then urged her into motion again. He glanced down at her in hopes that looking at her would aid in his understanding of the current emotion he felt coming from her. All he saw was her beauty, and it reminded him of how much he wanted her in his bed. A barrier spell kept the emotion to himself since Adrienne didn't need his emotions adding to her agitation.

Adrienne stopped the procession to the dining hall five more times. Malik had to explain the significance of tapestries adorning the walls and point out the high chancellor's room, which was located on the fourth floor of the palace along with the royal wing and their entourages' chambers. He was happy he hadn't placed the royal wing on the sixth floor as his chancellors had wanted, or else the trip to the dining hall on the second floor might have taken longer. Each new floor meant more stairs and even more questions from Adrienne, and he answered them as patiently as he could.

Malik finally realized the problem when he felt Adrienne's nails. Every step they took made her grip on his arm tighten that much more. Her hold on him loosened whenever they stopped to allow Adrienne to explore, only to have her tighten her grip when they started walking again.

He stopped the group and turned to Adrienne, this time really looking at her. She had a scared, cornered look in her eyes.

Fantasizing about the many ways he could strip off Adrienne's outfit without using his hands had kept him from noticing her growing agitation.

"You have nothing to fear from this dinner, my lady. Be at your ease," he said. Mushira started forward but he stopped her with a gesture. He didn't need help soothing his bride.

"Calm down. There's an idea. Why didn't I think of that?" Adrienne asked.

"You're shaking, Princess," Hani observed.

Adrienne glared at Hani. Malik was about to weave a calming spell around Adrienne when a chair appeared, making Nimat gasp and jump back. From Adrienne's thankful look, Malik guessed she had summoned it. He went to one knee as Adrienne lowered herself to the chair.

She said, "I can't do this. I don't know these people. What do I say? I don't know how to be a queen."

"You will be fine," Malik replied. He reached for her hands to keep her from hurting herself. Her nails were probably imprinted on his arm. He didn't want such marks on her body.

His smile turned to surprise when he felt her hands. "Karasi above! Your hands are like ice. It is not cold enough in this hall or your rooms to cause such a chill."

He enveloped her hands in his, but it didn't help. She seemed to be leeching his heat but not getting warmer. He generated a light heat spell in his hands.

Adrienne couldn't feel her feet, and her fingers were numb. Small quakes shook her body and she wanted to cry. The magicks had to be behind it all. Her anxiety attacks were never this bad, nor lasted this long.

She tried to present her case to Malik again. "There's no way this is going to work. I don't have a handle on my abilities or I wouldn't be trying to turn myself into a snowman."

"What has you nervous, my lady?"

"I can't do this. I don't know the customs. Hell, I don't even know if there is a different language spoken here."

Malik smiled. He raised her hands to his lips and placed a soft kiss on her knuckles. "Adrienne, you are not speaking English."

"Yes, I am...I..." she stopped in mid-sentence.

For the first time, she actually listened to the words that left her mouth. They weren't English. And that wasn't all. She had the distinct impression she could speak many other languages fluently should she have the need.

In English she asked, "What have I been speaking?" The words felt foreign after so many days. She had to force herself to focus on her mother language.

Malik answered in kind. "The language of Ulan, of course. Each kingdom has its own language and customs. You know all of them."

"How?"

"I gave them to you when I healed your body. From the moment you awoke until now, you have spoken only Ulanian. You never noticed?"

"No," she squeaked. She looked at the others—her constant companions for four days, and she had never noticed they weren't speaking English.

She switched back to Ulanian and asked, "What do you mean *gave* them to me? Gave me what exactly?"

The heat spell started working. Adrienne had stopped worrying about her lack of knowledge and her anxiety alleviated.

Malik answered in Ulanian. "Languages, writings, customs and laws of all fourteen kingdoms. You are to be queen. These are things you need to know. It would have taken too long to teach you in the conventional manner. As such, I put the information into your mind."

She didn't know what to say. How had she not noticed fourteen kingdoms' worth of info floating around her head? Easy answer—she'd never needed it. She hadn't met anyone from any other kingdom.

Malik stood. He pulled Adrienne to her feet and sent the chair back to wherever she had summoned it from. "Does that solve your dilemma, my lady?"

Adrienne didn't answer. Malik got the group moving again while she cycled through her newfound knowledge. It was a bit much to take in all at once. She knew histories, royal lineages and what made the fourteen kingdoms unique from each other. The info dump even had a map she could focus on if she closed her eyes, which she did, trusting Malik not to walk her into any walls.

The map in her mind's eye showed that Ulan encompassed Japan, Mongolia, the greater part of China and all the smaller countries between China and the ocean. That explained why everyone looked Asian. They were in Asia—Bron's Asia. The Ulanian royal palace was situated in the very middle of Japan.

After a while, Adrienne stopped going through what Malik had given her and worried about whether he had taken anything away. She still had her memories—some she didn't particularly want, but that couldn't be helped. So far as she could tell, everything was there.

But people don't destroy the originals when they make a copy. Malik could have delved into her most personal desires and dirtiest secrets and she would never know unless he told her.

Worrying about Malik peeking into her past made her forget her anxiety until the doors to the dining hall opened. The sounds of dozens of people conversing and the smells of varying foods jarred her back to the present.

Silence descended over the room when everyone noticed the royal couple. Men bowed and women curtsied, the servants lower than everyone else.

Adrienne looked at all the people in wonder. She thought dinner would consist of a handful of servants and a group of five or six. This was more like five or six *hundred*.

"Who are all these people?" she asked in disbelief. She didn't realize she had spoken out loud until Malik answered her.

"There are the chancellors, the entire Elite guard, generals of my armies and nobles from my kingdom who are currently courting my...*our* favor."

He had to adjust to think in terms of "we" instead of "me". Ruling alone and with complete authority for so many years would make that hard. As much as he wanted Adrienne for his bride, he didn't know how well he would handle sharing his kingdom.

"Why so many?" she whispered.

"Our wedding."

Malik noticed how Adrienne pressed against his side. It made him happy that she saw him as a source of protection.

He led her through the crowd to the inner dining hall where the tables were located.

Saj already waited atop the two-step dais with Adrienne's seat pulled back for her. She smiled in greeting and he bowed before helping her to her seat. Malik seated himself.

Mushira, Hani and Nimat took up positions standing behind the royal couple. Saj joined them while Malik dismissed the guards.

Adrienne asked in alarm, "Where are they going?"

"To eat with the other Elite guards," Malik answered. He indicated the table to their immediate right. There were fifteen men and women already seated at the table. With the addition of the Primaries and Khursid and Qamar, that made twenty Elite guards in all.

Adrienne watched the people file into the dining hall. It reminded her of a graduation procession. The Elite guards had been first and the chancellors followed after them to sit at the table on the left.

The room was situated in a giant "U" with the royal table placed at the curve. Thanks to the knowledge Malik had given her, Adrienne knew the closer tables were reserved for constant members of the palace household. She didn't mind that in the least. Temporary guests should be kept as far away as possible since one of them might be an assassin in disguise.

If Adrienne thought the people of Ulan would be upset at a non-Asian queen, she changed that thought upon seeing the varied races that entered the room. The majority of the people looked Asian, but one of the chancellors was black and many of the nobles looked Eastern European.

Malik said, "At present there are thirty-two noble couples—some in the accompaniment of their children—in attendance and more arrive every day."

Out of the side of her mouth, Adrienne whispered, "You didn't tell me there would be so many people. I don't like surprises like this."

"You would have used the information as an excuse to not attend."

Adrienne looked at him. In a low voice, she asked, "Do you really think you should start out our relationship by lying to me?"

"Omission is not lying."

"According to what dictionary?"

Malik chuckled.

Murmuring started in the back of the room and rolled over the crowd. To Adrienne's ears the murmurs didn't sound friendly. One woman blatantly pointed at her while her companion shook her head in a pitying manner. Were they comparing her to the past queens of Ulan?

They were all beautiful. Dione, Malik's mother, had led the pack, which explained Malik's devastating good looks. Adrienne didn't want anyone comparing her looks to someone else's. Soon they would be comparing her way of ruling to the other queens.

The food arrived and distracted Adrienne from spiraling into another magicks-induced anxiety attack. Everything looked wonderful and smelled even better, but her appetite waned under the scrutiny of Ulan's nobility.

Mushira served the first course, all the while explaining the dish and, in a low voice, how it should be eaten. The first course was a soup with large chunks of vegetables and meat in a thick brown broth. As silly as it sounded, the meat and vegetables were only decoration for the broth and shouldn't be eaten. Adrienne knew that already but she was thankful for the reminder.

She tried her best to ignore all the talking, but most of it was about her, and that made it hard. She also concentrated heavily on not using any magicks subconsciously. This wasn't the time to find out what her unconscious mind wanted to happen to the people speaking badly about her.

From the sea of faces came a high-pitched female voice. "It is good to see our future queen has a voracious appetite. That bodes well for the health of any children she will provide." Rumblings of concurrence came from several others.

Adrienne looked at her plate. It was empty. She kept her face relaxed so the horror of her mistake wouldn't show. It went against her upbringing to leave food on her plate, but eating everything the cook offered guaranteed she wouldn't make it through the next four courses.

Another woman, across the table from the first, added, "It is a shame the future queen isn't more particular about the foods she eats. I remember Queen Dione would barely touch the first three courses because she felt the cook rushed them in order to give the main course enough time to finish."

What was this "eat like a bird" nonsense? Had Malik brought Adrienne to the Civil War South and forgotten to tell her? She looked at the first woman who had spoken.

The woman, dripping with jewels that looked like they weighed more than she did, had less meat on her than a French runway model.

A man at the chancellors' table said, "To be fair, Lady Gen, Princess Adrienne must eat more. How else could she maintain her lovely figure? If Her Highness ate like you, her breasts would shrink— as yours obviously have." He smiled at Lady Gen's angered look.

Oh, this man was on her Christmas card list from now on. She asked, "And you are?"

The man stood and bowed with his arm swept out to the side. He didn't notice—or didn't care—that he nearly hit the man sitting next to him. His deep red robes made his amber eyes and tawny shoulder-length hair look almost golden. As he straightened from his bow, he ran his fingers over the thin mustache that adorned his upper lip. It curved around the outline of his mouth, dangling to his collar.

"I am Chancellor Valah, Highness. And, while I oft times speak out of turn, I hope King Malik will not perceive my words as impertinent?"

Malik said nothing. He toasted the man.

Valah smiled and retook his seat.

At the head of the chancellors' table, Travers cleared his throat. "I am High Chancellor Travers, Princess Adrienne."

Adrienne nodded at him with a smile. He seemed nice enough.

"I feel the need to say Lady Gen is right about Queen Dione not eating much of the first three courses."

"Ha," Lady Gen exclaimed with triumph. She smiled at her tablemates.

Travers continued, "However, Lady Gen is wrong about why. Queen Dione disliked soups, salads and breads, thus she viewed the first three courses as a waste. She preferred to save her appetite for the final course."

Valah added boisterously, "And her breasts were as full as yours, Highness."

"Are you the resident expert on breasts, then, Chancellor Valah?" Adrienne asked with amusement.

One of the women from the Elite guards' table called out, "He'd like to think so, Highness."

Valah shot back, "I did not hear complaints about my expertise from you last night, Keno." Laughter followed his words.

"You will hear complaints from me if your conversation continues to focus on my future queen's breasts for much longer," Malik said with a smile that held the same edge of warning as his words.

The mood in the room sobered quickly. Valah apologized, "Perhaps I took my joking too far."

"Perhaps," Malik agreed.

That brought an end to any further conversation with the royal couple. It also heralded the entrance of the second course. While Nimat took one dish and Hani replaced it with another, Adrienne went back to studying her dinner companions.

Valah, who seemed a little deflated, had acted as a great distraction and she wanted to speak to the man further but didn't know how to spark up a conversation. He wouldn't even look her way.

Laughter from the direction of Lady Gen's table drew Adrienne's attention. The woman looked right at her while commenting behind her hand to her companions, who all laughed again.

"You should share your joke with the room, Lady Gen. I am sure the rest of us would love a good laugh right about now," yet another chancellor said. Unlike Valah and Travers, he didn't introduce himself to Adrienne.

At first glance, Adrienne thought he'd sat at the chancellors' table by mistake. He wore his brown hair in the same severe ponytail as the Elite guards. All the chancellors were lean men whose ceremonial robes dominated them. This man let his blue chancellor's robes gape open, showing his bare-chested, muscled physique. He probably wanted everyone to see his perfect abs—why else go shirtless?

Travers agreed, "Yes, Lady Gen. I, like Chancellor Sabri, wish very much to know what is so funny." Anger colored his words and he glared at the woman.

Lady Gen raised her chin in the air. "Truth, King Malik. Is she truly the blood-spell-selected bride? Her magickal aura seems so much weaker than yours. Such a woman is unworthy to rule at your side."

Sabri jeered, "I'm sure you would volunteer yourself if that were the case. Everyone knows how desperately your family has courted his Majesty over the last year."

"We have done no such thing!" Gen jumped from her chair with her hands braced in front of her. The air around her shimmered as magicks gathered around her and awaited her commands.

Travers said calmly, "King Malik has not settled because of the nearness of his birthday. The blood spell chose Princess Adrienne." He glanced at Malik. "Besides, Chancellor Sabri, you insult the royal house of Ulan. Lady Gen's powers are weak. She would be wholly inappropriate as a queen at King Malik's side. She is barely a seventh-level mage."

"You are right, High Chancellor," Sabri said. "I had forgotten the weakness of Lady Gen's family. Her house sits so close to the royal table—and barely ever leaves the palace—that it is easy to forget their title wasn't earned like so many others present this night."

Adrienne didn't know what to say to all of the comments. Not that she needed to say anything, since the chancellors had come to her defense. They hadn't been formally introduced to her and yet they were ready to speak on her behalf.

Valah pointed out, "I fail to see what is so amusing about the misfortune that befell our king for so long."

"I would never make light of that," Lady Gen rushed out. "I merely observed Princess Adrienne's lack of a strong magickal aura. She feels weaker than me, despite High Chancellor Travers's claims to the contrary." This started the people whispering amongst themselves again. Many people had worry etched on their faces.

Malik shifted in his seat. All sound ceased. "This is Princess Adrienne's first time in Ulan, and she is unused to the wild magicks to which this land lays claim. I am shielding you all from her, as the magicks act on her impulses whether she calls them or not, much like myself."

"Like every queen who has come before her and every queen after her, Princess Adrienne is an equal to our king," Travers boasted. He pinned Lady Gen with a look of warning. "You would do well to remember that when insulting her."

"I did not—"

Sabri interrupted, "Sit down, Lady Gen. You are becoming annoying. I'd hate for you to lose the title your family begged so hard to achieve."

Lady Gen bristled visibly. "My family—"

"Sit down, Gen," Malik said in a low voice.

One and all noticed how Malik had dropped Lady Gen's title. If Sabri's warning wasn't clear enough, Malik's was. She would lose her title if she persisted.

The woman sank into her seat with wide and worried eyes. Likewise, her tablemates became overly interested in their food.

It was Adrienne's turn to be smug. Lady Gen had gotten exactly what she deserved. Where did she get off, attacking Adrienne like that? Sure, Adrienne embraced freedom of speech—and she was happy it existed in Ulan—but she hadn't thought people would insult her. On the list of stupidest things in the world to do, insulting your soon-to-be queen to her face had to be one of the top five.

Suffice to say, Lady Gen became the first person on Adrienne's list of people she didn't like. Judging from the disapproval she'd witnessed at the beginning of the dinner, that list would grow over the next few days.

A piece of paper appeared floating next to Adrienne's shoulder. She looked at it then laughed behind her hand. The paper had two columns, one titled "shit list" and the other "X-mas card list". Valah, Travers and Sabri had already made it to her X-mas card list, as well as Mushira, Nimat, Hani and Qamar. Khursid's and Malik's names were in the middle of the two columns with question marks after them, while Gen graced the "shit list" side with underlines and exclamation points after her name.

Malik looked over her shoulder at the paper. He smiled and whispered, "I shall ask you what exmass is later."

"Christmas." With a flick of her hand, Adrienne sent the paper back to her room. Saying the word aloud made her remember she would miss Christmas with her family this year. She sighed at her plate, her mood dropping several notches.

Mushira came forward. "Is anything amiss with your food, Highness?"

"It's fine," Adrienne answered mechanically. She hadn't touched it. It could be utterly disgusting and she wouldn't know because homesickness had replaced her appetite.

"You are not eating, Highness," Mushira said in a worried voice.

"I'm fine, Mushira."

"Have you lost your appetite, Princess Adrienne?" Sabri asked. "You seemed well enough a few seconds ago. You even laughed. It was a good sound." His fellow chancellors nodded.

The chancellor that Valah had nearly hit asked, "Was the message you received upsetting news, Highness?"

All the questions being thrown at her reminded Adrienne she had to be careful when in public. It didn't matter if she pouted and carried on in the privacy of her rooms, but in public it was different. People who wanted to find a flaw, and people who wanted to gain her favor, would watch her all the time. That thought depressed her more.

She looked at the chancellor who had spoken. He was the black man she had noticed before. Grey sprinkled throughout his close-cropped black hair made him appear to be the eldest of the chancellors. His robes were a true blue, which denoted him as second to Travers.

She answered, "No, Chancellor..."

"Riler," the man offered.

"No, Chancellor Riler. I conjured the note without meaning to. As Malik said, I tend to do things without realizing because I'm not used to Ulan."

"Where do you hail from, Highness? You look like a daughter of Braima. Or are you a descendant of Braima whose family traveled to another kingdom?" Sabri asked.

It was a near thing, but Adrienne kept herself from looking at Malik. They had never discussed a fake origin for her to impart to people who asked. Braima was Africa. While it would be easy to claim it, any further questions would reveal the lie.

She wanted to claim Biton, Bron's version of the United States, but she didn't know how to fight, and Biton was known for its warring clans. Males and females alike learned to fight as soon as they were strong enough to lift a weapon, if they wanted to live to see old age.

Malik answered, "As I wish to keep Princess Adrienne's family from harm or capture, questions concerning her birthplace will be ignored. She is not from Ulan and that is all anyone need know."

Crisis averted. The knot in Adrienne's stomach loosened.

"Will your family attend the wedding, Princess?" Riler asked. He laughed at his question as soon as he asked it. "Of course they will. That was a stupid question. Forgive me, Highness."

In spite of her wan smile at his words, Adrienne cried inside. She wanted her family to be there. Better yet, she wanted to be with them. Her earlier fears about dinner were realized. She didn't know what to say to these people and every time they asked her something, she got defensive or upset. As their new queen, everyone would want to know as much about her as possible so they could gauge what type of ruler she would be. She had no answers for them that she could give.

Adrienne gave a pained gasp and snatched her hand away from the table. Something had burned her. She looked at her hand to see if she would develop a blister. Mushira and Hani were immediately at her side to inquire as to her well-being.

She let them fuss over her while she looked for the source of the heat. Her eyes landed on Malik, who sipped his drink in a relaxed manner. His gaze met hers, and his eyes burned with the heat she'd felt. He was angry.

Adrienne didn't understand what triggered Malik's anger. Talk of his mother had ended a while ago. She opened her mouth to ask but said instead, "I think it's time for me to retire. I'm not used to this much excitement at dinner."

"This is normal for every meal, Highness," Valah said.

"Then I'll have to get used to it, obviously. But tonight is over for me," Adrienne said with a smile. She looked back at Malik. Would he let her leave?

Malik stood—as did everyone in the room—then helped Adrienne stand. "I will escort you back."

"We both don't have to leave. You haven't finished eating." Besides, she wanted to get away from him, not spend more time with him. "Khursid and Qamar are escort enough."

As soon as she said their names, Adrienne wondered if she had interrupted Qamar and Khursid's time with their fellows. They hadn't seen their cohorts in a while. The laughter that came from the Elite guards' table indicated Khursid and Qamar had been enjoying themselves. When Adrienne stood, she'd interrupted that.

It was too late to take it back. Not that Adrienne had any intention of recanting her words, since she wanted out of the dining hall with all speed. She would have to make it up to Khursid and Qamar another time.

Malik nodded. His grip on Adrienne's hand tightened when she would have turned away. He bowed over her hand. "I shall see you on the morrow, my lady. Have a good night."

Adrienne made a noncommittal sound, then disengaged herself from him and left the hall as sedately as she could. The heat from Malik's anger beating against her skin made her want to run, but she quelled the urge. She'd embarrassed herself enough for one night.

The doors to the outer dining hall closed and she breathed a sigh of relief. The amount of stress that accompanied the ordeal made it not worth repeating. She turned to relate her conclusion to Mushira and found the woman missing. In her place, the Primaries stood. As Malik's personal guards—for show or not—Adrienne had assumed their place was with him at all times, but there they were.

Mushira came out of the hall at a fast pace some moments later. She frowned at the Primaries but ignored them and went to Adrienne. She dropped a curtsy and said in apology, "I had the rest of your food sent to your rooms in case you become hungry later, Highness."

Adrienne snorted at that. "Hungry later, nothing. I'm hungry now. I couldn't stand another minute in that room. Those people staring at me, judging me, talking about me, insulting me... Most of it to my face." She didn't mention Malik's anger. No one seemed to have noticed but her.

She would have never noticed if Malik's anger hadn't come with a heat attachment set permanently on high.

"I'm sorry for that, Highness, I should have warned you."

"In the old days, such talk was forbidden and considered treason," Khursid said. "King Malik wants to know people's opinions. The better to—"

"Hush," Mushira bit out.

Muffled screams from the inner dining hall stopped Adrienne from telling Khursid to ignore Mushira and continue with what he planned to say. She stared at the double doors and a sense of dread settled around her. Had someone attacked Malik?

"Did you hear that?" she asked in a frantic voice, her feet already carrying her back to investigate.

Mushira and the Primaries barred her progress while Khursid and Qamar took up positions flanking her. She couldn't figure out why.

She looked at everyone in turn but no one would meet her eyes.

Mushira said in a strained voice, "It was probably nothing, Princess Adrienne."

"We should check to make sure," Adrienne insisted. She looked at the Primaries. "Don't you want to make sure Malik is okay?" The men said nothing. They didn't even acknowledge she had spoken.

She narrowed her eyes at them. "What's going on? You aren't telling me something."

"Nonsense, Highness," Mushira said with a laugh. "We should not dally in the open like this." She turned Adrienne gently and guided her away.

Something had happened. Adrienne would bet it was something she needed to know about. The screams she'd heard had come from more than one person, none of whom sounded like Malik. They were screams of pain.

Adrienne followed Mushira without another word. She had plenty of time to find out the truth.

Chapter Nine

Adrienne woke with a sense of dread for the new day. She would have to attend another meal in the dining hall and didn't know if her stomach could handle the stress.

"Good morning, Highness," Mushira said. Nimat and Hani echoed her greeting. All three women entered Adrienne's room and set about opening the curtains.

Mushira ran her hand over an orb near the bed. The ceiling went transparent, revealing the sky and flooding the room in light. "It's a beautiful day." Her voice was happy like her manner. She chuckled when Adrienne buried herself under the covers. "Hiding will not make the day stop, Princess."

"I don't want to have breakfast with those people," was Adrienne's muffled reply. She peeked out and added in a childish taunt, "And you can't make me." She reburied herself and dared Mushira to try and get her out.

"I have no intentions of making you do anything, Highness. If you would like to eat here, I will have Nimat fetch your tray."

That got Adrienne to peek her head out again. "Really?"

"Truly."

"Does Malik know about this?"

"King Malik is taking his meal in his chambers this morning. I do not believe he would wish you to face the court without him."

Adrienne emerged fully with a happy smile. She sat up and gave a good stretch. "Good morning, Mushira, Nimat, Hani."

All three women curtsied. Nimat said, "I shall see about your breakfast, Highness." She curtsied again and walked to the door.

"Wait, Nimat," Adrienne said as she got out of bed. She walked to the windows. The gardener-plant battles hadn't started yet. It might be interesting to see them up close. "It *is* a pretty day. How about I have breakfast in the gardens?"

Silence followed this question. She turned back to make sure everyone hadn't left. Mushira and Nimat stared at her in shocked silence. Hani nodded with a small, approving smile.

"Well?"

Mushira jerked and stammered out, "Of course, Highness. I...I will... If you allow a few minutes to—"

"Take your time, Mushira. I'm going to take a bath first." Adrienne tossed a wave over her shoulder and walked to the bathroom with Hani trailing behind her.

Mushira left Nimat the task of preparing a picnic-style breakfast while she spoke to Malik about Adrienne's plans for the morning. He opted to let her dine alone but sent the Primaries to keep an eye on her.

Adrienne entered the garden directly below her room and found it blessedly unoccupied. Hani explained that the location of the garden made it a security risk to allow anyone but the gardeners access. That said, Adrienne was happy she chose to stick with the familiar—and privacy—rather than exploring.

Her outlook on the morning brightened. She didn't even mind the Primaries' presence, and they gave her the opportunity to allow Khursid and Qamar the morning off. Khursid insisted on staying, but Qamar took advantage of Adrienne's generosity.

"Good Lord! Who is all this food for?" Adrienne asked as soon as she saw the picnic blanket. There were ten platters piled high with food.

"For you, Highness," Nimat answered. "The cook didn't know what you would like so sent one of everything." She shooed the remaining servants away, then signaled for Adrienne to make herself comfortable.

Mushira entered the garden, joined the others, and relayed to Adrienne, "King Malik sends his happy regards about your decision to leave your rooms this morning, Princess Adrienne. He hopes you will excuse him from attending you, as there are many preparations he must oversee for the wedding in five days."

"Not a problem," Adrienne said cheerfully. She sat on the blanket and stared at the food with no idea where to start. "Okay, everyone sit down. You're going to help me eat all of this."

Hani and Nimat obeyed. Mushira fixed Adrienne a plate first then sat. Adrienne looked at Khursid and the Primaries. "You're not sitting."

Khursid replied, "I did not think your invitation extended to me, Highness."

Adrienne rolled her eyes. She pointed to the blanket and commanded, "Sit." After Khursid obeyed, she turned her attention to the Primaries. "Let me guess, you three don't think I'm talking to you, either."

All three men wore clothing and weapons identical to Khursid's and Qamar's. The man in yellow was the shortest of the black-haired trio by two or three inches. He had one of those baby-like faces women always fall for. His soft brown eyes made him look as dangerous as a newborn puppy and just as cute.

The two remaining men were completely identical. They had the same green eyes, squared jaw and small mole on the left side of their chins. It was a good thing one wore red and the other blue, or Adrienne would have thought she was seeing double—or the magicks were at it again.

"Did you mean for us to join you, Princess Adrienne?" asked the man in yellow.

"I wouldn't have said it if I didn't mean it. Take a load off. Relax. I don't bite." The man in blue smiled at her words. He looked as though he wanted to say something, but held himself back.

All three men sat on their knees. They didn't relax, but Adrienne hadn't thought they would. "Introduce yourselves again. I don't remember your names."

The man in blue, who had smiled before, bowed. "I am Bayard, Princess. I am the Primary who wears all blue." He held out his hand to indicate his twin. "This is my Uncle Flavian, the Primary in red."

Adrienne choked on the piece of bread she had put in her mouth. A general uproar ensued before the bread was dislodged and Adrienne pronounced healthy again.

She drank a full glass of water then asked, "Your uncle? You look exactly alike. I thought he was your brother."

Flavian nodded. "That is to be expected. I am a shifting mage, Princess. My talent is changing my appearance to look however I choose. I don't really look like Bayard."

"Isn't that a little dangerous? For Malik, I mean? If you can change the way you look all the time, what keeps someone from impersonating you?"

"Very smart, Princess," Flavian complimented. He pointed to the side of his neck. He had a tattoo of Malik's crest below his ear. "This is a magickal imprint. It cannot be copied or forged. Malik wanted me for his Elite guards because of my particular talent, but he knew it might make him vulnerable. Thus, he marked me."

Bayard added, pulling down the collar of his shirt to show his tattoo, "Indivar and I opted to wear the tattoo as well, to show our solidarity. Ours are hidden and one of the best kept secrets of the Primary Elite."

"My talent also comes in handy with the females in the palace. I can look like any man they wish. It has made me very popular," Flavian boasted.

"I bet," Adrienne said. "I take it you're not married?"

"No, Princess. I am blessedly single. The only one of us with any type of familial obligation is Indivar. He has a four-year-old daughter."

"You're married?" Adrienne asked happily. She gave Indivar an encouraging look to elaborate.

"No," Hani answered quickly. Everyone looked at her. She cleared her throat. "Rena's mother does not acknowledge her and doesn't deserve to be called a lady of Ulan's court."

"Lady Piper is the heir of a prestigious noble family," Indivar said. "She cannot claim a child born of a momentary lapse of judgment. She has to marry a lord worthy of her family's power and produce legitimate heirs."

"Legitimate heirs again," Adrienne grumbled. "So Rena gets pushed aside? That's not fair. Why can't Piper raise her daughter even if Rena won't be her heir?"

Mushira explained, "Lady Piper is a distant relation of the royal family. As such, her family is under tremendous pressure to remain powerful and show that, though distant, their power still rivals the royal family." She shook her head in a pitying manner.

"Until King Malik, Lady Piper's family has always succeeded at their goal. Our king refused the Mage Guild's training. Trial and error were his teachers. Such learning made him one of the most powerful mages on all of Bron," Indivar said. "Lady Piper must find a powerful husband to produce children who will hopefully equal your children, Princess."

Adrienne muttered, "Always trying to keep up with the Joneses."

"Excuse me, Princess?" Bayard asked.

"I'd like to meet Rena," Adrienne said, changing the subject. They had gotten too close to her reality again. She smiled at Indivar. "Looks like you're going to be stuck with me all day. There are plenty of us here. I think we can keep an eye on one four-year-old. Who watches her, anyway?"

"The cook," Indivar answered. "You want me to bring her here now, Princess?"

"No time like the present."

Indivar bowed and left to retrieve his daughter.

Adrienne watched him leave, then turned her attention to Hani and asked, "So, how long have you had a crush on him?" It was a guess on her part. Hani choking on juice and blushing confirmed Adrienne's words beautifully. "Does he know?"

"No!" Hani clasped her hands in front of her and pleaded, "Oh, please, Princess Adrienne, don't tell him. I don't... Indivar is still in love with Lady Piper. He—"

"I don't mind if you want to watch Rena during the days. Don't let her distract you from your duties, though," Adrienne said with a wink.

Hani let her jaw drop. She recovered herself and said, "Thank you, Highness. Thank you so much."

"You should join them."

Malik, with Feyr beside him, watched Adrienne and the others from his perch in a nearby tree. He'd planned to watch for a short time then join her, but he couldn't get himself to move.

"Malik?"

"No," he whispered. "She is laughing and happy. My presence would ruin that."

"Since when has that stopped you?"

"Do you not need to be with your mate?" Malik snapped. He glared at his cat.

Feyr laughed. *"My mate attacks me whenever I go near her. Mulit females don't like males nearby when they are ready to give birth. I wouldn't hurt my cubs, but it is hard to argue with years of female instinct."*

"You do not need to be *here*. Leave."

"I will when you do."

Adrienne's laughter interrupted Malik's next comment. He turned his gaze back to her. "Soon," he whispered.

"Not soon enough." Feyr jumped to another branch when Malik lashed out at him. He laughed at Malik's growl. *"Temper, temper, old friend."*

Chapter Ten

The day of the wedding arrived. Adrienne had enjoyed learning more about the people who would be closest to her for the rest of her life. The only person she remained unsure of was Malik.

She avoided or ignored him and in doing so, she had lost the chance to learn more about him. Seeing him only reminded her of the inevitable.

Her reflection stared at her with sad eyes. She would be married soon, and thankfully Mushira had dictated modesty for the occasion.

There were no translucent fabrics or gaudy brooches—Adrienne wore a simple yet form-flattering long-sleeved white dress. It dragged the floor a good five feet in her wake. She was scared she might trip over the material and embarrass herself in front of the palace folk, who'd become less vocal in their disapproval of her.

Since the first time, she'd had every meal in the dining hall. That made Malik happy, but she didn't do it for him. It was the only way to learn. The more she interacted with her soon-to-be subjects, the less daunting they all seemed.

Her fear of screwing up because of lack of knowledge went away as well. The information download from Malik had an auto-update feature. Every time anyone mentioned something unfamiliar, she "remembered" the explanation. Malik had explained that was normal. If she had access to the information all at once, the overload might put her in a coma. Given the circumstances, she welcomed the drip feed approach.

While the spell was active from the first moment she awoke on Bron, she hadn't absorbed enough magicks to utilize it properly. Even now, her fount of knowledge stopped producing if she overexerted herself with too much magicks practice.

She moved away from the mirror and sat in the window seat. Khursid moved to stand behind her, but she ignored him. Outside, the garden lacked any gardener-plant battles to amuse her, since it had been tamed the day before. During one of her visits to the garden, she had coaxed a few of the plants into giving up their blossoms so she could decorate her room. The magicks that animated the plants wore off once the blooms were severed from the body. While the plants probably meant her no harm, they were still dangerous.

The same sentiment could be applied to her husband-to-be. She pushed away from the window seat and went to her bed.

Every thought led back to Malik and the wedding ceremony scheduled in less than an hour. The closer it got to sunset, the more agitated she became.

Anxiety had attacked her while she had gotten dressed. Tremors had coursed through her body and made the preparations harder. After Mushira declared Adrienne ready, the shaking stopped, only to be replaced by an overwhelming urge to jump out the window. A joke to that effect had Khursid standing in front of the windows and moving to her side whenever she got too close. Adrienne didn't scold him about it since she wasn't sure she might not try.

"Truly, Princess Adrienne, there is nothing to be so agitated over. You should eat so you are not lightheaded," Mushira urged. "You will not get another chance before the celebration feast later tonight."

Hani, who was polishing Adrienne's tiara, added, "That is three hours from now, Highness."

"Not hungry, and please stop mentioning food. My stomach is already trying to crawl out of my throat," Adrienne pleaded.

The sound of footsteps on the carpeted floor outside the bedroom made Adrienne jump from her perch and face the door. She wrung her hands until the footsteps passed then she slumped into her previous position with relief.

Adrienne put her head in her hands. A tiny stabbing pain started at the base of her neck. From experience, she knew it wouldn't take long for it to spread, and she would have a full-blown, take-no-prisoners adrenaline headache.

She wanted her mother. She wanted her father. Hell, she even wanted her bratty twin brothers, Castor and Pollux. A wave of homesickness hit her. Her family wouldn't see her get married.

They would never see her again, for that matter.

They were probably worried out of their minds about her and she had no way of letting them know she was okay—for now. Who knew what would happen to her after the wedding. Malik might turn into a real monster after she was legally bound to him.

Adrienne's headache doubled when Malik entered the room. She hadn't heard his footsteps—not that she'd ever heard him before, since the man moved as silently as his cat. She backed away from him and ran into the bathroom.

Malik looked after his retreating bride with concern. He'd felt her agitation all the way in his throne room where the ceremony would take place. He had rushed to her side in hopes that he could somehow help remedy her anxieties.

Mushira forced a smile. "Please, forgive her, Majesty. The princess finds herself—"

"I know, Mushira," Malik said in a reassuring tone. He shared Adrienne's case of nerves, if not their intensity, therefore he wasn't angry.

He went to the door of the bathroom and tapped lightly.

"Go away."

Malik smiled sadly. "You know I cannot, my lady. The ceremony is but moments away." He placed his palm flat on the door. "I have come to escort you."

"It's bad luck to see the bride before the wedding ceremony."

"That is a superstition of your world, my lady, not mine. I assure you, my escort is perfectly normal."

No reply, only tiny electric shocks running up and down his arms—Adrienne's panic.

This was a waste of time. She wouldn't see reason. Unfortunately, her time was up, as was Malik's. He'd allowed her to avoid him the past three days because that ensured he wouldn't rip the clothes from her body and find out what her passion felt like. Even the presence of her entourage wouldn't have deterred him.

He only had to be patient a little while longer. That was the mantra he repeated over and over to keep himself in control so he could deal with the situation at hand in a calm manner.

With a small push of power, Malik's hand passed through the door to grab Adrienne's arm. He pulled her through and made sure no part of Adrienne or her clothing remained in the door before he let her go. Releasing her too soon would have melded the two. He could separate them easily but the process was painful to a living creature and would only add to Adrienne's panic.

Adrienne stared at Malik in surprise. She hadn't imagined it. He had pulled her from the bathroom to the main room *through* her bathroom door. Through it! It hadn't hurt, but it was disconcerting.

She swatted Malik's hands away then stepped back. "You pulled me through the door."

"Would you have come out, my lady?"

"Hell no!" The look she gave him showed the stupidity of his question.

"Then it was necessary." He placed his hands on either side of her head at her temples.

She tried to pull away but found she couldn't move. "What are you doing?"

"Relieving your headache."

Of course, thought Adrienne. She had forgotten about her magicks, or else she would have stopped the headache herself.

Malik released Adrienne when her headache alleviated, and stepped back to give her room. Her panic remained but the pain was gone.

From the corner of his eye, he saw Nimat move in front of the bathroom door, barring Adrienne from fleeing back inside.

He looked over everyone in the room. Khursid and Qamar stood in front of the windows, Hani had moved to block the closet in case Adrienne thought to hide there and Mushira hovered behind him.

Though they could not feel Adrienne's agitation as Malik could, they responded to it by treating her like a caged animal ready to bolt at the first sign of weakness. That probably didn't help Adrienne's current state of mind.

He made a snap decision. "Out! All of you." His tone left no room for argument, though Mushira and Khursid both seemed as though they would. A single look made them keep their silence and follow the others out of the room.

After the door firmly shut behind the last retreating back, Malik spoke softly to his bride. "Adrienne, I know I have not given you much time to adjust, and an unfortunate happening marred your arrival here. I cannot change those things. However, I can make the rest of your time here happy, if you allow me."

He put his hands on her shoulders. It was all he could safely do, except he shouldn't even do that much. Touching her was dangerous without the others around to bring him back to his senses. He focused on Adrienne's agitation and tried to make it his own as a way to combat his lust. Only a few more hours and all his patience would be rewarded.

Adrienne looked up at Malik and knew he meant it. She could read the sincerity in his words, and in his eyes, and feel it of him. He was concerned for her.

"You really want to make me happy?"

"Yes." He breathed the word on a sigh.

"I want to see my parents," she demanded.

Malik's relieved look vanished.

Good, she thought. What did he have to be so happy about when she was miserable?

"I want my favorite stuffed animal from my bed. I want to yell at my bratty brothers for coming into my room without asking. I want to walk across the stage at my college graduation. I want to get my master's degree. I want—"

"Stop," Malik yelled over her tirade. He dropped his hands from her shoulders and stepped away.

"Why? That's what would make me happy. Some spell says I'm your queen and you just snatch me away from my life and throw me into yours. You didn't ask me! You still haven't!"

Adrienne didn't want to yell. The others were right outside the door and they might hear her. She couldn't help it. She'd held back her frustration and anger all this time, venting in her head but never aloud. With people always around, there was no privacy for her to tear into Malik like she wanted.

Except now.

The wedding day had arrived. This was her last-ditch effort. Even if it didn't work, she would have the satisfaction of telling Malik just what she thought about all of this, and of him.

"You wish for me to ask for your hand?"

"No! I *wish* to go home."

Silence.

Adrienne whirled away and went to the windows. She stared at her reflection. This was not the wedding dress she wanted for herself. It was nice but it lacked any fringe and flounce. She hadn't wanted the Cinderella deal but thought her dress would at least be made out of silk or satin, or a reasonable facsimile—not something that felt like cotton and looked like linen.

"Answer me something, Malik," Adrienne said in a soft, subdued voice. She was too tired to yell anymore. She had gotten no sleep the night before, anxiety had claimed her morning and it all caught up to her.

"Yes?" Malik answered, his voice equally quiet.

She looked at his reflection, which stood next to hers even though the man stood several steps away. He wore clothing as plain as hers.

His loose-fitting pants and shirt seemed to be made of the same white material, and the knee-length vest he wore over his shirt was pale beige.

"Would you have handled our introduction differently if those men hadn't been attacking me?"

His gaze met hers in the reflection. "Possibly not. I knew you to be mine, and I took you. I have ruled in a like manner since I was ten years of age."

Adrienne shrugged. "At least you're honest."

She looked past her reflection to the grounds below. She didn't see a garden, but her future. A spell and a spoiled king had decided her life, but that didn't mean she couldn't take advantage of the situation. She could be happy, barring the threat of imminent assassination.

She would be equal to Malik in rule and power—once she got control of her powers—and she could incite change. Her thoughts would be heard and heeded. In the end, wasn't that what everyone wanted? A chance to be heard?

Adrienne figured she had lost her mind. She was starting to entertain the thought of going through with this wedding and marriage willingly.

Her proof of insanity came when her reflection winked at her. She jumped back from the windows with a scared yelp.

Malik was there instantly. "What is it?"

She pointed at the window, but her reflection didn't mimic her. It smiled at them. "What in the..."

Malik touched the glass. The reflection of Adrienne smiled wider. He wrapped his power around the image but couldn't discern how it came to be there or how to get rid of it. Power from the image pushed him away. He stumbled back in surprise. His power knew no rivals, which included the heads of the Mage Guild. This couldn't be Adrienne's doing, as she hadn't learned to control her powers to such an extent.

The reflection pressed her palm flat against the glass of the window. She smiled invitingly and, with a crooked finger, beckoned

Adrienne forward. She pantomimed with her free hand that Adrienne should place her palm against the glass. Adrienne raised her hand but Malik pulled her back.

"No. The magicks of this realm take on many guises. Most of them have malevolent intentions." He left out the reflection's ability to manifest more power than him. That worried him. Had Hollace found out about Adrienne and decided to interfere and stop the wedding? But no, that made no sense, because Hollace abhorred magicks. Then who conjured this reflection, and what purpose did it have?

The reflection shook her head and rolled her eyes. She beckoned with her full hand. There was urgency in the motion, like the reflection had someplace to be.

No warning bells went off for Adrienne. She decided to trust herself, as it were. She pressed her hand against the reflection's.

Malik didn't try to stop her.

Adrienne leaned in close when the reflection did. She felt soothing warmth spread over her body. It was somehow familiar, so she opened herself to it.

The reflection spoke, and though there was no sound, Adrienne heard it. She quizzed the reflection and it answered her. She didn't like what it told her but decided to trust it. The reflection smiled once more then disappeared, and Adrienne's true reflection returned. The warm power from the reflection ebbed away and then vanished, leaving goose bumps in its wake.

Behind Adrienne, Malik lurched forward. Something had bound him to the floor and kept him from speaking. He rushed to the window and touched it. His powers picked up nothing. The magicks had come and gone without a trace. That was dangerous. Who had controlled the reflection?

Malik rescinded his power. "What did it say to you?"

"It... *She* said I'd be happy," Adrienne answered softly.

"It said more than that," he prompted. He grasped the hand she used to touch the window. The reflection had done something magickally to Adrienne, but he couldn't discern what from his contact with her now. She felt the same. No, she didn't feel the same. Her agitation and upset were less.

"You're right," she agreed. "She did say more. The only part that concerns you is the first part."

"I do not trust—"

Adrienne put a finger to his lips.

His skin tingled. He knew she felt it too.

In a husky voice, Adrienne said, "I'm not hurt and she convinced me to give in to the inevitable. You can take it at face value or we can go back to arguing. Up to you." She lowered her hand with a slow smile.

Malik looked back at the glass. Whatever the reflection was, it had given him what he wanted. The price of which would reveal itself in time. For now, he held out his arm to Adrienne.

She put her hand on his arm and they walked out to face the worried people who waited in the hall.

₧₨

Adrienne's calm wore off quickly in the face of all the people present for the wedding. She had never seen the throne room before and her first impression of it wasn't a good one—people filled every space.

She stood on the dais in front of twin thrones. Both high-backed chairs were polished wood with hand-carved serpents coiling around the frames. Adrienne wanted to sit down, but she and Malik had to stand for the ceremony. They faced the throng of people and Upala, the head of Ulan's Mage Guild and the woman who would perform the ceremony.

Since Malik had told her the ceremony didn't require her to speak, Adrienne let her mind wander. She focused on Upala's amulet, a flat metal disc with a small, ruby-looking jewel in the middle of it. Her gaze followed every facet of the jewel and she wondered if it was merely a decoration of Upala's station or an aid like the orbs. Malik's implanted knowledge turned up no ready answers since he hadn't attended the Mage Guild to learn how to use magicks.

Upala prompted Malik and Adrienne to lay their fingers on the jewel then she bowed her head and murmured some words. A tiny silver cord snaked out of the amulet and slithered over Malik's and Adrienne's fingers. Adrienne found she wasn't scared, since Malik wouldn't let her do something dangerous.

The cord wound around Malik's wrist, then Adrienne's, and tightened. Once taut, the cord disappeared but a tugging sensation remained.

Upala lowered the amulet. Adrienne tried to lower her hand and found she couldn't. She looked up at Malik.

He smiled and faced her. His manner indicated Adrienne should do the same. Upala moved down one step and to the side, removing a gold and silver dagger from her robes and holding it out to Malik. He grasped it and brought it up between himself and Adrienne.

Before Adrienne could ask what he planned to do with it, he stabbed her. With his hand directly beneath hers, Malik stabbed the dagger through the middle of their palms, pinning them together. The shock of the movement caused Adrienne to gasp.

She looked at their impaled hands and wanted to cry out, but there was nothing to cry out about. Sure, a dagger impaled her hand to Malik's, but there was no pain. She bled and he bled, but the pain didn't start. She looked back at Malik.

He said, "With a dagger blessed by Ulan Mage Guild Master Upala, I perform this blood spell. By deed, by magicks and by blood are we bound. None shall break this marriage, as our silver cord is now laced with crimson." As Malik spoke, blood slid down the dagger from their impaled hands. The blood curved around the invisible silver cord, then disappeared.

Malik touched the hilt of the dagger. It faded and reappeared in Upala's outstretched hand.

The wounds healed before Adrienne's eyes. Or, rather, the wounds closed. The only remembrance was the tiny scar on the back of her hand. She immediately turned her hand over to see the matching scar—it wasn't there. She saw the dagger go completely through her hand—hell, she felt it, too. But only the back of her hand had a scar.

Adrienne wasn't given time to fret. Malik pulled her gently forward so they both faced the crowd below and held up their joined hands. "Your new queen."

The resounding shouts of joy from inside and outside of the palace were near deafening compared to the silence attending the ceremony only moments before.

Adrienne would almost bet the entire kingdom cheered. She wanted to cover her ears but didn't know if that would be seen as rude. She soon forgot the noise as Malik took her in his arms and kissed her.

This wasn't the quick pressing of lips most people saved for weddings. No, this was a full-blown I-would-rip-your-clothes-off-and-have-my-way-with-you-right-now-if-it-weren't-for-all-these-people kiss. Adrienne ignored the roaring crowd—whose cheers had only gotten stronger—as she responded to Malik. Her arms wound around his neck and she returned his kiss with the same urgency. He felt right, and she wanted to feel more of him.

She felt her clothes shift but didn't pay any attention. She knew Malik wouldn't strip her in front of all these people—at least she hoped he wouldn't.

Adrienne leaned back to break the kiss but Malik followed her. She unwound her hands from his neck to push gently—and what she hoped was inconspicuously—on his chest. Sealing the marriage with a kiss was one thing. Sex in front of all these people was completely out of the question. She didn't know if the people of Ulan wanted proof of her virginity, but she wouldn't become an exhibitionist for their curiosity.

Malik backed away from the kiss with a reluctant look but continued holding her. Adrienne wondered if her eyes looked like his— dilated and full of passion. Her hands, still flat on his chest, felt the thundering of his heart. But she didn't need to feel it to know he was aroused. His lust slid along her senses and made her skin feel too tight. She looked away from him before she allowed him to go further with his seduction.

Slowly, the noise of the crowd returned to her, and reality settled in little by little. Her clothes had changed. An iridescent gown that shimmered with every breath she took and every movement she made had replaced her simple gown of white.

Something dangling in front of her eyes made Adrienne touch her forehead. A teardrop diamond suspended from a circlet adorned her brow. She hoped to pass a mirror soon so she could see her new outfit.

That was the shift she had felt earlier while she kissed Malik. He hadn't tried to undress her, he had changed their outfits. Malik's outfit had changed to the same iridescent material, but his vest was a soft grey. His brow sported a circlet similar to Adrienne's, but he had no annoying jewel to dangle just above his sight line. Instead the round blue jewel seemed to hold the two sides of the circlet together—it was utterly masculine, or Malik made it seem so.

Malik turned and said a few words to Upala while Adrienne stared out over the sea of faces. Her anxiety returned in cascades, but not the same as before. She was married to Malik. If his kiss was any indication, she would be getting to know him physically quite soon. She didn't know him personally—a problem partially her fault because she had avoided him.

She didn't know what to do. She wanted Malik to say something to her instead of words of ceremony. If this were an Earth ceremony, she and Malik would have walked back through the crowd to a private room to change for the reception. There, bridal party and parents would come to congratulate them and they could all relax away from the guests.

Adrienne wanted her mother. Hannah wouldn't have enjoyed seeing her baby impaled, but she would be even more upset if she knew her daughter had married without her. Right then and there, Adrienne vowed to do everything she could to get to Earth so her parents knew she was okay—and to have a proper Earth wedding.

She didn't know how she would do it. Malik said he wanted to make her happy but what if that didn't involve taking her back to Earth? Beyond letting her parents and brothers know she was alive and well, she wanted Malik to meet her family. All her thoughts led her down a road of homesickness that made breathing hard.

Malik's head jerked up as he sensed Adrienne's rising depression. He excused himself to Upala. The Guild master nodded with a smile and retreated down the dais steps. Malik tightened his arms as his attention returned to Adrienne.

"May I sit down now?" she whispered.

Malik looked over the crowd, who still cheered. He didn't care if leaving them was a faux pas. Returning to his bedroom would allow him to partake of Adrienne all the sooner.

He summoned an orb and opened a portal to his rooms. Once Adrienne stepped through, he followed and the portal closed behind them, effectively closing off the noise. The orb reshaped itself into its natural spherical state before it disappeared.

Malik watched Adrienne with concern. She sat on the edge of the bed with her head bowed and tears in her eyes. "Are you well, Adrienne?"

Had he scared her during the ceremony? He had explained about the dagger, but she might not have heard him since she'd insisted on ignoring his presence when he visited her. In hindsight, once she had started being more responsive he should have explained it all again.

Adrienne shook her head. She eased sideways and lay on the bed with her eyes closed and her arms cushioning her head.

Malik came forward and brushed his fingers lightly over her cheek. "Will you be able to handle dinner?" he asked.

"I have no choice."

"Yes, you do." He waved his hand at the door and explained, "If you wish, the celebration can wait until tomorrow." His eyes never left her face as he moved her hand from beneath her head and pressed a kiss against the scar. He hoped Adrienne would decide to skip the celebration feast so he could enjoy her body all the sooner.

"That makes no sense," Adrienne countered. "You're supposed to have the wedding dinner after the ceremony—directly after."

"It is your right as queen to postpone the feast until next year, if you so choose. Everything is your right as queen." Malik studied her features before coming to his own conclusion. "I will postpone the dinner." His reasons were purely selfish but they would benefit Adrienne as well.

"No."

"No?"

Adrienne stood away from the bed and Malik then smoothed her dress. Running her hands along the silken material reminded her that she wanted to look in a mirror. She looked around and didn't recognize anything. Malik hadn't taken them to her rooms. This was a bedroom, but whose?

It had to be Malik's. She had never seen his rooms before but nothing else made sense. They were bigger than hers—if that was possible. If the rooms got any bigger, she would need a golf cart to get from one end to the other.

Several large tapestries adorned the walls. Each depicted different scenes. The most intricate and detailed featured scantily clad dancing women in a field of pink. It straddled the line between art and the obscene. Adrienne knew it would be the first thing to go if Malik wanted to share the room.

The mirror, which was hard to miss, hung on the wall across from the bed and stretched from the floor to the high ceiling above. She headed for it and silently congratulated Malik for not following her like some duckling after its mother.

The first thought Adrienne had once she faced the mirror was that it didn't need to be so big. It was grand for grand's sake. The same could be said for Malik's bed—and hers. No one needed a bed big enough for twenty people.

It seemed Malik had a flair for the overdone, like her outfit. The dress was exquisite and made of exactly what Adrienne wanted, something silky. But the neckline, which plunged between her breasts to stop right above her navel, left much to be desired. Like everything else Malik commissioned the seamstresses to make for her, the dress revealed too much for her sense of modesty.

It was too late to change, though. Everyone had already seen her. Overall, the dress flattered her figure and made her look more regal than she really felt, and the iridescent material gave the illusion of glowing.

She looked at Malik's reflection and, with a steadying breath, she said, "I'm ready."

Malik held out his hand to her. She took it and he pulled her in close and gave her another kiss. She prepared to fend him off, but Malik kept the kiss chaste, a simple pressing of lips.

He pulled back and led Adrienne to the door. She coached herself into staying calm since she wanted to escape the bedroom. Besides, the addition of more people wouldn't make the reception much different from any other meal.

Adrienne gasped when Malik opened the door and their entire entourage stood on the other side. "How..." she asked, only to trail off with a shake of her head.

Mushira answered, "It is our duty to know where you are at all times, Majesty."

She had a new title. Adrienne had just gotten used to being addressed as "princess" and "highness".

She looked at everyone and they in turn looked at her. She gestured to the hall. "I don't know about the rest of you, but I'm starving." She looked up at Malik. "Shall we?"

Malik smiled at her as he placed her hand on the crook of his arm.

Chapter Eleven

The crowd of nobles who witnessed the ceremony had made their way to the outer dining hall. Adrienne took a calming breath and raised her chin a notch. She was a queen now and would damn well act like it.

Moments after Malik settled Adrienne on her seat at the royal table, Mushira informed Adrienne this was a royal celebration, not just any normal dinner, and many of the kingdom's people had made dishes as a present for the royal couple to sample. Adrienne looked at the long line of waiting people and knew she wouldn't be able to eat that much.

Malik waved the procession into motion. The families accompanied the dish they made. One and all offered well-wishes on Adrienne's long rule, while Adrienne and Malik sampled a spoonful of each dish once the food tasters approved it. Some dishes were better than others but Adrienne thanked the cooks for their consideration all the same.

She tried one dish despite her reservations about eating something that was still...swimming. The small fish, a little smaller than a sardine, swam in a bowl of boiling soup. It surprised Adrienne that the heat of the soup hadn't killed it. She was reluctant to eat it, but did, and almost choked as she felt the fish swim down her throat. It took all her willpower not to puke it back up.

Mushira handed her a goblet of purple, sweet-tasting liquid and a piece of bread to take away the taste. She would have preferred something to take away the feeling of the fish squirming around in her stomach. Boiling water hadn't killed it; would stomach acid?

116

Adrienne beckoned behind her for Mushira. The woman stepped forward and Adrienne whispered, "Make sure the cook never ever serves that ever." She couldn't emphasize her distaste of it enough. Mushira understood and sent Nimat scurrying to the kitchen with Adrienne's message.

Malik smiled in Adrienne's direction. He dabbed at his lips with his napkin then asked, "How does it feel to have given your first edict as queen, my lady?"

"I didn't..." She stopped. Her gaze went to the door Nimat had used, then back to Malik. "That wasn't a special Ulanian dish, was it?"

"No. The fish are abundant and easily caught. The dish is considered to be for poorer people. I am sure it was all the family could make."

"Oh," she whispered. Adrienne felt like a heel. She turned back to Mushira. "Make sure someone is taking down all the names of the people who brought presents and what they brought. I want to be able to send out thank you letters later."

Mushira nodded. She didn't get the chance to send anyone, as Saj left to see the deed done himself. Nimat returned moments later.

Malik noted, "You were born to give orders, Adrienne. I do not know why you were so worried."

Adrienne didn't say anything to that. She took a spoonful of the next dish and barely kept herself from spitting it back out—it had more salt than taste. The food tasters could have warned her. She forced a smile for the presenters and thanked them, then emptied the contents of her goblet three times before she could feel her tongue again. She hoped the drink didn't have alcohol in it. Though being drunk might make the latter part of the evening easier.

A male voice rang out over the crowd. "Very brave of you, Queen Adrienne, to sample the simple fare. You are no Queen Dione that is for sure. Verily, I remember Queen Dione sent many dishes to the servants rather than sample them herself. A smart move on her part, based on the faces you're making." He laughed.

It wasn't hard for Adrienne to spot the man. Not only was he the only person laughing in a room gone deafeningly silent, but his table companions had moved their chairs as far away from his as they could. His attire denoted him a noble of Ulan.

The man stopped laughing when he noticed no one joined him.

Malik lowered the fork that was halfway to his mouth. Everyone turned and stared at him. He stood, looking pointedly at the man who had spoken. "Lord Yuan, I know you have only recently returned from the Kingdom of Delu, and probably have yet to be apprised of what happened to the last nobles who insulted my bride. They too compared her unfavorably to my departed mother." He raised his hand. "It is only fair that you meet with the same punishment as them." Malik made a backhanding motion.

Lord Yuan flew out of his chair. His back hit the floor and he slid across the tile for a good five feet before stopping. The man remained sprawled with tears running freely down his cheeks. He blubbered out apology after apology for his stupidity and indelicate manner.

Adrienne looked from the man on the ground to Malik. She remembered the screams she'd heard after her first dinner with the court, and the subdued attitudes of the people upon the next dinner. Her guess was right—the screams were of people in pain. Malik had waited until she left the dining hall to discipline the people who verbally attacked her.

Malik looked calm, but Adrienne knew that was an illusion. She could feel his anger. While not as hot as the first time she'd witnessed it, it still burned.

Why was she so surprised? The same man had killed two men without a second thought or a bit of remorse. Had Malik enjoyed what he did to her attackers? Did he enjoy what he did to Lord Yuan? His people feared him, not loved, and it looked like he wanted it that way.

Her attention shifted to Lord Yuan, who stayed on his back like a flipped turtle. No one stepped forward to help him. To Adrienne's eyes it seemed like everyone pretended not to see him.

That was the last straw. This was her wedding day. She may not have wanted this wedding, but Adrienne wouldn't let violence ruin it. She stood and touched Malik's arm. The heat of his anger dulled when she touched him. She was happy for that.

With her free hand, Adrienne pointed at an attendant who stared at the royal couple in thinly veiled fear. The man flinched back.

"You there," she said with more authority than she felt, "pick Lord Yuan up and put him back in his seat."

The attendant bowed and quickly went to help. Lord Yuan continued crying. Adrienne had had enough. "Lord Yuan, stop crying. You're a noble, *act* like it."

The man startled as though she had smacked him again. He stared in astonishment at Adrienne. She stared back and dared him to say anything. He didn't.

Next came Malik.

Adrienne couldn't command him, but she could request. She moved her hand from his arm and touched his cheek lightly. "There isn't a door to muffle the sound this time. Even if there was, this is our wedding day," she whispered. She could tell her words shocked him. In that moment, she knew Malik hadn't realized she'd heard the screaming.

He whispered back, "I did not think... You were not supposed to hear that." He cupped her hand where it rested on his cheek. "I am sorry, my Adrienne. You are right."

Malik's anger abated to be replaced with a sense of peace. Someone was weaving a calming spell around him. He cast out with his power to find out who in his palace would dare. To his surprise, the spell came from Adrienne. He looked at her with amazement.

He searched her eyes and could see nothing there that indicated she even knew she had cast a spell. He gave into it and sat. Adrienne smiled at him as she resumed her own seat. Her hand left his cheek and the spell rescinded.

The people in the dining hall witnessed the calming of the beast and didn't quite believe it. Everyone knew their new queen saved them—if not quite *how* she saved them.

Chancellor Valah stood and raised his glass. Many others followed suit. "To King Malik and Queen Adrienne, and to the peace their joint reign shall bring," he said in a booming voice.

Everyone in the hall cheered their concurrence with the toast. Adrienne knew Valah hadn't meant peace from the threat of King Hollace and Kakra banging on the doors. He almost blatantly thanked her for the way she'd handled Malik and his temper.

In the same breath, he had charged her to continue in the endeavor every moment thereafter. She hoped she was up to the task. Malik had said so himself—he had ruled alone for years and gotten his way for too long. Adrienne hoped Malik would continue wanting to keep her from the rougher side of his temper for many, many years.

The atmosphere of the room turned back to a more jovial one. People laughed, made jokes and tossed comments up to the royal couple, who either responded with a raised eyebrow or a witty retort.

Adrienne continued to sample everything presented to her until she couldn't eat anymore. She didn't want to be full. Being full meant her wedding night was next.

Her anxiety returned in earnest. Around her the people talked in high, excited tones. No one seemed aware of their queen's new mood. She didn't want to spend the night with a man she knew next to nothing about. Sure, she knew his background, but she knew very little about his personality. For all intents and purposes, they had just met.

Malik's eyes roamed over the crowd but his thoughts were for Adrienne. She looked around the room as though an escape route would suddenly present itself. Malik needed to put a stop to this before Adrienne worked herself into an argument similar to the one before the ceremony. He didn't know if his patience would allow him to go through such a trial again, not when his goal of having her in his bed had come.

A hush went over the room when he stood. He ignored the crowd and looked at his wife. Resignation crossed her face as she met his gaze. He waited. Adrienne stood and he slipped his arm around her waist.

He faced the crowd of merry-makers who had risen when the royal couple had. "My new queen and I shall retire for the night. I trust you all will not destroy my hall in our absence." He turned and led Adrienne out of the hall with their entourage a few steps behind them.

Crude and bawdy jokes about Malik's virility and Adrienne's predicted inability to walk the next morning followed them. The door closed on the chatter and Adrienne sighed.

Now came the long walk back to Malik's room, during which time Adrienne planned to think of some way to stall Malik until she felt comfortable—and ready.

Malik formed a portal from one of the many orbs that seemed to be stored in thin air. His bedroom loomed before Adrienne, and hopes of a long walk were dashed. Adrienne wondered if Malik used portals all the time to get around the palace. It would explain why she'd never heard his footsteps outside her room.

Mushira offered, "I shall prepare Her Majesty for—"

"There is no need," Malik interrupted. "I will see to Adrienne. Retire, Mushira." His order was gruff and he didn't apologize. He didn't want to argue about etiquette and the proper dress for a bride on her wedding night. Malik had observed as much propriety as his patience could handle.

Hani placed a comforting hand on Mushira's shoulder, who gave an accepting sigh and curtsied. Nimat and Hani curtsied as well. As one, the women went back to the celebration. The Primaries and Adrienne's guards remained waiting for their orders.

Malik considered for a moment then said, "Return to the party. Enjoy it. No one shall bother us this night." The guards bowed but they didn't leave until Malik and Adrienne crossed over the portal threshold. The guards bowed to them. The portal closed.

Adrienne quickly put the width of the bed between her and Malik. She remembered how she'd responded to his kiss during the ceremony and knew if there was ever a time to talk, it would have to be before he touched her.

Malik followed her.

"Please," Adrienne said with an outstretched hand. She breathed a quiet sigh when Malik stopped his approach at the foot of the bed. "I...I want to talk. We've never talked."

He started towards her again, this time slowly. A step punctuated each word as he said, "I have talked. You chose not to respond."

"I'll respond now," she pleaded. She backed away from Malik as he drew nearer.

"I know you shall, my Adrienne," he rumbled with a slow smile.

"That's not what I meant," she said with dismay. He had purposefully misinterpreted her words.

Her back ran into a wall but before she could find a new direction, Malik was there. She didn't know how he'd crossed the distance between them so fast, but he had. His body pressed hers into the wall and she could feel the proof of his lust through their clothing.

"It is what I meant," he said before he claimed her mouth. He swallowed her whimper and tasted her fear. Not agitation, true fear.

He pulled away from her with a curse.

It took several ragged breaths and a silent prayer for control before he could meet Adrienne's gaze. "You wish to talk, then we shall talk," he gritted out through clenched teeth. "But we will talk in a setting of my choosing."

He pulled her away from the wall and across the room. Adrienne ran to keep up with his pace. Malik didn't stop until they stood in his bathroom. He closed and locked the door behind them so Adrienne couldn't run. Before turning back to her, he removed his vest and shirt.

Adrienne took a step back when he turned to face her. Malik reached for her and she squeaked in fear. He yanked the gown over her head in one fluid motion and tossed it aside. A little more patience was needed for her gloves and underwear.

After he stripped Adrienne, Malik scooped her up and carried her into the bathtub. He settled himself on a bench built into the wall of the tub, then stood Adrienne between his trouser-clad legs, turning her so she faced away from him.

"So talk," he demanded, breaking the silence. He soaped a sponge and pressed it to Adrienne's back. She jumped and tried to pull away, but he grabbed her arm. Once she stopped pulling against him, he released her and resumed washing her back.

The smell of flowers tickled Adrienne's nose. She shivered at the feel of the sponge. This was the first time anyone had ever bathed her—that she could remember. Her lady's maids had tried and failed, despite Mushira's many tiring arguments.

She held herself stiff and waited to see what Malik would do next. He simply washed her back, no other part of her body. This knowledge calmed her, a little.

She started, "I... Why are you still wearing your pants?"

"If I take them off this will be a short conversation," he answered matter-of-factly.

"Oh."

"Yes, 'oh'. I am being patient for your sake, Adrienne. Know that while I am a patient man, it has very nearly come to an end."

Adrienne tried to face Malik but he held her firmly in place. "That's just it. I don't know what type of man you are. I know that everyone is scared of you. Beyond what you did to my attackers, I've never seen evidence as to why—" she bowed her head, "—before tonight."

"I admit my methods of punishment are somewhat...harsh. I command respect from my people. Those in the palace especially, as most of the older members of the staff helped raise me."

"Some gratitude you've got there," she quipped. "'Hi, you helped me with math. That will be ten lashes.'" Malik caressed her thigh and the humor of the moment died. She needed to distract him, a task made easier if she were clothed.

She asked, "What happened after I left the first dinner?"

"I thought you already knew."

"I heard the screams. That's all. I thought you were in danger at first. None of the others would go back to make sure you were all right. What happened?"

Malik smiled at Adrienne's words. She'd admitted to being worried about him. "Something similar to what happened to Lord Yuan tonight. I do not wish to go into it. Talk about something else." He put down the sponge and moved his hands to her shoulders, kneading away the knot there.

"I want to see my parents. Ow!"

"Sorry. Sorry. I did not mean to hurt you." His grip on her shoulders loosened. It would be better if he stuck with the sponge. He didn't know if his control could handle the feel of her bare flesh. He retrieved it and continued his earlier motions.

"I mean, I *can* see my parents, right?" she amended. "They must be worried about me. I want them to know I'm okay." She looked over her shoulder at Malik, but he stared intently at a spot on her back instead of meeting her gaze. She couldn't tell his feelings on her choice of topics. There was no heat, which meant he wasn't angry—a good sign.

"That is all?"

Adrienne steeled herself for Malik's anger and said her next statement. "I want a real wedding."

Malik stopped his movements. "You had a real wedding."

"A real Earth wedding, with my family."

"What is involved in a 'real' Earth wedding?" He decided to ditch the sponge again to massage Adrienne's back. She needed to become accustomed to his touch. He would be more careful and this little bit of contact eased some of his annoyance. He hadn't thought seducing Adrienne to his bed would be this tedious.

"The wedding can be held on Earth. It would be easier," she said. She tried to turn again with the same results as before. Talking to the far wall annoyed her. "There is the minister—someone similar to Guild Master Upala. You can't bring him here, so it would be easier to hold the ceremony there."

Malik slid his hands to her lower back and the curve of her derriere. Her shiver made a small smile curve his lips. "What is so different about the two ceremonies?"

Adrienne tried to squirm away but that only made Malik's hands go lower. "Um... The vows. Yes! The vows. Usually, a couple says vows. Sometimes they are prepared ahead of time by the couple, or they just repeat a generic set the minister feeds them," she rushed out. Her plan to distract Malik hadn't worked. She had hoped an in-depth conversation would distract him long enough for her to either work up the nerve to go through with the night or find a way to put him off.

"What is said in these vows?" he asked. He let his hands dip lower to massage the top of her left leg.

She found it hard to concentrate. "Most couples promise to love and protect one another and to always be faithful and helpful... You know, that type of thing. And...and..." She looked to the ceiling for help. Finding none there, she closed her eyes. That only helped her to concentrate on Malik's hands and how right they felt. Her eyes snapped open. "Rings," she gasped out.

"What about them?" he asked with disinterest. His current task had his complete attention. He moved his fingers to caress up and down the backs of her thighs, moving near their juncture, then retreating.

"The couple exchanges rings."

"Why?"

Malik returned his hands to the middle of Adrienne's back. He may be distracting her but he didn't want to lose his own concentration, as well.

"The rings are a tradition and a symbol of the couple's vow to one another."

"Like the silver cord."

"No, you can't see the silver cord."

Malik held out his left hand. Adrienne mimicked his movement involuntarily. The cord, invisible until a second ago, shined between their outstretched wrists. "You were saying, my lady?" He returned his hands to Adrienne's sides just below her breasts and kneaded. Try as he might, he couldn't keep himself from exploring those parts of her body that would make her moan with pleasure. He could feel her lust. It almost matched his.

His hands on her flesh facilitated this reaction. He knew her nervousness would abate and she would respond to him once he touched her. This conversation had merit after all. Adrienne had given him the means to her seduction.

Adrienne continued, "Well, the rings are constantly visible. And there are other little traditions for the reception—the throwing of the garter, the throwing of the bouquet, the first slice of the wedding cake, the first dance—"

"I am trying to get to that now."

"That's not what I meant," Adrienne insisted in an agitated voice.

Malik felt Adrienne's lust waning in the face of her frustration at his words. He asked quickly, "Why do you throw things at the reception?"

"The bride usually carries a bouquet of flowers. Those flowers are tossed over her shoulder at the reception to waiting bridesmaids. The groom tosses the garter the bride was wearing to his groomsmen," she explained. "Usually the woman who catches the bouquet and the man who catches the garter are the next to be wed."

"And if these two people are already wed?"

"Only single people are allowed to..." Her statement ended on a gasp. Malik's hands slipped up to her breasts. The sensation of his thumbs teasing her nipples was wonderful.

"If I return to Earth to have this *real* wedding, will that make you happy?" he asked in a quiet voice. Adrienne didn't answer, so he assumed she hadn't heard him. He smiled knowingly and repeated his question a little louder.

Adrienne turned and faced Malik, successfully dislodging his hands from her breasts. She was about to speak but the words died in her throat. The raw passion in Malik's eyes scared her. She hadn't felt lust from him throughout their conversation and still couldn't. Was he blocking her somehow?

She tried to step back but Malik grabbed her arms and held her in place. In a small voice, she said, "I want to see my parents."

"I will take you to see your parents. You can have your *Earth* wedding."

Adrienne's smile was immediate and blinding in its intensity. She added, "*Before* I have the first child?"

"Before the first child, then."

Adrienne looked at him closely, her eyes narrowed. "You aren't just saying that to shut me up, are you?"

He laughed at her statement. "I give you my word. At the first feasible opportunity, before our first child, I shall take you back to Earth to see your parents and have your wedding." His laughter died as he felt Adrienne's power again. This time a contract spell surrounded him.

Malik cursed silently. He had not lied when he gave his word to take Adrienne back to Earth. Contract spells were ironclad, however. If he failed in one stipulation, the spell would punish him. Each contract had a punishment patterned to the person held to its terms, and the punishment promised to be painful. Malik didn't know if the first feasible opportunity would be before the first child. Now he had to make sure it was.

"What's wrong?"

"Nothing, my Adrienne," he soothed. He wouldn't dwell on it.

For now, he had a bride to bed. He rose from his seat and helped Adrienne out of the tub. Fine shivers cascaded down her spine, either from chill or anticipation. He hoped it was the latter.

It surprised Malik that Adrienne didn't protest going back into the main room. She walked calmly beside him and even sat on the bed without protest or argument. He didn't question her cooperation, just hoped it would last.

The time had come to claim his bride. He divested himself of his pants and heard Adrienne gasp.

Adrienne knew Malik was aroused but she hadn't expected the proof to be so daunting. Malik's height wasn't the only thing big about him. She jumped off the bed and practically ran to the other side, putting it between them once again.

Malik looked to the heavens and asked Karasi for help. He had never handled a virgin before. Every woman who ever came to his bed was a seasoned lover, and excited at the thought of being with a king. But he wanted his wife, not one of those women.

Adrienne stammered out, "I changed my mind. Can we do this some other time? I really don't feel comfortable—"

"You will not feel comfortable at any other time. This has to happen now, Adrienne. Talking will not soothe your fear of me."

She looked around for something to hide behind or in.

"Adrienne, listen to me," Malik ordered gently. He waited for her gaze to return to him. "You know my powers, or you know most of them. You have felt them before. If I wished to force your cooperation, I could, and easily. You are still as yet untrained and could not negate anything I do to you. I do not want that."

He searched her worried eyes for a sign she understood what he said. "I would never do such as that because I want never to cause you harm, my lady. I will never use my magicks against you, nor raise a violent hand to you. You have my solemn vow." He held out his hand and finished softly, "You are soul of my soul. Come to me, Adrienne."

He didn't lie. She felt exactly what he could make her do—or not do—that first day when they met. Malik's eyes showed she had nothing to fear, but some part of her wasn't convinced. Despite that, she forced her feet to move her in Malik's direction, but faltered a few feet from him. She couldn't bring herself to take the last few steps.

Malik took them for her. His arms encircled her body in much the same way they had at the ceremony. And like the ceremony, his kiss made her forget everything except the feel of his lips on hers and his tongue in her mouth.

He broke the spell when he slipped his hand between their pressed bodies and caressed her breasts. Adrienne jerked back with a strangled cry and crossed her arms over her chest. Tears came to her eyes. "I can't," she cried, then ran to the other side of the bed again.

Malik swore he was getting more exercise chasing his wife around the room than he had gotten in his last near-twenty-five years. He followed her before she could get too far and wrapped his arms around her from behind, pinning her arms down. Near her ear, he whispered, "I know you are scared. I can feel it in you."

He loosened his hold and allowed her feet to touch the ground. In a soothing tone he continued, "Our first meeting was not ideal. I have given you very little time to adjust to this life." He passed his finger lightly over her lips when she would have spoken, and felt her shuddering breath.

"There is nothing but time now." He turned her so she faced him fully. "I will not rush you. I will do nothing you do not want me to do. I mean this for all things, not only tonight, my Adrienne." He caressed her cheek. "I only wish to learn what will make you happy and give you pleasure. Will you allow me this?"

She nodded because she couldn't push the words past her lips.

Malik lowered his head and placed his lips against hers, though he learned from his past mistake and kept his hands on her waist. He had to go slow with Adrienne. So, he kissed her deeply and transmitted all of his lust into that single contact.

Adrienne responded to his kiss and placed her hands flat against his chest. Slowly, she hugged his neck, an action meant to keep her standing, as her knees had gone weak.

Just as she would have pulled away from him, Malik released her mouth and trailed kisses down her neck. He held the back of her head with one hand and cupped her thighs with the other.

She gasped when Malik lifted her into his arms.

He soothed, "I merely wish to make you more comfortable. There is no need for you to stand, my Adrienne." He placed her on the bed. As much as he wanted to drink in the sight of her naked body, Malik knew this would only make Adrienne more nervous. Instead he looked only at her eyes and smiled when she looked away from him.

He kissed her neck, then her collarbone. The next kiss landed still lower. His destination was her breasts. He laid a soft kiss on her left nipple before taking the taut bud into his mouth.

Adrienne wanted to squirm away but she stayed put. Malik's actions weren't uncomfortable. If anything, his mouth felt good. Her hand twitched by her side.

She wanted to run her hands through his hair but hesitated to touch him just yet. He might mistake her touch as an invitation to go further. As much as she enjoyed his kisses, she didn't want this to go too far, wedding night or not.

She stiffened when Malik caressed her thigh, moving his hand from her knee to her hip and back again. He made no other motions than that.

Malik felt Adrienne's fear ease and smiled. He could easily overwhelm her senses with his own lust, but continued shielding himself from her. Making her passion match his own was his goal.

He kissed her stomach and her thigh, then changed directions and pressed his lips against her navel. The next kiss landed right above the patch of black curls between Adrienne's legs.

When he would have let his kisses go lower, Adrienne pulled away from him. She asked in a breathy voice, "What are you doing?"

"Kissing you." He laid another kiss on her hip.

"You're not... Don't..." She stopped with a frustrated sound then tried again. "I don't want you kissing me there." She crossed her knee over her leg and turned slightly on her side, emphasizing her point.

Malik found her embarrassment amusing. He smiled at her and asked, "Why not, my Adrienne?"

"It's gross."

"Another man has kissed you there before?"

"No."

"Then how do you know it will feel gross?" He smoothed his hand up and down her thigh.

"I don't know how it will feel. It's just gross."

"Ah," was his only response. He kissed her hip and, with a gentle touch, pushed her side so she lay back. She complied easily enough but her legs remained firmly closed.

That wouldn't deter him as much as she seemed to think it would. And he knew she protested out of a misplaced sense of modesty—the anticipation tightening his stomach wasn't his alone.

He slipped his hand between her clamped legs and rubbed one finger over her most sensitive spot. His gaze stayed on Adrienne's face as he teased her.

Like before, Adrienne had to look away from the intensity of Malik's eyes. She closed hers, and all of her attention focused on the hand between her legs. Her body gave an involuntary shudder. She'd never felt a sensation like this before.

She wanted more of his touch, and opened her legs, giving him more freedom of movement.

Malik stroked Adrienne's leg with his unoccupied hand then lifted her knee, bringing it off the bed and moving her leg so she was open to him. Adrienne moved her other leg in a similar fashion without his prompting.

Keeping his eyes on her face, Malik lowered himself slowly. With a sly smile, he spread Adrienne's nether lips wide and drew his tongue over her sensitive flesh in a single stroke.

Adrienne gave a sharp, gasping moan. She slapped her hands over her mouth in embarrassment.

Malik took this as an invitation to continue. He flicked his tongue over and over her throbbing nub and was rewarded with breathless moans. It would seem Adrienne wasn't a quiet lover, and Malik wondered how loud she could be.

He slipped one finger into her depths to find out.

"Oh," cried out Adrienne through her fingers. She tried to close her legs but Malik blocked her. She didn't want him to stop but couldn't handle the feelings his fingers and tongue invoked.

"You will crush me, my lady," Malik joked. He laid a kiss on her inner thigh while he kept his finger moving. The teasing feel of her growing lust told him which motions pleased. Her vocalizations did the same thing, but weren't as rewarding.

"Do you still think my kiss gross?"

Adrienne said nothing.

"Is that a yes, my Adrienne? Shall I stop?"

"No," Adrienne yelled as she let her legs go slack again. Her hips moved of their own volition to meet Malik's finger. When she felt his mouth again, her back arched off the bed. This time her clearly audible moan originated deep in her throat.

Tremors moved over her body, and Malik caused them. He lapped at her then suckled ever-so-gently. That, coupled with his finger moving deep inside her, was her undoing. Her hands clawed the bed as her climax rolled over her.

Malik removed his mouth and his finger from Adrienne. He sat and watched her recover. Her eyes were closed and she panted. The rise and fall of her breasts drew his eyes and he knew where his mouth would go next.

Instead of immediately ravishing her breasts like he wanted, Malik asked, "Shall I continue, my Adrienne?"

It took a moment for Malik's question to register in her brain. She blinked open her eyes but couldn't focus on Malik's face. "Continue?"

"Are you still scared?" he asked, even though he knew the answer. The only thing he could feel from her was lust, and it finally matched his own.

She shook her head.

"Good," he rumbled. He lowered his mouth to her breast. When she arched into his mouth, he stole his arm under her back, keeping her arched. His other hand went back to the juncture between her thighs and stroked into her.

Adrienne opened her legs further and moved her hips to get closer to Malik's hand. He added another finger. She moaned. He stopped driving his fingers into her and made a beckoning motion. Adrienne screamed.

Malik couldn't help but laugh when she slapped her hands over her mouth again. It seemed his bride didn't want anyone to know of her pleasure. He had no sympathy for her embarrassment, and continued rubbing and caressing her. He returned his mouth to between her thighs.

With slow movements, he removed his fingers. Adrienne gave a tiny, upset whimper, and it only enticed him. He shouldn't enjoy teasing her this much, but couldn't stop. His tongue took the place of his fingers, thrusting into her depths then retreating. He hesitated to see if his bride would object.

The contact surprised Adrienne, but she didn't want Malik to stop. She reached out to him. He grabbed her hand and threaded his fingers with hers.

His tongue delved deeply only to retreat and wiggle inside her. She didn't care that his tongue didn't match the length of his fingers. The motions his tongue made inside of her more than made up for its lack of reach. Adrienne felt herself climax again.

Malik drank in her climax but continued his assault. He eased back on his shield and let his feelings mingle with his bride's. The immediate euphoric high made him freeze his motions and squeeze his eyes shut. He concentrated on not spilling himself onto the sheets while Adrienne bucked wildly beneath him.

Once he reasserted his control, Malik returned his mouth to its previous position. Every sound Adrienne made was music to his ears. Many of his motions were made to garner louder and louder responses from his bride. He was surprised the Elite guards had not tried to "rescue" Adrienne, her screams were so loud.

Adrienne's climaxes blended into one another until it seemed she was caught in one long perpetual one. She couldn't catch her breath and yet still vocalized her pleasure.

Malik was satisfied he had tortured his bride enough. Moving slowly, he positioned himself between her legs and pressed the tip of his arousal against her opening. With a whispered apology, he drove forward.

Adrienne screamed, with pleasure. The exquisite fullness that was Malik took her breath away. She thought the sensations of his fingers and then his tongue would be her undoing, but she was wrong.

She wrapped her legs around Malik's waist, pulling him closer. She wanted to feel more of him. Her arms weren't long enough to encompass his shoulders, so she settled on digging her nails into his back and hanging on to reality.

Malik braced his weight on one hand while he used the other to loosen the grip Adrienne's legs had on him, so he could move. He didn't really need to move—the velvety softness surrounding his member convulsed around him and drew on him. Adrienne had talents of her own.

Despite these talents, he still wished to move and did, slowly. He wanted his first time in Adrienne's embrace to last as long as it could. It surprised him that breaking her maidenhead didn't mar the beauty of the night and spark another argument. Adrienne hadn't even felt it. She was too far gone. Malik soon joined her.

His pace proved too slow for Adrienne as she met his every thrust and ground her hips against his. He sped up his pace. Still she demanded more.

Malik stopped his motions to change position. He sat on his knees, grabbed Adrienne and made her sit astride him. She didn't seem to mind the new position, as she immediately began moving.

Each time she sheathed him, she rotated her hips. Malik wondered where she learned such a trick. No virgin should move the way his bride did. She knew instinctively what would make him lose all reason.

Adrienne leaned forward and pressed her lips to Malik's. The kiss was chaste, but he didn't want a chaste kiss. He reached up and pressed her head forward. He slid his tongue past her lips and demanded her tongue dance with his.

Malik released her lips, hissing as she dragged her nails down his back. Though pleasure clouded his mind, he stopped his magicks from healing the wounds. He would keep them as a memento of his first time with his bride, and the proof of her pleasure.

A pleasure he increased when he reached between them and rubbed his finger against her nub.

Adrienne screamed Malik's name and clutched at him. It was the only thing she could think of to do. She wanted him to stop, but she also wanted these exquisite feelings to go on forever.

Malik gripped Adrienne's hips to hold her in place when his release came. If he thought that would stop her movement, he was mistaken. His bride convulsed around him. He sighed at the sensation then released her.

She started moving again, and he didn't stop her. His bride wished more of him—Malik could do nothing but obey.

Chapter Twelve

Mushira knocked on Malik's door promptly at sunrise. Adrienne rolled over with a groan and mumbled something incoherent before she returned to a peaceful slumber.

Malik smiled at her exhaustion. He had only allowed her to go to sleep four hours ago. Although it seemed more like she'd allowed him. He dozed off and on in that time, but found himself consumed with the need to watch Adrienne as she slept.

He pulled the cover over her nakedness and bid Mushira enter. Saj followed her.

"Majesties..." Mushira started before she noticed Adrienne was asleep. She corrected herself in a lowered voice, "Sire, the cook wishes to know if you and Queen Adrienne will be in the dining hall for breakfast."

Malik gestured to Adrienne before he answered. "As you can see, Adrienne is too exhausted to handle the court. We will be present at dinner."

Mushira, satisfied with this answer, bowed her way out of the room. Saj stood his ground and stared at the far wall. Malik knew what Saj wanted and also knew the man wouldn't leave him alone until he got it.

Saj was one of the servants who had helped finish Malik's upbringing. Ten years older and a foot shorter, Saj didn't fear Malik's temper or magickal prowess. Only a few servants could make that boast.

"The mess is in the bathroom, Saj. Truly, you can leave it until later," Malik suggested. He learned at an early age that he couldn't command Saj. The man did what he thought best, and nothing else.

"No, I cannot." Saj made his way to the bathroom with quick and precise steps. Before he closed the bathroom door, he added, "I will have a servant bring you and the queen a breakfast tray. You will not be able to beget heirs if you are hungry."

Adrienne stirred again. This time she curled into Malik's side, or tried to, at any rate. With Malik sitting up, it made the task somewhat difficult. She opened her eyes and blinked up at him. "What's going on?"

"Mushira and Saj wished to bid us good morning."

"Oh?" came Adrienne's reply. She lifted her head and looked around. "I don't see them."

"Mushira has gone already. Saj is cleaning the mess we made of the bathroom." Malik smiled at her instant embarrassment.

Though Adrienne seemed not to notice the tearing of her maidenhead, the blood was still present. Malik had taken Adrienne back to the bathroom and cleaned her. The task led to another encounter, which had ranged over the entirety of the bathroom.

He leaned down and captured her mouth with his. Against her lips he said, "Do not fret. Saj does not mind cleaning. He demands it, actually. Everything in its proper place." He cupped her breast, rubbing his thumb over her nipple.

Adrienne tried to pull away while she was still lucid, but Malik's other arm held her firmly in place. She turned her head from his kisses but her action only made Malik move his mouth to her nipple. She batted at his head and hands to no avail. Even if he released her, she couldn't escape the liquid warmth sliding along her skin.

"Saj is in the other room. We can't do this with him in here," she whispered in a pleading tone.

"He will not come out of that bathroom until it is clean. Even then, he will not exit the room until he is sure he will not embarrass us."

"He'll hear us."

"Correction, my Adrienne, he will hear *you*," Malik purred. His teeth clamped down lightly on her nipple, punctuating his sentence. Her resulting gasp proved his point, and he smiled.

"I don't want him to hear me," she whined. Understanding showed in Malik's eyes and Adrienne gave a relieved sigh. He sat away from her and she returned his smile. Once Saj left, Adrienne would have no problems allowing Malik to ravish her again. She had enjoyed it.

Malik had no intention of waiting for Saj to leave. He moved forward and kissed Adrienne's lips. He slid his hand down her stomach to steal between her legs. He could feel her dismay but knew soon she wouldn't care.

He stroked her until she stopped thinking about Saj. Once properly distracted, he entered her. Malik knew Saj heard every moan and cry because Adrienne was not a quiet lover. She vocalized her pleasure to the point where the distance between the bathroom and the bed wouldn't muffle the sound in any way.

Saj would approve of his queen's pleasure and his king's efforts to give her pleasure. Pleasure meant an heir would take root faster. Or it would if Malik hadn't employed a contraceptive spell to uphold his side of their bargain.

After their mutual climax, Adrienne rolled to face the windows. She couldn't see anything but sky from her vantage point, but it didn't matter. The afterglow of making love to her new husband had her too distracted to notice if the bed was on fire, let alone to notice the scenery.

Malik pressed himself against her back, draping one arm around her stomach and propping his head on the other. "Though the barrier was absent, you did not dream last night."

Adrienne ran her fingers over his arms. "I didn't sleep long enough to dream."

"I will not apologize for that."

"I didn't ask you to," she said. She looked at him over her shoulder. "I thought you didn't care about my nightmares? You didn't bother to show up on that first night when the others called you."

He caressed her cheek. "I could feel your fear and I knew what caused it. My presence would not have assuaged that fear but added to it." He kissed her shoulder. "Qamar reported you were well. I left your care to your maids."

The bathroom door opened. Saj came out with Malik's and Adrienne's wedding attire smoothed over his arm. He bowed. "The bathroom is cleaned, Majesties."

Malik nodded. "Thank you, Saj."

He tickled his fingers over her stomach before reaching down between Adrienne's legs and spreading her nether lips. She stiffened and looked over her shoulder at him. Before she could protest, he entered her from behind, forcing her to clamp her lips shut lest she cry out.

Adrienne closed her eyes as Malik moved. She didn't want to look at Saj. The distance between the bed and the door of the bathroom, as well as the blankets she and Malik were under, were enough to muffle Malik's movements from Saj—she hoped.

Malik continued to move his hips behind Adrienne and stroke her tiny nub. He felt her shiver and knew she fought with herself to remain quiet. His distraction at torturing Adrienne made him miss Saj moving to the foot of the bed. He asked in a breathy voice, "Was there something else you wanted, Saj?"

Saj looked pointedly at the bed. "I wish to take the sheets as well, Malik. The people will want to know Queen Adrienne was virginal."

Malik pointed at the side of the bed. "I anticipated your request. The sheet is over there." He returned his hand to Adrienne.

Saj retrieved the sheet. After he looked at the blood stain on the sheet, he nodded in approval. "The people will be happy."

Malik grunted. Adrienne wasn't the only one affected. He stopped his movements and finished his conversation with Saj. "The people will be happy but the chancellors will not be until they use their magicks to assure themselves the blood is Adrienne's virgin blood and not simply spilled from a wound."

Saj nodded in agreement. He turned to leave but said over his shoulder, "I shall have your breakfast tray sent up presently. I suggest you finish, Malik."

The door barely closed after Saj before Malik restarted his movements in earnest. Adrienne curled in on herself at her climax. Once they recovered, she swatted him on the arm. He fended her off half-heartedly and laughed at her assault.

"You jerk! It's not funny. Saj knew."

Malik pinned her arms and hugged her to his chest. "Calm down, Adrienne. Saj is discreet. And I do believe you enjoyed him watching you. Your climax was much stronger this time than any of the others."

Adrienne growled at him and struggled against his hold. In the end, she gave up. Her strength didn't compare to his. "I want a bath." She wanted to be dressed and out of bed before the breakfast tray arrived. Knowing Malik, he would try this again.

"Of course, my Adrienne."

ⅎ⃓

Adrienne and Malik spent four more days holed up in their rooms, enjoying each other. They only left to eat dinner with the palace folk. They never stayed for more than two courses before excusing themselves. One and all found their distraction with each other amusing and promising.

So it surprised some when, on the fifth day, Malik sat on his throne dais alone. Malik hadn't wanted to bring an end to his fun but his kingdom needed him. Adrienne pleaded to be left out of the proceedings.

She wasn't confident in her abilities to rule and would probably be a silent observer while Malik continued as he had before he married her. When the time came to sit before the court, Adrienne bowed out of the affair all together. She decided to take a walk with the promise she would be present the next day.

Malik didn't want Adrienne away from his side but he understood her anxiety. Her goal didn't involve hiding in their rooms, so he was happy to let her dodge her royal responsibilities.

Adrienne strolled in the main gardens off the dining hall instead of the ones below the royal wing. Mushira was right—they were even more gorgeous than the ones Adrienne had seen before.

Being out in the open didn't scare her as much as she thought it would. Khursid and Qamar, who walked five paces behind her, helped keep her fear at bay.

She threw comments over her shoulder at them every few steps and Qamar answered, but they made no move to keep pace with her. Adrienne figured her new status was the reason.

It was a beautiful but lonely walk. After an hour, she resigned herself to going to the throne room and sitting with Malik. Ruling made her feel apprehensive but it beat being lonely and bored.

"May I join you, Adrienne?"

Adrienne gasped and looked around. She would know that voice anywhere, especially since it spoke in her head. Feyr walked towards her.

"Hello, Feyr. I haven't seen you in days. Where have you been?"

"You have not seen me, but I did see you, at the wedding ceremony."

"I'm sorry I didn't notice you, but I was a little out of it," Adrienne admitted. She glanced back at Khursid and Qamar, who had stopped walking when she had. Actually, it looked as though they stood farther away. "They're scared of you because Malik uses you to punish people, right?"

"Correct." He glanced over his shoulder at Khursid and Qamar then looked up at Adrienne. *"Are you scared of me?"*

"No. I have no reason to be."

They started walking. Now that Adrienne had a companion, she could stand strolling around the gardens a little while longer. She asked again, "Where did you go? I wanted to spend more time with you but you disappeared."

"Yes," Feyr agreed with a nod. "*My mate's time was at hand. She gave birth to my cubs three nights ago.*"

"That's great," Adrienne gushed. "How many?"

"*Six total—two boys and four girls. A large litter for her first. She was exhausted.*"

"I can imagine." She gave a little laugh. "Well, I can't really imagine since I've never had children."

"*From what I've heard throughout the palace about yours and Malik's activities of late, that should change soon,*" Feyr said with a wink.

Adrienne didn't respond. Feyr had just voiced a constant worry of hers. Malik agreed to take her back to her family before their first child but Adrienne hadn't missed the lack of a contraceptive during their lovemaking. She could be pregnant even now.

Feyr snapped her out of her thoughts when he said, "*My mate says you can choose a cub in one month's time. They should be weaned by then.*"

"I'd almost forgotten about that," Adrienne said with a laugh. She looked down at Feyr. "What is your mate's name? I want to know what to call her when I see her."

"*She has no name. Naming is for kept animals only, such as myself.*"

"Oh."

"Queen Adrienne," Rena yelled as she ran towards Adrienne and Feyr. She waved her hand over her head frantically. Her movements dislodged her auburn braid from the top of her head. It had been pinned in the shape of a crown to match Mushira's. The little girl insisted on becoming one of Adrienne's maids once old enough. Until then she only dressed the part.

Adrienne called back, "Hello, Rena." Here was someone else she hadn't seen in days. She knelt and caught the girl, then hugged her close. "How have you been? Are you eating properly?"

"Yes. Cook said you said I have to eat more vegetables. They taste bad but I eat them because I want dessert," Rena admitted. She glanced at Feyr. "Hello."

Feyr nodded to her.

"Rena," came a frantic shout.

Indivar ran towards them with Bayard and Flavian not far behind. They seemed spooked about something. She looked around, expecting to see an attacker. Khursid and Qamar were relaxed. If she were in danger, they would be the first ones to try to get her out of it. What was going on?

Indivar grabbed Rena and pulled her behind him. Bayard tried the same with Adrienne but she stepped out of his reach.

"What are you doing?" she asked.

Bayard said, "Please come this way slowly, Majesty."

All of them stared at Feyr. He sat on his haunches and watched them. He looked bored. *They are trying to protect you from me, Adrienne.*

"Why?" she asked aloud.

"The cat is dangerous," Flavian answered.

"No, he's not. At least, he's not dangerous to me."

"You do not know Feyr, Majesty. The cat is dangerous," Bayard reasoned. He reached for her again. "Please Majesty, I—"

"Stand down, Bayard," Qamar said, finally coming forward with Khursid behind her. "Queen Adrienne and Feyr have met before."

"They have?" Indivar asked in disbelief.

Adrienne answered, "Yes we have." To Feyr, she said, "This is silly."

They only wish to protect you, he pointed out.

"And I'm grateful, but—"

"You can speak to the cat?" Flavian asked.

"Yes, yes, I know. Speaking to animals is a rare trait," Adrienne said. "I'm grateful to you all for trying to protect me but Feyr isn't going to hurt me." To Indivar, she added, "He won't hurt Rena, either."

Indivar blinked down at his daughter. She smiled up at him. He turned a horrified expression to Adrienne then went quickly to one knee with his head bowed. "I did not mean to consider my daughter before you, Majesty. I—"

"Was concerned for your daughter's safety, and I totally understand that, Indivar. You don't have to apologize. I'm fine and Rena is fine. Everyone is fine, and Feyr won't hurt anyone." Adrienne smiled at Indivar's concerned look. "It's okay."

"No, it is not, Adrienne," Malik gritted out later that evening. He paced in front of the bed.

Adrienne watched him from her perch on the edge of the bed. She had told him about the entire ordeal, thinking he would find it funny. Instead he got angry. She hadn't wanted to get Indivar in trouble, but couldn't take it back. "Rena is his daughter, Malik."

"You are his queen, Adrienne. Your safety comes before everyone else's, including his daughter. Rena should not be allowed in your presence if he cannot remember that."

"I like Rena," Adrienne said through her teeth.

Malik stopped pacing and looked at Adrienne. He tried to soften his words. "I did not mean to say you could not see her, my Adrienne."

"Then what did you mean to say, Malik?"

He sighed. "I do not want you in danger."

"I don't want to be in danger either. Believe me. But being with Rena is not a problem." She searched his eyes to see if he agreed with her. "Rena has already been denied her mother. Don't make me deny her, too."

"As you will, my lady," Malik conceded.

Adrienne smiled at him. Malik had started his lessons in compromise, and the ordeal seemed frustrating to him. "Besides, Rena is an integral part of my plan to get Hani and Indivar together."

"Excuse me?"

"Hani likes Indivar," Adrienne said plainly. "If Rena starts to see Hani as a mother, then Indivar will start to see Hani as a possible wife. Not to mention it'll get him over that silly infatuation he has with your cousin."

"Lady—"

"Don't say her name around me."

Malik chuckled. He walked over to her and pressed a soft kiss to her lips. He intended to make the kiss brief, but it changed the second he touched her. Suddenly, he couldn't get Adrienne's clothes off fast enough.

Adrienne gasped out, "What about dinner?"

"I have been with the court all day. I wish to spend my evening with you. *In* you," he growled against her neck.

Adrienne put her hand in his way before he could follow through with his plan. "You promised to take me home before our first child, Malik."

"I will, my Adrienne." He reached out to move her hand.

"Not if we keep doing this. How do you know I'm not pregnant already?"

Malik could feel her concern. He stopped trying to move her hand and laid a gentle kiss on her lips. "You are not pregnant, my Adrienne. I have used a contraceptive spell every time we have come together. I do not wish you to be disappointed in me, so I have taken measures to ensure I do not go back on my word."

"Really?" she asked. Her eyes searched his.

"Truly," he whispered back.

She hugged him close. Malik always thought about her feelings and her safety.

Chapter Thirteen

Adrienne sat on her throne next to Malik the next morning. Feyr sat between the royal couple and enjoyed head scratching from both sides.

Adrienne watched Malik preside over the many problems brought before them. He asked for her input every now and then, but she simply shook her head and remained silent. It was her first day and she wanted to observe. If anyone thought her attitude odd, they kept the opinion to themselves.

Observing went to the wayside when the Keeper arrived. Adrienne knew something was wrong when the man entered the throne room. First the woman announcing people with grievances only referred to the man as "The Keeper"—an obvious title, but the announcer didn't give the man's name or what he kept. Second, Malik stiffened, looked at her and then looked at the Keeper. The actions of a man caught doing something wrong.

The Keeper bowed to the royal couple and announced, "Your Majesty, King Malik, the women of the harem are becoming...restless. It's been some time since you required their services. They have asked if you would allow the men of the guard to seek entertainment with them." The man kept moving his gaze from Adrienne to Malik and back again.

Malik nodded sagely. "Perhaps this topic would be better left for later, Keeper."

"Begging pardon, Majesty, King Malik, but this is about as later as it's going to get. The girls are..." he paused to look at Adrienne and cleared his throat, "...well—"

"Harem?" Adrienne asked. It was the first word she'd said all morning.

Though she asked her question softly, the entire throne room grew quiet. All eyes were on Adrienne, including Malik's. She only had eyes for the Keeper.

"Well, yes, Majesty, Queen Adrienne. A harem is—"

"Keeper," Malik interjected in a vain attempt to keep the man from educating Adrienne should she not know the meaning of the word. The heat of her anger beating against his skin told him otherwise.

Adrienne smiled coldly. "I know what a harem is, Keeper. But thank you for attempting to explain." She moved her gaze from the Keeper to Malik. "I didn't know *my* husband," she said, her voice dripping ice, "had one. When did you plan on telling me?"

She didn't wait for his answer. "For days you came to my room and bombarded me with all types of information about your past and this kingdom. Never once did you mention a harem." She laced her fingers together in front of her and leaned forward in her seat. "Come to think of it, I was cooped up in my room for four days with nothing but my personal guards and my maids for company. For all the babbling they did, I never heard anything about a harem. Gardens, foods, the bazaar—yes. A harem—no."

The five people she mentioned were stationed at the bottom of the throne dais, and each one looked uncomfortable. "Why is that?" she asked no one in particular.

When Mushira would have spoken, Adrienne held up her hand for silence. The woman's mouth closed with a snap. Adrienne didn't want to hear any excuse Mushira would give her. In the end this all went back to Malik. Either he told her entourage not to mention the harem, or they felt the need to hide it from her and aid Malik's suit.

The Keeper chose to interject more news. "The ladies also wanted me to relay their...uh...displeasure at being made to stay in their chambers during the wedding and reception."

Malik gave the Keeper an icy glare the man blatantly ignored.

"Their chambers, Keeper? Where are the harem girls kept? I assume in the palace?" Adrienne asked calmly.

"The room directly below the royal chambers, Majesty, Queen Adrienne. There is an access staircase in King Malik's chambers—er, your chambers—so the women can come and go without having to trek all over the palace."

"Ah." Adrienne nodded and sat back. "The door to the staircase wouldn't happen to be hidden behind a tapestry of dancing women, would it, Keeper?"

"That would be the very one, Queen Adrienne," the Keeper said.

Adrienne turned her attention to Malik. She didn't just turn her head—she turned her entire body. Out of the corner of her eye she noticed Feyr slink out from between them with his tail curved around his body.

Her words were quiet, controlled, and dripped with every bit of the anger she felt at the situation. "Get rid of it." If this were a cartoon, there would be a bonfire behind her and her eyes would be glowing red.

The crowd gasped.

"What would you have me do with the women, my lady wife?" Malik asked.

"Short of killing them, I don't care. But either they go—and by go I mean out of the palace—or you're never touching me again. Is that clear?" She struggled to remain calm. She didn't want to show the people of the court how angry this situation made her. But she couldn't stop herself.

"I can't believe you never had the decency or the guts to mention you had a harem. No, I have to find out from the goddamned harem keeper!" Adrienne pointed at the man. The Keeper shrank back with a worried look. "And, to add insult to injury, the people I thought were becoming my friends didn't bother to mention it, either. I can only assume they decided to wait on you. Since it hadn't come up before the wedding, you would think *one* of them would've thought a *harem* was something important to mention to me, your wife!"

Khursid, Qamar, Indivar, Flavian and Bayard all went to one knee with their heads bowed. Nimat and Hani cried, while Mushira looked close to tears. Adrienne ignored it all and asked, "Is there anything else you've failed to mention that might make me angry? Might as well do it now. You can't piss me off more than I already am."

Adrienne didn't know what angered her more—that no one had bothered to mention the harem, or that it was directly below the chamber she shared with Malik. Had the harem girls heard her screams of pleasure at Malik's hands and been jealous? It would explain the Keeper's presence.

Malik wanted to see how his subjects responded to Adrienne's outburst but didn't dare look away from her. Her anger scorched along his skin. It would be an easy thing to shield himself from her emotions, but he deserved the pain, since he had deceived her.

He said softly, "I shall have the harem disbanded and the women relocated by nightfall."

One woman in the crowd of onlookers fainted. Never before had anyone seen Malik concede...on anything. There was no other movement.

"There is nothing else, my lady. You are right. I should have mentioned the harem earlier or disbanded it before I thought of bringing you here. I am sorry I caused you pain." Malik didn't bow his head or lower his eyes from Adrienne's gaze. Pride wouldn't let him, but his eyes showed his apology was genuine.

Adrienne whipped around in her seat and faced front again. She couldn't look at Malik so she stared at the far wall. Tears stung her eyes but she fought them. And, damn it, she would win. These people had just seen their new queen lose her temper. They wouldn't see her cry.

She took a cleansing breath and, in a normal voice, she said, "Thank you, Keeper. You can go." She watched the man bow uncertainly and leave the room. Slowly, murmuring started, soft at first, then it grew into a roar.

Everyone was shocked. Their queen had a temper that matched their king's, and said king had apologized after being chastised like a child. The day would be talked about the kingdom over.

Malik continued watching Adrienne. The heat of her anger subsided and he wanted to comfort her, but he knew it would be rejected, since he had caused her pain. Still, he wished to do or say something to make the situation better.

He whispered, "Adrienne—"

"Burn that bed," she interrupted him. Adrienne knew no one heard her soft command over the noise of the crowd. She wanted it that way, because the last was for Malik alone. She sniffed, then dabbed at her eyes with her sleeve, blinking rapidly several times to keep the tears at bay.

"Of course," Malik agreed. He signaled. Flavian appeared and knelt at his side. Malik whispered his orders to the man, who nodded, sketched a quick bow and quit the throne room with six other men behind him.

Malik said for Adrienne's benefit, "They will take the bed someplace where the fire will not be seen. It will be replaced by tonight."

Adrienne gave the barest of nods. She looked down at her entourage. Hani and Nimat cried openly. Mushira glanced up at Adrienne then looked away. Minus Flavian, the Elite guards remained on one knee with their heads bowed.

She didn't feel the least bit sorry for what she had said. They owed her an explanation. If she felt like hearing it, Adrienne would ask them later. Something told her she would just want to put the whole thing behind her.

"'Whatever doesn't kill you makes you stronger'," she quoted.

Feyr returned to his previous position, ready to bolt if the need arose. He looked from Adrienne to Malik. Until her outburst, he thought Malik would rule over Adrienne as he did everyone. Now Feyr felt Malik might be ruled over instead.

ଔୠ

Flavian and his men burned and replaced the bed in a day's time.

Adrienne kept silent the rest of the day. When it came time to retire, she allowed Malik to escort her to their rooms. She hadn't expected to see a new bed. While the same size as the first, the frame and headboard had different carvings, and a tapestry of serpents replaced the one of dancing women.

Without being asked, Malik left Adrienne alone that night. The bed's size meant Malik and Adrienne could share it without touching, and that suited Adrienne fine. She didn't know how long she would want it that way.

Two weeks passed and things remained strained between them. The harem girls were employed in different trades outside the palace walls. And Malik had the harem chambers remodeled into a recreation room for Adrienne as an apology gift. Adrienne hadn't visited the room and didn't know if she ever could. A new set of furniture and quick but thorough cleaning wouldn't change the room's past.

The weather turned perpetually overcast. The magicks did this to mirror Malik's somber mood. When Malik retrieved Adrienne from Earth, the weather became bright and warm. Ulan entered a time of rebirth and growth after years of winter.

But spring had reverted and storms raged across Ulan's lands. The people of Ulan decided to solve their own problems until the weather improved, leaving the throne room empty.

The bad weather and poor traveling conditions didn't deter everyone.

Malik sat before those still brave enough to seek him out. For the first time, he noticed the loneliness of his throne without Adrienne seated next to him. He couldn't keep himself from glancing over at her empty throne. The distraction he felt made him dismiss five cases outright.

He had to figure out a way to get Adrienne to forgive him. At first her silence frustrated him, but then her silence turned into avoidance. She refused to sit before the court, and took her meals in the secluded gardens. He only saw Adrienne at night, and that was across the width of their giant bed. A bed he had thought small until the distance kept him from his bride.

"Announcing Ambassador Kerest from the Kingdom of Sondo," called the court attendant. He bowed to Malik then stepped aside, allowing the woman to pass.

Malik stiffened and looked at Kerest in disbelief. She was truly there. The years had been kind to her. He hadn't seen her since he was fifteen.

A few strands of grey sprinkled her floor-length black hair and were the only indication of her true age. Her full breasts, slender waist and round hips were exactly as he remembered them. The laughter in her manner made her black eyes sparkle.

Malik stood and yelled, "Clear the throne room." People filed out. "Except you, Kerest."

She smiled up at him, running one of her perfectly manicured hands across the naked flesh of her barely concealed bosom. A series of ribbons intertwined around her body constituted her clothing, and left nothing to the imagination.

Malik descended the dais. He grabbed Kerest's wrist and pulled her along in his wake.

She laughed at the pace he set. "There is no need to hurry, my love. We have time to play," she purred.

He didn't respond. He entered his study and whipped his arm forward, throwing Kerest in front of him.

"No one is to disturb us under any circumstances," he barked over his shoulder, then slammed the door.

The two guards gave each other knowing looks.

One said, "Looks like the weather will be improving soon."

"Looks that way," the second guard agreed with a grin.

Kerest pressed her front to Malik's back. She licked out her tongue, tasting his neck. He jerked away and faced her with a dark look.

"Come, now, Malik. Don't be that way. We are old, old friends, you and I," Kerest said as she sashayed over to him. She slipped her hand inside his shirt and caressed his bare skin.

Malik stepped back, out of her reach. "Keep your hands to yourself, Kerest. I am not interested."

"Not anymore," Kerest agreed with a pout. "When I heard of your harem being banished, I couldn't believe it. Not my Malik. He would never—"

"I am married now, Kerest," Malik interrupted.

"So?"

"This is not Sondo."

"Your father had a harem. I remember he and Dione quite enjoyed it. Perhaps your queen might enjoy the same," she suggested with a knowing smile. "You taught her about sex. Teach her the enjoyment of multiple bodies intertwined and bringing exquisite pleasure." She grasped Malik's arm and jerked him forward.

Her lips melded to his, but Malik kept his firmly closed as he tried to get away from Kerest without hurting her. That would only entice her.

Kerest was a masochist. Her love of pain endeared her to Malik when he was younger. Bouts of rage had overcome him, and that rage found an outlet in his father's harem with Kerest. She'd allowed him to vent on her flesh until she bled, then he would heal her. Once his rage had cooled, she would love his body and drown his senses in pleasure. Kerest was his first teacher in the carnal arts.

Malik got older and became better at dealing with his grief. He had learned to hide his emotions, and thus he hadn't needed Kerest anymore. She'd returned to Sondo. Malik hadn't seen her since, but Kerest was not a woman to be forgotten—or denied.

Adrienne frowned at the empty throne room. She knew Malik was there. She had finally decided to stop her childish pouting. The harem existed long before Malik knew about her, and she'd given him the cold shoulder for two weeks. The time to forgive and forget had come.

Truth be told, she hadn't thought Malik would let her keep avoiding him the way she had. He forced his attentions on her before they were married—she thought he would do the same after. Instead, he kept his distance, even in bed. She didn't know how to bridge the gap between them.

It had taken her all day but she finally convinced herself to just talk to him. She had overreacted. The guards burned the bed, Malik dismissed the harem and several palace servants had renovated the room the harem used. Only Adrienne's grudge remained, and that needed to end.

Two nervous-looking guards caught her eye. She walked across the throne room towards them. As she got closer, she realized they stood before the door that led to Malik's study. It made sense that if the court was in recess and Malik hadn't called lunch, he was probably in a closed session with an ambassador or dignitary.

"Is Malik in there?"

The guards exchanged looks before one answered, "Yes, Majesty, he is."

"Good. I need to talk to him," Adrienne said. She waited for one of them to open the door. "Well?"

"King Malik said not to disturb him," informed the guard.

"Open the door."

The guards exchanged one last look. The one who had spoken opened the door for her. She passed him without another word. She would have a talk with Malik about these guards. They had to know Malik didn't mean her when he said he didn't want to be bothered.

After a deep, steadying breath, she opened her mouth to apologize for her behavior—then stopped.

Heat scorched over Malik's back and told him his private conversation had ended. He shoved away from Kerest, heedless of whether he hurt her or not, then turned and faced the door. Sure enough, Adrienne stood watching him.

She met his gaze for the length of a breath then she whipped around and stormed off the way she came.

Malik gave chase. He grabbed her arm and pulled her to a stop. "Adrienne—"

Adrienne spun and slapped Malik across the mouth. "Let go of me!"

Her attack caught Malik off guard and he released her without thinking. She fled before he could correct his mistake. He turned back to his study and glared at its occupant.

Kerest smiled at the enraged display of Malik's bride. "She's lovely, Malik, and so full of fire. She must be wonderful in bed. Perhaps I should stay tonight and help you convince her to reinstate your harem. You know I am a master of—"

Malik's hands surrounded her neck and choked her words to a stop.

She smiled at him and rumbled, "I see you do remember how I like it."

Malik let her go quickly. His anger at being caught with Kerest, coupled with the incident with the harem, had overridden his good sense. Pain didn't work on Kerest, not the way he wanted.

"I know you have not come to offer yourself to us. And it is an offer I would refuse. Why are you here?"

Kerest pouted. She tried cuddling up to Malik but he backed away and gave her a warning look.

"King Ravalyn wishes to know how he will repay his debt to you now that you've sent back the concubines," she said.

"His debt is repaid."

"He doesn't think so. Your aid put him on the throne of Sondo. He thought you would keep the harem forever, as they were the best girls from the most prestigious schools. Since they are banished from your palace, he finds himself in your debt again."

Malik didn't want to deal with this. His situation with Adrienne had taken a turn for the worst. He had kept his distance all this time.

So many times, he had to stop himself from demanding Adrienne acknowledge him and take him back into her embrace. Their problem wouldn't be solved that way and it might have made it worse. He waited for her to come to him, and when she did, Kerest's actions ruined everything.

"Ravalyn did not need to send you, of all people, to relay this message. He could have contacted me with an orb."

"Oh, he tried but you didn't acknowledge his calls. But his renewed debt is not the only reason he sent me," Kerest said. "Iniko also tried to contact you. Your foul mood has the magicks in a frenzy, and that has made travel into Ulan all but impossible. Only I could attempt it, and it nearly killed me."

"More is the pity it was only nearly," Malik mumbled. He didn't give Kerest time to react to his insult. "What does Iniko wish of me?"

"A meeting. It is time for the three monarchs to meet and greet one another at last. You are married and Chisisi has returned from her training."

"This meeting will have to wait until my queen and I are on sanguine terms once again."

Kerest laughed. "It may never happen, then. She looked ready to kill you. I remember that look in your eyes when you were younger. It landed me in the most delicious places."

Malik growled at her.

Kerest smiled. "What shall I tell King Ravalyn?"

"I will think on it. But his repayment and this meeting will have to wait," Malik snapped. He could feel Adrienne's anger waning. In its place came sorrow and despair. Malik needed to find a way to set things right.

"I shall relay your message, then." Her seductive look vanished. A look of concern marred her features and she whispered, "I never thought I'd see you this upset over a woman, Malik. I'm happy for it. I'm happy your parents' assassination didn't render you incapable of love."

She reached out to him again. This time her kiss landed on his cheek. She whispered against his skin, "Be patient. She won't stay angry forever."

Malik hugged her for that. He stepped back from her and called forth an orb. A portal opened to the middle of Ravalyn's throne room. The least he could do was see Kerest safely home, and a portal would get her out of the palace all the quicker.

Ravalyn looked surprised by the portal's sudden appearance. He stood up and peered through it. Once he caught sight of Malik, he smiled.

Malik ignored him and said to Kerest, "I am happy to see you are well, Kerest. But you will understand when I tell you not to return to my kingdom, ever again."

"The Malik I knew is gone. Love has gotten him past his grief. There's no reason for me to return." Kerest walked through the portal.

Malik closed it after her then faced the door. A sense of doom settled on his shoulders. Adrienne may have forgiven him the harem, but the kiss she'd witnessed had hurt her anew.

He didn't know how to fix it. His every action only seemed to anger his bride. He wanted to explain himself but he knew Adrienne wouldn't hear him out.

"This is a nightmare," Malik said to the empty room.

Thunder crashed outside. Malik looked out the nearest window. A storm brewed in response to his darkening mood. For the sake of his people and continued trade with other kingdoms, he needed to resolve this.

No—not for his people, and not for trade. This was about Adrienne's joy and the happiness he received when he bore witness to it.

For now, his people would have to suffer the storms and hope Malik didn't continue to make the situation with his queen worse. He had thought he couldn't upset her more, and he was proven wrong.

A sound drew his attention to the two guards who stood on either side of the doorway. Malik's anger at this new mistake suddenly had a target. He advanced on the guards, a cruel smile curving his lips when the two men shrank from him.

Adrienne ran until she reached the royal chambers. She burst into the room and ran straight for the bathroom, locking the door behind her.

Mushira witnessed this with horror. She turned to look back at Khursid and Qamar, who had followed Adrienne. "What happened? What is wrong with our queen?"

"Kerest returned to Ulan, acting as an ambassador on King Ravalyn's behalf," Qamar answered in a deadpan voice.

"Queen Adrienne happened upon Kerest and King Malik kissing," Khursid finished.

Mushira's shoulders dropped and she sank into a nearby chair. She whispered, "She was ready to forgive him."

"And now the hurt is made fresh," Khursid said.

"This can't go on," Nimat pleaded. She pointed to the window and the weather outside. "The weather has gotten worse in the last three minutes. Ulan will be devastated if—"

"I will go speak with Saj," Mushira announced. She stood and squared her shoulders. "We will solve this, as our queen and king seem to botch the job whenever they try."

Chapter Fourteen

"*When will you forgive him, Adrienne?*"

She said nothing. Adrienne and Feyr had gotten in the habit of spending time with one another over the last four days. Her guards trailed her out of sight and her maids busied themselves whenever she was near. She didn't want to talk to them anyway. This new slight from Malik reminded her of their betrayal and she had become angry with them again, as well.

Feyr remained the only one not scared of Adrienne's mood. He purposefully sought her out—since she refused to go to the throne room anymore—and brought Rena with him because he hoped the girl would cheer Adrienne.

He said, "*You two have not enjoyed each other since that time. I cannot smell it on you.*"

"Not in front of Rena, Feyr."

"*She cannot understand me,*" he reminded Adrienne. "*Your lessons on how to speak to animals are, as of yet, ineffectual.*"

Rena asked, "What's not in front of me?"

"Nothing," Adrienne said quickly.

"Everyone always says 'not in front of Rena'. Is there a reason things shouldn't be in front of me, Adrienne?"

"You're still a child, Rena. Everyone wants to keep your innocence intact for as long as possible. Many of the adults will try not to mention certain things around you," Adrienne explained in a way she hoped the child would understand.

"Is that why they apologize?"

"Yes."

"Like Sir Bayard did two days ago," she said with a nod.

Adrienne stopped walking and looked down at the girl. "What did Bayard say in front of you that he would apologize?" And had the man made the same apology to the girl's father?

"I saw Sir Bayard and Sir Khursid kissing. Sir Bayard had his hand on Sir Khursid where Father told me no one should touch because that is a private place. But Sir Bayard touched Sir Khursid there. Sir Khursid was angry about it. I think he was angry. He made angry noises and asked Sir Bayard to stop. But he didn't." She stopped her explanation and looked up at Adrienne. "Why didn't he stop if Sir Khursid asked him to? Father says people will do things if you ask them nicely. Sir Khursid wasn't nice when he asked, but he did ask."

At that moment a slight breeze could have blown Adrienne over. She didn't know how to answer the little girl's question. Only Rena's expectant look made her respond. "Sometimes asking isn't enough, Rena. Some people won't do what you ask no matter how nicely you ask it of them."

"Oh," the little girl said. "Sir Bayard even licked Sir Khursid's neck. I laughed and Sir Khursid saw me. He said a bad word then ran away. Sir Bayard apologized and told me not to tell Father. I don't know why I shouldn't tell Father, but Father said I should always listen to what Sir Bayard and the other Elite guards tell me to do."

Telling his daughter something so general made Indivar an idiot. Adrienne would inform him of that later. For now, she had another complaint.

She smiled down at Rena and said, "I think it's time for lunch."

Rena's stomach growled and she laughed. "What is Cook making?"

"I don't know. Why don't you go find out?"

"Okay." She ran off towards the palace and waved at Khursid when she passed him.

Adrienne watched her go.

Feyr chuckled and shook his head. *"I shall speak to you at a later time, Adrienne."* He was three steps away when he turned back and said, *"My mate has weaned the cubs. You can come to see them at any time."*

"Thank you, Feyr," Adrienne said absently. Khursid had her complete focus. Her face must have betrayed her thoughts, because he snapped to attention. Or maybe it was a guilty conscience, since he looked nervous when Rena ran past him.

"Khursid, come here, please," Adrienne called. Khursid rushed forward with Qamar close behind him. "Qamar, you can go."

"Majesty?"

"Leave," Adrienne clarified. She didn't mean her harsh tone, but it did the trick. Qamar bowed and retreated, but Adrienne knew she wouldn't leave completely. The woman would go into hiding with the Primaries.

Adrienne looked around but saw no sign of them. She just knew they were there.

She called out, "Bayard."

He dropped out of a nearby tree. She beckoned him to her. His look was as nervous as Khursid's. He walked towards her but continually glanced over his shoulder. His actions told Adrienne that Indivar was in a nearby tree.

Good, she would need to talk to him later about Rena.

She ordered, once Bayard reached her side, "Walk with me, gentlemen."

Both men walked on either side of her.

"Majesty, I—"

Adrienne cut off Khursid's words, "Bayard, the next time you tell Rena not to tell her father something, I'll give you to Feyr. Do I make myself clear?"

Bayard stopped walking and went to one knee with his head bowed.

"Get up," Adrienne snapped. He obeyed quickly. "Do you understand me?"

"Yes, Majesty. I meant no insult to Indivar—"

"This isn't about insulting Indivar. This is about putting Rena in danger. For some stupid reason, Indivar has told Rena to listen to and obey the Elite guards. If one of them does something to her and then tells her not to tell Indivar..." she trailed off with a pointed look at Bayard. "Do you understand my complaint now?"

"Clearly, Majesty. It won't happen again," promised Bayard. "I didn't think... I didn't know Indivar had given his daughter such a command."

"He'll rescind it soon enough," Adrienne said.

They walked in silence for a few steps while Adrienne collected her thoughts. She didn't know how to start her main topic now that she had initiated the conversation. The direct approach seemed best, since both men already knew Rena had told their secret.

"You two have rooms. Why don't you use them instead of making out where impressionable children can see you?"

Bayard offered, "The fault is mine, Majesty. I forced Khursid. He didn't want to be out in the open but I insisted."

"So Rena told me." She laughed at Bayard's horrified look. "Rena saw more than you think. I doubt she's told anyone but me, since the news hasn't gotten back to Indivar yet, but who knows how long that will last."

"I should make my apologies to him," Bayard said.

"Yes, you should. *Now*, as a matter of fact. And do it someplace people won't see if he decides to hit you," Adrienne said in dismissal. By "people", she meant her. She didn't want to see Indivar fighting with Bayard if the man took exception at what his daughter had witnessed.

Bayard bowed and reversed direction. He went to the tree line and called out. Indivar dropped out of a tree. After a few words, Indivar looked at Adrienne, then turned back and argued with Bayard.

Adrienne called out to him, "I need to speak with you, Indivar, once you are done talking with Bayard."

Her words were enough to get Indivar to follow Bayard.

Khursid noted, "King Malik will not like you sending away your guard, Majesty."

"You and Qamar and Hani are my guard, not the Primaries. They belong to Malik and should be with him."

"Hani is not here."

"Stop trying to change the subject, Khursid. We're going to talk about your lack of discretion."

"Discretion? I thought your complaint would be for my choice of partners. My sexual preference does not offend you, Majesty?" Khursid asked in surprise.

Adrienne shrugged in complete indifference. "It's your body. I couldn't do it, but I won't begrudge you your fun." She smiled at him. "Why? Is Ulan prejudiced to people who like the same gender?"

Khursid relaxed. "No. King Malik's father, King Iasion, saw it as a curse, as did most of the kings before him. However, his father didn't raise King Malik—the palace did. As such, he learned to accept many things in life if they didn't cause him harm." His manner became stiff when he added, "My father disdains me. I do not know how he found out, but he sees my preference as a bane. He wishes me to produce heirs and I cannot do that with a man. I will not deny myself by marrying a woman."

Pain shone in his eyes. "I wish my father to be proud of me but I do not wish that praise to come from a lie."

"I understand. I'm glad you feel you can tell me these things, Khursid."

He blurted out, "I should have told you of the harem, Majesty. I wanted to tell you a great many things, but Mushira said I would scare you needlessly. Forgive me—forgive us. We meant no harm."

"It's okay, Khursid."

"You forgive too easily, Majesty," he urged, contradicting his earlier plea.

Adrienne shook her head. "It's true I was mad at all of you for not telling me, but the blame falls solely on Malik. I see that now. It was his secret and he should have imparted it." He probably didn't volunteer the information because the women were still in his employ, as Adrienne witnessed the other day.

She held up her hand when Khursid would have argued the matter. "Tell me about you and Bayard. When did you meet? In Kakra while you trained?"

"We met in Kakra. Bayard instructed me in close combat."

She laughed, unable to help herself. The irony of that statement was too rich. She giggled out, "Close combat? Is that what they're calling it nowadays?" Her statement made her laugh harder.

"That was not what I meant, Majesty," Khursid said stiffly.

"I know, I know," she admitted. "I can't help teasing you, though. Please go on. So Bayard was a teacher? How did he end up coming to Ulan?"

"No, Bayard was a student like me. Students close to graduation, like Bayard at the time, help the instructors as part of their training. It teaches them how to interact with a subordinate."

"That makes sense. Did you figure out you were gay then, or did you know before your close combat training with Bayard?" She tried to keep a straight face and failed miserably.

"Gay?"

"Homosexual. We call it 'gay' where I'm from—among other things."

Khursid nodded. "I like that title better. And no. I knew of my preference for men before I went to Kakra. I wish I hadn't found out until after though, because I had to keep it a secret and act contrary to my desires. If a woman is treated roughly for being female, men such as me are treated worse."

"Hollace doesn't like homosexuals, then?"

"No. Most who find themselves attracted to the same gender immediately move away from Kakra in order to escape punishment."

"Punishment? It's that bad?" she asked in disbelief. Adrienne didn't know why it surprised her. As soon as she asked the question, it jogged a "memory"—by Hollace's decree, all homosexuals, whether male or female, would be punished for their crime against nature and the natural order of male and female relations. Punishments were severe enough to cause people to uproot and leave their entire way of life to avoid persecution.

Not knowing Adrienne had already received the answer, Khursid responded, "Yes. Some are tortured until they renounce themselves to live a lie, only to be put to death when they lapse. Others are put to death immediately. It is yet another sore point between Ulan and Kakra."

"Malik has laws that protect same-gender relations, and they can marry and live like any other married couple. He even punishes those who would see them harmed, but those laws didn't come about until six years ago. What changed?" she asked, not truly seeing the answer.

"Sondo and Iniko."

Adrienne closed her eyes. Her reference map popped up so she could see the countries Khursid had named. North of Ulan were the Ashon Mountains and Kontar, to the west was the Tano River and Kakra, and Iniko resided on the other side of Kakra. Sondo, the kingdom to the northwest, shared approximately three hundred miles of border with Ulan. Malik had made allies six years ago.

Khursid explained, "King Malik entered into a treaty with Iniko and Sondo six years ago. Part of the treaty called for Ulan's dismissal of any and all laws against same-gender relations. Sondo is the kingdom of carnality—they feel all forms of sexual pleasure are acceptable, and they explore them in depth. And though they would never force such compliance onto another kingdom, for they are wholly unique on this world, they do ask their allies to revoke laws that would seem unjustly harsh towards those wishing to participate in same-sex relations."

Fact after fact about Sondo bombarded Adrienne. Every fact spawned another question, which spawned another fact. She could barely keep up. What she saw almost turned her stomach.

She cried in a high voice, "They condone incest and sex with children and...rape."

Khursid steadied his queen when she swayed. He looked around for a place to sit. The bushes parted to show a hidden bench. He guided her to sit and knelt before her.

"Majesty?" he asked in concern.

"Why? How could Malik want to have any type of treaty with those people?" She didn't understand. The answer didn't come to her and that scared her. In all other things, the answers came if she simply thought of the question.

She saw part of the treaty Malik had signed with Iniko and Sondo, but not all of it. She saw Ulan's concessions to accommodate Sondo—full acceptance of same-sex relations and couplings, as well as punishments to those who would persecute them. She saw Ulan's concessions to Iniko—the presence of one their ambassadors in all negotiations, as Iniko was the land of mediators.

But she stared at a page with words blacked out—parts of the treaty were missing. The information was there, but her brain wouldn't access it.

"Sondo's views are their own. Ulan's power is its magicks, Iniko's is its mediators, Kakra's is its soldiers and Sondo's is its knowledge of sex and what it can do to people. There are strict rules concerning Sondo's citizens and those of visiting kingdoms," Khursid said in a worried voice. "Citizens of Sondo must have the consent of the visitor before they can do anything to them. And Sondo's people live with the knowledge of what their kingdom is and how it functions. If they didn't like it, they would leave."

Adrienne looked at Khursid with hopeful eyes. "I wouldn't be in danger of being attacked if I visited Sondo?" she asked softly.

Khursid shook his head. "No one in *any* kingdom would be stupid enough to attack you, Queen Adrienne. Most fear King Malik, and those who don't are fools. Any citizen of Sondo who even suggests the idea would meet a horrible death when King Malik found out." He patted her hand in reassurance. "Our king will let nothing happen to you."

Adrienne hoped he was right. With a calm she didn't feel, she stood and smoothed her dress. Everything had happened too much, too fast.

"I'm tired. I think I'll go take a nap before lunch." She didn't wait for Khursid to agree before walking away.

She didn't remember the walk back to her room, because she was in too much of a daze. How could a kingdom like Sondo exist? Khursid said its citizens were there willingly, but children didn't have the power or means to leave. She wanted nothing to do with a kingdom who abused children in such a way.

It took her a moment to realize Malik stood in the room waiting for her. She blinked at him several times, forgetting her anger at him to ask what possessed him to sign a treaty with Sondo—any treaty. The words didn't get past her lips.

Suddenly she saw the treaty in all of its glory and knew exactly why she hadn't before. Adrienne could only view the complete treaty when she and Malik were in a secured room together. Before they were wed, Malik only had to be alone to read the treaty. Getting married changed the terms of the spell that bound it in secrecy.

Adrienne considered the information before her and knew it should be forgotten until the time came to use it, because lives were at stake.

"You are confused," Malik said, breaking the silence. He kept his voice soft because he didn't know how Adrienne would react. He had wanted her to speak to him first—to forgive him.

"I'm tired." She didn't mean from her walk, but from everything. It was one stress after another.

Malik ushered her to the bed. Once he had her settled beneath the covers, he sat by her side and held her hand. She didn't pull away from him and that gave him hope.

"You have nothing to fear from Sondo."

"How did you know I was thinking of Sondo?"

He moved her hand to caress his temple. "I felt your laughter and knew happiness. Then I felt your horror and I came here to meet you. As soon as you entered the room and shut the door, the treaty appeared in my mind. Specifically the parts about Sondo." He smiled at her. "I took an educated guess."

"They force children to—"

"No, they do not," Malik interrupted. He smoothed a hand over her forehead in a soothing manner. "Sondo's laws are strict because of the freedoms its people are allowed to take. Children under the age of ten are not to be touched."

"They're still children."

"I agree—they are still children. However, at the age of ten, the children are given the choice to stay or to leave. They are not forced or swayed in any way. Those who choose to leave become wards of Iniko or Ulan, their choice. That is what our treaty states."

Adrienne closed her eyes to digest all of this info. It was wrong and went against everything she believed. She didn't know how to deal with a country whose policies raised strong moral objections within her. Malik seemed to see nothing wrong.

"Why your sudden interest in Sondo, my lady?"

"Rena told me Khursid is gay. It kind of snowballed."

Malik chuckled. "I take your meaning and I am as yet still confused, my lady. Please elaborate."

Adrienne repeated everything Khursid had told her. She sat up during the middle of the telling so she could judge his reaction better.

He nodded and said, "I knew Travers had issues with Khursid. I did not think Khursid's sexual preference was it."

"Travers? What does High Chancellor Travers have to do with this?"

"Travers is Khursid's father."

Adrienne fell over, the bed cushioning her short fall. Malik couldn't have surprised her more if he had said Saj was Khursid's father.

He laughed at her reaction. "Is their relationship so surprising?"

She righted herself and answered, "Yes! They look nothing alike. They act nothing alike. Are you sure it's Travers?"

"Positive, my lady. Khursid takes more after his mother—Travers's wife—than his father."

Without thinking, Malik leaned forward and placed his lips against Adrienne's. He couldn't help it. Her cute antics overwhelmed his sense. He'd held her hand throughout their conversation and she hadn't pulled away from him. They hadn't been this close in weeks.

He didn't come back to himself until Adrienne pulled away from him.

"Malik, I think—"

"Forgive me, my lady. I did not mean to take advantage of this moment," he whispered. He searched her eyes to discern her emotions. He felt nothing from her. Not anger or upset, but not lust either. "I understand I betrayed your trust, but know I did not mean to."

"You should have told me about the harem," she whispered.

"Yes, I should have. You must believe I would have told you, if I had but remembered."

"How do you forget an entire harem consisting of nearly one hundred women?" she asked incredulously. "You obviously remembered them long enough to bar them from the wedding." She tried to retrieve her hand from Malik but he wouldn't let her go.

"I did not bar them from the wedding, Adrienne."

"You wanted them to come?" she yelled.

Malik shouted, "No." He lowered his voice to a normal tone. "The moment Travers announced he had found you, all thoughts of any other women fled my mind."

"What about that other woman? She looked like she was on more than your mind."

"I will not discuss Kerest with you. She is a part of my past that I am ashamed of."

"You didn't look—"

Malik interrupted in a ragged tone, "You walked in on a one-sided kiss, Adrienne. Kerest was my first, and she used that designation to take liberties. I neither encouraged nor wanted her to touch me. I have asked her never to return to Ulan, because I do not wish to hurt you again." He touched her cheek and whispered, "I want only you, Adrienne. I have wanted you since the blood spell found you."

She pulled away from him. "You didn't know me then."

"That did not matter. You are mine. The blood spell said as much."

"So it didn't matter who, so long as the blood spell chose her, then, huh?"

"You twist my words."

"I'm calling it like I see it, Malik. You would be having this conversation with some other woman if the blood spell hadn't chosen me."

Malik nodded in agreement, though he hated to concede to Adrienne's point. "You are soul of my soul, Adrienne. We were meant to be together. Dimensional space could not separate us."

"Soul of my soul? What does that mean?"

Malik searched for a term or phrase Adrienne would understand. He answered, "Your people would call us soul mates."

"Wait. What?"

"That is what that particular blood spell does. It searches for the one woman who is my soul mate. She alone is my equal, and worthy of being my queen. For me there is no other but you, my Adrienne."

Adrienne's marriage to Malik didn't happen randomly. The spell picked her because she was his soul mate. This news made all her tension disappear. All this time she'd thought any woman from Earth could rule with Malik, and the blood spell had clued in on her first. But if she was Malik's soul mate, there could be no other.

That news made her happy, but there was still the matter of the harem with which to contend.

"Why didn't you disband the harem, if I'm the only one for you?"

"I told you, I forgot their presence. I ceased caring for them—I did not care for those women to begin with. I retrieved you and never gave them another thought, not until I saw the Keeper in the throne room."

"You expect me to believe that?"

"It is the truth. I would have told you and I would have disbanded them had I but remembered. You drove thoughts of any other woman from my mind. My attention, my entire being, is focused solely on you."

A knock at the door interrupted whatever Adrienne would have said.

Malik yelled, "Not now."

The door opened anyway. Saj and Mushira entered and closed the door. They faced Adrienne and Malik solemnly.

Malik stood and said in a deadly quiet voice, "I said not now. Get. Out."

Saj responded, "I barred the ladies of the harem from the wedding, both ceremony and feast."

"I kept everyone from even hinting about the harem to you, My Queen," Mushira said. "As I kept them from mentioning anything that might have made you think badly of King Malik. I did not mean to deceive you, and I ask for your forgiveness."

"You?" Adrienne asked. She looked between them.

"I make no apologies for my actions," Saj said. "I thought only of the good of the kingdom. We needed our queen. If she found out about the harem, Queen Adrienne would have protested the marriage longer. I would have dismissed the girls outright, however I did not have the authority to do such as that."

Malik said through his teeth, "If you had reminded me, Saj, *I* would have dismissed them."

"True. I wished to conceal them, not remind you, since you had forgotten. I exercised the full extent of my power to keep the girls hidden and relations sanguine between my king and queen," Saj replied. He bowed at the waist as though to say "you're welcome" for the favor he had rendered.

Adrienne couldn't believe her ears. She pointed to the door and said, "Get out. Both of you leave. Now. Don't say anything else, just get out."

Mushira opened her mouth to plead her case.

"She said not another word," Malik growled.

Saj urged Mushira from the room and closed the door behind them.

Malik stared at it in confusion. In the history of his rule, Saj had never done anything like this. These past few weeks of misery were because Saj elected to hide the truth rather than let Malik deal with it and abolish his harem.

Several explosions in rapid succession made Malik whirl around and face Adrienne. She'd destroyed every vase in the room, which Hani had placed there in case Adrienne ever needed them.

"Adrienne?"

"I'm sorry," she whispered, staring at her hands.

Malik went to Adrienne's side. He took her hands in his and brought them to his lips. "You have nothing to be sorry for. I should not have forgotten the harem. My carelessness caused you pain. I will not be so forgetful in the future."

He laid a gentle kiss on her hands then he turned and scanned the mess Adrienne had made. He released her and moved towards the first vase. The glass would need to be cleaned up and Adrienne was not in the mood to suffer the presence of their servants. He would clean it himself.

"Leave it," Adrienne said softly.

"Adrienne?" He looked back at her.

She stood and walked over to him. Taking his hand, she pulled him into the bathroom, away from the broken glass, and closed the door. She looked into his eyes and asked, "Did you go to the harem after you brought me here?"

"No. Adrienne, I have already—"

She placed a finger over his lips. "Am I being an idiot for trusting you?"

He removed her finger to answer, "No, you are not, my Adrienne."

"I don't want it mentioned ever again. What's done is done. I don't want to think about this anymore, either."

"Allow me to help you forget," Malik said in a low voice. He tilted her chin so she looked at him.

"Please."

His lips met hers and the world faded away.

Chapter Fifteen

Adrienne smoothed her dress over her knees as she knelt in front of the she-cat. The cat was dark burgundy with a sprinkling of pale yellow spots across her shoulders. Belatedly, Adrienne wondered if mulits had any set color scheme or patterning.

Today she would choose her cub. The last few days had been spent getting to know Malik all over again. Now that their relationship was back on track, she wanted her bribe.

She smiled at the she-cat as it eyed her. "Hello."

"*You do not reek of the power of which Malik lays claim,*" the she-cat finally said.

Adrienne nodded. "You're right, I don't."

"*Who are they?*"

She glanced back at Chancellor Riler and Chancellor Sabri. She'd hoped the men would stop following her when they found out her destination. No such luck.

"They are children asking for mommy's permission when daddy already said no," Adrienne said. She smirked at the chancellors' insulted looks. It served them right for trying to get her on their side so she would convince Malik.

Sabri asked, "You can understand the she-cat, Majesty?"

"Can't you?" She would have thought the chancellors powerful enough to understand and communicate with animals.

Travers answered as he entered the room, "It is a rare mage who can understand animals, especially the animals of Ulan, Queen

Adrienne. In my experience, only the Mage Guild masters and King Malik are capable of such a feat." He sketched a quick bow and smiled at her as he straightened.

"Oh." She looked back at Feyr. She'd understood him from their first meeting and thought her entourage had exaggerated her abilities to make her feel better. Was communicating with animals really all that rare?

"Yes, Adrienne, it is," Feyr answered.

She frowned at that. "Could you only answer questions I ask out loud, please?"

Feyr gave his usual feline smile. He stuck his muzzle in her face, his grin growing when their audience gasped. *"The volume of your thoughts made me think it was a question asked aloud."*

"Sorry," she said softly. She gave Feyr's nose a pat and he retreated to his previous position. Her attention returned to his mate. Given the expression on the she-cat's face, Adrienne could tell the cat wasn't happy. She asked the obvious question, "He didn't ask you, did he?"

The she-cat snuffed at that. *"Oh, he asked. Though his request left no room for refusal."*

Adrienne nodded. That sounded like Malik. "Do *you* want me to have one of your cubs?" she asked and hoped the answer was still yes.

Travers answered before the she-cat could. "If it is King Malik's wish, the she-cat has no say in the matter. He is King of Ulan, and she resides in Ulan."

The matter-of-fact quality of Travers's voice made Adrienne mad. Nothing gave Malik the right to separate a child from its mother, especially not to pay Adrienne's bribe.

"My child was a bribe to you then, Malik's mate?" the she-cat asked in a curious tone. She cocked her head to the side.

Adrienne shrugged. "In a manner of speaking. He saw my interest in Feyr and thought a younger version would cheer me up. For my part, I had to leave my room."

"*A bribe then,*" the she-cat agreed. She cast her gaze away from Adrienne and looked at her sleeping young. One cub with blue and grey tiger-stripes was fully awake and watched the newcomers with fascination. "*I do not think my mate weak, not anymore,*" she began.

Feyr explained, "*She thought my life in the palace made me less than the free mulits of Ulan.*"

"In other words, she thought you were tamed," Adrienne clarified, mostly for herself, and nodded. "I can understand how you would fear something like that for your cubs. But—"

"*But Feyr is not tamed. He proved that during the challenges when he won the right to court me. His time with Malik did not turn him into a kept animal.*" She looked at Adrienne. "*I cannot say the same for you.*"

And suddenly the real problem presented itself. The act of giving up one of her cubs wasn't the she-cat's issue—the she-cat feared Adrienne would turn it into a weakling.

Adrienne would probably baby the cub beyond reason. Just looking at all of them asleep made her want to cuddle them close. A feat that would prove hard once the cub was Feyr's size, but she doubted she would stop.

"But?" asked Riler when Adrienne didn't finish.

Adrienne rose and dusted off her dress, frowning at a little brown spot that didn't shake loose. Looks like she would be changing before lunch...again.

"I respect your decision," she said to the she-cat. She gave Feyr's head a pat and left the room.

She crossed the threshold then stopped. Malik leaned against the wall to the immediate left of the doorway, his arms crossed over his chest and his eyes closed. He looked like he was asleep. She thought to walk past without waking him, but Malik had other plans.

"I meant for you to have one of Feyr's cubs, Adrienne," he said without opening his eyes.

Adrienne turned back. "What you meant and what truly happened are two totally different things, Malik."

Chancellor Riler and Chancellor Sabri inched past the royal couple and escaped quickly down the hallway.

"Do you usually back down so easily when someone tells you no?" he asked with an edge of scorn.

She narrowed her eyes at him. Why did he want to pick another fight when they had just made up? Or was this to be their relationship, one fight after the next followed by amazing make-up sex?

After a calming breath, she said, "You promised me something that wasn't your right to give in the first place, Malik. She said no. I'm not bully enough to take a child from its mother by force."

He finally opened his eyes, and they shone with his anger. Straightening away from the wall, he stepped close to her. "I am King of Ulan. *Everything* is my right," he said quietly.

She didn't back down, because she could do pissed as well as he could. She looked up at him with her knowing smile and countered, "I am Queen of Ulan. Everything is *my* right, too, and I *choose* not to separate a child from its mother." She turned and continued back to their rooms.

Khursid and Qamar, who had waited a little ways away, bowed to Malik and followed Adrienne. They parted ranks so Adrienne could say over her shoulder, "Consider this a learning experience, Malik. Don't give away something that isn't yours to give in the first place." She tossed a wave over her shoulder.

Feyr and Travers joined Malik. Travers put Malik between him and Feyr, which made Feyr smile. The cat turned his attention to his longtime companion and asked in an amused tone, *"How do you like marriage so far, my friend?"*

Malik growled and entered the room, glaring at the she-cat as he stalked towards her. She shrank from him and shielded her cubs with her body while Feyr sat between her and Malik.

"Move, Feyr," Malik commanded softly.

"Make me." His manner was relaxed but he was ready to spring should Malik try to hurt his mate or cubs. It wouldn't be the first time he and Malik fought physically.

176

"*I would never hurt your mate and cubs. I expect the same courtesy,*" he said.

Malik gave another growl and left the room. Travers made to follow him, but Feyr stepped on the tail of his robes. The man looked at Feyr with a startled yelp.

It truly is like a drug, thought Feyr. But he hadn't stopped the mage to revel in the man's fear. When Travers tugged lightly on his robe, Feyr extended his claws and sank them through the fabric, gripping the floor beneath. That got Travers's attention, and he stopped trying to free his robe and went still as a statue.

Feyr nodded. Let Travers think Feyr meant him harm. It was better than the harm Malik would do to the man in his present mood. Feyr found amusement in this situation, since Malik had thought the scene in the throne room was a fluke. Feyr knew better.

His gaze turned to his own mate. She relaxed. Without loosening his grip on Travers's robe, he reached out and nuzzled her neck. "*He will not harm you,*" he soothed.

"*You cannot be so sure of that,*" she challenged. She looked out the door. "*Adrienne does not fear him?*"

Feyr thought on this. "*She did at first. I smelled it on her.*" He paused to remember when it had changed. He finally said, "*Adrienne is a match for him. I think her outburst in the throne room some time ago showed her how much power she has, over Ulan and over Malik.*"

Mushira's scream got Adrienne's attention. She stood in front of the windows and watched the gardener-flower battles. She turned to ask what was wrong, but surprise stopped the question on her lips. Feyr's mate stood in the doorway with the little blue and grey tiger-striped cub clutched in her mouth.

"Mushira, shut up," Adrienne said when the woman didn't stop screaming.

Mushira's mouth snapped shut but she started whimpering instead.

"Go hide in the bathroom, if it'll make you feel better." She had to keep herself from laughing when the woman ran flat out to the bathroom and slammed the door shut. Adrienne shook her head at the absurdity. "Why she's more scared of you than Feyr, I'll never know."

The she-cat placed the cub on the floor and sat on her haunches. She replied, "*The people of the palace believe Malik only sends Feyr after those who anger him, because Feyr is his pet. I have no such bonds in this place.*"

"A loose cannon, then," Adrienne said with a shrug. "To what do I owe the honor?" She signaled the she-cat to come fully into the room.

"*You do not fear him,*" she said from her perched position by the door.

"Feyr? No, he's been nothing but—"

"*Malik.*"

Adrienne was confused. "You do." She nodded then admitted, "I did at first, too. He killed two men right before my eyes. I'd never seen a dead body before that moment."

"*Why do you not fear him now?*"

Adrienne sat on the window seat. "He promised to never hurt me. I didn't believe him until my little temper tantrum in the throne room the other day. We may get pissed off with each other but he'll never hurt me."

"*He would hurt me.*"

"Feyr wouldn't let him."

The she-cat nodded then looked at the cub who sat patiently between her front paws. She gave it a push. "*I have changed my mind.*"

Adrienne stared at the little cub as it ran to her. She slid from the window seat and sat on her knees. The little cat jumped onto her lap, purring loudly. "Why?" she asked.

"*You showed courage when I did not, could not. Though it is as you say, Feyr would protect me, I cannot stop being scared of Malik. None of us can,*" she admitted. "*I cannot have reservations about giving up a son to a female who shows more courage than me.*"

"Malik hasn't given you the same promise as me," Adrienne offered.

The she-cat shook her head. "*I see it in you. Even if you had no such promise of him, you would still defy him,*" she said. She gave her cub one last look then looked up at Adrienne. "*Take good care of him.*"

"He won't be weak. Feyr will ensure that he isn't."

The she-cat gave another nod and left.

Adrienne looked down at her new acquisition with wonder. The tiny cub had already fallen asleep. She stroked his head and smiled. It had made her angry when the she-cat had denied her, and Adrienne placed all the blame on Malik for getting her hopes up. Her little argument with Malik wasn't planned—or wanted—but it had worked in her favor. In the end, her way was best.

"It would seem our argument had merit after all," Malik said from the doorway. He stepped into the room, regarding her and the cub. His expression showed relief at the sight they afforded him.

He regretted his outburst after Adrienne refused to simply take the cub. But Malik's anger was at his lack of control of late, not at Adrienne. First Saj and then the she-cat. Everyone had started to disobey him. Did they think marriage weakened him somehow? He would have to disillusion his subjects of that misconception before this whole situation got out of hand.

Still, it was stupid of him to anger Adrienne so soon after getting her back and he realized that.

He'd decided to return to their bedroom and make amends when Feyr's mate passed him headed in the same direction. Malik had hung back to see the she-cat's intentions.

Adrienne looked up at Malik. She wanted to give him a nonchalant look but couldn't pull it off. Her happy mood wouldn't allow for superiority. She did manage to say coyly, "Were we arguing?"

Malik moved to her side, stooped and laid a kiss on her cheek. "What will you name him?" he asked.

Adrienne closed her eyes at the kiss and sighed as she felt Malik's anger soothing. She hated when he was angry, and not just because she felt it. "I'm not sure yet."

He nodded.

Malik's joy at Adrienne's new pet didn't last long. The little cub wouldn't leave Adrienne's side. When Feyr finally came to retrieve him so Adrienne and Malik could retire for the night, the cub latched onto her and wouldn't let go.

"*No, no, no,*" the cub cried. His small claws dug into the ground near Adrienne's feet to keep Feyr from picking him up. "*Wanna stay! Wanna stay!*"

Feyr reasoned, "*You cannot stay, my son. Malik and Adrienne wish privacy.*" He grabbed his son in his mouth and gave a quick tug. The cub lost his grip on the ground with a perturbed kitten noise. Feyr nodded to Malik and Adrienne before leaving with his son.

Adrienne chuckled at Malik's relieved sigh. "He's just a baby, Malik. You can't blame him for wanting to stay. His mother left with his siblings after she gave him to me."

"Oh, I understand the little one's need to be near you better than you know, my Adrienne," Malik said in a husky voice. He moved towards her. The look in his eyes told her exactly what he planned to do when he reached her.

She giggled as she dodged to the side. He gave chase, as she knew he would. Malik caught up with her near the bathroom and pulled Adrienne back against his chest.

He whispered, "Shall we continue this on the bed or in the bath?"

Adrienne tilted her head to the side. "I can still hear him." Finding out the cub could speak at such a young age had surprised her. He sounded like any baby, mispronouncing words and stumbling over syllables, but he could speak. Malik explained it was the magicks of Ulan at work again. Everything could be traced to the magicks of Ulan, it seemed.

"Who?" He pressed a kiss to her neck, then caressed up her side and cupped her breast.

"Feyr's cub," she answered. She turned in Malik's arms. "I can still hear him crying."

"He will stop," assured Malik. He bent to kiss her and stopped. The concerned look on Adrienne's face coupled with the feel of her worry did nothing for his amorous mood. He sighed and let his head fall forward to rest on her shoulder.

Adrienne kissed his cheek. "If you're this frustrated over a cub, you're going to hate having children." She gave him another kiss then turned away from him. She called out, "Feyr, bring him back. He can sleep here tonight."

"I do not wish to make a habit of this, Adrienne," Malik grumbled.

"You wanted me to have him, remember?"

"A decision I regret more and more as this night wears on." He waved his hand towards the door, opening it for Feyr.

The cat entered, cub in tow.

"Are you sure you want him here?"

Malik opened his mouth to say no, but Adrienne cut him off. "It's fine, Feyr. Malik will get over it."

೫෬

Adrienne sat on her throne and totally ignored the goings-on around her, focusing on her cub and his antics. Currently her little one amused himself by running up and down the stairs of the throne dais.

She was all smiles and didn't notice that her joy had rubbed off on Malik. Despite having the little cat in their bed every night for the last five days, Malik enjoyed Adrienne's happiness at owning the cub. The people of the palace, noticing the fair weather and Malik's good mood, decided to take advantage of it and have problems resolved they would normally suffer with.

The woman who currently aired her problem before the throne wrung her hands and rushed her explanation in the hopes that she would get through it before Malik's good mood wore off. There were two other equally nervous women behind her.

The woman continued with her explanation, "That is why I have come before you this day, Your Majesties. No matter what spells are cast, the animals continually return to decimate our crops. We have brought the problem to the attention of the Mage Guild but—"

"Stop," Adrienne yelled.

The woman stopped with a gasping breath.

Adrienne's command wasn't for the woman. She ran down the dais steps, past the woman. Her cub had decided to claw his way up a tapestry towards a window—an *open* window. Normally she wouldn't worry so much, except the throne room was on the second floor of the palace, a very high second floor. Cat or not, the fall would kill him.

The cub ignored her command and continued to climb. He got to the ledge with a look of satisfaction. His satisfaction turned to an angry kittenish whine when Feyr jumped up on the ledge and grabbed him.

Feyr jumped back to the ground and dropped his son at Adrienne's feet. She picked him up and headed back to her throne. Everyone watched her, but she ignored them, saying to Feyr, "I think your mate gave me this cub because she didn't want to deal with him, not because she respected me."

Feyr laughed. "*You might be right, Adrienne.*"

The cub lazed in Adrienne's arms, content despite his earlier upset. Feyr took up his regular position between the two thrones. Adrienne stepped around Feyr and went to Malik.

She smiled at Malik when he raised a questioning eyebrow. "Portal, please," she requested.

Malik pointed slightly to his left and an orb appeared, forming into a portal that led to their room. Adrienne peeked in and spotted Hani and Nimat pulling out clothes for lunch. They curtsied to her when they noticed her. "Is the door closed?" she asked.

Hani looked over at the door, then back at Adrienne. "Yes, Majesty. Why?"

Adrienne gave the cub a good toss. She knew he would land on his feet so she didn't bother aiming for the bed. Besides, that would mess up the clothes. "He's grounded," she explained. She nodded to Malik and he closed the portal.

She took her seat again, smoothing her skirts and smiling at the waiting people. The woman in front of her continued wringing her hands in agitation.

Without preamble, Adrienne asked, "Has anyone tried talking to the animals?"

"*Only you would think of that,*" Feyr said with a chuckle.

Adrienne looked down at him. "What? It only makes sense. Everything in Ulan is magickal. Maybe those squirrel things have a reason for being such a nuisance. Did anyone bother to ask them?"

"I did not think you were listening, my lady," Malik said. He rested his head on his hand as he regarded her.

She waved that off. "I'm a woman. I can multitask." Her attention turned to the woman at the bottom of the throne dais. "Well? Has anyone tried talking to them?"

The woman shook her head quickly.

"Okay, so someone from the Mage Guild who can talk to animals will be sent to your farm to see if an understanding can be reached," Adrienne declared. "If that doesn't solve the problem, let us know and we'll try something else." She looked at Malik for his agreement. "Right?"

"It sounds like a viable plan to me, my lady," he agreed with a smile. He looked at the nervous woman and asked, "Did you have another matter?"

The woman shook her head again. She curtsied and her friends behind her followed suit. They fled from the edge of the throne dais in obvious relief.

For her first act as queen, Adrienne thought it went well. Maybe ruling wouldn't be so bad after all. She smiled at Malik and he nodded.

The next case was about to be announced when the crowds parted. Adrienne couldn't believe her eyes. "What in the..." she started.

Her cub ran towards her as fast as he could. He ran all the way up the steps and jumped on her lap, snuggling his head under her breasts. "*Again.*"

Not far behind him was Nimat, who fell to her knees at the foot of the throne dais steps in exhaustion. "I'm sorry, Queen Adrienne. I opened the door to run a short errand and the little one got out." She took several breaths before she finished, "He runs so fast."

Adrienne looked down at the cub. He cocked his head to the side with a grin that could only be described as mischievous. She gave his head a pat. "You're a little ball of mischief, aren't you? You know good and well I wasn't playing with you." She looked up at Nimat with a smile. "It's okay, Nimat. I'll take care of him. Go ahead and return to what you were doing."

Nimat got to her feet, curtsied and left the throne room.

Adrienne lifted the cub in front of her face. He stared at her as she stared at him. He purred. She said, "Mischief."

He replied, "*Adri.*"

"*Adrienne, my son,*" Feyr said.

"It's all right, Feyr. Many of my friends back home called me Adri. It's good to hear the old nickname again. Do you like your new name, Mischief?"

Mischief purred louder.

"Good, because it suits you," she said as she lowered him back to her lap. After a moment, she put him on the floor in front of Feyr. When he jumped back on her lap, she put him back in front of Feyr. He didn't try a second time, since Feyr placed his paw on Mischief's back and held him.

Malik got the proceedings underway again. They presided over three more cases before Malik called a recess for lunch. Everyone, except Feyr and Mischief, filed out of the throne room and left Malik and Adrienne alone. Malik pointed to his side to open another portal to their bedroom, since they would have to change before lunch.

Adrienne placed her hand on top of his. "Let's eat in the garden." Then it wouldn't matter what she wore, since no one would see her. This constant changing of outfits had gotten old.

"If you would like, my Adrienne," Malik agreed. He changed the portal's destination to the secluded gardens below the royal chambers.

Mischief zipped past them with Feyr hot on his heels. Adrienne laughed at him. Everything excited Mischief. He explored everything, whether he should or not. Any new room was a mystery to be solved.

The only room Mischief went out of his way to avoid was the bathroom. In true cat fashion, he didn't like water. Malik used Mischief's aversion to his advantage and secluded himself and Adrienne there whenever he wanted privacy.

Malik mused, "With the little one thusly engaged, it would be so easy to whisk you away to our rooms so I can ravish you." He laid a kiss on her neck.

"Malik," Adrienne scolded with a mock frown.

"May I, My Queen?" he asked in a deep, rumbling voice. He laid another kiss on the curve of her shoulder.

"No. I'm hungry."

"As am I." He slipped his arm around her waist and pulled her closer.

Behind them, someone cleared his throat.

Malik gave an annoyed sigh. He said without turning, "Adrienne and I are taking lunch in the gardens, Saj."

Saj replied, "Very well, Majesty." He bowed and left.

Malik escorted Adrienne through the portal and closed it behind him.

Adrienne asked, "What about our guards?"

"Do you feel so unsafe around me that you must have your guards?"

"That's not what I meant, Malik," she rushed out.

He said in a soothing tone, "I merely jest, my Adrienne. As for our guards, they are hidden so we can enjoy our time together with the illusion of privacy."

"*Food,*" Mischief squealed with glee.

Saj directed the servants on how to set out the picnic. Adrienne wondered if Saj used portals to get around the palace as Malik did. It would explain how he had gotten to the secluded garden first.

Mischief wove in and out of people's feet as they placed the different platters. Some servants were brave enough to shoo Mischief away when he would have tried sampling the food, then cast wary looks at the cub's father. Feyr merely lay on the edge of the blanket and watched.

Malik and Adrienne sat on the blanket. Adrienne took off her shoes with a sigh. Malik pulled her feet onto his lap and massaged them.

Saj made a huge display of choosing three of the servants at random to sample all of the food. Once Saj declared the food safe, everyone bowed and left.

Adrienne decided to feed Malik, since he wouldn't stop rubbing her feet to feed himself. He insisted she use her hands instead of the utensils provided. Every piece of food she offered allowed him the opportunity to suck on her fingers.

Feyr cleared his throat and asked, "*You two do remember there is a child present, do you not?*"

"I do," Adrienne answered. "But I think Malik doesn't care."

Malik winked at her.

"*Birds,*" Mischief yelled. He ran after a flock of birds that had taken flight from a nearby tree top.

Feyr watched him go with a shake of his head. He turned back to comment to Adrienne on his son's tendency of being easily distracted but the words didn't come. He witnessed another's tendency of being easily distracted. He cleared his throat again and asked, "*You do remember I am present?*"

Malik said against the swell of Adrienne's breasts, "You can leave." He slipped the sleeve of Adrienne's dress down so he could have better access.

"*And your guards?*"

"Oh," Adrienne exclaimed with dismay. She pulled away from Malik and straightened her dress quickly. The hidden guards had slipped her mind once Malik started kissing her. She pulled her feet from his lap and slid slightly to the side, putting some distance between them.

Malik grumbled. "Thank you, my friend. Remind me to repay you in kind when your mate returns."

"*You know I will do no such thing,*" Feyr said. He looked up. "*It would seem my son has caught something.*"

Mischief ran back to the group with a bird in his mouth. He jumped over food platters and presented Adrienne with his catch.

She stared down at the bird in Mischief's mouth and tried to smile for the cub's sake. He looked so proud of himself. The poor bird squirmed in Mischief's mouth, screaming in pain for him to let her go.

Adrienne held out her hands for the bird. "Thank you, Mischief. How sweet."

Mischief opened his mouth and the bird dropped into her hands. It cried out in pain and tried to fly, only to scream louder. Adrienne couldn't show how much the gift upset her. Mischief thought he had done something good and she couldn't punish him for hunting. Adrienne had promised Mischief's mother he wouldn't be weak.

Malik took the bird from her gingerly, pretending to look the bird over and praising Mischief for his hunting abilities. In truth, he was healing the bird's injuries.

Adrienne smiled at him for his consideration to the cub and his kindness to the bird. She turned her attention back to Mischief. In an exaggerated manner she looked all around then back at him. She asked, "Where's your father's present?"

Mischief stared up at her with a confused look. "*Papa?*"

Feyr gave an affected sigh. "*I must not rate, for my son to forget me so easily,*" he stated in a dejected voice.

Mischief ran back towards the trees. He yelled, "*Present for Papa.*"

Adrienne sat next to Feyr. A flash of color caught her eye and she looked up in time to see her present from Mischief flying away as fast as it could. She smiled at Malik in thanks.

Malik pointed out, "He will notice the bird's absence."

She shook her head. "No, he won't."

"But if he does?"

"I'll tell him the truth and the reasons behind it. He's a baby but he'll understand," she said. She scratched Feyr's head absently and leaned into his side. His purring made her relax.

"*Back,*" Mischief yelled as he emerged from the woods.

Adrienne's welcoming smile faltered then turned into a horrified gasp. She screamed, "Mischief."

She scrambled to her feet and ran to the cub.

Malik caught her and pulled her to a stop. "No, Adrienne, it might still be alive."

Mischief didn't seem to notice everyone's unease. He came forward happily with his prize in his mouth—an awez, a very poisonous snake, possibly one of the most poisonous on all of Bron.

Feyr went to his cub slowly, ready to kill the awez if his son hadn't done the job. He took in how Mischief held the snake behind the neck and how the snake didn't move.

He scented the air, then pronounced for Malik's benefit, "*It's dead. Mischief killed it. Though not without injuries of his own.*"

Malik released Adrienne and she rushed over to Mischief. She wanted to take him in her arms but blood covered his body—his blood and the snake's. She didn't want to hurt him since it seemed he didn't feel any pain. He had a particularly nasty-looking gash over his right eye.

Mischief dropped the snake at Feyr's feet in triumph. "*Present for Papa.*"

Feyr nodded. "*Thank you,*" he whispered. He didn't take his eyes off his son as he said, "*Malik.*"

Malik had reached for Mischief before Feyr said anything. "You know you do not have to ask," he said softly. His magicks surrounded Mischief as his hands surrounded the cub's body, and he said with wonder, "He has no poison within him."

Feyr looked at his son in surprise. He looked back at the snake and remembered the way his son had carried it. He gave an amused chuckle. "*He has good instincts, it would seem,*" he said in a proud, relieved voice.

Adrienne placed her hand on top of Malik's when she noticed his magicks had started healing the wound over Mischief's eye. "Wait, Malik. Can you heal him so he keeps the scar and his ability to see?" She looked at Feyr to see if he understood what she asked.

Feyr nodded in agreement. "*He's earned his badge. Let him keep it, Malik.*"

"As my Adrienne wishes," Malik agreed.

Once Malik finished healing him, Adrienne grabbed Mischief in one hand and the awez in the other. She took them both back to the royal chambers through one of Malik's portals.

She congratulated Mushira for not screaming about the blood covering her clothing.

Adrienne held out the awez to Mushira, who took it hesitantly.

"Could you have someone make this into a collar for Mischief? Have them make it big enough so he won't grow out of it. I want the fangs to hang from it, as well."

Mushira looked at the snake, then back at Mischief. "The little cub killed this awez?"

Adrienne gave a proud affirmative then carried Mischief into the bathroom. Fully clothed, she walked with him into the tub. Her dress would have to be soaked anyway, might as well start the process. Undoubtedly, Mushira had prepared a bath so Adrienne could clean up before she changed for lunch. Adrienne liked to be clean as much as the next person but a bath before every clothing change was a bit excessive.

"*No, no, no, no,*" Mischief screamed as soon as the water hit his fur.

Adrienne gripped him as tight as she could without hurting him. She warned, "Scratch me and I'll have you declawed." An empty threat, but it worked.

Mischief stopped fighting and started crying as she rubbed soap into his fur. He cried through the whole ordeal and wouldn't even let up when Feyr entered the bath to show it wasn't as bad as Mischief made it out to be.

The little cub didn't stop crying until Adrienne dried him with a towel. Mischief took several sniffling breaths. *"Mischief bad. Got punished,"* he whined.

Adrienne gathered him close and kissed him. "I didn't punish you, silly. I just wanted you clean. I can't cuddle you if you're covered in blood."

"Mischief not bad?"

"No, Mischief very good," she complimented. She put him on the ground and gave him a push towards the door. "Off you go," she urged in a warm voice.

Mischief recovered quickly, as was a child's wont. He ran out of the room with Feyr walking slowly after him. Adrienne sagged visibly. Her legs stopped supporting her and she dropped to her knees.

Malik crouched behind her, gathering her close. "Your heart is beating so fast, my Adrienne. Were you truly that scared for him?"

Adrienne rested her hands on his arm where it circled her chest. She said, "I saw the blood... He's just a baby. I don't want to coddle him too much and make him weak like Feyr's mate feared, but I might be letting him do too much too soon. She won't forgive me if I get him killed."

"You are doing fine," Malik soothed in a soft voice. "Will you be this frantic over our own children?"

"No, I'll probably be worse," she admitted. "I may know the facts but I don't know this world. I can never relax. And they'll use magicks. What happens if the baby starts crying and blows up the throne room?"

Malik kissed her neck. "We will have the construction mages fix it."

"Just like that?"

"Just like that," Malik agreed. "If the people of the palace could put up with me, a parentless tyrant, putting up with children with two parents should be easy." He gave her a squeeze as he added, "You and I will live to see our great-great-grandchildren. That I promise you, Adrienne."

Adrienne pulled away from him. She got to her feet and faced Malik with a sad expression. He stood with his own look of concern. She said softly, "You know what I said about promising something that—"

Malik placed a finger over her lips to stop her words. He vowed, "I will tear open the gates of the afterlife and bring you back if I have to, my Adrienne. But I will keep my promise."

Chapter Sixteen

After fretting over it for the last half hour and finding no way around it, Adrienne stood. All conversation in the throne room stopped and all eyes turned to her. She had known this would happen. She couldn't urge them to keep going as she snuck out of the room. She couldn't *sneak* out of the room.

"Adrienne?" Malik asked with concern. He stood and went to her side. Once there, he wrapped his arms around her waist and brought her close.

She leaned into him and whispered, "I'm going for a walk."

"I can go with you," he said. He turned to the crowd, but Adrienne stopped him.

"You're needed here."

"Do I not deserve a break also?" he asked with a smile. He didn't wait for her answer. Instead, he laid a kiss on her cheek then opened a portal to their rooms.

Adrienne thanked him and left. She didn't know what everyone thought of her departure, but she needed a break before she fell asleep. As embarrassing as it was to simply walk out in the middle of royal proceedings, it would be even more embarrassing to fall asleep in front of everyone.

She had no problem sitting for long periods of time and listening to people speak. Being a senior in college meant sitting and listening to lectures for hours on end. She tended to zone out and eventually fall asleep if her hands weren't busy. Whether she took notes or crocheted an ever-growing scarf, her hands had to be busy in order for her to stay awake. Her college days had ended so she didn't need to take notes any longer. And she didn't own materials to make a scarf, ever-growing or otherwise.

She'd ask Mushira about procuring something that resembled a crocheting needle and thread later. If Bron was a parallel Earth, they had to have crocheting. At least Adrienne thought Bron had to.

She wandered around the palace with no destination in mind. Movement out of the corner of her eye revealed Khursid and Qamar a few paces behind her. She didn't bother telling them to catch up with her since she had nothing to say to them.

Her wanderings took her to the High Chancellor's wing, located on the fourth floor like the royal wing. The other chancellors had rooms on the third floor, but High Chancellor Travers had earned the right to be near his monarchs.

Most of the chancellors were in the throne room with Malik, but not all of them. Specifically, Travers was absent. Adrienne found that strange. Out of all of the chancellors, she would think the High Chancellor would always be present at Malik's side.

On a whim, she decided to drop by Travers's room. Adrienne rounded the corner and noticed his door open.

"High Chancellor Travers?" she asked. She poked her head around his chamber door and smiled when he looked at her.

Travers jumped out of his seat and gave a deep bow. He stumbled out, "Majesty! I didn't know... How good of you... Come in, please." He pulled out a chair for her. "I didn't know you wished to see me. I would have gladly met you in the throne room or..."

Adrienne took the chair he offered. She waved him back down to his own seat. "It's okay. I didn't know my destination until I arrived. I mean, it's just me being a busybody. So I didn't need to make it an official visit." She looked around the room. Papers and books and random glass containers of varying shapes, contents and sizes were scattered everywhere. "I'm not interrupting," she started, then trailed off.

"Never, Majesty. My time is always yours to do with as you see fit," he said quickly.

"You can sit down, High Chancellor Travers. As I said, I'm just being nosy."

Travers lowered himself into his chair. "Nosy about what, exactly, Majesty?"

"Your son. Khursid."

Travers's expression instantly turned dark. "He hasn't done anything to endanger—"

She rushed out, "No, no, no. I...I wanted to talk to you about him. He's done nothing that would cause alarm." She glanced over her shoulder at the door. Khursid and Qamar had stopped at the end of the hallway and couldn't hear the conversation.

That was a good thing because she'd approached it all wrong. She looked around the room again. She had seen Khursid's room. It was immaculate. She didn't even think the palace vermin would dare set foot there. In contrast, Travers would break his neck walking from his door to his bed if he didn't watch his step. These men really had nothing in common.

"Khursid feels you...disapprove of his choice in lovers. He knows you want him to carry on your family lineage and that he can't do that if he's with a man."

Travers leaned back in his chair and stared at her for a long moment. He blinked several times and laughed, then slapped his hand over his mouth with a look of apology. "Forgive me, Majesty. I don't laugh at you. I laugh at my son's stupidity."

"You aren't mad because he's gay, uh, homosexual?"

"If I disdained him for taking men to his bed, then I would be a hypocrite, as I do the same."

Adrienne let her mouth drop open in shock. "I thought you were married to a woman, High Chancellor," she said.

"I am. My wife and other two children are teachers in the Mage School of Ulan. My marriage was of convenience. I needed children to satisfy my family and my wife needed a husband her parents would not disapprove of outright."

"You don't love her?"

"I am fond of my wife. We are friends after all these years. But we both married for obligation." Travers smiled at Adrienne's disapproving look. "Don't think I am benefiting alone, Majesty. My wife has lovers, as well. We have had our children. We stay married for the sake of our families, but our life together is that of friends, not spouses."

"Then I don't understand. Why doesn't Khursid do the same thing? Marry a woman, have kids and take a lover on the side, I mean?" asked Adrienne.

If she were back on Earth, there would be a hint of impropriety in her question. Ulan, however, embraced a form of consensual adultery. So long as both spouses agreed, a lover could be added to the household as a legal family member.

"He doesn't see it as an option. As you have just enlightened me, my son thinks I disdain him for sleeping with men. He obviously doesn't know of my predilection. My daughters do, but that is only because they know of their mother's lovers. As they all teach at the same school, it is hard not to notice."

"You live in the same palace as Khursid—down the hall from one another, no less—and you two don't notice anything about each other. I didn't even know you were related until Malik told me. You act and look nothing alike. Well, except for liking men." Adrienne studied Travers and tried to see any of Khursid in him, anything at all. Malik must be right—Khursid took after his mother.

Adrienne asked, "If it's not his preference for guys, then what's the problem?"

"He is a soldier."

Adrienne waited. When Travers didn't continue, she shrugged and asked, "And?"

"My family and his mother's family are all mages."

She looked to the ceiling for help. Of all the stupid... "You're telling me that you and your son can't stand each other because he decided to 'be all he could be' instead of casting spells for a living?" She slumped into her seat and let her head fall against the high back.

"Be all he could be? I don't understand your meaning, Majesty."

Adrienne replied, "Never mind." She pushed herself back to an upright position and straightened her skirts. She mumbled something about men and stupidity and the hard way before she said, "Get over it."

"Majesty, I don't think you understand."

"I understand enough. Do you even know how lucky you are? I can't even *see* my parents unless Malik takes me to them. And you... You're not twenty feet from your son—he's standing at the end of the hall—and you can't even look at him." Adrienne stood and paced in the little space in front of her chair, which consisted of three steps, turning and repeating. "Both of you are idiots and that's what you have in common," she finally pronounced.

Adrienne plopped back into her seat. She met Travers's worried gaze. "Okay, look, Travers. You and I both know in order to be in the Elite guard—let alone one of the chosen few to guard the royal couple exclusively—you *have* to know how to use magicks. Khursid is a mage and a soldier. Don't know if you've noticed, but Malik prefers his guards to be both."

She searched his eyes to see if he comprehended her words, then continued, "It doesn't matter that Khursid became a soldier and chooses his blade before magicks. He still has magicks and uses it if he has to." She thought back to his nose dive out of her window but didn't mention it. "That's all that should matter."

Travers bowed. "I know the Elite must have knowledge of magicks. I know that, Majesty, but I have seen Khursid in battle before. He never uses his magicks, even if his opponent does."

"So what? Be happy he can cover his ass with his blade even if the other guy is throwing fireballs at him. I think that speaks volumes about his combat skills."

Adrienne rose once more and walked over to Travers. She laid her hand on his shoulder. She felt him jerk and smiled at him. "'It's better to have it and not need it than to need it and not have it'. That's a saying where I'm from." She gave his shoulder a pat and backed up a step. "In my opinion, though a strong mage you may be, it's you who's lacking in skills, not Khursid. Not to mention, isn't this soldier versus mage crap what got this feud between Ulan and Kakra started in the first place?"

She didn't wait for his answer before she turned and headed for the door. A thought brought her to an abrupt halt. She turned back to Travers, who had risen when he realized she intended to leave. "Khursid will be at dinner tonight, like always. You two have my permission to step out and have a talk. You will explain to your son about your relationship with his mother and about what the real problem is. He will give you the heirs you wanted and you'll start treating him like he means something to you. Be thankful you can see him at all—it's more than my parents have." She gave a slight nod and left.

Travers stared after his queen in stunned silence. Before, his silence was to save himself from upsetting her—now his silence was from shock. He didn't have any time to recover before Malik stepped out of a portal directly in front of him. Travers opened and closed his mouth many times.

"Calm yourself, Travers. I simply want to know what my wife found more important than the welfare of the kingdom," Malik said. He smiled at Travers's state. Adrienne had that effect on people.

"Majesty..." Travers stopped, passing his hand over his face. "I don't envy you, My King. She truly is your equal."

"You felt it then?"

"As soon as she touched me, Majesty. When did she learn to forge contract spells?" He waved his hand in front of himself. "Strong contract spells, at that. I will be near death if the spell perceives I am not following her orders to the letter."

"She has not."

Travers stared at his king in stunned shock. "You...you mean... She forged a contract spell of this power, this magnitude, and she has not yet learned—"

"Yes. She has this capability. That is not my worry, Travers," Malik dismissed. He sat in the chair Adrienne had vacated.

"Majesty?"

"Something is wrong with Adrienne's powers. She was more powerful before we wed. She imagined what she wanted and it would happen. Now all her magicks are unconscious. She seems to not have noticed the change."

"I don't understand, Majesty," Travers said.

"She wanted me to be calm during our wedding dinner and wove a calming spell around me. She wished for you to follow her words without hesitation and bound you in a contract. Her magicks are acting on inner desires. It is my theory her magicks will not work if she actively concentrates on a specific goal. I do not plan to test this theory and alert Adrienne to her impediment."

"How did this happen?"

Malik recounted the incident in Adrienne's former chambers before the wedding ceremony. He finished, "I have never known any mage who could hold me silent and immobile. Whoever the mage, they did something to Adrienne to stunt her powers."

Travers nodded. He almost mentioned the interference spell placed on the blood spell that found Adrienne, but he stopped himself. This didn't sound like the work of the same person. Why would they stunt Adrienne's powers? Making her weaker would only make Malik guard her more closely. Anyone who wished to do her harm would want Malik to be overconfident in his wife's abilities and thus protect her less.

Instead, Travers said, "I shall look into this matter, My King."

"Do not bother," Malik said as he got to his feet. "There is no trace of the mage who cast the spell and no trace of the magicks used. If I had not felt Adrienne's true powers before our marriage, I would have thought she was fine—weak, but fine. I know better. But what mage can cast spells and leave no trace of their power afterwards?"

"None."

"Someone on Bron is more powerful than me, and they showed this by affecting Adrienne. But to what purpose?"

"I do not know, My King."

"Keep all I have told you to yourself, Travers. I do not want even the other chancellors to know. They will think Adrienne is not my true blood-spell-chosen bride."

"I will breathe not a word, Majesty." Travers bowed. After all, he hadn't told the other chancellors about the possible traitor in their midst, as they were all suspect. Not telling them of Adrienne's now-stunted powers would be easy. As a matter of fact, he wouldn't even mention these visits to anyone—Adrienne's or Malik's.

Malik returned to the throne room through a portal, leaving Travers alone. He looked around his rooms. His king and queen must think him a slovenly person for having his rooms in such disarray. He was not usually so disheveled. The search for the traitor made him frantic, and he didn't have time to clean.

And now it seemed he had to worry about another who may or may not be a traitor. Malik told him not to search for answers to Adrienne's stunted powers, but Travers didn't believe as his king. The two incidents were related.

Chapter Seventeen

"Mushira."

Mushira stopped searching the closet and looked at Adrienne. "Yes, Majesty?" she asked.

"I want you to come with Malik and I this weekend to visit my parents," Adrienne said. The day Malik would take her back to her parents had arrived, six days before Malik's birthday. The whole kingdom had started preparations for a huge party. They would celebrate not only Malik's birthday, but another heir's ability to hold Ulan.

Court matters lulled, since nothing was more important than planning the celebration. Malik thought it was the perfect time to take Adrienne home.

Adrienne couldn't agree more.

"As you wish, of course, Majesty. May I ask why? I would think you would like this chance to be alone with your family and away from reminders of court," Mushira said.

"Away from reminders of court?" Adrienne asked and laughed. "We're taking Feyr and Mischief. If they aren't a huge reminder, I don't know what is." Mischief came over to her at the mention of his name. He rubbed against her ankles and purred. She picked him up and absently started petting him. "I think my mother will take this whole situation much better if she knows there is someone here taking care of me, namely you."

Mushira looked shocked. "Majesty, I...I am only your maid. It is the king who—"

"That's not what I meant, and you know it," Adrienne interrupted. "I know you and my mother will get along, because you're a lot alike. She'll be happy to know you're by my side."

"It is my honor," Mushira said with a deep curtsy.

Malik entered the room. Travers, who looked pale and carried himself like he was in pain, trailed behind him.

Malik stopped short and whirled around. "You are not going, Travers. It is a three-day trip to visit Adrienne's family, not a diplomatic mission to another kingdom. Even then, you would not accompany me."

Before Travers could open his mouth and argue, Adrienne said, "You aren't coming, High Chancellor. I distinctly remember telling you to talk to your son, which you still haven't done. This would be the perfect time since I won't be here for him to protect. He has three days' free time. Use it wisely." There was a warning in her tone. From the way Travers snapped his mouth shut and took a step back, she knew he heard it.

Adrienne put her smile back in place with a nod. She looked around the room. "Are we ready to go then?" she asked Malik.

He came to her side and kissed her neck. "At your command, my lady," he agreed.

Mushira said frantically, "I have yet to pack for you, Majesty." She returned to searching through the closet.

Adrienne waved that away. "You don't have to. I have clothes at my parents' house. They aren't what you're used to dressing me in, but I don't need to dress like a queen at home. Pack what you need for yourself and we can go." She watched Mushira rush out of the room.

"I want to go," Rena said.

Adrienne smiled at the little girl. "Not this trip, sweeting. I promise you can come next time, though." Adrienne didn't know what would happen on this trip. Whatever it was, she didn't want Rena exposed to it.

Feyr said, "*Mischief will tell you all about it upon our return. Though you must remember what we told you, Rena. No one is to know Adrienne is from a different dimension.*"

"I won't forget, Master Feyr. I won't say anything to anyone. Promise," Rena vowed with a hand over her heart. With Malik's help, as Adrienne couldn't seem to get the job done, Rena had learned to communicate with Feyr. This little ability surprised her father. Rena could use very little magicks since she hadn't started her schooling yet, but at the whim of her queen, she had surpassed almost every mage on Bron with her ability to speak to Feyr and any other animal she wanted.

"Good girl," Adrienne praised. She smiled as Hani came forward and retrieved Rena. Both of them moved to stand near the others.

Her attention returned to Malik. "You did pack enough for Feyr and Mischief to eat, right?"

Malik held up the orb for her to see. He had ordered the cook to prepare the meals, not offering an explanation for their purpose, and the cook not asking for one.

"Good," Adrienne said. With an excited squeal, she hugged Mischief close. He purred at her affection. She was going home. It had taken three months but she was going home.

Adrienne's excitement thrilled along Malik's skin. He liked the feel of it. Suddenly this errand didn't seem as trying as it had an hour ago. He'd had to practically cause his chancellors bodily harm when they insisted on knowing where he planned to vacation with Adrienne.

Only Travers, Adrienne's entourage and the Primaries knew of her true origins, and Malik planned to keep it that way. Now Rena was added to that list.

Malik didn't like the little girl knowing, most of all. She was a child. She could mistakenly tell someone without thinking. But Adrienne told him not to worry about it.

"Oh, that reminds me," Adrienne said. She faced Malik fully. "I'm pretty sure my parents are not going to be the least bit happy with you for kidnapping me. You aren't allowed to get mad, since you brought it on yourself. Understood?"

"I have no intentions of harming your parents, my lady," Malik said in answer to her true worry. It annoyed him a little that Adrienne thought he would hurt her family.

Mushira returned and mumbled out a quick apology for taking as long as she had.

"Mushira, you can drop my title while we're at my parents' house."

"But—"

"This is not the time to be arguing, Mushira," Malik said.

Mushira corrected herself, "Of course, Majesty."

Adrienne continued, "Also, think of this as a vacation. You don't have to do anything, because I'm pretty sure my mother won't let you. Just relax and try not to get too annoyed with my brothers."

"I will try, Majesty," Mushira promised. Her face showed her worry. "The language is close to that of Otieno's, correct?"

"Yes," Malik answered. "Do you require a translation orb for Adrienne's particular dialect?"

"I will manage, Majesty."

"Good." He opened the portal to Earth.

"That's my room," Adrienne said.

"Yes." He made to step over the portal threshold.

Adrienne grabbed his arm and pulled him back. She rushed out, "Not my room. I can't just show up at home, the shock might give my parents a heart attack or something. Can't we—"

"There is no unobserved location around your parents' home. It has to be your room, my lady."

She released him with a sigh. This would start the visit off on the wrong foot for sure. She followed him through the portal. Feyr and Mushira brought up the rear. Travers and the others bowed to them before the portal closed.

Slowly, Adrienne lowered Mischief to the floor. She scanned everything around her. Her queen-sized bed was situated underneath a long picture window that overlooked the backyard. Her lavender curtains were closed and the blinds were shut behind them. The entire room was dark and felt a bit somber.

Her parents hadn't touched her room since she'd come home for winter vacation.

Her desk and bookshelf were bare because her laptop and books were at her apartment near the college. It looked like someone kept the dust away, though. For some reason that made Adrienne want to cry. Had they visited her room over the past few months just to feel close to her again? Did they think she was dead somewhere?

A high-pitched meow on the other side of her bedroom door snapped Adrienne out of her growing sadness. A loud, angry male voice from down the hall commanded the feline to shut up. The cat didn't listen. It continued meowing in earnest.

Adrienne heard the meowing, but she also heard the voice that went with it. The cat said frantically, "*I smell Adri, you dumb ass. Come over here and open this door.*"

"Why do I understand him here?" she asked softly.

Malik answered just as softly. "You do not lose the ability now that you are away from Bron. If we stay on Earth too long, the magicks will fade. That is not a worry on this trip, though."

"*I hear voices,*" the cat yelled. He scratched at the door.

"Stop that, Sheds. Dad sees you scratched the paint on this door and he'll skin you alive," said the male voice from earlier.

"Castor," Adrienne whispered. Her breath caught when she saw the knob start turning. Had he heard her? She wasn't ready for anyone to see her.

The door swung open. Castor yelled, "Look. There's no one..." His words died as he saw the crowd standing in Adrienne's room. "Holy shit!"

Adrienne reached for Castor to stop what he was about to do next. She pleaded, "Castor—"

"Mom, Poll. Come here quick," he yelled over his shoulder.

"I'm busy," Pollux yelled back.

Castor insisted, "Move your asses. Adrienne's home."

Two voices mingled to yell, "What?"

Hannah called up the stairs, "Castor, you are not too old to get a whuppin'. I don't care for jokes like that or your language."

Adrienne spoke up then. She called in a choked voice, "He's not joking, Mom." She blinked furiously to keep from crying. She was home.

She hadn't known her mother could move so fast until that moment. Hannah was up the stairs and standing in the doorway next to Castor in ten seconds. The exertion had her breathing hard and doubled over trying to catch her breath. She choked out, "I don't—"

"I'm home, Mom," Adrienne interrupted. She walked over to her mother and embraced her. The woman's shock wore off and she returned Adrienne's hug.

"You're home? You're home. You're home! Where the hell have you been for the last three months?" Hannah demanded. She pulled away. Her hands wandered over her daughter frantically to make sure Adrienne indeed stood there. Finally, Hannah's hands framed Adrienne's face and she smiled at her daughter.

She said softly, "Your father and I were worried sick about you. You could have called or something to let us know you weren't dead. What's wrong with you?"

Pollux poked his head in the room. He asked, "Did anyone else notice there's a panther-thing in here, or is it just me?"

Castor added, "And two other people?"

Hannah frowned at Malik and Mushira. "Who are you?"

Adrienne pulled away from her mother and answered, "Can we talk about this downstairs? It's getting crowded in here." She didn't wait for her mother to agree before turning the woman towards the door and pushing her out of the room. Castor and Pollux shrugged and followed her. Malik and the others brought up the rear.

Once everyone settled in the living room, Adrienne introduced Malik and Mushira properly. She explained what happened to her, and with Malik's help, she gave her mother plenty of proof that she wasn't nuts. She left out large portions of the story, namely the feud and possible assassination attempts.

Hannah took it pretty well. She looked Malik up and down. "So, you're the one who killed Adrienne's attackers."

Malik answered, "I make no apologies for my actions. They deserved worse, but I did not have time to punish them properly."

"I agree with you," Hannah admitted without embarrassment. "But we have a problem."

"What?" Adrienne asked.

Castor answered, "The cops."

"What about the cops?" Adrienne demanded.

Pollux shot back, "Don't be dumb, Adri. You're snatched off a dark campus at midnight, there's a camera with pics of you getting jumped and the two guys doing the jumping are dead. The campus rent-a-cop called the real cops. The real cops called us."

"Then Mom half-kills us driving down to the police station near the college to hear you got snatched," Castor finished. He turned his attention to Malik and added, "Thanks for the shortened lifespan, by the way. I'd kick your ass, but I don't pick fights I know I can't win."

Hannah reached over and smacked Castor on the back of the head. She pointed at him and said, "Language."

"Sorry," he bit out in an insincere voice.

"The police said we should contact them if... God, they actually said if..." Hannah's words trailed off and she took a shaking breath.

Adrienne got off the couch and went to her mother. She knelt in front of Hannah, hugging her around the waist. "I'm right here, Mommy. I'm right here. I know it was scary. Believe me, I was terrified. But Malik saved me before anything happened. I went to my wedding day a virgin."

Hannah hugged her daughter close and rocked her back and forth. She whispered, "My baby. My sweet, sweet girl."

Pollux whispered, "That was a bad scene, Sis. The cops showed us the pics from a digital camera found near one guy's body." He rose from his seat quickly and walked to the far end of the living room away from everyone.

Malik watched them all. He felt Adrienne's sadness but it dulled in comparison to her joy at being home. Her sadness only echoed her mother's, and that was why Malik didn't call an end to the visit. He asked, "The authorities wished you to contact them why, Hannah?"

"Call me Mom," Hannah ordered. "You're not old enough to use my given name."

"As you wish, Mother."

"Close enough," Hannah said. "The police told us to contact them if Adrienne came home before they could find her. They wanted to question her to get an ID on the killer of her attackers. You may have done us a favor but you still broke the laws of our land, of this Earth."

Adrienne looked at Malik. He had a thoughtful expression. She started to explain about murder being murder even if the person deserved it or had it coming, but he rose from the couch and walked through a portal before she could say anything.

"Malik?" she asked in astonishment. She pulled away from her mother and went back to the couch. She looked at Mushira and asked in a scared voice, "Where did he go?"

Mushira shook her head. She looked as shocked as Adrienne felt.

Adrienne didn't have time to work herself into a state over Malik's disappearance, because he returned and resumed his seat moments later.

He said in a calming voice, "I did not mean to alarm you, my Adrienne. I simply solved the problem causing Mother so much worry."

"Solved the problem? Solved it how exactly?" Adrienne asked. Her surprise over his disappearance turned to worry.

Malik took her hands in his and kissed them. "I understand your authorities must punish all who commit murder. I gave them someone to punish."

"Gave?" Hannah asked.

"There is a man who has occupied my dungeon for quite some time. He committed travesties in my kingdom. I captured him myself when the mages I sent after him proved too inept to see the deed accomplished," Malik explained. "I implanted the memory of the killing in his mind, gave him a sword and placed him near the location of

Adrienne's attack. He will be arrested and tried. Your problem is solved, Mother."

Hannah asked, "Just like that?"

"Yes."

Adrienne countered, "The police are going to know he's not from Earth, Malik. Sure, they might think he's nuts and lock him in a loony bin, but what about his magicks?"

"I took them away. Magicks fade or they can be taken away if the subject is removed from the source. That is why Ulan is so important to mages across Bron. It is the center of all magicks, and the orbs created in Ulan are wells of magicks a mage can use anywhere. Those mages practicing their trade in Biton, for instance, must purchase hundreds of orbs a year to ensure their magicks will not run out when they need them most," Malik said.

"This isn't the time for lessons, Malik. Besides, that knowledge became evident to me as soon as I asked the question. What I want to know is how—"

"I gave him enough knowledge to be tried as a sane person and took away a large portion of his memories from his time on Bron," Malik interrupted.

Castor asked, "How the heck do you know anything about Earth? You didn't even know about the justice system until Mom brought it up."

Malik answered, "All I know, I learned from Adrienne."

"I knew it," Adrienne said loudly. She pulled away from him. "I knew you didn't give me all that knowledge without taking something from me."

"Knowledge for knowledge, my Adrienne. It is a fair trade. The information I gained has made it easier for me to interact with you," Malik argued. He grasped her hands again and held her firm when she tried to get away from him. After he kissed the backs of both her hands, he said softly, "I took only knowledge, my lady. I did not delve into memories or desires—no matter that I wanted to."

"Huh?" Castor and Pollux asked in unison.

"Never mind," Adrienne said. She allowed Malik to pull her onto his lap. He hugged her close and her worries and anger went away. Whether from a spell or his nearness, she didn't care.

She faced her mother and said, "That's one problem solved. Now all you have to do is call the cops and let them know I'm safe. They'll probably want me to fill out some forms or something, which I hope I can do from a police station near here."

Hannah blinked at her daughter. She opened her mouth, paused, closed her mouth and then shook her head.

"What?" Adrienne asked.

"And you're my daughter's head lady's maid?" Hannah asked Mushira, ignoring Adrienne's question.

"Yes, my lady."

Hannah waved that off. "Call me Hannah. I'm not any type of royalty."

"As you like, Hannah," Mushira conceded quickly. She looked uncomfortable at the request but didn't voice her misgivings.

"Your father's going to be home in another hour," Hannah said.

"Why not call him and let him know I'm home, Mom?" Adrienne asked.

"No, no. It's okay. He'll find out when he gets home."

"Ouch," Castor said.

"I don't want your father getting into an accident trying to rush home to see Adrienne," Hannah snapped. She pointed at her son and ordered, "Shut it."

He grinned at her but kept silent.

Hannah got out of her seat and went to the fireplace. She took down a framed document and gave it to Adrienne. She explained, "Your father accepted it on your behalf. Your teachers said, even though you missed the last few weeks of classes and the exams, your grades didn't suffer enough to hinder you graduating."

Adrienne's hands shook as she took the degree. Her name was scrawled in the middle of a bachelor's degree of art for literary history. She smiled at it and then laughed. "It's so silly now."

D. Reneé Bagby

"You worked hard for it," Hannah said firmly.

"I'm not arguing that fact, Mom. But all those years of education and all that money were pretty much wasted since I can't use any of it on Bron." She hugged the degree to her chest. "Still, I'm happy to have it. Thanks for attending my graduation for me."

Malik distracted her from the sorrow of missing her graduation when he plucked the degree from her arms and looked at it. She explained the significance of the paper to him then remembered he probably already knew. If the information he garnered from her worked like the information she got from him, every time he had a question about Earth it was automatically answered if Adrienne had knowledge of it.

Malik suggested, "You should hang it in our room, my Adrienne. Even if what you learned has no usefulness on Bron, you cannot deny all your hard work."

"What if someone sees it? Someone other than the people who already know I'm not from Bron."

Malik tapped the glass of the frame. The degree inside shifted and changed into a picture of the royal crest. He said, "Only those who know of your secret will be able to see the truth. Others will see the crest." He smiled when Adrienne placed a small kiss on his cheek.

Hannah nodded. She looked at the middle of the living room. Feyr occupied a huge part of the floor with Mischief trapped in front of him. It was the only way to keep the cub from running all over the house exploring.

She asked, "What is that?"

Malik answered, "He is Feyr and the cub is his son Mischief."

"Fear?"

Adrienne corrected, "It's pronounced *'feh-er'*, Mom. Think 'fair' instead of 'fear'. I made the same mistake, too. The magicks in Ulan combined some animals, and mulits are the results of one of those combinations."

Pollux turned to Malik and asked, "Any chance I can get one? You know, a gift to the brother of the bride and all that. Hook a brother up."

210

"No," Hannah and Adrienne said in unison. Hannah went over and looked down at Feyr. He stared back up at her. "I don't have enough food to feed this thing *and* your brothers, Adrienne."

"Stop feeding Castor and Pollux, then," Adrienne quipped. She grinned at her brothers and they glared back. "Got it covered, Mom. We brought food for Feyr and Mischief."

"I'm going to assume you named him Mischief for a good reason. I'm also going to assume he won't be living up to his name while you're home," Hannah said with a warning look in Adrienne's direction.

"He'll behave. That's partially why Feyr came along."

Hannah said sarcastically, "Just what your father always wanted, another cat in the house. Speaking of which, where are the cats?"

"Hightailed it when Sir Sheds-a-Lot sounded the alarm on Feyr over there. Little punk," Castor said.

"*Sir Sheds-a-Lot?*" Feyr asked with a disgusted look. "*It would seem you have a tendency of naming your pets for their traits, Adrienne.*"

"Don't pin that on me," Adrienne shot back. "Castor named him. Sphinx is my cat...sort of...was my cat. But, I named Sphinx."

Pollux asked, "Are you talking to Feyr?"

"Yes."

"Kick ass," Castor said. He dodged Hannah's hand a second later. She pointed at him instead with a warning look.

"What else can you do?" Pollux asked.

Malik answered, "Whatever she likes. Though it would not be wise to expend magicks frivolously."

Hannah walked over and held out her hand to Adrienne. She pulled Adrienne to her feet and said to Malik, "Does that mean you'll be cutting up the vegetables in the kitchen the old-fashioned way? With a knife, I mean. Or do you only know how to chop up people?"

"Mom," Adrienne yelled.

"Oh no, Adrienne. He may be royalty where he's from, but here he's a person just like everyone else. And people in this house help out if they want to eat."

Mushira stood.

"Except you, Mushira. You're on vacation. Sit down and rest." Hannah looked back to Malik. She dropped Adrienne's hand and crooked a finger at him. "Let's go, Malik."

Malik stood and followed Hannah without argument. Adrienne stared after them with a small smile on her face. Her gaze traveled over to Mushira, who looked very worried. Adrienne soothed, "Relax, Mushira. I warned you my mother wouldn't let you do anything while you were here."

"I should be the one helping, Ma—" She stopped when Adrienne frowned at her, and corrected, "Adrienne."

"Don't worry about it. It'll do Malik good to see how the other half lives for a little while," Adrienne said with amusement. She looked around. "I guess I better go find the cats."

Castor asked, "Can I pet Feyr? Does he mind? He ain't gonna tear a chunk out of me or something?"

"Go for it." At Castor's wary look, she said, "Feyr won't hurt you unless you try to hurt him or Mischief. Keep that in mind and it's all good." She didn't wait to see if Castor would pet Feyr, before she jogged up the stairs in search of her cats. She knew where they would be hiding. She may have changed over the last few months, but home hadn't.

Hannah handed Malik a knife, the cutting board and a bowl full of rinsed cabbages. "I want them thinly sliced, and don't be all day about it."

Malik was tempted to use magicks, but then thought better of it. He had stopped Adrienne from using her magicks because he knew they wouldn't come to her call as readily as before the wedding. She hadn't noticed this fact and Malik wanted to keep it from her as long as possible.

He began chopping the cabbages and asked, "Why are you hiding your anger?" He couldn't feel Hannah's anger as he could Adrienne's, but he recognized the signs of someone hiding their true emotions.

Hannah gaped at him. She crossed her arms before she answered, "I don't want to upset my baby. Adrienne said you all are here for three days and I'm going to enjoy them. If that means not giving you a piece of my mind over your high-handed, insensitive and overly spoiled actions where my daughter is concerned, I'll hold my peace." Grudgingly, she added, "Besides, Adrienne looks happy with you. That's enough for me."

"I will not apologize for taking what is rightfully mine."

"Then you can't get mad when someone calls you on it."

"Adrienne warned me of that very fact before we arrived."

Without warning, Hannah reached up and pulled Malik down to her level. She kissed his cheek and gave him a quick hug. She released him and said, "You saved my baby. You brought her home—even if it took you a while. Thank you."

"You understand, we are not staying."

Hannah nodded, stepped away and started chopping carrots. "I know. I also know you'll be coming back for visits. I may not have magic or magicks or whatever, but I'll find a way to get to Bron if you don't bring my grandbabies here to see me."

"I believe that of you, Mother," Malik said with a smile.

A thought made him open another portal and retrieve an orb, which he held out to Hannah. She took it with a confused look on her face.

"Is this that orb you were talking about earlier? You sell these to people?"

"Yes," Malik answered. "This will be your way of contacting Adrienne after we have gone. Simply sit the orb by any mirror and speak Adrienne's name. It will open up a communication portal."

"Like talking on the phone."

"Like talking on a video phone."

"Even better." Hannah turned the orb this way and that. She smiled at it then turned her smile on Malik. "You're a good son. I know your parents would be proud of you. Even if you are spoiled, you still know how to place someone else's happiness before your own."

"Only Adrienne's. It makes her happy to see you happy. Therefore, it makes me happy."

Hannah placed the orb in the middle of the fake flower center piece on the dining room table. She asked, "Will this thing break if it gets dropped?"

"No. It may look fragile, but the orbs do not break. They fade after the power inside them is used up, but I shall make sure to replace yours before that happens."

"Thank you."

Malik nodded. He went back to chopping the cabbage.

૪ઝନ୍ଧ

A car pulled into the driveway an hour later and caught Hannah's attention. She gave the stew one last stir. "I'm going to head him off. You finish those apples," she said on her way out the door.

Malik stopped peeling the apple in his hands and watched Hannah through the kitchen window. Listening to what Hannah told Benjamin would be easy, but he knew the story already.

Hannah spoke to Benjamin as he got of the car. He looked elated at what she said. When he would have run into the house, Hannah grabbed his arm, stopping him. She continued relaying the news of Adrienne's return. Benjamin's attitude steadily darkened the longer Hannah spoke. When he argued with her, Hannah tried to get Benjamin to keep his voice down, as some of their neighbors were watching them.

Malik lost sight of them when Hannah pulled Benjamin in closer to the house. He turned his attention back to the apples. It would seem his new father-in-law wasn't as forgiving of Malik's actions as Hannah.

Benjamin slammed into the house. He stalked into the living room and took in the scene there. Castor half-petted, half-wrestled Feyr. It looked like Castor had tried to give Feyr a noogie and Feyr decided to return the favor. Pollux ran Mischief around in circles with a kitty toy

214

he found under the couch. Adrienne, who had Sphinx asleep on her lap, and Mushira were engrossed in a lesson on television and remote usage.

Adrienne smiled at her father. "Dad!"

Benjamin growled out, "Upstairs. Now."

"Dad?"

"Move!"

Malik came out of the kitchen but said nothing. Benjamin didn't even look at him. Adrienne saw this and knew her father hadn't taken the news of her whereabouts well. She pasted a smile on her face to lighten the mood. "Dad, this is—"

"Don't care," he snapped. He pointed up the stairs. "Don't make me come get you."

Adrienne gathered Sphinx close and walked up the stairs. Benjamin followed behind her.

Hannah shook her head and said, "I don't understand why he can't be happy Adrienne is home, and leave it at that."

"What angered him?" Malik asked.

"Adrienne got married without his permission," Castor said from beneath Feyr. He pushed at the cat, but Feyr wouldn't let him up.

"He'll get over it," Hannah predicted. She turned to Malik and asked, "You finished with those apples?"

"No," he said quietly.

"Then get back in there and finish. Benjamin and Adrienne will be a while. He didn't like the short version of the story so he'll make her go through the entire thing all over again," Hannah surmised. She headed back into the kitchen, pushing Malik in front of her. "There's nothing to worry about. Benjamin is all show. He had to pretend to be mad or he would have cried all over Adrienne in front of everyone and embarrassed himself."

Malik allowed her to push him back into the kitchen. He even went back to preparing the apples. He pointed out, "Benjamin's anger was not a ruse."

"Okay, so he is angry. He'll get over it."

A muted crash sent Hannah running out of the kitchen back to the living room.

Pollux said quickly, "Don't worry. The clock fell over. Nothing broken."

"Yet," Hannah finished in an angry mother tone. She put her hands on her hips and regarded her sons and their new playmates. "Why not take them out back if you're going to roughhouse like that?"

"Sure," Castor said. Feyr rose off of Castor, and then all four of them trooped to the back door and left the house and all breakable items behind.

Mushira stopped fiddling with the remote. She looked back at Hannah and asked, "Is that wise, Hannah? Adr...Adrienne said there are no big cats like mulits on Earth."

"There aren't," Hannah agreed with a shrug, "but we have a high fence around our backyard. No one should see them. Do you worry this much when you're on Bron?"

"Yes, I do," Mushira answered. "It is part of my duties to think of everything."

"Like I said earlier, you're on vacation now. Give your head a rest and let me and Benjamin worry about Adrienne for a while. We had the job first, after all." She waited for Mushira's nod before returning to the kitchen and Malik. Something had distracted him.

He stood in front of the cutting board and stared at nothing. Hannah walked over to him but he didn't acknowledge her. She waved her hand in front of his face. "Hello? Anyone home?"

"Adrienne is amused."

"Huh?"

He turned his attention to the apples. "The bond I share with Adrienne allows us to feel each other's emotions."

"Is that normal on Bron?" Hannah asked. She added the thinly sliced apples to a frying pan of sizzling butter.

"Only among blood-bonded mates."

"Between what now?"

216

Hannah listened as Malik explained the blood spell that found Adrienne and the ritual they performed during the wedding ceremony.

She was silent during the whole recital.

Adrienne stood, hugging her father. He returned her hug while he tried to hold back his tears. She pulled away and asked, "Do you feel better, Dad?"

He grumbled, "I would feel better if you were here longer."

"I'm sorry. Malik and I have responsibilities as the rulers of Ulan. It took this long to arrange three free days to visit." She wished they could stay longer too, but she wouldn't complain about the amount of time given. It served to let them know she was healthy and happy.

"I didn't even get to give you away. I was looking forward to that," he complained.

Adrienne frowned as she remembered the wedding ceremony on Bron. "That isn't part of the Ulanian marriage ceremony. We didn't even say vows or anything."

"Then you aren't married," he said firmly.

Adrienne held up her left arm. A pulling sensation preceded the silver cord's appearance. She held up the cord for her father to see. It glinted in the light, showing off the red blood stripe. "This means we're married. It's a cord of marriage."

Benjamin fingered the cord. He asked, "You had this on the whole time? I didn't see it."

"It only turns visible and tangible when Malik or I want it to."

"What's this red?"

"Blood," she answered honestly. Like with her mother, Adrienne hadn't told her father about the assassinations of Malik's parents or her danger from the same. He wouldn't want her going back. She had no problem telling him about the marriage ceremony since he would handle it better than her mother.

"He stabbed you!"

Adrienne rushed out, "It didn't hurt, and healed almost as soon as he took the knife out. We needed the blood to make ours a marriage of equality. It also reinforces that we're soul mates."

He crossed his arms and grumbled under his breath about how he wanted to stab Malik. "There won't be any stabbing at the wedding ceremony your mother and I hold for you."

"Dad?"

"When Hannah found out she was pregnant, we started a college fund. When we found out you were a girl, we started another fund for your future wedding. We've been looking forward to throwing you one hell of a bash ever since. You aren't going to go and disappoint us, are you?"

Adrienne hugged him again with a happy laugh. "I wouldn't dream of it."

"Is that husband of yours going to let you?"

"He already promised to let me have an Earth wedding. We only have to pick a date."

"Your anniversary would be perfect. That gives us enough time to get it right and make sure everyone can come. It also makes one hell of a first anniversary present."

"Thank you, thank you, Dad."

He patted her back and gave her one last squeeze before he let her go. They headed to the door together. He stopped and regarded Adrienne with a thoughtful look. "Do I have to like him?"

"Dad," Adrienne scolded.

"Fine, fine. I won't hate him, how about that?"

Adrienne pushed him out the door. They joined Hannah and Malik in the kitchen. Hannah grabbed Adrienne's left hand as soon as she cleared the threshold. Her mother looked at the back of her hand, then her palm.

Adrienne glared over at Malik. "I told you not to tell her."

Hannah demanded, "Is there anything else you haven't told me?"

"No," Adrienne said quickly. She gave Malik a warning look, then smiled back at her mother. "Dad says you two started a wedding fund for me. Thank you, Mom."

Just like that, she'd distracted Hannah. Adrienne planned to keep her that way for the rest of the visit. Her parents had a hard enough time accepting Adrienne's new life without the added worry of assassination attempts.

Chapter Eighteen

Dinner conversation involved a huge brainstorming session for the upcoming wedding. Hannah and Adrienne left no topic untouched— guests, food, location for the ceremony and the reception, time of day, music, etc.

When the topic of the dress came up, Mushira offered her services. Hannah turned her down, stating she and Benjamin had more than enough saved up to pay for a nice dress. To which Mushira insisted the seamstresses in the palace would be able to make the dress better and more to Adrienne's liking than anything bought in a store.

Mushira's show of backbone impressed Adrienne, though she didn't know why it surprised her, since Hannah had stepped on Mushira's territory. Earth wedding dress or not, Mushira would oversee the making of it.

After Adrienne relayed this bit of information to her mother, the subject died with Hannah upset that she'd lost. Adrienne knew her mother wanted to go shopping with her to pick out a dress.

She suggested, "How about we peruse dress shops tomorrow? That way we can give Mushira some ideas of how Earth wedding dresses and Bron wedding dresses differ."

"Good idea," Benjamin seconded quickly. He smiled at his wife.

Hannah agreed, grudgingly.

Adrienne added, "If we leave early enough in the morning, we can stop by the DMV and I can sign ownership of my car over to Castor or Pollux."

"Don't joke," Pollux warned.

"Who's joking? I can't use it anymore. It might as well be given to someone who can." She smiled at her brothers' stunned looks. "So which of you is getting my car?"

"Me," they said in unison.

They glared at each other.

Pollux said, "Slow your roll, man."

"You slow yours. The only way you're getting that car is over my dead body," Castor countered.

"That can be arranged," Pollux threatened. He brandished his fork at his twin.

Castor beckoned. "Bring it."

"You got a car."

"It's a piece of crap. You can have it. I'll take Adrienne's."

"I'm older."

"By two minutes," Castor yelled.

"Boys," Hannah called over their yelling.

Malik observed, "My understanding of the feud between my ancestors is becoming clearer now." He sat back and watched the argument, his food forgotten.

Castor and Pollux bickered back and forth.

Benjamin got up from the table and went to the living room, retrieving a coin from the mantle over the fireplace. He held up the coin. Castor and Pollux continued to argue. He said in a normal tone, "Winner gets Adrienne's car."

It didn't seem as though either boy heard him, since they continued to threaten and defame one another.

Benjamin tossed the coin. "Call it."

Pollux stopped arguing and yelled, "Tails."

The room went silent as Benjamin caught the coin and announced, "Pollux gets it." He returned the coin to its place on the mantle then returned to his dinner. To Malik, he said, "This is how I keep peace in my family. If they keep arguing about it now, neither of them gets the car. Isn't that right, boys?"

"Yeah," the boys agreed solemnly. They returned to their food.

Adrienne said, "Too bad we can't solve some of the problems of Ulan like that."

"Too many magicks would interfere with the tossing of the coin. Or those depending on its outcome would influence it, Majesty," Mushira pointed out. She realized her mistake too late.

Castor teased, "Hoity-toity now, aren't we, big sis? Your Majesty this and bowing that. Does she wipe your butt for you, too?" He couldn't attack Pollux anymore so Adrienne was the next best target.

"I bet Mushira normally chews Adrienne's food," Pollux added.

Castor laughed, "Yup, can't let little miss queeny get... Ouch! You kicked me!"

Adrienne kicked him again. She'd wanted to avoid this. Not to mention it embarrassed her if Mushira used her title while with her parents.

"Ow, damn it," Pollux yelled. He leaned quickly to the side to dodge a flying spoon from Hannah's direction. He glared at Adrienne as her next kick landed on his shin. "Can't you take a joke? You've gotten a little high-strung." He pushed his chair back, getting out of range of Adrienne's legs.

Feyr came around the table. He grabbed Pollux's chair leg in his teeth and yanked. The chair toppled over and sent Pollux sprawling. Feyr knew Pollux couldn't hear him, but he said anyway, *"Be nice to your sister, boy. Else I might have to stop being nice to you."*

"Boys, stop teasing your sister. Adrienne, we don't kick people at the table. Feyr, you better not eat my son," Benjamin scolded.

Adrienne said, "Feyr doesn't eat humans, Dad. He just mauls them." She beckoned Feyr back to her side of the table and gave his head a pat. "My brothers are brats. That isn't going to change because I became a queen. If anything, it gives them new material to work with."

Feyr purred under her touch. His eyes stayed on Pollux as the boy righted his chair and returned to the table. *"If it doesn't bother you—"*

"I didn't say it didn't bother me. But you're not allowed to hurt them, so getting mad about it does you no good," she reminded him. She glanced at Malik. He inclined his head but said nothing.

"Fine. I won't play with them anymore," Feyr said.

Mischief whined from Adrienne's lap, *"Not play? I like play. Want play, Adri."*

Adrienne scratched under his chin and cooed at him, "You can play in the morning. Right now is dinner." She gave him a spoonful of cabbage to emphasize her point.

Hannah asked with concern, "Should you be feeding him that, Adrienne?"

Malik answered, "Feyr and Mischief can eat whatever we eat, and usually do. It would probably help if you do not think of them as normal cats."

"Sure don't look normal," Benjamin allowed.

Adrienne asked nonchalantly, "By the way, Castor, how's your boyfriend doing? What was his name? Philip?"

Benjamin choked on his food. "Boyfriend?" he yelled.

Castor hissed at Adrienne, "You're a real bitch, you know that?" An empty cup sailed across the table and hit him on the head. He mumbled an automatic apology.

Adrienne smiled smugly at him.

"Well?" Benjamin demanded. He looked at his twin sons in turn.

Pollux complained, "What are you looking at me for? Cast is the gay one. I'm straight."

"Calm down, honey," Hannah said.

Benjamin asked, "You knew about this already?" He stood up. "You know what. Never mind. I don't want to know. I've reached my excitement quota for the day and I'm going to bed. I'll see you in the morning." He took his dishes to the kitchen then went up the stairs.

Everyone continued to eat in silence. Mushira apologized, "I did not mean to cause this, Adrienne. Forgive my lapse."

Adrienne smiled at Mushira kindly. "This is normal, Mushira. No harm done."

"Why'd you have to tell him about Philip?" Castor growled.

"Oh, please," Adrienne shot back. "Dad's being a dad. He'll be over it tomorrow. You know he has no problem with gay people. You should have told him a long time ago."

"Figured Mom would do it when she found out," he mumbled.

"You can do your own dirty work," Hannah said. "Speaking of which, those dishes aren't going to clean themselves. Get to it." She rose from her seat and came around the table to kiss Adrienne's cheek. She did the same to Malik and gave Feyr and Mischief a pat. "I'm off to bed, too. You all better be here in the morning."

"We will," assured Malik.

Hannah was halfway to the stairs when she turned back. She went to Mushira's seat and pulled the woman to her feet. "Come on, Mushira. I'll show you where you'll be sleeping."

"Of course," Mushira said. She bid good night to Malik and Adrienne and followed Hannah.

Adrienne looked around. Castor and Pollux wolfed down the rest of their food and cleared the dishes. Feyr made his way to the living room. The cats followed him—they had come out of hiding once Adrienne explained Feyr wouldn't hurt them. Mischief bounded off Adrienne's lap and joined his father. The television fascinated him. He liked trying to catch the people inside.

"I was mistaken in thinking this trip would be a relaxing break from our regular duties," Malik stated. He sat back in his seat with his eyes closed.

That got a chuckle from Adrienne. "Are you referring to the peace treaty we negotiated between my family and the cats, the renaming of Sir Sheds-a-Lot to Knight or the dinner battle royale?"

"I have dealt with countries less demanding than your family's cats."

"Feyr thought it was funny."

"As did I...for the first twenty minutes. It became tiresome after the second hour passed."

Adrienne leaned over and kissed him lightly on the lips. She whispered, "Thank you for healing Sphinx. I never knew she was so sick. I took her to the vet so many times and they insisted nothing was wrong with her."

"I do whatever I can to make you happy, my Adrienne." He rose, pulled her to her feet and walked with her to the couch. There they spent the rest of the night, watching television with Feyr and the cats.

Castor and Pollux surprised Malik when they joined them. They said nothing, simply watched whatever Feyr chose. And Malik watched them. He couldn't feel the boys' emotions and he didn't need to. They were relieved and happy to be with their sister again. It was enough for them to sit with her in silence.

Before Adrienne, Malik never felt the need to be near anyone. His parents' deaths closed him off from others, and he kept them at a distance to protect himself. He had forgotten what a real family felt like. At this moment, family surrounded him and it felt right. That realization made Malik decide to make time for Adrienne to see her family as often as he could. He wanted to relearn how to be part of a family before he had one of his own.

Too soon, the three days ended. This time Malik opened the portal in the middle of the living room. The bedroom on the other side of the portal impressed Adrienne's family.

Castor asked, "That's your bed?"

"Yup," bragged Adrienne. After three nights on her old queen, she missed her other bed.

"You and what army?" Pollux asked.

Feyr urged Mischief through the portal and followed after him. Mushira went next and waited with the rest of the entourage for Malik and Adrienne to cross.

Hannah asked, "Who are they?"

"I'll tell you about them the next time we visit. Heck, I may even bring them along," Adrienne answered cheerfully.

"Thanksgiving," Benjamin insisted.

Adrienne looked at Malik. He smiled and nodded.

Hannah added, "Christmas and New Year's too."

Adrienne hugged her parents. "You'll see us as often as we can get away."

Malik allowed Hannah to hug him then shook hands with Benjamin. Without prompting, he said, "She will be safe and happy with me. You have my word on that."

"That's all we ask," Benjamin said.

Through the portal, Hannah called, "I'll leave her to you, Mushira." She smiled when Mushira nodded. She hugged Adrienne again and whispered, "At least this time I get to say goodbye."

Though Castor and Pollux had annoyed her as usual, teased her relentlessly and argued over nothing just to argue, they still hugged Adrienne fondly. Pollux bent over to tie his shoes so no one would see him wipe tears from his eyes.

Malik handed Adrienne over the portal and followed her. They took one last look at her family before it closed.

Adrienne continued staring at the spot, tears forming in her eyes. She turned and buried her face in Malik's chest. Behind them, everyone bowed and filed out of the room quietly.

Malik turned Adrienne's face up at him. He kissed away the tears on her cheeks, then trailed his kisses to her lips where he laid claim to her mouth. Only time would take away the sadness of leaving her family. He knew that. That wouldn't deter him from trying to relieve that sadness faster in his own way.

He whispered against her lips, "Out of respect for your parents and their house, and because I know how loud you can be—" he chuckled when she hit his arm, "—I refrained from making love to you. I intend to make you pay for my three days of celibacy."

She kissed him and said, "You make it sound like a threat. I choose to take it as a promise."

Chapter Nineteen

A week later, Malik had to go to the Kingdom of Iniko on urgent business. The Kings of Sondo and Iniko marked the message urgent because they noticed Ulan's return to good weather, but neither had heard from Malik.

He tried to persuade Adrienne to accompany him, but she didn't feel ready to face other monarchs yet. Having to stop in Sondo and retrieve King Ravalyn further turned her off to the idea. The thought of traveling to Sondo—even briefly, as Malik insisted—was out of the question.

"You will not embarrass yourself, my Adrienne. There is nothing to worry about," Malik urged.

Adrienne sat on a chair in front of the ceiling-high mirror and combed out her hair. She looked at Malik's reflection. "I've barely gotten used to this kingdom. And Iniko—hell, all of the other kingdoms—are so different from Ulan."

Malik pressed a kiss to her hair. "I will bend, but next time you are coming. The other monarchs will wish to meet my new queen," he said before he retired to the bed. "I will be gone for no more than four days. If I traveled by land instead of portals, I would have to go around Kakra to get to Iniko, which would make the trip a month or longer."

"Why doesn't everyone else use portals? It seems like a lot less hassle," she pointed out. She put her brush down and joined him on the bed.

Malik stretched before he answered, "They would, but portals are unwieldy. They take a control and power most mages cannot manage.

And, portals respond to emotions. The slightest shift in emotion would send an inexperienced mage careening off course."

"You use them so easily, though."

"I use them easily because I am not afraid to use them. I have always used portals indiscriminately and, some would say, carelessly. Only a few other mages can make such a boast."

"You're right. I do think using a portal to get from the throne room to the bedroom is a bit lazy on your part," she chided with humor.

Malik pulled her into his arms and kissed her. He asked in a sly tone, "How else would I be able to return quickly enough to bed my beautiful wife?"

Adrienne giggled as she succumbed to Malik's lust. They made love every time they were alone. Her period had started last week, but it didn't surprise her.

Malik told Adrienne he would continue to use the contraceptive spell until after their first anniversary. Though Adrienne said he'd fulfilled his promise, Malik knew better. The contract spell remained. Malik had to give Adrienne an Earth wedding before he could give her a child.

Adrienne saw Malik off the next morning. It upset her that he left the Primaries behind even though she asked him to take at least one. He wanted her to be guarded extra closely in his absence. While his worry about her safety made her happy, she wanted him to think of his own. She didn't want to rule this kingdom alone, and had a feeling she wouldn't, since Derex's will stipulated it would default to Hollace.

The more Adrienne thought on the subject of Malik's recklessness, the more agitated she became. She decided to think happy thoughts and trust that Malik would be careful. When he returned, they would have a conversation about his reckless habits.

The portal barely closed before Adrienne felt a marked difference in the attitude of the patrons of the palace. Everyone laughed easier and smiled more.

The day after Malik departed, Adrienne decided to see if she could run the palace on her own, and found out how much Malik shielded her. She and Malik usually presided over upwards of twenty hearings before lunch. Actually, Malik presided over them, and Adrienne offered her opinion when she thought her reasoning was valid. Even after a few months on the throne, she still didn't feel qualified to rule.

On her first solo try, Adrienne barely made it through six cases. Her major had been literature, not law, and legalese in any language was confusing and boring. She had retrieved her crocheting supplies on the trip to her parents', but no amount of needlework would keep her awake.

The chancellors thought to take advantage and presented her with law amendments and city requisitions she knew Malik wouldn't pass. At least, she thought Malik wouldn't pass them. Being equal in power meant the chancellors only needed one monarch to approve something for it to take effect. Adrienne didn't want to approve something then regret it, so she decided all matters should sit until Malik returned.

No one questioned her decision. She didn't know if they were scared to ask her or if they felt she was incapable of ruling. Whatever the reason, she used the reprieve to her advantage. Or, she tried to.

Mushira sequestered Adrienne against her will in the royal chambers with twenty seamstresses chosen to make her wedding dress. Reminding Mushira that she had eight months was a waste of time and words, so Adrienne didn't bother. She gave in and allowed one whole day for fittings and the like.

If the seamstresses wondered at the purpose of the dress, they kept their questions to themselves. Mushira ordered them to keep the entire affair quiet. Adrienne hinted she wanted to surprise Malik, which meant if too many people knew about the dress, he would eventually find out. Her explanation wasn't a total lie—Malik shouldn't know what her dress looked like until the day of the wedding. And the hint of conspiracy kept the ladies silent on the matter.

The following morning, Adrienne escaped to the gardens before Mushira could corner her. It was a beautiful day and she wanted to enjoy it.

"May I walk with you, Majesty?" Khursid asked, moving one pace away instead of five.

Adrienne waved him forward. "What's on your mind, Khursid?"

"Thank you."

"You're welcome."

Khursid glanced at her before saying, "You do not know what I am thanking you for, My Queen."

"You and High Chancellor Travers have come to an understanding and you are thanking me for that, right?"

"Yes."

"I'm glad that's fixed. How is Bayard taking your impending marriage?"

"Well," Khursid answered with a growl. "Bayard enjoys men and women. He wishes to find me a wife who will want two men in her bed instead of one."

Adrienne chuckled at this. *You can't win for losing,* she mused.

"It's for the best," Khursid conceded. "Women do not arouse me. Bayard's presence will make it easier for me to conceive the heirs my father wishes of me."

"How do you feel about your father being gay?"

"We have a subject on which we both agree—now. Before, we could speak of nothing and therefore we never spoke. I thank you again, My Queen."

"Glad to be of service."

Khursid bowed then rejoined Qamar. She didn't walk alone for long. Rena came running out of the palace with Mischief hot on her heels. Feyr followed a little while later.

Adrienne glanced over her shoulder and smiled. As she expected, the Primaries had come out of hiding. Indivar probably wanted Rena to know he was in the area so she would behave. With Indivar out in the open, Flavian and Bayard had no reason to hide.

The Primaries walked with Qamar and Khursid, but everyone dropped back more than ten paces, giving Feyr room. Despite

Adrienne's assurances that Feyr wouldn't hurt them, her guards continued to give the cat a wide berth.

"Does the day find you well, Adrienne?"

"I'm not being bored out of my mind or poked with pins, so I'd say yes. The day finds me very well. You?"

"I have spent most of the morning chasing after the cubs. Mischief is a bad influence on Rena, I am saddened to say."

"They're children. They'll grow out of it," she reasoned. She contradicted her accepting attitude a few minutes later when she yelled, "Rena, Mischief, you're getting too far away. Come back this way."

Rena waved then chased Mischief back towards them. The cub ran slowly so Rena could match his pace.

At three months old, Mischief was half-grown. Adrienne had to stop holding him, which upset them both. He didn't weigh too much, but Feyr thought it wise to wean Mischief off being carried sooner rather than later.

"Thank you, Adrienne," Feyr whispered.

Adrienne gave him a surprised look. "What did I do?" This was a day for people to thank her, it seemed.

"In all honesty, I did not wish you to have one of my cubs. Though not for the same reasons as my mate."

"Why?"

"My experience as a kept animal made me vow never to let my cubs suffer the same."

"I don't understand."

"I am not free to leave the palace."

"But, I thought—"

"Malik needs me. Though he has you now, Malik still needs me. I cannot be amongst my own kind for more than a few days at a time. My fellows alienate and shun me because I am a kept animal," Feyr explained. *"I faced many more challenges than other males just to gain the right to be amongst the others. The challenges to have my mate went on for days."*

"I'm sorry, Feyr. You should have said—"

"My mate changed her mind when she saw your argument with Malik. I changed my mind when you decided not to take the cub if my mate did not wish you to have him. Malik would have taken the cub and I would have had to fight him."

"I thought you liked Malik?"

"I do," he agreed. *"I do not like the way he acquired me, and I would not have it repeated with one of my own."*

Some part of her didn't want to ask, but she did anyway. "What happened?"

Feyr explained in solemn tones, *"A few months after the assassination of Malik's mother, King Iasion decided to cheer his son with a rare gift. He ordered his men to capture a mulit cub. They completed the task to the king's satisfaction. They killed my mother in the process, and my siblings were left to fend for themselves. We were only a few weeks old. I am sure they did not survive."*

Adrienne didn't say a word since nothing seemed appropriate.

"I hated Malik at first. We fought constantly...physically. Everyday, Malik and I sported new wounds for the palace mages to heal. It impressed me that a mere human could hold his own in a fight against me.

"I started enjoying Malik's company, though the pain of my loss was forever with me—as his loss is with him. We learned to speak to one another shortly before his father's assassination. From that day forward, we were inseparable. I am a physical manifestation of Malik's anger and I enjoy my job."

"You still can, Feyr. If there is someone deserving of your kind of punishment, I will send you after them myself," she promised. "You'll forgive me if I don't watch. I want to continue in my naiveté of your true power for as long as I can."

Feyr was about to say something when he stopped walking instead. He lifted his nose and sniffed.

Adrienne stopped walking when he did. She spared him a glance before her attention went to Rena and Mischief. They had run to the far end of the garden during Feyr's story. She opened her mouth to call them back.

Her voice froze in her throat and her knees gave out beneath her. Instinctively, she raised her hands to break her fall. White noise crackled all around her in a deafening cacophony. Her vision blurred.

She heard the voices of her guards calling to her. A screaming woman drowned them out.

Adrienne realized she was the one screaming moments before she passed out.

In the shadows, a cloaked man clenched his fist around the orb he held. He watched in delight as the confusion spell wove around Adrienne without hindrance. He had worried Malik would leave a barrier orb with her, or something else to mess up his plans. He gave praise to the goddess Yatima—queen of the gods on high—for his good fortune that nothing interrupted his plan. Soon, his mistress would have her prize.

He snapped out of his happy stupor and erected a barrier around Adrienne before the Elite guards could help her. He smiled as they tried futilely to break the barrier. No mere Elite guard could break his spell. Malik's chancellors were not even up to the task.

From the depths of his cloak another orb appeared. This one opened a series of portals beneath Adrienne. He couldn't chance opening a portal directly to the destination he wished Adrienne transported to, because someone might see and then later alert Malik.

His task was almost done. Soon he would...

"Damn," he cursed as loudly as he dared.

He watched in horror as Malik's cat Feyr held the girl's hand firmly in his mouth and kept her from dropping. The confusion spell should have affected Feyr, as well. The cloaked man had heard rumors Malik endowed the damn cat with powers to rival those of the chancellors. The rumors now had proof. Thankfully, he had a backup plan.

He pulled out another orb. This one—unlike the others, which were clear—was metallic. With a push of will, the orb sped towards Feyr. The cloaked man's smile of triumph grew as he watched the cat drop in obvious pain.

No matter how powerful the mage, no one—not even Malik—could fight the neutralizing effects of mage metal. If worn, mage metal nullified any and all magicks the wearer might try to use.

Wearing mage metal did not make a person immune to magickal attacks, however. To be immune from magickal attacks, the mage metal had to be embedded inside the body. But this would also render the individual unable to use magicks.

The cloaked man wanted to keep the cat from contacting Malik, if it hadn't already. He thought he would have to reveal himself and attack the cat openly. But the mage metal worked and the cat suffered terribly, from the looks of it. He kept to his hiding place and watched, his task almost finished.

Adrienne woke as she started falling. She opened her eyes and blinked repeatedly to clear her vision. Everything remained fuzzy, but she saw Feyr. His jaws were wrapped around her hand.

Through her confusion, she managed to grab the edge of the hole. Just as her fingers brushed the edge, Feyr collapsed. Another scream wrenched from her lips as she dropped into eternal blackness. The light from the opening disappeared. The portal closed.

There was no wind and yet Adrienne knew she was falling. Her head pounded from the noise, which remained constant even though she covered her ears. It affected her whole body. Her vision had crackling fuzz over everything, though there was nothing to see, and her skin tingled painfully. She twisted her body this way and that, trying to relieve the discomfort. She felt herself losing consciousness again.

She clenched her fists against her temples and screamed, "Stop."

Her scream was the last thing she heard before she lost the battle with the madness and fainted.

Guards rushed up the throne dais to aid their king. He looked at the woman sprawled across his lap in confusion. She had dropped out of thin air and surprised the hell out of everyone in the room, including him.

"Your Majesty," one of the guards yelled. They pulled their swords, ready to do battle.

A mere gesture from him stopped them.

The queen, who stood slightly behind his throne, stepped forward and laid a hesitant hand on the girl's forehead. "She seems feverish. Perhaps a student from the mage school who misused a spell, my lord husband?"

He stood with the girl in his arms and regarded her. "No errant spell can breach the barriers in place around this palace. You know that, wife. This girl is not here by accident." With a nod to the man closest to him, he handed the girl over, relieving his burden.

The man looked at the girl and then his king. "What would you have me do with her, King Hollace?"

"Take her to the infirmary and contact Caradoc to see to her. Keep her under close guard. I want to know the instant she awakes," he ordered gruffly. "She has some explaining to do." His gaze followed the girl as the guard carried her away.

How had the girl breached the barrier spells around the palace? The mages who constructed the barrier had made sure it was impregnable. Hollace knew of no one with enough magickal prowess to break it.

Chapter Twenty

"She's coming around. Get King Hollace," Caradoc said. He leaned over the girl when she looked at him. "You're okay now."

"Whe... Where am I?"

King Hollace answered from the doorway, "You are in my palace, young woman. The question is how did you open a portal into my throne room, and for what purpose?" He searched over her with an angry brown gaze.

Caradoc opened his mouth to speak.

"Silence, old man. I want to hear from her," Hollace barked. "Answer me, woman."

"I don't know what you mean."

King Hollace took a threatening step towards the bed. The queen stopped him with a hand on his arm. He glared back at her and she smiled in response. She turned to the girl on the bed and said, "I am Queen Tacita. This—" she motioned to Hollace, "—is King Hollace. Who are you?"

Caradoc glared at the woman then bowed his head to hide his expression when she looked at him. He couldn't stand her. She was too tall. Her height matched her husband's and that put her head over Caradoc. She shared Hollace's red hair color, but her eyes were blue instead of brown. Her frame was toned and her clothes were cut to show it. She would be a beautiful woman if not for her height.

He glanced at the mystery woman. She smiled at Tacita and Hollace. The girl was either too stupid to realize the trouble she was in, or a very cunning actress.

She answered, "I am..." And stopped. She whispered, "I...I don't know."

"You have forgotten your name?" Tacita asked with concern.

Hollace snorted. "Don't encourage her, wife. She is faking to get out of punishment." He signaled to Caradoc.

Tacita turned to her husband in shock. "Is that necessary? The child obviously has gone through an ordeal."

"And she will go through much more if I find out she is lying to me."

Caradoc pulled an orb out of the air and held it up to the girl. It turned dark grey, which caused him to push an agitated hand through his dark brown, close-cropped hair. He rubbed his bare chin, missing his beard in that moment. He had to shave it off when it revealed his age by going grey, but he missed how stroking it helped him concentrate.

This was a mess.

He turned to Hollace and shook his head. "She isn't lying, Your Majesty. She has no memory the orb can discern. Someone used magicks to wipe it clean—for what purpose, we can only guess."

"See, my lord husband, the child is not lying to you," Tacita said. She stepped forward and took the girl's hand. "Can you remember anything about yourself—anything at all? Perhaps the spell did not fully do its job."

The girl closed her eyes. "Ad...Ad..." She stopped with a grimace of pain.

"Adele. Does that sound familiar?" Tacita asked hopefully.

The girl shook her head.

"Well, Adele shall be your name until you can tell us what it really is. Alright...Adele?"

"Adele," she whispered back.

Tacita stood and turned to Hollace. "My lord husband, please meet Adele," she introduced.

Caradoc chose that moment to interject. "I don't know if it is wise to be so jovial, Your Majesty. The girl... Adele has an abundance of latent magickal power. It is true her memory loss is magickal in nature and the process can be reversed, but she could have easily inflicted this amnesia on herself to avoid persecution."

"Doesn't the Guild usually use memory erasure spells as punishment?" Hollace asked in a bored manner.

Caradoc tried not to show his surprise at Hollace's question. He didn't know Hollace knew anything about the sole Mage Guild he allowed on Kakra's soil. "Yes, yes. But, Your Majesty, the Guild would usually put a tracking spell on the individual. There is no such spell on...Adele. The spell could easily be someone's idea of revenge. Though that doesn't explain how she ended up in your throne room."

Hollace glared at Adele. "No, it doesn't." He turned his attention to Caradoc. "She is under your charge, Caradoc. She will stay with you. You will find a way to reverse the spell, and then you will give me my answers."

Tacita placed herself in front of Adele. "A spell this powerful cannot be ignored. The person casting it is strong and they cast it on Mistress Adele, which means she is important to them. If they find that we have treated her badly, it could be equally bad for us."

Hollace responded with a snort. "I wouldn't call sending her to live with Caradoc treating her badly, wife."

"If she is the daughter of a powerful mage, do you think her father would see living with Caradoc as ideal?" she asked with her eyes lowered. "Remember, my lord husband, not all kingdoms are like Kakra and Ulan. Other kingdoms allow their daughters to inherit positions of power. If she—" she motioned to Adele, "—is from one such kingdom, casting her out would make her guardians our enemies."

Hollace's gaze rested on Adele. His fist clenched at his side. "Your council is sound, wife. She can stay. Messengers will be sent to make inquiries as to her true identity. Satisfied?"

"Thank you. Until such time as that happens, Adele is no threat to anyone," she said quietly.

"Now that you have gained her entry to my palace, wife, what shall she do? I will not have a listless mage wandering about my palace unchecked."

She clapped her hands together in delight. "Chandra," she answered.

"What of our daughter, wife?"

"Chandra has need of a companion. Adele could fill that role while Caradoc figures out the mystery." Tacita smiled at Adele. "You will like Chandra, Mistress Adele. She has recently had a child and is in dire need of company close to her own age, since her husband is away. I shall retrieve her now."

Adele stared after Queen Tacita as she ran from the room. Her gaze turned to Hollace, who glared at her. She held his gaze until he looked away.

Tacita returned quickly with Chandra in tow. Chandra did not take after her mother. She didn't seem to take after either parent. She was shorter, with blonde hair and green eyes. Where Tacita was tall, toned and willowy, Chandra was of average height and curvaceous. Her ample breasts were probably the envy of her mother, as Chandra filled out the halter top more than her mother ever could.

Chandra took one look at Adele and turned to her mother. She spoke in an angered voice, but the language differed from what everyone had used a moment ago.

Hollace raised an eyebrow at his daughter's words. He opened his mouth to reply but Adele said, "Amnesia is not catching, Lady Chandra."

Everyone in the room looked at her in surprise. Hollace spoke first. "How do you know Kontarian?"

"I...I don't know. I simply understood the words and responded in like fashion."

Hollace asked in Inikon, "And how many languages do you know?"

Without hesitation, Adele answered in kind. "I'm not sure, Your Majesty."

Hollace tried Nashan next. "Your accent seems flawless no matter what language you speak. That is a useful talent. One could never tell where you are from."

"I accept the compliment, Your Majesty, but I don't know why I remember these languages and yet cannot remember my own name."

Hollace switched back to Kakran and asked Caradoc, "Is this part of the spell?"

"I cannot be sure, Your Majesty. There are different types of erasure spells. This one might have only erased her identity and memories of herself while it left everything else intact," Caradoc explained. "Until I start trying to crack the spell—"

Hollace cut him off with a gesture. "Fine," he barked. He turned to Chandra and said, "She is your new companion. You have complained incessantly of wanting one. And, though your status as princess has diminished to a mere lady, I have listened. She is your only option, *Lady* Chandra."

Chandra showed her distaste at being called lady. She whispered, "Thank you, Your Majesty. I accept Mistress Adele as my new companion." She bowed and departed the room. Tacita followed after her.

Hollace glanced briefly at Adele before he left, as well.

Adele looked at Caradoc and he stared back at her. He sighed and shook his head. She mimicked his sentiment.

ಬಿಂ

Mushira waited for Malik's return in the throne room. The Elite personal guards, already on one knee with their heads bowed, waited with her. They had waited like statues, not moving a muscle, for the last five hours.

Nimat opted not to be present. She was too scared. Hani stood beside Mushira with her head bowed, ready to face her punishment for failing as Adrienne's guard.

Malik was scheduled to return any minute. Mushira dreaded what she had nominated herself to do. Her hands were sore from wringing them together all through the night and most of the day. While contacting Malik and informing him of Adrienne's kidnapping would have been easier, she didn't have the courage. She had hesitated so the

Elite guards could search for Adrienne and bring her back before Malik found out. All their searching was in vain, as there were no leads.

She looked at the throne dais. Feyr sprawled in his usual spot between the thrones with Mischief beside him. The cub pushed at his father and whined, but Feyr wouldn't move. Seeing this, Mischief cuddled close to him.

Feyr didn't wish to sadden his son, but he couldn't summon up the strength to move. He focused all his energy on breathing, the mage metal lodged in his body causing him tremendous pain. The chancellors had tried to remove it but with no luck, since it negated all the spells they tried. One and all decided that Malik would have better luck. If not, the metal would have to be cut from his body, which might kill him.

Mushira thought back on the recounting of the incident. The barrier that kept the Elite guards from Adrienne collapsed without warning and they arrived at the portal in time to see it close. No amount of tracing spells could determine the destination of the portal, or the originator.

None of this would be news Malik wanted to hear. News Mushira had to impart...now.

A portal opened behind Malik's throne. Mushira had planned to face her king on her feet. She found her legs wouldn't support her, and she dropped to her knees, folding in on herself.

Malik passed through the portal. He only had to look at the people before him to know something was wrong.

He asked in a quiet voice, "Where is Adrienne, Mushira? Why are you here and not her?"

Mushira couldn't answer. Fear held her silent. Tears tracked down her cheeks and she shook her head in answer to Malik's words. It was all she could do.

"Mushira?"

She glanced up and gave Malik full view of her tear-stained features. Before she could say anything, Malik shouted, "No. Where is she? Where is Adrienne?"

"Gone, Majesty," Hani answered. She remained on her feet. "She was stolen out of the gardens yesterday."

Malik rushed down the dais to stand in front of Mushira and Hani. "What do you mean she was stolen from the garden? How?"

Mushira took a shaky breath. On her third attempt, she answered, "A confusion spell, My King. A confusion spell hit her before a portal opened beneath her."

"Where were you?" Malik spat.

Indivar answered, "We were unable—"

"Not you," Malik roared. He turned his full attention to Hani. He stepped into her and grabbed her by the throat. "Where were you?"

Hani answered in a raspy whisper, "Preparing Queen Adrienne's clothing for lunch, Majesty."

Malik released her then backhanded her across the face. The force of his blow sent her flying. She uttered not a sound. "I did not hire you to be her lady's maid, you little bitch. I hired you to be her third. It does not matter if the entire Ulanian army followed her every step, you should be there, as well." He advanced on Hani.

Mushira rushed out, "Feyr tried to hold her... He tried to hold Queen Adrienne, but the attacker used mage metal on him."

That stopped Malik and he looked up at Feyr, noticing the tired expression on his cat's face. He lifted his hand and made a sweeping motion. The mage metal ripped from Feyr's body and caused the great cat to scream in pain. Mischief ran from his father's side and hid under Adrienne's throne.

The mage metal floated to Malik's hand. He stared down at it. Someone attacked Adrienne in the palace. Who?

His gaze turned to the Elite guards. "And where were you?"

Again, Indivar answered. "Because Feyr walked with Queen Adrienne, we allowed her distance as she strolled in the garden. As soon as the confusion spell hit her, a barrier appeared around her. We couldn't break it to reach her."

Flavian added, "We looked for the origin of the attack and found no one, Majesty."

Qamar concluded, "We are prepared to die for our failure to protect our queen, King Malik."

Hani knelt beside the Elite guards. The Primaries hadn't known her true role. Indivar had looked surprised when Malik attacked her first.

Malik raised his hand to deliver the spell. The guards had failed in their duties. So far as he was concerned, that meant a sentence of death.

Mushira grabbed his hand. He turned burning eyes on her and yelled, "You dare."

Mushira didn't meet his eyes. She shook her head and continued to cry. She muttered, "Queen Adrienne has grown fond of the Primaries...of all the Elite guards, and Hani. She would be distressed if she found them dead upon her return."

Her return?

Malik lowered his hand. Adrienne wasn't dead, but kidnapped. There was a difference. He had to remember that.

He snatched his hand out of Mushira's grip. While she was right about sparing the guards, Malik needed satisfaction. He summoned an orb, held it in front of him and squeezed it. Before him, the guards hit the ground in agony. Their screams of pain filled the throne room. His grip on the orb tightened and their pain grew.

"*That will not make you feel better, Malik. You should stop before you damage them,*" Feyr said.

Malik ceased his torment of the guards. When they recovered enough to kneel once more, he said quietly, "Get out. You will find out who attacked my queen or no amount of Adrienne's grief will keep me from killing you all."

They nodded as one and quit the room.

Malik turned to Mushira. She cringed back from him in fear. He whispered, "Leave me, Mushira."

She complied, happily.

When she closed the door behind her, Malik turned to Feyr. "Tell me," he demanded.

Feyr shook himself out, now fully recovered from the effects of the mage metal. *"The attack was sudden. The confusion spell had no effect on me, as you well know. I tried to help Adrienne when the portal opened beneath her but the mage metal hit me then. Before I blacked out, I felt a great surge of power. It wasn't from the attacker."* Feyr watched as Malik came back to his throne. After Malik sat, he continued, *"Adrienne is safe. I would bet my cubs on it. Something happened before the portal could finish its task, and I think that 'something' was Adrienne."*

"How come I do not feel her, then? I should be able to track her anywhere through the power of the silver cord that binds us in marriage. I do not feel even a hint of her."

"If she were dead, you would feel it. You feel nothing. That, in and of itself, is hope."

Mischief came out from underneath Adrienne's throne. He walked over and stared up at Malik. He said, *"Me and Rena were bad. We ran too far away. Adri told us not to and then she went away. We're sorry."*

Malik reached over the arm of his throne and stroked Mischief's head. While not in the mood to comfort the cub, he said in a soothing tone, "You are not at fault, Mischief."

A knock sounded at the throne room doors. Malik bid the person enter. Travers stepped into the room as he had done so many weeks before. He bowed to Malik then said, "We have a traitor in the palace, Majesty."

"I had surmised as much, Travers," Malik said flippantly. He was seconds from using the pain orb on Travers if the man didn't get to the point.

"I knew of the traitor before Queen Adrienne disappeared."

Malik surged out of his throne and bellowed, "You what?"

"The blood spell should have found Queen Adrienne at the moment of her birth, regardless of the different dimension. A powerful interference spell, amplified by its proximity to you, caused the delay. I broke it once I became aware of it."

"Someone tried to keep me from finding her. Hollace?"

Feyr shook his head. "*Hollace abhors magicks, you know that,*" he reminded Malik.

Travers repeated Feyr's words, not knowing the cat had spoken them. He admitted, "I would have come forward with this news before now, but I wished to have a list of possible suspects to the treachery."

"Where is this list?" Malik held out his hand.

At this, Travers bowed his head in defeat. He replied, "My search has turned up nothing, Majesty. The only reason I have come forward with this news now is because of the queen's kidnapping."

Malik smiled slowly. His smile grew when Travers stepped back. Outside, dark clouds gathered, lightning split the sky and thunder shook the earth. "No, this is a perfect time to find out exactly who is loyal to me." He sat back on his throne, moving his lips as he invoked a silent spell.

An invisible shield materialized around the palace. Eighteen people appeared in the throne room before him. They all looked confused and scared—as they should be.

Malik explained, "You all were in the palace at the time of my wife's disappearance. The barrier spell I created around the palace brought you back. You are to be my guests until I find out who the traitor to my throne is and kill him."

The people called out denials and pleas for mercy. Malik turned a deaf ear to their complaints. He would find the person or people responsible and they would know a new definition of pain.

Chapter Twenty-One

The cloaked man huddled in the shadows, a new desperation in his conduct as he waited to be acknowledged. His fingers curled and uncurled around the orb he held.

"You have failed me—again," the shadowed woman said in an annoyed tone. Her fingers drummed on the desk in front of her. Little sparks of blue fire scattered from the places where her nails hit the desk.

The man shook his head in fear. He pleaded, "I had her, Excellency. She was to be delivered to your prison mere moments after she fell into the portal. A power disrupted the portal. Not even Malik can track her."

"Return to me here and we will find a way to track her. I will not have your incompetence ruining my plans."

This time, the cloaked man's head shook in denial. "I cannot, my lady. Malik sealed the palace. If anyone tries to leave, they are immediately returned to the palace's throne room and under extreme suspicion." The man didn't add that he was in no hurry to find out what punishment the woman on the other end of the orb had waiting for him.

"You try my patience—"

"My lady, the confusion spell remains active. Even now the orb vibrates against my body. I cannot pinpoint Adrienne's location with it, but I do know—wherever she is—she is in pain."

The woman was silent for a time. She stared at something beyond the orb's view. "As you cannot come here, send the orb. Surely Malik hasn't guarded the palace against objects leaving. My soldiers will track her down."

The cloaked man bowed in relief. He held out the orb that contained the confusion spell and it disappeared then reappeared in the woman's hand. The communication orb faded and the cloaked man made his way back to his chambers. He had to get out of the palace before Malik questioned him.

Malik systematically interrogated everyone, starting with the most recent guests to the royal palace then progressing to the servants. Each person was interrogated individually and under the influence of a truth orb. Screams of pain could be heard from those who tried to lie.

There had to be a flaw in Malik's barrier. He needed to find it before his time of questioning came. And, that was soon.

Chapter Twenty-Two

Hollace slammed into his bedroom, his face contorted with fury at the situation.

"No luck, still, Father?" asked Oringo, Hollace's one and only son.

Hollace looked up at his son and his anger switched targets. He hated his son's beauty. Oringo took after his mother in that respect. He was tall and lanky. No amount of training put any muscle on his frame. However, Oringo wasn't a weak man. He only looked it.

His face further pronounced this weakness. No one would fear a man who looked pretty enough to shame most women. Oringo's red locks were cut above his shoulders to frame his heart-shaped face. His jewel-green eyes were always wide and innocent looking, a trait that endeared every woman in the palace to him.

That was the main reason Hollace wanted the boy married. He wanted an heir for the throne before Oringo started making bastards. At the rate Oringo had worked his way through the female servants of the palace and the noblewomen who visited the court, Hollace wondered if he wasn't already too late.

In answer to Oringo's question, Hollace ground out, "It has been four days. No one knows where the girl is from. I have contacted the Mage Guild. It took them this long to tell me they are missing no students."

Contacting the Mage Guild and waiting so long for their answer had only added to Hollace's bad mood. The school took up a large amount of land that could be put to better use. He'd have it demolished tomorrow if that wouldn't constitute a breach of Derex's stipulations to have a Kontarian representative—namely the Mage Guild master—at every birth and wedding. Since neither he nor any of his predecessors wanted a mage in the palace, a school was built.

Tacita asked, "Will the Mage Guild contact other mage guilds of the surrounding kingdoms?"

"Yes, wife, they will. Are you questioning my intelligence by asking such a profoundly stupid question?"

"No, my husband. I was merely curious—"

"Silence, woman," Hollace growled. He gave a nod when Tacita closed her mouth and bowed her head. His gaze went to his son. "Have you found a wife yet?"

Oringo looked back at the pictures on the desk in front of Tacita. He scanned them with a look of indifference. "Does it really matter who I choose, Father? They are all the same." He looked back at his father. "Why don't you simply pick one for me? It's not as though any of these women will keep my attention for very long. No woman has before."

"She'll keep your attention long enough to beget Kakra's heir, boy," Hollace snapped.

"Of course, of course, Father," Oringo soothed in a bored tone. "It's a shame Chandra wasn't born male. She seems a better choice for the throne than me."

Hollace stalked over to his son. The back of his hand cracked across the boy's cheek. "Bite your tongue, boy. No woman shall sit on Kakra's throne."

"I said if Chandra was a *male*, Father," repeated Oringo.

"Get out. Go back to whatever it was you were doing...or whomever," Hollace dismissed. Disappointment colored his words. His son had a point. Chandra was everything Hollace could ever want for Kakra's throne—responsible, strong and able to fight close to a first blade's level. But she was a woman. Hollace was stuck with Oringo, the son who would rather be in a woman's bed than on the throne.

Hollace's attention went back to Tacita. She sifted through the pictures of potential brides.

She said, "Lady Sovenne is quite beautiful, and from a Kakran noble family. She even trained as a warrior. I do believe she graduated as a fifth blade, my husband." She picked up Sovenne's picture to show Hollace. "And she has red hair."

"Do not think I have not noticed how much time you spend with Chandra of late, wife."

Tacita lowered the picture with a confused look on her face. "I do not understand, my husband, what you mean. Chandra is still our daughter and I like spending time with our new grandson, Devon."

Hollace gave his wife a sly smile. He taunted, "You forget to mention Adele, wife. You forget to mention how you spend almost every waking moment near her to feel her magicks instead of standing behind my throne where you belong."

"I do not—"

He hauled her up from her chair and grabbed the chain around her waist to give it a good yank. He nodded when it didn't give. "If I ever catch you not wearing this, Tacita, you will rue the day."

"I would never take it off, my husband. You know this."

"You envy her, don't you, woman? You want the freedom I have granted her—her and Caradoc. The only mages within this palace without mage metal adornments." He fingered the chain again before shoving Tacita away from him. "Take off that chain and it will be the last thing you ever do."

He left the room then. He didn't want to sleep there tonight. A palace maiden had caught his attention earlier that day. He only hoped he had seen the girl before his son had. Having a woman after his son did annoy him.

ಬಂಚ

Adele bounced Devon on her knee and smiled as he cooed at her. The babe had the red hair his mother envied so much. Every other member of the Kakran royal line had red hair. It was a trademark of sorts. Chandra believed if she had it, her father wouldn't treat her so coldly. Adele thought otherwise but kept her opinion on the matter to herself.

Her days with Chandra had shown the woman didn't want a companion so much as someone to listen to her and agree without comment. Chandra's maid did nothing but frown disapprovingly at her constant complaints about her situation in life. The woman thought Chandra should be thankful Hollace allowed her to stay in the palace after her marriage and subsequent demotion.

Adele listened to Chandra rant while she cared for Devon. It was an easy enough task. Chandra only wished an affirmative from Adele on the odd occasion, but mostly it was Adele's lack of censure she liked best. And Devon was happy with anything Adele did. He seemed starved for attention.

Across the room, Chandra smiled at them in the mirror. It confused Chandra that she found herself fighting off Caradoc's presence whenever he came to whisk Adele away to conquer the mystery of her amnesia.

Everyday after lunch, Caradoc took Adele back to his cottage in the woods outside the palace. There he tried spell after spell to find some way to break through Adele's amnesia. They always returned in failure. Despite Caradoc's promises of a speedy resolution, Hollace's foul mood at the lack of progress ruined dinner after dinner.

So far as Chandra was concerned, he could keep failing. Despite her earlier misgivings, Adele turned out to be the perfect companion. She also filled the role of nurse for Devon quite nicely.

Adele made faces at the baby to get him to smile. It worked. He laughed and flailed his arms with each new face. The baby's laugh turned to a grunt and his smiling face to a frown. Then he whimpered.

Adele stood quickly. She cooed, "Oh, I know that face, young man. No crying, now, I'm moving as fast as I can."

Chandra watched Adele in the mirror with disgusted disinterest. She was glad Adele was there or she would have had to listen to the boy cry until the nurse or a maid came to change him.

She couldn't understand how Adele could be so nonchalant about the entire affair. Adele never made faces or complained. She changed the diaper and that was the end of it. Even Chandra's maid would make a comment about the smell.

She rolled her eyes and went back to preening herself. "I swear all he does is eat, sleep and crap...excuse my language, Mistress Adele."

Adele laughed at that as she pinned the new diaper in place. She looked up from the baby to Chandra and said, "Your tone reminded me of my mother. She said the same thing about my brothers and me."

Chandra turned from the vanity to face Adele fully. She asked with wonder, "You have brothers?"

"Yes, two," Adele answered. She picked up the baby to deposit him in his crib. It was his bedtime. "Their names are Castor and Pollux."

"Strange names."

Adele didn't take offense. She laid Devon down and tucked the blanket around him. He kicked it off. She tucked it in around him again. He kicked it off and laughed. He thought this was a game. To Chandra, she said, "You can blame my mother. She loves Greek mythology and named them after the twins in the Gemini story."

"The what?" Chandra asked in complete confusion. "What is a Greek?"

Adele laughed again. "Oh, they..." her words trailed off as she fell into a faint.

Chandra jumped up and rushed to her side. "Adele? Adele," she yelled, tapping the woman's cheek. Adele gave a loud moan of pain, her face twisting in agony. Chandra went and pulled her personal alarm.

Something was very wrong with Adele.

"Ah, there she is," Caradoc said in a thankful voice.

Adele blinked open her eyes and stared at the people surrounding her—Caradoc, Chandra, Tacita, three physicians and Hollace.

"What's going on?" she whispered.

Hollace snapped, "That's what we'd like to know." He glared at Tacita when she placed a hand on his arm. She smiled at him in response.

Chandra came forward hesitantly. "You fainted, Mistress Adele. When I tried to wake you, you looked to be in immense pain. Do you remember?"

Adele shook her head in complete confusion. She didn't remember fainting. Though she doubted people would remember fainting. It was probably like trying to remember falling asleep. "I remember changing the baby and then waking up here."

"Yes. I made...a comment that you said reminded you of your mother," Chandra supplied in an urging tone.

"I said something about my mother?"

Caradoc cut in to the conversation to ask, "You don't remember?"

"No. What did I say, Lady Chandra?"

"You said my comment resembled something your mother said about you and your brothers, Castor and Pollux."

Tacita said, "Those are strange names."

"I said the same. Adele told me her mother named them for a story in Greek mythology. When I asked what a Greek is, she fainted." Chandra looked at Adele. "Do you remember what you planned to say?"

Again, Adele shook her head. Her voice showed her confusion as she said, "I have no idea what a Greek is. Or that I had...have brothers. It's nice to know. I wonder if I have sisters, as well."

Hollace barked, "You mean to say you don't remember the very words you said to Lady Chandra last night?"

"I'm sorry, Your Majesty. I can't recall any of it. As I said, I remember changing the baby and then waking up here," Adele said defensively.

Chandra whispered, "You looked to be in so much pain, Adele. I was so scared."

Caradoc asked, "Do you still have any pain?"

"I have a slight headache," Adele said. She put her hand to her head.

Caradoc nodded. "It only makes sense, since you missed several meals. Your headache is probably from hunger."

"What time is it?"

"Twenty minutes to dinner," Hollace said in an exasperated tone. "You have no memory of what you said to my daughter or of these supposed brothers?"

"I'm sorry, Your Majesty, but no," Adele answered. "I wish I did."

"I, as well. If you remembered, you could tell us who your family is and be gone from here," he snapped. After glaring at her for a few breaths, he quit the room. Tacita followed him.

Caradoc excused himself to Chandra and Adele and followed the royal couple.

Chandra sat on Adele's bedside and held her hand. "I am so happy you are awake. We were so worried."

"I can imagine. Dinner had just ended when I was with you and now it's almost dinner again," Adele said in amazement. What had happened to her? Her concern for herself vanished with a thought.

She sat up in the bed with a scared look. "I didn't hurt the baby when I fell, did I?"

"No, no," Chandra said quickly. She patted Adele's hands. "He's fine. He cried when you fell but you didn't fall on him. I'm thankful you weren't carrying him when you fainted."

Adele nodded at that and settled back on the bed. She would have to be more careful from now on. Whatever had made her faint could happen again.

Hollace barked, "Report."

Caradoc stared at the orb in his hand in confusion. "It makes no sense, Your Majesty. We all saw her pain when she arrived at the infirmary. Something that strong should have left a mark on her of some kind, but there is nothing, absolutely nothing."

Hollace stopped walking and glared at Caradoc. "How can there be nothing?" he roared.

"The erasure spell seems to have slipped with her glimmer of memory. That slip caused her to faint. During her slumber, the spell corrected itself and erased the memory of the slip so it wouldn't happen again. Or that is my theory, in any case," he explained.

"Theory? That's all you have. What good is a theory?" Hollace gritted out. He resumed walking.

Caradoc followed. "I don't know what else to say, King Hollace. I have never seen a spell like this one. It changes and evolves to suit Adele's condition. Spells just don't do that unless the caster is physically changing the spell."

Tacita asked, "Does that mean the caster of the spell is nearby, perhaps even spying on Adele somehow?"

Hollace snorted. "Not likely."

"But, husband—"

"No mage would be in my palace without me knowing it," Hollace said, cutting off her argument. He thought on what Caradoc had told him, though. The spell had changed because she'd started to remember. The caster had to be close, just not in his palace. "Caster...caster..." he mumbled to himself.

"Your Majesty?" Caradoc asked.

Hollace stopped again. He commanded, "Send out a new notice about Adele. Add in that she has brothers by the names of Castor and Pollux. Mayhap this will speed up the search for her true family and she can get out of my presence once and for all."

Caradoc bowed. "I will see it done immediately." He turned and almost ran down the hallway in the opposite direction.

"First, messengers sent to every mage guild, and now this," a soldier grumbled. He shifted his arms to relieve the burden of the heavy paper.

His partner demanded, "Shut up before someone reports your complaints to King Hollace. You will get us both in trouble." He stopped near his horse and opened the saddle bag to unload the papers.

A strong wind rushed by and ripped several of the flyers out of the man's hands. He cursed and ran after the pages.

His companion yelled, "Leave them. The wind can spread the word faster than we can."

The man cursed and returned to his horse. He looked one last time at the papers. A frown marred his features. The only thing the wind affected was the flyers. The leaves of the trees nearby didn't stir.

"Come on!"

"Right behind you," the man said. He spurred his mount in the opposite direction the wind had taken.

Chancellor Sabri watched as the guards carried away a man in too much pain to walk on his own—Malik's latest victim of interrogation. Hundreds had been questioned already, and there were still no leads as to the traitor or Adrienne's whereabouts.

"There has to be a better way," Sabri said. The other chancellors edged away from him. He sneered at them for being cowards. He looked up at Malik on the throne dais and said again, "There must be a faster way to find Queen Adrienne, Majesty."

Malik rasped, "What would you suggest, Chancellor?"

"Ask for the other kingdoms' aid. Queen Adrienne has not left the planet. She is still on Bron. Someone in one of the kingdoms must have caught sight of her."

The suggestion made Malik laugh. Feyr roared. Everyone in the throne room took a collective step back.

Malik rose from his throne and descended so he could stand in front of Sabri. "If I were to ask for aid from the other kingdoms, Hollace would find out Adrienne is missing. He would divert all of his resources to find her before me. Once he found her, Hollace would kill Adrienne without hesitation."

"This is true, Majesty. I hadn't thought of—"

"I would be forced to level all of Kakra and kill every man, woman and child within its borders, starting with Hollace. Such an action would upset Kontar and I would have to destroy them next before they decided to retaliate." He stepped into Sabri and his tone dropped to below freezing as he finished, "The remaining eleven kingdoms would take exception at the destruction of both Kakra and Kontar and band together to stop me from destroying other kingdoms. That would mark the beginning of a world war.

"You can believe, Chancellor Sabri, that I would not be killed until I had seen most of this world laid to waste. That is how strong my grief would be should Adrienne die before I can find her. And that is why no other kingdom will be apprised of her kidnapping. Do you understand me, Chancellor?"

"Clearly, King Malik," Sabri whispered. He didn't back down but did notice that he and Malik were alone, since everyone else in the throne room had moved to stand along the walls.

"Good." Malik returned to his throne. He barked, "Bring forward the next."

The other chancellors rejoined Sabri. "Not even when his parents were killed did he act like this," Riler whispered.

Valah said, "We must remain vigilant for any signs of Queen Adrienne's presence. The sooner she is found the better it will be for all of us."

"Once he is done with the Elite guards, he plans to interrogate us," said Travers.

"I'm surprised he didn't start with us," said Sabri.

A maid carried a basin of water towards the guest wing of the palace. She dodged people who milled in the halls. Everyone was nervous. No one wanted to be next on King Malik's list. Her mistress had already faced the orb of truth and come out of it unscathed. But the ordeal had put her under a great deal of stress.

The maid hoped a cool cloth would calm her mistress, hence the water she carried. She passed by an open window. A strong gust of wind blew her skirts up and caused her to squeak in dismay. She couldn't keep her skirts down and hold the water at the same time. Something brushed her leg and she screamed.

She dropped the water basin to swat at whatever had brushed her leg. Her hand came into contact with a piece of paper. She lifted the paper and scanned the contents. Her eyes went wide.

Her mess forgotten, she rushed to the throne room. One of the guards stopped her before she could enter. She waved the paper at the man and pleaded, "King Malik must see this. It might be—"

The man snatched the paper from her and read over it. He asked, "Why would this Adele person interest King Malik at all? His queen's name is Adrienne."

"Maybe she hid her true identity to remain safe. This message is from Kakra. If she is there—"

The throne room doors opened and Valah stormed out. He glared at the maid and the guards. "Why are you out here gossiping? You have jobs to perform—all of you. You disrespect our king in this trying time with your flagrant disobedience."

The guard started, "This woman—"

The maid snatched the paper from the guard and held it out to Valah. She said, "It came in through an open window. I thought King Malik should see it. Queen Adrienne might have needed to disguise her name since the message is from Kakra."

Valah took the note from the woman and read over it. He whispered, "Castor and Pollux? What types of names are those?"

"What's going on here?" Travers asked. He came up behind Valah.

"Nothing," Valah rushed out. He crumpled up the paper. When the maid would have pressed the issue, he ordered, "Get back to your mistress and stop wasting our time with fanciful tales."

The maid looked stricken. She opened her mouth to voice her theory to Travers. Surely he would hear her out. Her logic made sense.

The guard who stood closest to her shoved her away and yelled, "You heard the chancellor. Get!"

"High Chancellor Travers, the..." The maid's words stumbled to a halt as Travers and Valah re-entered the throne room and closed the door behind them. Her shoulders slumped.

"Guess they don't care," the guard taunted.

The maid walked away. She must be wrong. Now that she calmed down and thought about it, her logic made no sense. Queen Adrienne had to know her life would be in danger if she remained in Hollace's palace. She wouldn't hide there, false name or not. But the woman had hoped her queen was found and this madness would come to an end. It would seem her mistress wasn't the only one overcome with stress.

Chapter Twenty-Three

Caradoc and Adele returned for dinner to report another failed attempt at restoring her memory. She took her normal place at Chandra's table, situated five tables down from the royal table. It was a topic Chandra bemoaned almost daily. But then the woman bemoaned everything almost daily.

Adele was ready to endure another dinner of listening to the same whispered complaints as usual. A new member at Chandra's table caught her attention—Oringo. He sat next to the spot Adele normally occupied.

His rightful place was at his father's right hand. Adele chanced a glance at Hollace. Based on his displeased look, she could tell Oringo's change in seats hadn't annoyed only her. Adele heard many stories about Oringo and his tendency of bedding every willing woman who crossed his path. Adele wasn't willing, and she hoped Oringo would see that and leave her alone.

Three years separated Oringo from Chandra. But, as the firstborn *male*, only he qualified to be Hollace's heir. The topic represented the bulk of Chandra's angst. The list of complaints she bombarded Adele with included a rant on how much she hated her ancestor for the stipulations he had laid down for his descendants.

Adele couldn't shake the feeling that she knew the story of Chandra's ancestor, but she couldn't quite figure out how she would come to know about it. She didn't mention this to Chandra as it would be construed that she had gotten her memory back, and she hadn't. That frustrated Adele more than anything. Everything was familiar and yet none of it jogged her memory.

"So, Mistress Adele, how goes the search for your memory?" Oringo asked as he reached over her to get a plate of bread. The movement was intentional so he could brush up against her.

Adele tried to edge away from his nearness only to be brought up against the man seated on the other side of her. From his attitude, the man didn't seem to mind.

Adele answered, "Master Caradoc tries day after day with little luck."

Oringo made a *tsk* noise. He said in a pitying tone, "That is too bad. Perhaps it would be best if you simply stay here."

Chandra glared at her brother as she asked, "How is your *betrothed*, Oringo? Isn't she supposed to grace us with her presence at the next ball?"

Adele grasped at the out Chandra had given her. She turned a genuinely happy expression to Oringo. "You are to be married, Your Highness? That is wonderful. When is the happy day?"

If Oringo got married, he would stop focusing on her. He was very handsome, she couldn't deny that. But his attentions made her nervous and a little guilty. What she had to be guilty of, Adele didn't know.

Oringo returned his sister's glare with one of his own. He didn't get the chance to answer the question since Hollace answered for him. "Prince Oringo is slated to marry Lady Sovenne before this year is out."

Adele glanced up at Hollace. She met his gaze as she always did. And, like always, he looked away first. She sensed that Hollace found her presence more of a pain than he admitted. To his statement, she said, "I hope, by that time, I have found my proper place and have amply returned the courtesy you have extended to me, Your Majesty."

"So elegantly put, Mistress, and yet you are still an unknown. One wonders at your sincerity."

Oringo laughed to lighten the mood. He said, "Father, you speak as though Mistress Adele has caused her own memory loss and could cure it if she so chose."

Hollace didn't share in Oringo's jovial nature. "We don't know that not to be true, do we, Mistress Adele?" he asked.

Adele felt all eyes on her. The feeling was singularly familiar. A headache started behind her eyes. For once, the pain constituted a blessing in disguise. The excuse of it allowed her to get away from dinner, the prince and everything else. Somehow that felt familiar, too.

With a whispered apology, Adele left the dining hall to go hide in her room.

Once dinner ended, Chandra cornered Oringo. "Are you mad, brother? To openly show your desire for Mistress Adele is to court father's displeasure."

"Mind your own business, Chandra," Oringo said coldly. "What I do to or with Mistress Adele is none of your concern."

"Mistress Adele is not a toy, Oringo. She isn't a palace maid to be bedded and forgotten, either. What if her memory returns and she is a person of import to another kingdom? How will you apologize?"

Oringo's laughter rang through the halls. He taunted, "You are mad. If she were important, the news would be banded out far and wide to ensure her safe recovery. No such news has reached our ears, has it?"

Chandra faltered in her arguments. She was uncertain how to keep Oringo from molesting Adele. She grasped at the last straw. "Father will not allow you to have her. He distrusts her. He will not risk his only heir on a chance such as Adele, and he will take steps to ensure you never get near her if you prove too arduous."

"Father will never know," he said, eyeing her, "unless you decide your loyalty lies with Mistress Adele and not your family."

Chandra's chin lifted haughtily. "Telling Father of your intention shows the purest loyalty to my family." She lowered her chin and her voice as she added, "I will not feel the need to involve Father so long as you leave Adele be." With that, she departed his company.

Oringo stared after his sister. He didn't care what she thought or did. Even if she told Hollace, that wouldn't unmake the experience Oringo planned to have with Adele tomorrow night.

ॐ

Mushira smiled wanly at the images of Hannah and Benjamin in the mirror before her. She reiterated, "I know it has been some time since Adrienne has called you, but she and Malik are still, as yet, traveling around Bron. It is hard to pinpoint their current location, else I would immediately inform them of your calls."

Hannah nodded. She smiled to show she wasn't upset with Mushira. She said, "I know, I know. But I hoped they'd returned." She gave a frustrated, motherly sigh. "Well, give them my best and tell Adrienne to call me back as soon as she steps through the door. I don't want her doing anything before she calls me, okay?"

"Of course, Hannah. I will relay your message," Mushira agreed. She inclined her head to the woman then waved her hand in front of the mirror, blanking the image. Her whole body sagged.

From the shadows of the room, Malik apologized, "I am sorry to make you lie like this, Mushira."

"I understand the necessity of it, Majesty. This can be done no other way," Mushira said sadly. She looked at her reflection in the mirror. "I only wish we could tell them."

"That is not an option," Malik snapped. He softened his tone. "I do not wish to worry Benjamin and Hannah in such a way. I promised them their daughter would be safe with me. I will not give them cause to think I am breaking that promise."

Mushira whirled to look at Malik. She pleaded, "Majesty, please. Such news should not be withheld from her family."

"She is not dead, Mushira!" The woman shrank from him. He continued in a cold voice, "She is not dead. She is alive and she will return. If she chooses to tell her parents of her ordeal, I will answer for my subterfuge then, and only then. Until that time comes, Hannah and Benjamin will believe Adrienne and I are touring Bron, and you are unable to contact us. Do I make myself clear, Mushira?"

She went into a deep curtsy with her head bowed but said nothing. The grief in Malik's voice was a tangible thing.

"Leave me."

Mushira rose and left.

Malik waited for the door to close before he fell to his knees. He whispered, "I should have never left your side. You were safer in my presence." He shook his head, and tears splashed onto his fists where they rested on his knees. "I will find you, my Adrienne. I will find you and make those who took you pay."

ℴℴ

Adele smiled at Caradoc's confusion over her particular conundrum. He had failed to break the spell on her memory yet again. He decided to stay in his cottage to ponder another plan of attack for tomorrow. Adele knew better—he didn't want to face Hollace. She couldn't blame him since she didn't want to tell Hollace the bad news, either.

She bid Caradoc farewell and returned to the palace. Despite Caradoc's constant arguments that she should reside with him, Adele enjoyed the exercise. Staying in the palace also meant she didn't have to worry about the way Caradoc looked at her when he thought she wasn't paying attention.

She saw in Caradoc's eyes some of what she saw in Oringo's. Both men made her nervous. When she tried to find a reason for her reaction to them, her head began to hurt. That alone made her wonder if remembering her past was worth it.

Her new headache made Adele change course and go to her room. She would meet up with Chandra in the dining room later. For now, she needed sleep. Hopefully it would alleviate the pain in her head.

Adele needed a nap before she could face Chandra and her incessant ranting about the unfairness of her marriage and demotion to a mere lady, anyway.

Her short rest was not to be. Adele opened the door to find Oringo waiting for her. He smiled as she came up short in the doorway.

Adele curtsied quickly. She asked, "Your Highness, I... Is there a reason you have sought me out?"

Some instinct told her to run. Something about the look in Oringo's eyes made Adele nervous. She'd seen that look before. This feeling of familiarity made her headache get worse.

Oringo beckoned her further into the room. Adele stayed defiantly by the door and the safety it offered.

"Come, Mistress Adele, I will not bite. I merely wish to speak to you in private," he said as he pulled her into the room and closed the door. "I have come with a proposition to get you away from my nagging and ever-complaining sister."

Adele put some distance between them before she asked, "And what would that be, Your Highness?"

Oringo closed the small distance with ease since Adele's room was not that large. He wrapped an arm around her waist and pulled her close. He told her in a low voice, "I wish to make you my concubine. I have to marry some noble's daughter, but the taking of concubines is a common practice, and expected of royals."

Adele's expression darkened. She asked, "You would disgrace your wife in such a way?"

"My wife is merely there to bear me heirs and look pretty. Queens serve no other purpose," he scoffed.

His words made Adele want to slap him. He had such a low opinion of women. She pushed against his chest. "There must be other women waiting with baited breath for such an invitation. I am not one of them, Your Highness. I would ask that you leave now."

Oringo was solid and unmoving. He grinned at her attempts to get him to release her. Many women mistook his slight form as a sign of weakness. They had learned differently.

"Given your current circumstances, when Chandra leaves with her husband next month to return to his keep, I will be your best way to stay in the palace and close to Caradoc. That should give you more incentive to consider my offer, Adele." He lowered his lips to hers. His free hand grasped her chin to keep her from turning away.

Adele pushed as hard as she could on his chest. Oringo wouldn't let her go. She entertained ideas of biting him. Thoughts of treason and punishment banished the idea. She was satisfied with keeping her lips firmly pressed together and making the kiss a chaste one. She felt his tongue beckoning her to open for him. She folded her lips around her teeth and bit down to make it even harder for him to gain entry. It didn't hurt...much. Anything was better than his tongue in her mouth.

"Stop fighting me, damn it." He tried again with the same results.

Oringo pushed Adele onto the bed. Instead of trying to kiss her lips again, he ripped away her blouse and suckled her breasts.

Adele tried futilely to push his face away. She pleaded, "Stop this. I don't want to be your mistress." She didn't add that his mouth on her body made her feel disgusted. Her feeling of guilt returned in force.

Oringo ignored her pleas. His hands roamed over her body. He pushed his hand underneath her skirt and around her undergarments to caress between her legs.

When Adele felt her legs being pried apart, her mind snapped back to another time when she was assaulted. The flash of memory caused her mind to rip apart in pain. The slight headaches of before were welcome compared to this pain. She felt as though her head would explode. As the memory tried to grab hold, so too did the pain get worse.

She screamed and writhed on the bed as though possessed. It took Oringo a moment to realize her screams weren't because of him. He stared at her in horror. He pinned her arms to her sides to keep her from tearing out her hair. After five minutes of continuous screaming, Adele finally passed out.

Oringo stared at her. She was limp beneath him and he almost thought she had stopped breathing until he saw the rise and fall of her chest. He gathered her up and rushed her to the infirmary.

Once there, he ordered a guard to fetch Caradoc.

৪০৪

Malik's head snapped up, his attention momentarily distracted from the woman he interrogated. The orb in his hand dulled and the woman slumped.

He had felt Adrienne. But too soon the feeling vanished. She was alive and a spell masked her, he knew that for a certainty. He turned his attention back to the woman on the ground.

He said quietly, "Get out. You may not be part of the conspiracy to do my queen harm, but neither are you, nor have you ever been, loyal to me or my throne. You are hereby banished. Return to Ulan and you will be killed."

The woman crawled out of the throne room. Malik stood and addressed the rest of the people in the room. "This day has ended." He ignored the murmurs of relief and returned to his rooms via a portal.

In his chambers, Mushira aired out Adrienne's closet. Malik had commanded her over and over to stop. She stubbornly refused to be separated from the only part of Adrienne left in the palace. Even Feyr's presence on the bed couldn't deter her.

With Mushira were Nimat, Rena and Mischief. Like Mushira, Nimat and Mischief had a need to be near something of Adrienne's. Mushira had taken up the task of caring for Rena since both Indivar and Hani searched for Adrienne.

Malik regarded them and knew he couldn't keep his news to himself.

"She is alive."

Mushira froze. The dress in her hands fluttered to the ground. She whipped around to face Malik. "What?" she demanded.

Malik ignored her impertinence, for he knew Mushira's joy was akin to his own. "Only moments ago, I felt Adrienne. You were right, Feyr. There are magicks hiding her from me. And, for a time, those magicks weakened. We can only hope next time the weakening will be long enough for me to track her."

"*It would be better to hope the traitor will be found soon.*"

Malik mirrored his sentiment. "Tomorrow the interrogations will be harsher and faster. I want my wife back."

Nimat asked, "Do you still think it wise not to seek help in the search from the other kingdoms?"

Malik shook his head. "No. Hollace's spies are many—as I have found out over the last few days. The traitor will be revealed soon."

"I only hope you are right, Majesty," Mushira replied solemnly.

ॐ

Hollace looked at Adele lying prone on the bed. He turned his gaze to his son. "What happened *this* time?" he asked in a clipped voice.

"She collapsed."

"That's it? She collapsed?" Hollace asked incredulously. "And you happened to be there to catch her?"

Both men looked up as Chandra entered the room with a crash. The door to the infirmary bounced off the wall and shook on its hinges. She had a look of horror on her face. Chandra's eyes swept up from Adele to her father and her brother.

When her gaze rested on Oringo, a look of loathing crossed her face. Oringo shook his head at her and looked pointedly at Hollace. That was all the incentive Chandra needed to lose what little composure she had.

Tacita entered the room in time to hear her daughter scream, "You bastard." Chandra launched herself at Oringo with her hands clawed. Oringo fended her off while he called for the guards. The guards seemed confused about what to do.

Hollace made the decision for them. He grabbed Chandra and held her in a bear hug. He put his mouth close to her ear and growled, "You will calm yourself, girl. Adele collapsed. That is all."

Chandra pulled away from her father and looked at him. "Are you blind?"

"You will watch your tone with me, *Lady* Chandra," Hollace warned.

Chandra sliced her hand through the air. "No. He," she yelled, pointing at Oringo, "attacked her. That's what brought on this fit."

Tacita—ever one to try to keep peace between her daughter and husband—stepped forward to lay a hand on Chandra's shoulder. "You don't know that, Chandra," she said in a soothing manner.

Before Chandra could insist that she did know it, Caradoc confirmed her suspicions. "Lady Chandra is telling the truth. Prince Oringo did attack Mistress Adele." He'd planned to wait until Hollace was alone before revealing the true source of Adele's seizure, but Chandra's outburst rendered his tact unneeded.

"Liar," Oringo yelled.

Hollace calmly asked, "You have proof?"

Caradoc held up the orb he'd used to examine Adele. "This orb replays recent events from within the last few hours."

Hollace demanded, "If you've had such a thing, why did you not use it to find out where this girl belongs when she first arrived?"

"I could not, Your Majesty. The spell of erasure would not allow the re-enactment spell to do its job," Caradoc answered quickly. "However, the erasure spell is not taking away Adele's memories from the time she arrived until now. Adele cannot tell us herself what happened and I thought the attack might have triggered a buried memory which caused this faint. I could repeat it and gain some insight into how to break the erasure spell if I could see what caused the attack." He beckoned Hollace forward and held the orb slightly up. "This is what I saw."

The orb's sound was muted and only loud enough for Caradoc and Hollace to hear. Hollace watched the tiny playback in stony silence. His expression betrayed nothing. When the playback finished, Hollace confronted his son.

"Stay away from Mistress Adele from now on."

Oringo looked from his father to Caradoc and back again. "Father—"

Hollace backhanded Oringo for daring to talk back. He took a deep breath and said, "There are strong magicks at work here. Your attack could have made what is afflicting her spill onto yourself." He glanced back at Adele and added, "I find I must protect you from yourself. If anyone reports that you were found even looking at Mistress Adele, I will be forced to punish you. Is that understood?"

Oringo held himself rigid. He managed a curt nod but nothing else.

Chandra gave Oringo a superior look. Tacita grabbed her daughter and pulled her out of the room before she angered Hollace more.

A moment passed before Hollace and Oringo followed. Caradoc stayed behind with an excuse that he wished to do more tests. And, like most excuses, it was a lie.

Caradoc had seen something in the playback of Adele's memories. Something Hollace had missed or else he would have made mention of it.

Caradoc traded the orb he held for another. He held this orb to Adele's head and pushed his power into it.

The air around Adele shimmered. A knowing smile creased Caradoc's lips when he saw what he had only glimpsed before. He rescinded his power from the orb and the confusion spell fell back into place. He couldn't break the confusion spell—it was too powerful and he didn't want to try.

His question had an answer. Adele had caused her own amnesia. The only way to escape the pain of the confusion spell woven around her was to forget everything about herself.

Her spell was a work of art. It not only hid her memory, but changed itself to make sure she would never remember. If Caradoc had not seen Adele while in the throes of an attack, he would have never glimpsed the silver cord of marriage. And the scar on her left hand had intrigued him. A scar that had faded once he let the confusion spell fall back into place.

Caradoc knew what a marriage cord and that scar meant together—Ulan. Only the royal line of Ulan practiced such, because only the royal line of Ulan went out of their way to find their soul's mate.

It would seem Caradoc had found King Malik's bride. It would also seem that someone had tried to take her and failed. That same someone would pay handsomely to have her now.

Caradoc wasted no time with the information he uncovered. After he returned to his cottage, he started his search. He used every bit of power at his disposal to find out who had tried to kidnap Malik's new bride. In the end, his search led the party in question straight to him.

An orb appeared with the rising of the sun. It floated before Caradoc's face, shadows obscuring its occupant. Based on the voice, Caradoc knew the person talking to him was a woman. Not just any woman but a woman with power of magicks, and of station, as well.

"I have felt your magicks. I surmise you have something of mine," the shadowed woman said confidently.

Caradoc nodded slowly. He answered, "Yes, my lady. I have found a girl. She has a confusion spell wrapped around her like a swaddling blanket—not easily broken."

The woman chuckled. "That is as it should be. Since you have not returned her to her rightful location, I assume you wish to barter with me. Am I correct?"

"I presumed the maker of the spell shared her true home," Caradoc lied, easily. It didn't do to let the woman realize he knew too much. Too much knowledge often led to pain and death.

The shadowed woman was silent for the span of five breaths. She put her hand into the light on top of her desk and leaned forward. Not enough to illuminate her face but far enough to let Caradoc know what she said next was of vital importance. "I will send one of my people to retrieve my girl. You will make sure nothing happens to her in that time."

Caradoc could barely speak around his pent-up breath. He managed, "Do you need my location?"

"Not necessary. You are in Kakra near Hollace's palace," she said. The shadowed woman leaned back in her chair once again. "I will send a reward and it will be handsome. Our conversation is at an end."

271

The orb disappeared.

Caradoc cast out with his powers. He felt no trace of the orb or who sent it. If that was true, it meant the shadowed woman no longer watched him.

He sagged to the ground in fear. He had made a deal with a monster—a monster he knew all too well. And he had to confront a devil to reveal the monster's identity. He felt damned.

Chapter Twenty-Four

Nimat looked around before she ducked into an alcove. Sneaking away had become much easier since Mushira continued to fret about Adrienne's safe return. Nimat missed her queen like most everyone else in the palace, but that didn't stop her from wanting to meet with her lover.

She heard footsteps approaching and knew they belonged to her lover. She debated jumping out at him but decided against it. It was better to let the suspense build. That was part of the fun of these secret interludes—the ever present fear of being caught.

Being caught would mean Nimat might lose her post as the queen's maid, and she would never find work again. No one would want a lady's maid the queen cast off. Her lover, however, would have to deal with the wrath of his wife, as he hadn't asked her permission to have a lover on the side.

Nimat held her breath as her lover passed the alcove she occupied for the next one. She frowned at his stupidity. They had met in the same spot for the last five months. It was ridiculous that he would get it wrong now.

She pushed back the tapestry and stepped softly out of the alcove to surprise him. Then she stopped cold. The man who spoke in the next alcove wasn't her lover.

She hurried back behind the tapestry and listened.

"My lady, I barely had time to hide myself when you called. Is there something amiss?" the cloaked man asked shakily. He feared his mistress would be angered at his continued absence. It was true he hadn't tried very hard—or at all—to get out of Malik's binding spell but he couldn't let his mistress know that.

"No thanks to you, I have found your missing queen. She is currently in Kakra under Hollace's roof...of all places," the shadowed woman said with no small amount of humor.

"How?"

"I don't know how! I do know you will get her and bring her to me. You fail me again, Sabri, and I will personally hand you over to Malik."

The orb disappeared before Sabri could say more. He closed his eyes and tried to think of what his next move would be. He pulled out an orb from his robe and waited for the person on the other end to acknowledge him.

When she did, he said, "Good. You're in Kakra, correct?"

"Of course I'm in Kakra. After that bitch kicked me out, where was I to go? Thankfully, there is a lord in Kakra who recognizes my skills and pays me handsomely for them," the woman boasted.

"I don't care. Adrienne is found. She is in Hollace's palace. Go there, get her and deliver her to Kontar. Fail me in this and I will drag you through Hell in my wake," Sabri promised.

The woman nodded and the orb went blank. Sabri replaced it in his cloak and pushed aside the tapestry to leave the alcove. He looked around then hurried back to his chambers.

Thanks to a suggestion he had made, Malik decided to forestall the interrogation of the chancellors in favor of his generals. Sabri's reasoning was simple—the generals leave the palace more frequently than the chancellors. If there was ever a suspicious party, it would be them.

That had bought him some time. Now that Adrienne was found and his mistress no longer wished to see him covered in pain, he needed to get out of the palace.

Nimat kept her hands clamped over her mouth. She couldn't believe what she'd heard. Her breath came in shallow gasps and fear froze her limbs. Chancellor Sabri... But why?

The tapestry to the alcove ripped back and Nimat screamed.

Her lover rushed into the tiny space and covered her mouth with his hand. He hissed in her ear, "Are you mad? Why are you screaming, you little idiot?"

Adrenaline rushed through Nimat's veins. She pushed past her lover and ran straight to Malik's chambers. The Elite guards were not there to guard his door because they were still searching all over Bron for Adrienne, and he had appointed no others to take their place. No one barred her way. She didn't even think of the consequences of waking her king so early in the morning.

She pounded on the door until her fist went numb, and still she pounded.

Malik came to the door, his eyes blazing mad. He asked, "Why—"

Nimat rushed past him and slammed the door behind her. She looked around and then back at her king. She shook her head over and over.

"Nimat?" he asked in confusion. He ran a hand through his hair. Knots impeded his path and he gave up. His eyes were half-closed with sleep. It was hard-won sleep, as his worry for Adrienne remained ever-present.

"He did it," she whispered frantically.

Malik came instantly awake. He asked slowly, "Did what? Who?"

Nimat stared at her king with disbelief as she answered, "Chancellor Sabri."

Malik grabbed Nimat's shoulders and shook her. "Is this a game to you?"

Tears rolled down her cheeks and she shook her head. She stammered out, "Heard him. I...I was meeting someone in the south corridor alcoves of the servants' wing. I thought my lover had come. It was Chancellor Sabri. He spoke to someone."

Malik released her. "Who?"

She shook her head again. "I don't know. It was a woman. The woman said Queen Adrienne is in Hollace's palace. Chancellor Sabri called another woman in Kakra. She is to find Queen Adrienne and deliver her to Kontar."

"Kontar?" Perplexity showed on Malik's face. "Why Kontar?"

"I don't know, Majesty. I..." She stammered to a stop and fell to her knees. Tears overwhelmed her.

Malik shimmered. He went from naked to clothed in a single instant. He closed his eyes and opened five portals. The Elite guards used these portals to answer his call.

Footsteps running down the halls heralded Mushira and Hani's arrival. Malik grabbed Nimat and deposited her in a chair.

He wasted no words in his explanation once everyone arrived.

Mushira dabbed at her happy tears with a tissue Hani handed her. She asked, "What shall we do, My King?"

Malik ignored her to speak to Nimat. "You said the second woman Sabri spoke to mentioned being kicked out of the palace by Adrienne?"

Nimat nodded.

"One of the concubines, perhaps, Majesty?" Hani suggested.

Malik nodded. "They are the only ones to have suffered any ill happening at Adrienne's hands. It has to be one of them, but who? I had several."

No one had an answer for him. Absently, Malik listed off the names of his concubines. Before this moment, such a feat would be beyond him. He hadn't cared what their names were, he'd only cared that they were good at their jobs. He forced himself to remember every one of the women in his harem and their demeanor while in his presence.

Hani interrupted his mumblings. "Did you say Juven, Majesty?"

Malik looked over to Hani. "You know her?" he asked with hope.

"I hope you do not mean the Juven I know, though."

Khursid pointed out, "It is a unique name, Hani. The woman you are thinking of and the woman King Malik named might be the same."

Hani looked down.

Malik yelled, "What? Speak already."

Hani glanced at Indivar. He looked away from her. She turned her gaze to Malik and asked, "You remember my title, do you not, Majesty? The one that caused you to seek me out?"

"The Assassin's Assassin," Malik answered impatiently. "What of it?"

Hani sighed and explained, "In the history of the Assassin's Guild, there have only been seventy-eight people granted such a title. Training to be an assassin is rigorous and deadly. Those who pass are excellent at the work. Then there are those who surpass excellence. Those who are hired to hunt the hunter. They are granted the title of Assassin's Assassin. Two of them are alive today—myself and Juven."

"No," Malik gasped. He dropped to his knees.

Mushira hurried out, "It may not be the same woman."

Malik held out an orb. In it, Juven stood wearing a floor-length orange loincloth and nothing else. She had her light brown hair was swept up in her arms and a smile on her face that made her light brown eyes twinkle. The lights in the room made her honey-colored skin glow. She started dancing.

The scene depicted the past. A time when Malik had needed distraction. A time before Adrienne.

Hani sighed. "That is her. I only met her once. We were not trained at the same time, she and I. But for two to be named Assassin's Assassin within the same year, within the same generation, is unheard of. We met and were tested against one another to see if one deserved the title more than the other."

"Who won?" Qamar asked.

"It was a draw."

Malik's head dropped into his hands.

Nimat reminded him, "Chancellor Sabri only told Juven—if that is the woman with whom he spoke—to retrieve Queen Adrienne and deliver her to Kontar, not to kill her."

"Yes," Mushira agreed quickly. "We are only guessing it is Juven. It may not be."

Malik stood. He wiped his hand down his face then turned to his Primaries. Each man snapped to attention. He ordered, "Bring Sabri to my throne room. Make no indication that he is suspect."

The Primaries nodded quickly and rushed out of the room.

Next, Malik turned to Khursid and Qamar. He held out the orb with Juven pictured in it and blanked it. He then shaped the orb into a portal. "This portal will put you in Hollace's palace. See if you can get to Adrienne before Sabri's hound."

They ran through the portal after a quick bow. Hani made to follow. Malik stopped her and said, "I want you to track down Juven. And this time, I do not want it to end in a draw. Whether she is the woman who is after Adrienne or not, she still remains a threat."

Hani nodded and pulled out an orb of her own. She didn't shape a portal. Instead, she concentrated. With a tiny flash, she disappeared.

Malik opened another portal to his throne room. Feyr already waited for him.

Caradoc nearly jumped out of his skin when a woman separated from the shadows of the woods that surrounded his house. Tight black clothing swathed her entire body and a mask covered her face. All he could see were her brown eyes. He sensed no magicks on the woman but somehow she had kept her presence hidden from him. Every alarm bell in his mind screamed *assassin*. Assassins were notorious for their ability to get close to and kill anyone—even mages on constant guard.

He stammered out, "Who are you?"

"My name doesn't concern you. Where is she?" the woman demanded.

Adele peeked out of the cottage at Caradoc. She had come to his cottage at his request. It was early in the morning, but she hadn't minded. Sleep had eluded her as memories of her near miss with

Oringo continued to plague her. Going to Caradoc's cottage to muddle through her memory loss was just the distraction she needed.

Caradoc said he had seen something after her attack and wished to study it more. Once she arrived, he'd done nothing to study her. He'd only looked out his window. After a while, he left the cottage altogether.

When she heard voices, Adele decided to come out and see who had come.

She asked, "Is someone here, Master Caradoc?" She looked at the black-clad woman with interest.

The woman smiled. "Well, well, well, if it isn't Queen Adrienne." She gave a mock bow and sneered, "Your Majesty."

Adele frowned in total confusion. She tried to make sense of the woman's words. That only brought on a headache. The headache grew steadily worse and she dropped to her knees with the pain of it.

The woman *tsked* as she drew closer. She asked, "Does your head hurt, dear? Maybe this will help." The woman snapped a mage metal collar around Adele's neck. Once the collar was secured, the woman removed an orb from her clothing and said to it, "Release."

The headache disappeared. Adrienne's memories came crashing back into place. She also retained the memories of everything that had happened to her over the past twelve days. What confused her was how the spell that surrounded her had vanished.

The woman explained, "Your memories are back because I have cancelled the confusion spell placed on you. The party interested in you supplied me with the orb that contained the spell. I also bound your powers under mage metal." The woman grabbed Adrienne's arm and hauled her to her feet. "Move," she barked.

As the women passed Caradoc, the assassin tossed a small sack to him. He threw up his hands and made a shield. The sack bounced off the shield and hit the ground with the jingle of coins knocking together. He realized it was his payment.

He looked at the sack on the ground then back at the departing women. Once they were out of sight, he bent down and opened the bag. Five thousand in gold coins minted in Kontar stared back at him.

Was that the worth of his soul? When he reported to Malik, he would find out.

Caradoc made ready to journey to Ulan.

Malik closed the portal behind him. He took his time to get settled on his throne then smiled at the men who waited for him. The Primaries had retrieved Sabri, and Travers had seen fit to tag along. Both chancellors being present would mean Sabri wouldn't be on his guard. That would make what Malik planned to do that much easier.

Travers spoke upon Malik's entrance, "You called for us, Majesty?"

Malik laid a lazy hand on Feyr's head. No one noticed the mage metal orb Feyr carried in his mouth. The same mage metal orb Sabri had used to incapacitate Feyr the day Adrienne was kidnapped. Malik palmed it while he stroked Feyr's head.

"One of my operatives in Kakra has located Adrienne. I need a pass of peace from Hollace to retrieve her without bloodshed or hassle," Malik said nonchalantly.

"That is wonderful, Majesty. Is there any news of how she came to be there?" Travers gushed.

Malik flicked his wrist. The mage metal orb disappeared and reappeared behind Sabri's head. Malik smiled at Travers. He said, "No, there is not. But perhaps you can shed some light on that particular subject, Sabri."

Sabri sputtered, "Whatever does Your Majesty mean? I am just as in the dark about all of this as everyone else."

"Funny you should mention dark, Sabri. It was in darkness that Adrienne's maid heard you conversing with a personage from Kontar about the retrieval of my wife. Care to tell me the identity of said personage?" Malik again flicked his wrist. The mage metal hit Sabri seconds before the man pulled an orb out of his robes.

Sabri screamed as the mage metal entered his body. The orb he had hidden in his robes dropped to the floor and rolled away. His eyes blazed as he looked up at Malik. He spat, "You'll never make me talk. You can do nothing to me with this mage metal embedded in my body. If you take it out, you'll have to fight me on equal footing. I don't fear you, Malik. I endured worse pain in preparation for infiltrating your kingdom as one of your chancellors than you could ever summon up."

Malik descended the stairs. He pointed out with a shrug of indifference, "Ah, but you do not know all of my secrets, Sabri. If you did, you would look upon me with fear, because what I am about to do to you will far surpass any tortures your training might have introduced you to."

A black orb appeared in Malik's hand. He held it out to Sabri. "This orb has never been marketed. It is one of Ulan's greatest secrets, and Ulan has many. A majority of those secrets originated with me." He caressed the orb lovingly. He smiled as Sabri winced in pain but still stared at him in defiance.

"If that is all that little black ball can do, you have failed before you have started, Malik," Sabri said with a sneer.

Before Malik could say more, a knock sounded on the throne room doors. Flavian entered and went to one knee. He announced, "A mage from Kakra has come bearing news of the queen."

"Enter, then," Malik commanded impatiently. His attention turned to the mage who entered his throne room. "Who are you?"

"I am Caradoc, Your Majesty. I am palace mage to King Hollace."

"You have news of my wife?"

Caradoc nodded. He threw the bag of money he had acquired only moments before in front of him. "An assassin retrieved her from my home to take her to Kontar, Your Majesty. I was paid handsomely for not interfering."

Malik's anger grew. "You obviously knew her identity, why did you not contact *me*?"

"I thought," Caradoc said softly, "you would rather know the kidnapper's identity so you could exact your own revenge and retrieve your wife personally."

"Your logic is flawed, old mage. I want my wife in the safety of my palace," Malik snapped.

"True, true. But she would have killed me and possibly retrieved your wife personally if I had contacted you *before* Nadid contacted me. Queen Adrienne would still be gone and you would have remained ignorant of whom to blame."

Travers spoke in disbelief, "Nadid? The Queen of Kontar?"

"The very same," Caradoc affirmed.

Malik—forgetting Sabri—walked over to Caradoc. He said in a low, lethal voice, "How do you know it was Nadid? You are hefting a serious charge against a woman who is third in ranking of the Mage Guild's masters."

"I know my accusation is steep, Your Majesty. That does not change the fact that I saw her ring. I studied in Kontar for a short time in my early years. I had an opportunity to meet Nadid. She was a little older than you are now and had not yet become queen. The woman who contacted me about Queen Adrienne stayed in the shadows, but she made the mistake of putting her hand in the light. It held the crest of Kontar. Only Nadid—and the other Kontarian rulers before her—wear such a ring."

Malik turned back to Sabri. His gaze promised death as he held out the black orb. This time he gripped it tightly. Sabri arched off the ground with a bloodcurdling scream. Malik enjoyed the sound for three breaths before he let off the pressure.

Sabri sagged to the ground. His eyes, once they had cleared, showed disbelief. "What..." was all he could manage before his throat closed and he coughed.

"The black orb is pain. It does not matter if you have mage metal embedded in your body or not. My magicks can overcome such an obstacle. The black orb has ripped away four years of your life. The longer the pain, the more life you lose. Eventually, it will kill you," Malik informed Sabri.

He crouched down in front of the man. His smile was something only the devil himself would wear. He said in a low, husky voice, "You will tell me why Nadid wants my wife. You will tell me about all who have helped you up until this point. You will tell me many, many things, Sabri—" he paused and retrieved a white orb from the air, "—or I will keep giving you life simply so I can rip it away again."

Sabri looked at him with fear. On the dais, Feyr mirrored his master's smile.

Chapter Twenty-Five

Hollace stared at Khursid and Qamar with humor. His guards had captured them a few minutes ago. They were stupid enough to think they could move around his palace freely.

Once the guards roused Hollace from his sleep to confront Khursid and Qamar, the two immediately told him who they were and why they were there. Hollace couldn't believe it. He'd had the Queen of Ulan, Malik's queen, in his clutches all this time and didn't even know it. And now she was gone. A maid in the kitchen had reported seeing Adele leave the palace for Caradoc's cottage. Hollace had sent his soldiers to arrest her, but they returned with news of her and Caradoc's absence.

Hollace had nothing but questions for his captives. Questions they would answer upon threat of torture. He asked, "How did you come to be in my palace?"

Khursid and Qamar went to one knee with their heads bowed. Hollace looked at them with amusement. They showed homage to him. He started to gloat when his smile froze.

A portal opened two feet in front of the kneeling guards and Malik stepped through. The portal closed. Malik signaled to Khursid and Qamar and they rose to stand at attention behind him.

Hollace came off his throne in a rage. He roared, "How dare you, Malik. You shouldn't be able to get into my palace."

Malik looked around himself in amusement. "You mean that flimsy piece of nothing you call a barrier?" He laughed. "I broke through stronger when I was twelve. I let you think you were safe behind this barrier, but I could always come and go as I pleased." A gasp drew his eyes to Tacita. He inclined his head at Hollace's queen. She took a defensive step back.

"What do you want? Your queen isn't here," Hollace said quickly. He was thankful he had not called for Oringo. Hollace didn't care if he died so long as his son survived to keep Kakra out of Malik's hands.

"I know that. She is in Kontar...now a guest of Nadid."

Hollace looked incredulous. "Nadid? What would the Queen of Kontar want with your wife, Malik?"

"We Kings of Ulan do not think our queens are useless like you Kakrans do. They are equal in rule, in wisdom and in power. My queen is very powerful, indeed. She wove an erasure spell around herself to fend off the effects of a confusion spell...all unconsciously," Malik said in a proud voice. "If I have my facts right, she even disrupted a portal and landed directly on your lap, Hollace. How is that for power?"

Hollace turned a sickly shade of white. He sank back onto his throne.

Tacita sat heavily on the floor, not having a throne of her own on which to sit. She stared at Malik and asked, "Adele was that powerful and I couldn't even feel it?"

Malik frowned. He asked, "Who is Adele?"

"I gave her that name when she couldn't remember her own."

"Her name is Adrienne, Queen Tacita. And what do you mean sense?"

"I am a child of Kontar. My father was a powerful noble, and high ranking in the branches of the Mage Guild. Hollace conditioned that I should never use my powers again when I became his bride. I had to renounce my powers by wearing this—" she fingered the mage metal chain around her waist, "—leash. But I cannot forget years of training because of my husband's biases and fears. I remove the chain from time to time. I did so once to see if I could ascertain Adele...Adrienne's true identity and proper place."

"You sensed no power in Adrienne?"

"I sensed the magnitude of the spell that bound her mind, and a second spell that I couldn't identify—"

"The confusion spell," Malik supplied.

"Yes. But nothing in me sensed the erasure spell came from her," she said in wonder. An admiring quality came to Tacita's voice. "It was flawless. The silver marriage cord and the scar of the blood binding spell were absent. I suppose that is why you didn't know she was here—you couldn't track her."

Malik shook his head. The discussion had gone off course. "Yes, the spell was powerful, but we waste time. Nadid has my wife. She means to siphon Adrienne's magicks in order to make herself more powerful. With that power she intends to assassinate the current Mage Guild head, take his place and then level *both* Ulan and Kakra to take as her own."

"The hell you say," Hollace yelled, coming back from the shocks Malik and Tacita had given him. He was beaten and betrayed all in the same breath. He thought himself clever to bind his wife's powers with a mage metal chain. A chain she took off whenever she pleased and as often as she pleased, it seemed. His anger at her defiance and at Nadid's audacity merged. "That *woman* couldn't make Nadid that much more powerful."

Malik said in a conspiratorial voice, "Nadid is third ranking in the Mage Guild. My wife...my Adrienne is an equal to my power. I walked into your palace as though your barrier did not exist, Hollace. A barrier, I am sure, your mages informed you was powerful enough to stop even the strongest Guild member."

"You are that strong?" Hollace asked, disbelieving.

"The measurement for my power is off the Guild charts. Believe me when I say, if Nadid is able to harness my wife's powers, neither Ulan nor Kakra will survive her attack." He clenched his fists at his side. "We need to join forces and stop Nadid now, before it is too late."

"You're so damn powerful that you can fight Nadid on your own. Why should I help to save your wife? You may have married her but she has not begotten your heir yet. If she dies and you are killed trying to save her, I get your kingdom," Hollace sneered.

"You truly are scared of magicks," Malik observed with a nod. "That is why I came to you, actually."

"What do you mean?" Hollace asked in a guarded voice.

Malik opened a portal in the floor. It overlooked a room, somewhere in the bowels of Hollace's palace that was full of mage metal orbs. He said, "That same fear caused you to stockpile mage metal. You have the biggest cache in the world. It is the only reason I have never attacked you. I may have power, but that much mage metal would daunt even me." Malik closed the portal. "That much mage metal would also stop Nadid and save my wife. The siphon will kill her."

Hollace laughed at Malik's words. "Tell me more good news."

"I could simply tie Oringo's life to that of my wife's. The minute she breathed her last, so too would he," Malik suggested. He raised his hand to do just that. "With the spell binding Tacita's reproductive abilities, you cannot have anymore heirs and Chandra cannot inherit. I would win."

"Spell? What spell?" Tacita asked in confusion. "You are mistaken, Malik. I had a difficult birth with Oringo. It rendered me unable to bear more children."

"Because Hollace would not allow mages in his palace to ensure the safe delivery of his heir?" Malik asked.

Tacita nodded.

Malik arched an eyebrow at Hollace. "You are an idiot, cousin. There are mages aplenty in your palace. A reliable source informed me of the spies. One such spy attended Oringo's birth to make it more difficult and thus hide the placement of a binding spell on Tacita's womb."

"I feel no magicks," Tacita said. She threw the mage metal chain away. Her hands splayed in front of her belly, she tried to sense the spell Malik mentioned.

"You did not take off your shackle nearly enough if you cannot sense such a simple spell, Tacita," Malik said. He made a beckoning motion with his hand. A light surrounded Tacita then shrank to focus on her belly. It whizzed down to Malik's waiting hand. "This spell is from Kontar, Tacita. It is from Nadid's father. He placed it on you so no other male heir would be born to take Oringo's place if he died." He crushed the ball of light and the magicks dissipated.

"That is no simple spell," Tacita said. "Only a Mage Guild master could cast such a spell."

"It is simple to me," Malik said without a hint of bravado. He turned his attention back to Hollace. "Tell me, cousin. If one of us fails in Derex's stipulations, what happens?"

"Then the other gains his kingdom."

"Once the two kingdoms are rejoined, what happens if there is no male blood heir to inherit?"

Hollace answered in a quiet voice, "Kontar gains both kingdoms."

"At some point, they became ambitious. Kontar does not want to see Ulan and Kakra joined unless it is under Kontar's rule." In a pain-filled voice, he said, "The spell they put on Tacita did not work on my mother. She sensed it. Instead, they killed her and blamed you. My father was killed so he would not find another bride. As a child I posed no threat and Kontar thought to control me through the Mage Guild. I quit to learn and control the magicks on my own, and it made me more powerful."

Malik met Hollace's eyes. "Do you understand what I am telling you, Hollace? Kontar has fueled the feud, not us. Kontar ordered the assassinations—all of them—and has done so for many generations. This was a plan long in the making. With the aid of my wife's powers, Nadid will see the plan to its fruition."

Hollace looked at his wife. Tacita remained stunned she had not felt the magicks that bound her womb. Hollace descended the throne dais and held out his hand to Malik. He said, "I don't much hold with mages and their practices, but I know a blood oath is binding. A blood oath to prove what you say is true."

Malik drew his dagger. He sliced his hand and then Hollace's. He grabbed Hollace's hand. Their blood meshed and intermingled. He said, "The blood will reveal all. Let the blame fall on whom it truly belongs."

With those words, the men were taken over their respective histories. Assassinations, sneak attacks and plots of generations past were all laid bare for the other to see. And what they saw was the betrayal of a father's trust.

"Our ancestors didn't care anymore. But Kontar needed them fighting, needed the feud to remain fresh," Hollace said once the spell finished. It felt like years had passed but the spell had done its job in mere seconds.

All heard and understood the implications of his words.

"I propose an end to it. No more blood. No more wasted life. Let us be joined as family, as Derex always meant us to be, instead of forever fighting. Help me save my wife and your kingdom will have a new ally, Hollace."

Hollace gripped Malik's blood-soaked hand. "Done... Cousin."

80CR

Juven pushed Adrienne to the ground in front of the throne dais of Kontar. Offhandedly, Adrienne wondered if a kingdom existed that didn't have its throne on a dais. She looked up at the woman who stared down at her.

Adrienne could see some of Malik and Hollace in the woman. She had black hair and slanted eyes like Malik, but her eyes were the same deep brown as Hollace's. Unlike Malik and Hollace, Nadid was white. Literally. The woman looked like a corpse.

Nadid was swathed in the ceremonial robes of her station as third ranking in the Mage Guild, but the robes didn't hide her curvaceous figure. She also had the height and the look of arrogance that seemed to be a family trademark. Adrienne had gotten sick of seeing it, to be perfectly honest. All this fighting and killing was all about family. Being married to Malik made Adrienne more family than she wanted to be, at the moment.

Nadid stood and walked down the dais steps. The lights in the flickering orbs that floated around the room made shadows and highlights play off Nadid's jet-black, silky-straight hair. Her Guild robes, a deep royal purple, rolled and convulsed around her feet.

Nadid reached towards Adrienne but pulled back when Adrienne snapped at her hand.

"Little she-devil, aren't you, Your Majesty?" Nadid asked. "It only makes sense. Malik wouldn't have married you if you weren't equal to him in attitude."

The glimmer that shone in Nadid's eyes gave Adrienne just enough time to brace herself before Nadid's open hand made contact with her cheek. The woman put her full weight behind the blow. Adrienne's head snapped to the side but her gaze stayed on Nadid. She hoped the hatred she felt showed in her eyes. Adrienne could feel the heat of it just beneath her skin. She knew the mage metal collar was all that kept her from turning Nadid into a writhing ball of flames.

"Let that be a warning to you, Queen Adrienne. I don't care that you are a queen. I don't care that you are Malik's bride. I am Nadid, Queen of Kontar and third elder of the Mage Guild. Once I have your power, I will be so much more."

Adrienne faced her fully to ask, "What do you mean? What do you want with me?"

Nadid turned away from Adrienne. She pulled a small sack from her robes and held it out to Juven. She said, "I know this is not what you are normally paid for, Assassin. But you did your job well."

Juven bowed before she took the money. She said with a smile, "Call me back when you want her dead. I would be more than happy to do it for free."

"I have no need of you to kill the likes of her. You may go," Nadid said. She didn't wait to see if Juven left or not. She turned her attention back to Adrienne. Signaling two waiting acolytes, she walked out of the room. They hauled Adrienne to her feet and pushed her to follow Nadid.

Juven taunted after Adrienne, "Die knowing I will return to my previous assignment of comforting your husband, Queen Adrienne." She laughed when Adrienne tried to look back at her but the acolytes shoved Adrienne to keep her moving.

The sack of gold jingled as Juven tested its weight. She said in satisfaction, "One thousand pieces." She gave another bow in the direction Nadid had taken. "A pleasure to be in your service, Your Majesty."

She headed out of the throne room. As she walked, she pulled out an orb and concentrated. A tiny flash later and the pre-made transportation spell placed Juven directly in front of her horse. She'd left it at Caradoc's cottage and used her orb to get Adrienne to Nadid quickly.

Retrieving and dropping off Adrienne had taken Juven less than an hour. She had enough time to do another job that had come her way before Sabri contacted her.

Juven grabbed her horse's saddle and had readied to pull herself up when she jumped back instead. The horse gave a scared whinny and ran. Juven clutched her arm, blood seeping through her fingers. She glared at the lance embedded in the ground a few feet away.

Hani stepped out of the shadows. She said, "You're getting sloppy, Juven. You should have had your horse meet you, not leave it where anyone could see and wait for you to come back for it."

"Hani," Juven hissed. She released her wound and crouched at the ready. "What do you want? Have the elders decided to test us again?"

"No. This is work," Hani answered. She smiled with her normal good-natured manner. "It is funny to think we served in the same palace for well over a year and never knew the other was there. Maybe I'm getting sloppy, as well."

"What?"

Hani pulled her dagger and her smile vanished. Her eyes narrowed and her voice dropped to one degree below freezing when she said, "Malik doesn't appreciate you handing his wife over to Nadid." That was all the warning she gave before she attacked.

Juven's dagger met Hani's a few inches from her throat. The blades threw off sparks when they clashed. Both women stared at each other.

"Haven't we done this once already? It ended in a draw. This is pointless," Juven said.

"It was a draw because a title wasn't a good enough reason to kill you." Hani added her weight and pressed her dagger closer to Juven's neck.

"Your mistake. And not your only one, Hani." Juven squeezed the orb in her hand. She disappeared and reappeared behind Hani.

Before the woman could react, Juven buried her dagger in Hani's back. She smiled at the resulting scream.

Nadid and Adrienne walked down several corridors in silence. Finally they came to a door with a shield embossed on the outside. The shield showed a bird of prey looking down from a tree branch at a serpent coiled around a flaming battle-axe. Adrienne recognized the serpent as Malik's family crest. She had a seen a flaming battle-axe all over Hollace's palace—Kakra's crest. It would seem the bird of prey portrayed Kontar in the role of watcher over the two intertangled kingdoms of Ulan and Kakra.

"Your curiosity is for the family crest, is it not, Queen Adrienne?" Nadid asked. "Kontar has always been the watchdog of Ulan and Kakra. But no more." She waved her hand over the shield. The image changed—the bird of prey now stood on a broken battle-axe and had the serpent caught in its beak. "Soon, Kontar will take its rightful place as the leader of Bron. It will rise from the ashes of Kakra and Ulan's destruction."

"You're no phoenix, Nadid," Adrienne whispered.

Nadid faced Adrienne. Behind her, the door creaked open and revealed stairs that led into an unbroken darkness. Nadid said, "It's funny you would liken me to a phoenix, Adrienne—since you have dropped my title, I shall do the same for you. For, Kontar, before Derex, had a flaming bird for its crest. That symbol changed when my ancestress, Derex's daughter, became queen. Soon it will change back."

She descended the stairs. The acolytes and Adrienne followed.

"You are probably wondering why I wanted you so badly, Adrienne."

"I'm Malik's wife."

"True, you are. But, even if you hadn't married Malik, I would have wanted you," Nadid corrected. She paused to smile back at Adrienne. Again, she reached out to touch Adrienne's face. This time the acolytes held her head in place and her mouth firmly shut. Nadid's fingers caressed up and down Adrienne's cheek. She purred, "You are from the Earth dimension. We have waited for someone from the Earth dimension, male or female, to come back to Bron for a very long time."

Nadid turned to continue down the stairs. As they descended, torches flamed to life.

Adrienne asked, "So what if I'm from Earth? What's that got to do with anything?"

"My great-grandfather, King Andsaca, met a woman from the Earth dimension once. She was a powerful mage—far beyond any on Bron. Possibly even Malik. My great-grandfather told me she immobilized the entire Mage Guild council with a mere gesture of her hand. Through sheer force of will, she gathered enough magicks around herself to tear open dimensional space and go home. She did not use a portal or transportation spell."

The stairs emptied into a small circular room made of black marble. It had no windows. Torches adorned the walls. In the middle of the floor, someone had drawn a giant circle with rune-like symbols written along the outside. Each rune had a line drawn from it to the middle of the circle, and the circle segments contained even more symbols.

Nadid continued happily, "The woman impressed King Andsaca very much. He decided she—or someone like her—would be the key to fulfilling Selene's greatest wish. Selene was Ulan and Kakra's younger sister."

"I know that," Adrienne said through her teeth.

"Good. Then you know her brothers and father treated Selene like dirt. She did not signify until Kakra and Ulan needed a keeper. Even then, Derex didn't trust her to see the job done. He entrusted the job to the man he married Selene off to."

Nadid's features twisted in anger. She clawed her hands in front of her then fisted them.

Adrienne paid no attention to Nadid's antics. She had eyes only for the circle painted on the black marble floor. Thanks to the knowledge Malik had given her, she could read the runes etched around the border of the circle. It was a spell to transfer power.

"You've gone mad," Adrienne said when she could finally speak.

Nadid came back to herself. Her anger dissipated and she smiled again. She said, "That's where you're wrong, Adrienne. I am quite sane, like all of my line before me. Selene wanted to repay her father and brothers for their treatment of her. When Ulan and Kakra started growing content with their kingdoms, she'd had Kakra killed. Kakra's sons killed Ulan and his wife in immediate retaliation. That wasn't enough. Their kingdoms still stood. Selene wanted them to suffer and she charged her descendants to find a way to enact the ultimate revenge.

"That revenge will be realized through you, Adrienne. You are from the Earth dimension, like the other woman. Your magicks added to my own, just as my great-grandfather wished, will make me powerful enough to level both Ulan and Kakra without ever stepping foot out of Kontar," she boasted. "Once they are gone and Selene's soul is finally at peace, I will make all of Bron bow at my feet."

"I may not know much about Bron, but I do know magicks are like blood—if you try to take my power, your body will reject it."

"This spell—" she gestured to the circle, "—will siphon your powers." She pointed to the runes around the perimeter, "And those runes will purify the siphoned power and enable me to feed on it just as I would my evening meal. Like my evening meal, I will feel no ill effects, and my hunger for revenge will be sated."

She swept her hand towards the circle. Adrienne was ripped out of the hands of the acolytes and went flying. She landed in the middle of the circle with a thud and a cry of pain.

Nadid smiled at Adrienne's glare. She offered, "Be angry, Adrienne. I don't mind. For, once the siphon is finished, you will be dead. Regrettably so, for your only crime is being of the Earth dimension."

Adrienne felt the heat beneath her skin and embraced it. She was an innocent in all this, except for her dimension of origin, which made her the perfect weapon for Nadid. Yet again, someone used Adrienne for their purposes and to hell with how she felt about it. As of this moment, she was sick of kingdoms and royalty and everything in between.

The collar around Adrienne's neck cracked. The snap resounded throughout the room. Nadid jumped visibly. The collar clattered to the floor.

Adrienne glowed with her anger. Heat rose off the floor around her in waves. Beside Nadid, one of the acolytes screamed in pain and fell to the ground.

Flames erupted around Adrienne and rushed at the fallen woman like a ravenous wolf. In seconds, the acolyte was ash. The flames moved towards Nadid.

She raised a barrier around herself, all the while staring at Adrienne in amazement. She murmured an incantation and slowly balled her outstretched hand into a tight fist.

Adrienne felt justified when the flames killed the acolyte. She'd wanted Nadid, but the acolyte was just as guilty. Adrienne focused and tried correcting her aim.

Her body slammed into the ground and she watched in horror as the flames died around her.

"You are amazing, Adrienne. I have never seen anyone throw off a mage metal collar before. And, even unschooled, you called up hellion flame," Nadid complimented with genuine awe. "You truly are everything my great-grandfather said you would be."

Adrienne struggled against the spell that held her to the floor. She heard footsteps rushing towards her. Now what? Wasn't her imminent death enough to worry about?

Another acolyte—male this time—rushed into the room. He skidded to a halt. The edge of his shoe stopped right before the outer edge of the circle.

Nadid lashed out at him. She threw an arc of power at the man that smashed him against the far wall away from the circle. She screamed, "Watch your step, you fool. You nearly made yourself part of the siphon spell and killed us all. Why are you disturbing me?"

The man took several deep breaths before he said, "Ulan's and Kakra's armies are headed this way, sire."

"Both?" Nadid asked in disbelief.

The man gave a curt nod.

"Together?"

"Yes, sire. They crossed the border only half an hour ago."

Nadid growled out her frustration. "Why haven't the mages taken care of them? Even Malik and his lack-wits can't withstand the might of the Guild's strongest."

"Mage metal, sire," the man answered. "Malik is using mage metal to incapacitate any who step forward. The rumor is it came from Hollace's stockpile. They have teamed together, sire, and their destination is clearly the palace." Fear made the man's voice change octaves several times over his recital.

Nadid gnashed her teeth. Malik must have found her spy and thus realized the identity of his wife's kidnapper. In all Nadid's planning, she had never thought Malik would seek Hollace's aid in retrieving Adrienne.

"Malik has sent back Lord Sabri, sire."

"Sabri," Adrienne gasped. "What do you mean sent back?"

"My spies are many in the palaces of Ulan and Kakra, Adrienne," Nadid replied. "Sabri is merely one of them." She turned to the man. "Where is he, then? I shall torture the fool for revealing my secrets to Malik."

The man held out the orb in his hand. He pointed it towards the ground in front of him. Sabri's body appeared. His face was frozen in a mask of pain. He'd clenched his jaw enough to crack his teeth and his eyes bugged out of his head. The man said, "That won't be necessary, sire. Malik has already done it."

Nadid's curiosity turned to horror as she studied the body.

She curled her fingers towards herself. A mage metal orb rolled out of Sabri's prone body. She stared at the orb. "A mage metal orb embedded in Sabri's body did not stay Malik's magicks? How?"

"I do not know, sire, but Malik sends a message with it," the man replied. He waited for Nadid to look at him. When she did, he continued, "His message orb said, 'You are next'."

"Get out," Nadid screamed. She watched the man flee, then looked down at Sabri's body. Her hand glided in the air above the twisted remains and they were gone. Next, she turned to Adrienne. "It would seem your husband does not want you dead, Adrienne."

Nadid faced her palm towards Adrienne and barked out an incantation.

Adrienne screamed. She wanted to squirm, wanted to claw the floor, but she couldn't move. It felt like someone dragged nails down every inch of her body.

"I am sorry I can't accommodate him. Malik's arrival in Kontar has only sped up the time of your death, I'm afraid," Nadid said in feigned concern. She said another incantation. Adrienne's screams grew. Nadid began to glow. She whispered, "I had thought to take my time. However, I haven't that luxury anymore."

She said the final incantation. Adrienne's powers transferred to Nadid.

Chapter Twenty-Six

Malik halted. All of his troops stopped with him. Hollace looked back then wheeled his horse around. "What is it, Malik? You're pale. Don't tell me this little bit of fighting has gotten you tired already?" Hollace joked.

Malik's eyes were only for the palace. He rasped, "Nadid has started the transfer. Adrienne is in pain...terrible pain."

Hollace followed Malik's gaze to the palace ahead of them. "Damn it, then, open one of your blasted portals. The scare tactic has worked too well."

"Do you not think if I could portal to Adrienne's side, I would have by now, you idiot?" Malik snapped. "Siphon spells are dangerous, as are portals. Mixing the two could make one or both unstable."

"Meaning?" Hollace asked in a peevish tone. He understood Malik's anger but he didn't want it taken out on him.

"Meaning, Adrienne could be killed and the resulting backlash would take the entire Kontar palace and most of the countryside with her in the explosion." He spurred his horse forward. By his side, Feyr ran with unnatural speed. Malik looked down at him. He yelled, "You can travel faster than I, old friend. Get there. Help her."

Feyr doubled his speed.

Hollace spurred his horse to catch up to Malik. He said, "If she's going to explode, I don't want to be around to see it."

Malik gave him an evil smile. "Come now, Hollace, where is your thirst for excitement? I thought Kakra was the flaming battle-axe of war and retribution."

298

"We are," agreed Hollace. He gave his horse a kick to get it going faster. "Well, let's go save your bride."

Feyr had little trouble finding Adrienne—he followed her screams. Everyone who got in his way fell beneath his claws. Those who were dumb enough to try to use magicks on him were greeted with a nasty reversal spell, which sent all their attacks back at them.

He entered the transfer room and stopped dead in his tracks. The fur on his body stood on end. The magicks in the room brought him to his stomach since his legs were unable to support him under such enormous pressure. He struggled to stay lucid enough to send one thought.

"Malik, she's in danger. Nadid has made a mistake."

"A mistake?" Malik asked in confusion.

"No time for mistakes, Malik. This war has already begun," Hollace growled.

"Not mine. Feyr—" Again, Malik reined in his mount, but this time for a wholly different reason.

Hani had dropped out of thin air directly in front of him. Blood covered her body and she looked to be in immense pain.

Hani said for all to hear, "Juven is dead, Majesty." Then she fainted.

"Indivar," Malik roared. He didn't wait for the man to gain his side. He pulled out an orb and imbued it with power. When he finished, he tossed it over his shoulder.

Indivar caught it.

"Get far enough from the Kontarian palace and use the orb to portal her back to Ulan. See to her wounds." Malik steered his mount around Hani's body and continued to the palace. He hoped she lived but his first concern was Adrienne.

"Majesty," Indivar agreed with a bow of his head. He dismounted and gathered Hani close. With a shaking hand, he wiped some of the blood from her face. He whispered, "You'll be all right, Hani. I will see to that."

As gently as he could, he lifted her onto his mount and sped away from the battle.

Malik and Hollace barely let their horses stop before they jumped down and charged the open gates. Feyr had effectively cleared a path to the throne room for them.

Hollace asked, "Should we be following the cat's trail if he's made a mistake and gone to the wrong location?"

"That is not the mistake," Malik corrected. "Nadid is the one who made a mistake. The spell she invoked is wrong. She did not allow for Adrienne's true power. She—"

Malik tackled Hollace to the floor seconds before a shock wave of pure power from an open doorway rushed over them. Two women could be heard screaming in perfect harmony with each other. One scream was cut short while the other continued.

Malik wasted no time rushing down the stairs. The power in the room brought him to his knees beside his pet. He laid a hand on Feyr but had eyes only for Adrienne, who shrieked and thrashed around the floor in pain.

Nadid's charred remains stood smoldering only a few feet away. Malik could only guess the backlash from the mistaken spell had surprised Nadid. So much so that she didn't have time to create a shield before her body combusted. It looked like the power had burned her from the inside out.

"Adrienne," Malik whispered. He looked on in helpless horror. He couldn't fix the mistake unless he could read the runes Nadid had used. He couldn't read the runes because the power in the room kept him in his place at the bottom of the stairs. It took all his strength to remain upright.

"Please," he whispered. Tears ran down his face. He watched Adrienne. Wave after wave of power flowed off of her with no place to go. Each wave hit Malik like a kick in the gut from his stallion, but the pain was minimal compared to what he felt through his renewed connection with his wife. Still he stayed seated on the stairs. If she died, he would die with her.

"Not so fast, Malik. It isn't your time," said a distant voice.

Malik looked around. He had just heard Adrienne speak. That couldn't be. Adrienne was on the floor a few feet away.

A ghostly figure shimmered into view in front of him. It was Adrienne. She wore a flowing white gown similar to the one he dressed her in on their wedding day, and a veil attached to the back of her head.

"Yup, it's me...sort of. You'll understand in a few months," she said with a smile. Ghost-Adrienne turned to her physical self lying a few feet away. She grimaced then whispered, "I remember this. This pain... I remember it." She held out her hands. The waves of power in the room targeted her.

Malik found himself able to stand. Feyr stood, shook himself out and watched. Ghost-Adrienne took in the power corporeal-Adrienne spilled off. The air in the room cleared. Adrienne stopped screaming. Ghost-Adrienne let her arms drop. She seemed more solid, more tangible.

She stepped forward. Malik rushed over to stop her but his hand passed right through her.

"I choose who and what touches me. And don't worry, I can't affect the circle," ghost-Adrienne assured him with a smile. She knelt beside corporeal-Adrienne and took her in her arms. "Remember me?" There was a slight tremor in her voice.

"Wha—" croaked Adrienne.

Ghost-Adrienne made shushing noises. She urged, "Don't speak. After all that screaming, you won't be able to speak until Malik heals you. I'm going to tell you something. You have to remember this, okay?" She smiled as corporeal-Adrienne nodded, then ghost-Adrienne lowered her head and whispered something Malik couldn't make out.

Once she finished, ghost-Adrienne kissed corporeal-Adrienne's cheek and lowered her back to the floor.

She straightened and gave Malik one last look. He got the feeling she wanted to say something. Instead she winked at him then disappeared.

Malik watched as the circle vanished. He rushed to Adrienne—*his* Adrienne—and took her in his arms. He felt his magicks spill over her as he soothed her pain and healed her wounds all at once.

Adrienne held tight to him and cried.

"It is over, my love, it is over," he said again and again.

Hollace descended the stairs. He'd tried earlier, but Adrienne's power had pushed him back. He looked at Feyr, who looked back at him. He nodded then went back up the way he had come. The war was over...truly over.

"I can walk, Malik," Adrienne complained.

Malik's arms tightened around her. He walked out of the Kontar palace with Adrienne held firmly against his chest. He said, "You have been through an ordeal."

"You've healed me. I'm fine now," she pleaded. When he still didn't put her down, she put a hand on his cheek. He stopped walking and looked down at her. "I'm okay, Malik. I'm right here and everything is fine." She smiled at him then added, "Now put me down."

Grudgingly, Malik lowered her feet to the ground. He kept his hand on her waist in case Adrienne wasn't as well as she seemed to think.

Adrienne felt a bit shaky, but that was probably nerves and nothing else. She looked around. Soldiers on foot and on horseback milled around. Some of the soldiers led away chained prisoners while others tended to the dead. Malik had done all this for her, to get her back.

He hadn't done it alone, though. Her gaze rested on Hollace. He sat atop his mount and Oringo stood next to him. They noticed her looking at them and stopped talking to watch her.

Her gaze still on Hollace and Oringo, Adrienne said to Malik, "I want to talk to Hollace and Oringo."

"Come then," Malik agreed. He started forward.

Adrienne pulled him to a halt. "I want to talk to them alone."

"Why?"

"I want to thank Hollace for his hospitality."

"You do not need to be alone—"

"And I don't want you glaring at him when you find out I acted as a servant to his daughter," she finished. As she suspected, Malik's expression went dark. "See?"

Malik sighed. "Fine. I shall remain here. Feyr will—"

"Alone, Malik," she insisted. She looked at Feyr and apologized to him silently. He nodded at her and sat on his haunches beside Malik. It seemed Feyr accepted her terms more readily than Malik did.

They stood quietly as Malik contemplated her request. Adrienne waited. He would give in. He would concede or she would make him, but he would give in.

"Do not take overly long, my Adrienne," he said with a growl.

Adrienne kissed his cheek then walked over to Hollace and Oringo.

Hollace dismounted wearing a grin that spanned his face. He boomed, "No need to thank me, Mistress Adele...excuse me, I mean, Queen Adrienne."

"I didn't come over here to thank you," she snapped. She remembered to keep herself calm because Malik would feel her anger. It was a hard task. She had her memories back and tearing Oringo's head off seemed like the best way to celebrate. While the thought kept her mood upbeat, it would have to wait.

"You should. My mage metal made—"

"Shut up, Hollace." His eyes narrowed on her face. Before he could respond to her outburst, she warned, "Whatever you say to me, you had better keep it civil."

"You think I fear you because you're a queen now, woman?" Hollace scoffed. He crossed his arms over his bare chest and raised his chin to look down his nose at Adrienne.

"You fear my husband, Hollace. You fear what he'll do when he finds out Oringo attacked me."

She nodded when Hollace paled. His arms dropped slack at his sides. Oringo shot a look at Malik then took a step back. Malik hadn't moved. He didn't react because he couldn't hear the conversation.

In an impish tone, Adrienne urged, "Smile, gentlemen. You don't want my husband to think there's something wrong and come over here, do you?"

Their smiles looked forced. If Malik couldn't hear them because of the distance, he wouldn't be able tell a fake smile from a real one.

Hollace asked, "What do you want, woman?"

"I want peace."

Oringo shot back, "You threaten us and then say you want peace. You have a funny way of showing it."

"I will keep what *almost* happened to myself so long as Ulan and Kakra sign a peace treaty. It will be fair and equitable for both sides. All this assassination and taking each other's kingdoms crap ends *now*. I will not live the rest of my life looking over my shoulder."

"That's all you want?" Oringo asked.

"You're never to set foot in Ulan," she answered him. "Give whatever excuse you need. I don't ever want to see you again. Maybe in the far off future when this is a distant memory I never think of, I may change my mind. But, for now, stay on your side of the Tano River."

Oringo bowed to her. "Done. I am sorry."

"You're only sorry because I turned out to be attached to someone who's detrimental to your health. You should've thought of that before."

"I liked you better as Adele," Hollace said.

Adrienne laughed with genuine humor. "Considering you didn't like me at all when I was Adele, that says volumes, Hollace."

Malik charged forward and scooped Adrienne into his arms once again. "Enough of this. I take my leave of you, Hollace. I trust you can handle the rest on your own."

A portal opened behind him. Mushira and Nimat waited on the other side. Tears ran down their cheeks.

Hollace nodded. He said, "When you are ready to discuss the peace treaty, I will be as well." His gaze met Adrienne's as he said the last. He nodded to her and she returned the gesture.

Malik carried Adrienne across the portal threshold. Feyr followed them.

ℙ℞

Adrienne lay in bed with Mischief sprawled across her legs and Rena seated beside her. The little girl chatted away happily about anything that came to her mind. Adrienne happily listened. Rena was her first non-entourage-related visitor in a month.

It had taken three days to get Malik to let her out of his sight. Her intention to contact her parents and let them know what had happened provided incentive for Malik to leave her alone. He had all but run out of the room.

Adrienne didn't blame him. Hannah and Benjamin were furious. First, they were mad at Adrienne for not warning them about the danger surrounding her new role as queen of Ulan. Second, they were pissed off with Malik for keeping them in the dark. It was a trying six hours. Adrienne had to promise her parents it would never happen again. She didn't bother to point out the silliness of her promising not to be kidnapped again. She did it nonetheless to make her parents happy.

Satisfying her guards and maids as to her general health was much harder. Feyr or no Feyr, Khursid and Qamar were ever-present. Hani—who still pretended to be a lady's maid—never did any errand that would take her from Adrienne's side. Mushira had ordered

Adrienne to bed rest. Adrienne wasn't allowed to go farther than the bathroom for an entire month.

The situation had gotten old. Her mandatory bed rest—which Malik endorsed—made it impossible for Adrienne to go to the peace talks held in Iniko. Malik wanted to opt out so he could stay with her, but Adrienne wouldn't let him leave such an important task up to his chancellors. He didn't like leaving Adrienne and came back every few hours to make sure she remained in bed.

Today the peace talks ended. And, thanks to some fancy negotiating, Adrienne's bed rest ended also.

She smiled when Malik returned and signaled the end of her captivity. Before he could fully cross the portal threshold, she asked, "Well?"

"Well, my impatient wife, the treaty is signed," he said. He shooed Mischief and Rena out of the room so he could speak to Adrienne in private. Khursid and Qamar left to stand outside the bedroom door, while Hani went to the far end of the room with Mushira to prepare Adrienne's lunch attire. The outfit for her first meal with the court since her return required extra preparation so Adrienne would look perfect.

Malik wished the women would leave. He wanted to be alone with Adrienne, truly alone. His anger dissipated once he took Adrienne's hands in his own. He related, "Hollace has agreed to put an end to Derex's stipulations. We have both decided to keep the male heir—"

Adrienne snorted.

Malik ignored her to continue, "—and the proof of legitimate birth."

"You mean the crest birthmark?"

"Yes," he answered. "We will split Kontar in half. But, instead of each half joining the respective kingdoms, Chandra will rule with her husband the one half of Kontar closest to Kakra, and our second born—no matter the gender—will rule the other half. Hollace has agreed to let you act as regent until our second born is of an age to rule."

"Why me and not you?" she asked. "We're equal in rule."

Malik rolled his eyes. "He does not trust me."

Adrienne laughed. "What else?"

"I hope the last part of the treaty will not anger you too much," he started. He took a steadying breath. "I have promised our last-born daughter to Oringo's firstborn son. The marriage will reunite the families and prove our commitment to this peace."

She thought on this for a little while. If Oringo's son would take after his mother and not his father, the situation might turn out well. Adrienne didn't know the woman, but anyone was an improvement over Oringo.

"It's not me you have to apologize to, Malik. It's our last-born daughter," she finally said in a sage tone.

"But you agree?"

"For now."

Malik leaned over and kissed her. He wished to do more but knew Adrienne wouldn't want an audience. When he leaned back from her, he noticed her features were marred with a frown. He asked, "What is wrong, my Adrienne?"

"Just thinking of Nadid."

"Why?" Malik demanded.

Adrienne laughed at his insulted look. She soothed, "That's not what I meant, Malik. I remembered what she told me about why she kidnapped me. She and Andsaca thought being from Earth meant I—or whoever they caught—would be powerful, but I didn't get my magicks until I came to Bron."

"Perhaps the woman King Andsaca met came from another alternate Earth," Malik reasoned.

"Huh? What do you mean?"

"There is more than one Earth, my Adrienne."

She agreed, "Yes. Bron."

"No, my lady. I mean to say there are others called Earth. They are more similar to yours than Bron is."

"There are?"

"The woman King Andsaca met more than likely came from an Earth where magicks are used freely, as they are here on Bron."

Adrienne couldn't believe it. Other alternate dimensions existed and some had Earths similar to hers. How many were there, and from which had Nadid thought Adrienne arrived?

Malik chuckled at her surprised look. He said, "You may be from the wrong Earth, my Adrienne, but you were still a powerful mage."

"*Were* being the operative word."

Malik said nothing. True, Adrienne had survived, but the ordeal had diminished her powers. That was a secret he kept from the kingdom. No one needed to know.

Chapter Twenty-Seven

March 28, 2007

Malik knocked on the bedroom door then peeked into the room. "I know your mother says this is bad luck, but we are already married..." He stopped as he saw Adrienne.

Twenty floating orbs surrounded her. The same orbs Malik had brought with him to ensure he didn't run out of magicks during their visit to Earth, which would strand them there.

Adrienne had insisted he bring enough to accommodate those who accompanied them, which consisted of everyone who knew her true origins. The proof of her true intentions for the orbs was evident now.

Malik came fully into the room. He watched as Adrienne's outfit shimmered and changed into a dress he found all too familiar. A ghostly apparition had worn it while she saved his wife.

He asked, "Adrienne, what—"

She smiled at him and held a finger to her lips. The room around them changed. Suddenly, Malik watched the scene from Nadid's palace again, just from a different angle.

Adrienne spoke to past-Malik then went to her other self. She held out her arms and gathered to herself the power her other threw off. Once complete, she went to her past self and held her.

Tears sprang to her eyes as she witnessed the true horror of the pain she had gone through from the outside looking in. Adrienne gave a shaky smile and whispered, "Remember me?" When her past self would have spoken, she rushed out, "Don't speak. After all that screaming, you won't be able to speak until Malik heals you."

She was satisfied when her other just nodded and gave a small smile. Adrienne smoothed the hair from her face. "I'm going to tell you something. You have to remember this, okay?" She leaned over and whispered, "You read the runes when you entered the room. Never forget them. Don't forget any of this. Leave the forgetting to me. I need you to remember so I can stop this and keep you alive. Do that, and all will be well."

She kissed her past self's cheek. Gently, she released her hold on her and stood. She glanced over at past-Malik. The events seemed to be confusing him. She couldn't help smiling at him. She gave him a wink and then she let the image fade away.

The orbs that floated around Adrienne dropped to the ground. They were no longer needed since she had all of her powers back. She hadn't completely depleted the orbs, but she would exchange them for new ones later. Her work wasn't done yet.

With a deep breath and an exhaling sigh, Adrienne squared her shoulders. As she did, her flowing, ethereal robes shimmered again. This time she wore the linen gown from the beginning of her wedding ceremony in Ulan.

Behind her, Malik started to ask why she didn't change back to the dress Mushira and the ladies of the palace worked so diligently on, when he felt her power spread around them again.

Unlike before, the room didn't change. Instead, what looked like a portal opened before Adrienne in the mirror. Malik watched as another past-Malik ran forward to protect his soon-to-be wife. He watched Adrienne throw off his seeking magicks as though they were nothing, then signal her past self to step forward.

Malik remembered the frustration he felt at not being able to counter the magicks used against him. It all made sense now. Everything. He could not trace the magicks used because they had come from the future.

He didn't know time magicks. Malik knew if he had tried to master them he would have gone back in time and saved his parents.

Knowing this of himself, he left time alone. It would seem his wife had no such fear.

Adrienne placed her hand on the glass of the mirror and smiled at her past self in encouragement. When her other's hand touched hers, she said, "Don't worry, he can't hear us."

"You're me, aren't you? And why can't he hear us?" asked her past self.

"Yes, I'm you. I'm you in the future." She glanced at past-Malik and stuck her tongue out at him. "And, because I don't want him to hear us. He'll hear us later. Right now, this is girl talk," she explained. She leaned into the mirror and her other leaned into the window. It was interesting to see this from the other side. She remembered how scared and lost she'd felt. And then her future self made it all better.

Like she planned to do now.

"I want you to stop whining and go get married," she commanded.

"I don't know him," her past self complained.

"You will in time."

"I don't want to die."

"He won't let you."

"He scares me," her past self whispered.

She whispered in return, "He loves you. You may not believe that now because you just met, but he does." She smirked and gave a little wink before adding, "Besides, when it comes to being pissed off enough to kick ass and take names, you two are evenly matched. Or, you will be." She let her magicks flow around her past self. With an ease that surprised her, she cast a barrier spell. Her powers would be stunted and she would never notice.

When her past self still hesitated, Adrienne added, "You'll be happy. In the end, that's all that matters. Now get going." She let the image drop with a sigh. She was done. She had saved herself and her marriage all in the half hour before the start of her second wedding.

Malik embraced her from behind and kissed her hair. He said, "That was why your powers changed after we married. You placed a barrier spell on yourself."

"In the end, it saved my life." She rested her hands on top of his and leaned back into him with a sigh.

"You are far too clever for me, my wife."

"This is true," Adrienne agreed. She rested her hand on his cheek. "On the day of our wedding, my future self came back in time to stunt my powers so when the time came, they would overwhelm and kill Nadid. And, once again, my future self traveled back through time to correct the siphon spell and take the power into herself...myself." She turned and looked at Malik. "I had to play the role of my future self to get my powers back." She caressed his cheek. "I know you were worried but I've retrieved my powers and no one need ever know they were gone."

Malik pulled her back into his arms. "I would have saved you, my Adrienne, if you had but trusted me."

"I do trust you, Malik," Adrienne soothed. "But this damsel had to save herself from distress. I can't call myself your equal if I have to keep waiting around for you to save me."

Malik released her. He studied her before he said, "You travel through time as easily as I travel through portals. Though my portals are unruly, time travel is dangerous."

"I'm only following your reckless example, my love."

"Love?"

"Yes. Why do you look so surprised?"

He took her hands in his. He pulled her close to say, "I thought you would become even more afraid of living on Bron after—"

She placed her fingers over his lips. "That is the past and that's where it will stay. I don't ever want to think of that again, ever. It may have taken me a while to realize what I felt, but I do love you, Malik."

"I love you, my Adrienne," he whispered. He pressed his lips to hers.

The door to the room swung open and Rena rushed in. She said in an excited tone, "Grandmother Hannah told Father to tell Mother and Mother told me to tell you to hurry up before the preacher gets angry." She sucked in a deep breath after such a long sentence.

Malik ended his kiss with Adrienne and regarded Rena. He said, "We are coming. Go back and tell them that, Rena."

"Okay," the little girl yelled before she ran off.

"Is it my imagination or are Hani and Indivar taking advantage of their time away from Bron to forget I am their king?" Malik asked.

"Don't be grumpy on our anniversary, Malik."

He chuckled. "I merely jest, my Adrienne. I am glad Rena has found a true mother in Hani, and Indivar a wife worthy of him."

"I'm glad Bayard found a wife Khursid liked. Good lord, that man is picky," Adrienne said. She went to the mirror and straightened her veil. She wore the wedding dress she had always wanted.

It was an off-the-shoulder number that hugged her body all the way to her knees then flared out. While the front of the dress stopped at the floor, the back trailed behind her forming the train. The entire ensemble was completely handmade, from the lace to the silk itself. Mushira and the seamstresses had worked hard.

Adrienne gave her veil one final tug to get it situated the way she wanted. She stood back and looked at herself. Her eyes went wide when her reflection winked at her. It took her a moment to realize why, and then she smiled. She nodded and her reflection did the same, just delayed.

Malik noticed all of this. He asked, "Was that—"

"Me from the future."

"You take too many chances, my lady."

"I'll be careful," she promised. "Besides, you've only yourself to blame. You taught me to have little to no regard for the rules. And, as I said already, I am following your reckless example. Just as our son will." She walked past Malik to leave the room.

Malik caught up with her and pulled her to a stop. "You have seen this? You have seen our son?"

"No, I haven't seen him. Every version of myself in every time agrees that the past should never know about the future." She moved his hand to her stomach. "But I do know that I'm carrying your son, and I have no doubt he'll be like you."

"The contraception spell," Malik argued.

"I didn't do it. I mean, *I* did do it, but not *this* me. One of my future versions voided our contract a while ago and nullified the contraception spell," she said with a shrug.

"What else have you seen and done on your travels through time, my Adrienne?"

She walked away from him. Over her shoulder, she said, "You'll have to wait and see."

About the Author

D. Reneé Bagby is the type of woman who lives in her imagination. She visits the real world only long enough to spend time with her husband and two cats and go to her day job. If it weren't for bills, hunger and fatigue, Reneé would more than likely spend all her time trying to get the stories that are in her head onto her computer.

Reneé is also the type of woman who looks forward to getting lost just so she can find a new way home. She approaches her stories in much the same way. If there's a roundabout way to get from girl-meets-boy to girl-and-boy-live-happily-ever-after, she's sure to find it and write it.

Check out Reneé's website at: http://dreneebagby.com. Email Reneé at: DReneeBagby@gmail.com

Look for these titles by
D. Reneé Bagby

Coming Soon:

Serenity

She doesn't know who she is or where she came from.
But she knows she's in love with the man who found her.

The Wolverine and the Jewel
© *2007 Rebecca Goings*

From the moment the Wolverine knight, Sebastian, finds the unconscious, badly beaten woman he nicknames "Jewel", all he wants to do is protect her—no matter the cost.

Jewel wakes with no memory of who she is. The only clue to her identity is a lavender-colored jewel around her neck—a jewel which the dragon, Mynos, recognizes as the talisman made by his long-dead mate. Through the jewel's magic, they discover that the man who attacked Jewel is none other than her fiancé, Lord Merric.

Violent and ambitious, Merric was enraged when Jewel mysteriously vanished on the eve of their arranged marriage. Now, he'll do anything to force her to return. Even dark magic—or murder.

Available now in ebook and print from Samhain Publishing.

Their uneasy alliance could lead to love—if the demon will allow it.

Serenity
© 2008 D. Reneé Bagby

Melchior, King of the Bhresyas, is quickly growing tired of the war between his kind and the humans who view them as demons. He proposes a peace treaty with the most powerful human kingdom. His only stipulation? Once she comes of age, the human queen's daughter must be his bride.

Serenity has spent her entire life preparing for her role at Melchior's side. Other women might be frightened, but she embraces her destiny, knowing in her heart that she and Melchior have been twined together by fate.

While he wants cooperation between their two peoples, his union with Serenity cannot and should not lead to love. The more she tries to bring them together, the harder he pushes her away—until she lands in the arms of those who would do her harm.

Love is the answer. But before Melchior admits to his, it may be too late.

A Gezane Universe Novel

Available now in ebook from Samhain Publishing.

GET IT NOW

MyBookStoreAndMore.com

GREAT EBOOKS, GREAT DEALS . . . AND MORE!

Don't wait to run to the bookstore down the street, or waste time shopping online at one of the "big boys." Now, all your favorite Samhain authors are all in one place—at MyBookStoreAndMore.com. Stop by today and discover great deals on Samhain—and a whole lot more!

Samhain
Publishing, ltd

WWW.SAMHAINPUBLISHING.COM

GREAT cheap fun

Discover eBooks!
THE FASTEST WAY TO GET THE HOTTEST NAMES

Get your favorite authors on your favorite reader, long before they're
out in print! Ebooks from Samhain go wherever you go, and work with
whatever you carry—Palm, PDF, Mobi, and more.

Samhain
publishing, ltd

WWW.SAMHAINPUBLISHING.COM